DEATH WITH A DOUBLE EDGE

May, 1911. Daniel Pitt is summoned to a murder scene in the slums of London's East End. He identifies the dead man as Jonah Drake, a distinguished senior barrister who has been killed with a double-edged sword. With the police holding out little hope of finding Drake's killer, Daniel and his friend Toby Kitteridge rise to the challenge. They have leads that take them from the underbelly of the East End to the very highest echelons of society. Then Daniel's father, Thomas Pitt, receives a warning from Special Branch to cease the investigation. But Daniel and his father will not be deterred — despite the risks involved in the pursuit of justice . . .

SPECIAL MESSAGE TO READERS

THE ULVERSCROFT FOUNDATION
(registered UK charity number 264873)
was established in 1972 to provide funds for
research, diagnosis and treatment of eye diseases.

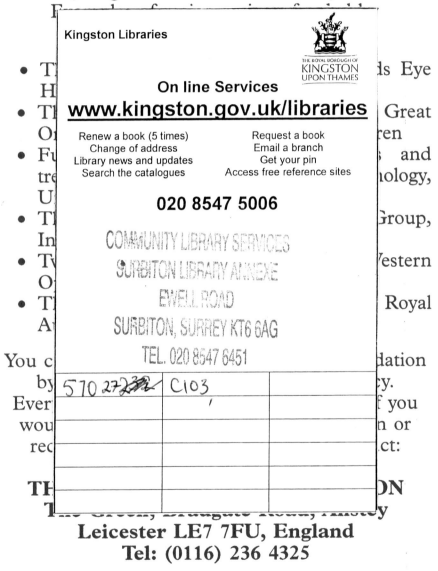

- T... ...ls Eye
  H...
- T... ...Great
  O... ...en
- Fu... ...and
  tre... ...ology,
  U...
- T... ...Group,
  In...
- T... ...estern
  O...
- T... ...Royal
  A...

You c... ...dation
by... ...y.
Ever... ...f you
wou... ...n or
rec... ...ct:

TH... ...ON

Leicester LE7 7FU, England
Tel: (0116) 236 4325

website: ...on.org.uk

ANNE PERRY

DEATH WITH A DOUBLE EDGE

Complete and Unabridged

CHARNWOOD
Leicester

First published in Great Britain in 2020 by
Headline
London

First Charnwood Edition
published 2021
by arrangement with
Headline Publishing Group
an Hachette UK Company
London

A catalogue record for this book is available
from the British Library.

ISBN 978–1–4448–4704–8

Published by
Ulverscroft Limited
Anstey, Leicestershire
Set by Words & Graphics Ltd.
Anstey, Leicestershire
Printed and bound in Great Britain by
TJ Books Ltd., Padstow, Cornwall

This book is printed on acid-free paper

To Rob Daly

Character List

Daniel Pitt — junior barrister at fford Croft and Gibson

Impney — chief clerk at fford Croft and Gibson

Toby Kitteridge — senior barrister at fford Croft and Gibson

Jonah Drake — skilled, senior barrister at fford Croft and Gibson for thirty years

Marcus fford Croft — head of fford Croft and Gibson

Inspector Letterman — Mile End police chief

Sir Thomas Pitt — Daniel's father, head of Special Branch

Charles Hobson — clerk to Jonah Drake

Miriam fford Croft — Marcus's daughter

Dr Evelyn Hall — British forensic scientist, trained in Holland

Charlotte Pitt — Lady Pitt, Daniel's mother

Lionel Peterson — the defendant in a previous murder trial

Evan Faber — acquitted of murdering Marie Wesley

Erasmus Faber — Evan's father, shipbuilding magnate

Mrs Portiscale — Daniel's landlady

Roman Blackwell — a private enquiry agent and ex-policeman

Mercedes (Mercy) — Roman's mother

Sir James MacPherson — member of the House

of Lords and Home Office
Dr Octavius Ottershaw — forensic pathologist
Belinda May Blades (Bella) — tobacconist's
assistant
Minnie Maude — the fford Crofts' housemaid
Grandma Blades — Bella's grandmother
Patch — Grandma Blades' black and white dog
Jacko — a kidnapper, with accomplice
Emily Radley — Charlotte's sister
Lieutenant Livesey — Special Branch
Sergeant Judd — police officer

1

Daniel was worried. Toby Kitteridge was almost
an hour late, which was extremely uncharacteris-
tic of him. He was untidy, no matter how hard
he tried not to be. His hair never lay flat. He
found it difficult to buy a shirt whose sleeves
were long enough to cover his bony wrists, and
occasionally he wore odd socks without noticing
it. But he was meticulous about time. He was
never late. He considered it to be not only rude,
but incompetent, a fatal flaw in a lawyer.

Daniel looked at the office clock. It said eight
minutes before ten.

There were two light taps on the door. He
knew who it was: Impney, the chief clerk at the
legal chambers of fford Croft and Gibson.

'Come in,' Daniel said quickly.

Impney entered and closed the door behind
him. Normally his face was completely professional, polite but unreadable. However, this
morning he looked decidedly grim.

'What is it?' Daniel asked, his voice sharper
than he meant it to be.

'There is a policeman outside, Mr Pitt, and he
is asking to see you.'

'Me, or just someone?' Daniel asked.

'You, sir, quite specifically,' Impney replied.
'He has one of your cards.'

Kitteridge. Something had happened to
Kitteridge. Daniel swallowed hard and kept his

1

voice steady. 'Ask him to come in, please,' he instructed.

'Yes, sir.' Impney withdrew, and a moment later opened the door again. A young, profoundly unhappy policeman came in.

'Mr Pitt?' he asked.

Daniel found his voice hoarse. 'Yes?'

'I'm sorry to ask you, sir, but they found this card.' He fished in his pocket and produced a calling card.

One glance told Daniel it was his own. 'Where did you find it?' Daniel asked.

The policeman shifted his weight from one foot to the other. 'In the pocket of a man who is unfortunately dead, sir. At first, we thought it might be his own, but one of our officers knows you by sight and said it wasn't you.'

'You don't know who it is?'

'No, sir. If you would come and look at him, sir? It appears that he is someone you know.'

Daniel stood up a trifle unsteadily.

'Are you all right, sir?' the constable asked with concern.

'Yes, thank you,' Daniel answered. He straightened his shoulders.

The young man gave a sigh of relief. He glanced at the coat rack. 'It's already quite warm outside; you won't need a coat.'

'It's a long way,' Daniel pointed out. The morgue was well over a mile from Lincoln's Inn Fields, which housed the most prestigious law chambers in England, including that of fford Croft and Gibson.

'I have a taxi waiting, sir.' The policeman

opened the door and stepped out into the passageway.

Daniel left the coat and followed him, explaining to Impney that he was going with the constable to help him in an urgent matter. He did not want to put it into words. Impney was anxious enough already.

'Yes, sir, I'll inform Mr fford Croft.' Impney inclined his head slightly.

'Thank you,' Daniel acknowledged, and followed the constable out of the front entrance, down the few steps to the pavement, and into the waiting taxi. It was one of the new shiny black automobiles that were slowly taking over from the horse-drawn hansom cabs. It was May, 1911, well into the new century, not even Edwardian any more, now into the reign of King George V.

At another time, Daniel would have enjoyed riding in the black taxi. He thoroughly approved of them. But this could have been a vegetable cart for all the pleasure it gave him. He stared out through the window at the street. He did not want to talk to the constable. He was choked with fear, emotion, memories of Kitteridge who had been in the law chambers several years longer than Daniel, and knew so much more. He was excellent in court. Once he began to argue a case, all his nervous tension was mastered and he had flashes of positive brilliance. Only Daniel knew he probably had odd socks on, and that he had been too absent-minded to eat breakfast. They had solved cases together, complicated and emotional ones, as well as simple legal arguments. They had shared successes and failures, long hours researching into the night. There had been one or two dangerous and tragic cases, and people he would never forget.

The last thing Daniel had felt towards Kitteridge was anger because he was late. And now he felt fear. What was the final thing Daniel had said before parting? Please heaven it was not something he would regret for ever, now that it was too late to take it back.

Now they were caught in traffic, as if to illustrate his fears. There were new automobiles, as well as older horse-drawn vehicles, barrows, drays, or hansom cabs. He was in a hurry, impatient to get there. And yet he had to endure the crawling through the mass of engines, the shouting of insults. He fidgeted in his seat. The constable glanced at him but said nothing. He made as if to say *sorry*, then changed his mind. This must be one of the worst parts of this man's job: having to fetch people to identify the dead body of someone they knew, even loved.

At last they were there. The cab stopped, the constable paid the fare and led Daniel across the pavement and through the doorway of the morgue. The smell of it enveloped him immediately. The carbolic and lye caught in his nostrils and the back of his throat. He could still smell death here. It lingered long after the corpses were removed.

A morgue attendant appeared from one of the doorways, closing it softly behind him.

'This way, sir,' the constable said, glancing at Daniel anxiously.

Daniel nodded without speaking, knowing the

4

poor man was doing his best. He looked about twenty-five, Daniel's own age. They walked side by side and passed through a doorway at the end of the passage and into an anteroom. And then Daniel saw it. It was like a blow that knocked all the air out of his body. There was a boldly checked coat hanging up on a railing. There could not be two coats so ugly in exactly that loud, clanging check. Kitteridge had just bought it, and Daniel had been very rude, calling it an eyesore. And so it was. But he would give anything now to be able to take that back. It had been meant carelessly, teasing. Kitteridge had little sense of style, and had trouble getting decent clothes that fitted him.

Daniel felt a pull on his arm. It was the constable, gripping him as if to hold him up in case he collapsed. Daniel wanted to shake him off, but the grip was too firm.

Unprotestingly, he was led into the morgue itself. How could people work in a place like this? Everybody had once been living, somebody's child, or brother, or wife . . . or friend.

The police surgeon smiled at him grimly. Daniel had seen the man before but couldn't remember his name. It did not matter now.

'Thank you, sir,' the man said gently. 'Just look at his face, if you don't mind. Are you ready?'

No, he was not ready; he never would be. He steadied himself. He must not give in to emotion. 'Yes . . . '

The surgeon pulled the sheet back. It was stained with blood in patches all the way down. Daniel forced himself to look. He knew the face, in spite of the knife slashes across the cheek and nose, and another over the neck, dark with congealed blood. It was not Kitteridge — although he was about the same height, as well as Daniel could judge of a man lying down — but it was Jonah Drake, one of the senior lawyers in his own chambers, one of the cleverest in court. Not a particularly likable man, but one with skills Daniel could not deny. In fact, reluctantly, he had admired him.

Daniel was ashamed of himself for the wave of relief he felt that it was not Kitteridge. It was as if a physical pain had vanished, to be replaced by mere discomfort.

'Sir?' The surgeon's voice broke through his thoughts.

'Yes . . . ' He paused as he released a breath he didn't know he'd been holding. 'This is not Kitteridge. It's his coat on the rail, but that's Jonah Drake, a senior partner in our chambers.'

'Are you sure, sir?'

'Yes. Kitteridge is in his mid-thirties; Mr Drake is sixty, at the very least. It's Mr Drake. I don't know why he had Kitteridge's coat. He must have borrowed it . . . ' His voice sounded awkward, faraway.

'Jonah Drake. Has he any relatives we should inform? A wife, perhaps? Or children?'

Daniel tried to clear his mind of the violence, and the reality of death, and think clearly. 'No. No, I don't think so. I'll tell Mr fford Croft, the head of our chambers. He'll know.'

'Would you like us to do that, sir?' the surgeon asked.

'Thank you, but I'll go straight back now and tell him.' He swallowed hard. 'What happened? Do you know?' He stared down at the face again. It was misshapen with the violence of what had been done to him, but he was still recognisable. Jonah Drake had an unusual nose and a small, dark mole on his cheek, just to the right of it. His neck was usually covered by a shirt collar and an old-fashioned cravat. That neck was unusually ugly now, with sagging skin, unshaven. Daniel knew that hair and nails go on growing for a little while after death, as if they had not received the message that the heart had stopped. There was no one there any more. Drake had been a very clever man, had won most of his cases, even when they seemed impossible. He knew the law as Daniel knew the alphabet. The vanity of covering an ugly neck made him somehow human . . . and vulnerable.

He dragged his eyes from the dead face and stared at the surgeon.

'Someone attacked him with a knife — a long one,' the surgeon replied. 'Or possibly even a sword. I should think it was all over in a matter of seconds, if that is any comfort. I'm afraid he was found in a pretty bad part of the East End. I don't know precisely where, but the police will tell you. They are looking into it, of course.' As he spoke, he lifted the sheet to cover the face again. 'You are quite sure of the identity?'

'Yes, I am,' Daniel answered. 'How . . . how tall is he?'

'I measured him at six feet two inches.'

'Yes, that's about right,' he said aloud. 'That is

Kitteridge's height, too. May I speak to the police? Do they know what happened? Who did this?' He turned to look at the constable.

'No one knows yet, sir,' the constable replied. 'Delivery man found him this morning. Or someone like that, up and about early.'

'So, it was a residential street? People's houses?' Daniel asked quickly.

'Not exactly, sir. The man was taking a shortcut through an alley. His horse stopped suddenly: animals smell death.'

Daniel had a sudden vision of the animal shying away from the corpse, possibly scaring the man out of a daydream.

'Any idea what Mr Drake might have been doing in the East End?' The constable's voice was shaky. 'He must have been lying there a good while.' He looked at the surgeon for confirmation.

'Died about two o'clock in the morning, but that's only an estimation,' the surgeon replied. 'He was found at about six. Well daylight by then, this time of year.'

'Nobody saw him before that?' Daniel said curiously.

'Nobody reported it, sir,' the constable said, shaking his head. 'Not the same thing as not seeing it.'

'Where, exactly?' Daniel asked.

'Mile End. Little alley off Anthony Street. Not a very healthy neighbourhood. Any idea what he might have been doing there at two in the morning, Mr Pitt?'

'None at all. I don't know where he lived. But

it won't have been in Mile End or the Whitechapel area.' Daniel realised as he said it that he knew nothing at all about Jonah Drake, except for his professional skill and a sharp, rather twisted sense of humour. He would have to tell Marcus, of course. And Impney might know Drake better. Not that the police would get a great deal out of him. Impney was always courteous, even pleasant to people, and managed to speak very freely, without ever giving anything away. He was one of the best legal clerks in the business, discreet, without ever appearing to be so.

'If you're feeling well enough, sir, I'm sure Inspector Letterman would like to speak to you,' the constable said. 'You might know something as could help us.'

Daniel jerked himself back to the present. 'Of course,' he agreed. He could not reasonably refuse. He said goodbye to the surgeon and followed the constable out into the street and the fresh air. Even the horse manure was a living smell, relatively sweet compared with the sourness of disinfectant and death.

They walked to the police station in silence. It was only a few streets away. Daniel did not want to talk, and the constable was tactful enough not to try to make idle conversation. Daniel wondered briefly how many times he had had to do something like this.

They went inside and the constable left him with the desk sergeant, who took him up to the inspector's room. 'Like a cup of tea, sir?' the sergeant asked.

Daniel was about to refuse when he realised his mouth was dry, and a cup of tea was about the only thing he could imagine drinking. 'Yes, please. No sugar.'

'Right you are, sir.' The sergeant disappeared and came back ten minutes later with an enamel mug, steam rising from it. 'Mind the handle. It's hot.'

Daniel accepted it and thanked him.

Five minutes after that, Inspector Letterman came in and introduced himself. He sat down on the other side of the desk. He was a smart, self-satisfied man, with well-groomed hair, greying a little, and a deceptively mild manner. 'Understand you identified our corpse for us? Fellow from your chambers in Lincoln's Inn Fields, fford Croft and Gibson, eh?'

'Yes, sir,' Daniel agreed. 'It is Jonah Drake, one of our senior lawyers.'

Letterman grimaced. 'I'm sorry. Nasty shock. Did you know him well?' There was a professional pity in his voice. He must have had to do this many times.

'No, sir,' Daniel replied. 'He was . . . not particularly sociable. Worked extremely hard, most of the time in court.'

'Good, was he?' Letterman asked with a sudden flicker of interest . . . more than just the normal degree of courtesy required.

'Excellent. He very rarely lost a case.' That was the truth.

Letterman pursed his lips. 'Any idea what he was working on at the moment, specifically, that might take him to Mile End, or thereabouts?

Whitechapel, perhaps? It could be very important, sir.'

'No, I haven't. I expect Mr fford Croft will know.'

'If it was legal business,' Letterman qualified, with a ghost of a smile.

'I don't know what else would take him to Whitechapel at two in the morning,' Daniel answered, then immediately thought how naïve that sounded. And yet the assumption annoyed him, reasonable as it was. Drake was dead, and could not answer for himself.

Letterman gave a twisted little smile. 'Then you are a singularly unimaginative young man, Mr . . . ?'

'Pitt.' Daniel felt himself colouring. 'I would have thought Drake could do better for himself than that.'

Letterman let out his breath. 'Any relation to Thomas?'

'My father.'

'Ah. Worked with him once, when he was a mere policeman. Maybe you're not so unimaginative, then,' Letterman grunted. 'What do you know of Drake? I'm afraid this was a very violent attack, as if it were personal, not just a robbery gone wrong.'

'If I knew, I would tell you,' Daniel said a little more sharply than before.

'Would you indeed? Rather than keep the name of fford Croft and Gibson out of any nasty gossip? That's a little disloyal of you, isn't it? Got a grudge against him, have you?' His face still wore the same pleasant expression, but there was a sharp glint in his eyes.

'My first loyalty is to the law,' Daniel replied, and then realised how pompous he sounded, and spoke a little more softly. 'And if Drake were doing anything he should not have been, we would be better advised to admit it now than lie about it and look as if we were part of it, when it all comes out . . . and it will. If you do your job.'

'So, you bite, Mr Pitt.' Letterman appeared amused. 'Son of Sir Thomas Pitt, head of Special Branch. Are you trying to follow in his footsteps, by any chance?'

Daniel felt the colour rise up his face. 'I'd like to do as well, but I'm not in the police. I'm a lawyer.'

Letterman changed his tone. 'Well, we'll do our best to find out who killed your Mr Drake, but I can't promise anything. In that area, people don't talk to the police much. I understand you've undertaken to inform Mr fford Croft? He will have a record of Drake's family, if there is any. And no doubt one of you is his solicitor for other affairs, distribution of property, et cetera.'

'Yes,' Daniel answered flatly.

'We'll come by to question everyone who knew him. See if they have any idea what he could have been doing there. And we'll ask around the neighbourhood. But don't raise your hopes too high. He was probably investigating something that turned out worse than he realised. Although, why in God's name he did it at that time of night, I'll never know. Some people just don't realise what risks they run.' He stood up, signalling that the interview was at an end. 'Thank you, Mr Pitt.'

Daniel rose also. Letterman clearly wasn't going to tell him any more. 'Yes, sir. I'll inform Mr fford Croft. I dare say he will be in touch with you.'

★ ★ ★

Daniel took a taxi back to Lincoln's Inn Fields and went inside. Impney met him in the hall, his face expectant. He was too professional to ask outright what had happened. 'A cup of tea, sir? And perhaps a lemon tart?'

'Yes, that's exactly what I would like. Get the taste of the morgue out of my mouth,' Daniel said, thanking him.

'Yes, sir. Would you like it in your office, or perhaps in Mr Kitteridge's room?'

'Is he in, at last?' He had almost forgotten his anxiety about Kitteridge.

'Yes, sir, about a quarter of an hour ago.'

'Then bring it there, thank you.'

Daniel walked down the short corridor to Kitteridge's rooms and knocked abruptly on the door. Then, without waiting for an answer, he flung it open and walked in.

Kitteridge was sitting behind his desk with a sheaf of papers in one hand. He looked startled, and then indignant. He drew in a sharp breath to say something, but Daniel pre-empted him.

'So, you're alive and well then?' Daniel said, more acidly than he had intended. He had been so distressed to think that Kitteridge was dead. Now he found him alive, and completely unaware of the fear he had caused, and it made him unreasonably angry.

Kitteridge looked startled, then offended. 'Of course I'm all right. Where have you been? You look dreadful.'

Daniel found he was shaking. He pulled out one of the visitors' chairs and sat down abruptly. 'To the police morgue,' he replied. 'To identify a corpse wearing your God-awful coat!'

Kitteridge looked at him sharply. 'What are you talking about? I lent it to Drake . . . '

'And he was wearing it when he was killed,' Daniel said grimly. 'I've just come back from identifying his body.'

'What?' The blood drained out of Kitteridge's face.

'Do you need me to say it again?'

Kitteridge slumped against the back of his chair. 'No. No, I don't. But how did this happen?' His voice was suddenly hoarse.

'I don't know. The police are investigating it. There was one of my cards in the pocket of your coat, but nothing of his own to identify him. That's why they sent for me.'

'Why would Drake have one of your cards?' Kitteridge looked puzzled, as if he were struggling with a problem that mattered.

Daniel could understand that. They had neither of them worked much with Drake, but they had known him as long as they had been with their chambers, and for Kitteridge that was eight or so years, even if it was only two for Daniel. The death of anyone they knew would affect them; a violent death like this would leave a deep and ugly mark on the memory. It was unimportant that they had neither of them particularly liked Drake. In fact, it was irrelevant now. It was sudden death. Savage, frightening, unforeseeable.

'More to the point,' Daniel replied, phrasing it as if it were important, 'why did he have your damn coat? It's enough to scare the crows!'

'He took it without asking me,' Kitteridge said with puzzlement. 'He was pretty rude about it, too. I dare say he meant to return it . . .'

'You won't want it back,' Daniel told him, this time avoiding his eyes. 'Even if they could clean it up and mend it. He didn't — ' He stopped. He had been going to ask if Drake had been mistaken for Kitteridge. They were the same height. Now he regretted the clumsiness. He looked at his friend apologetically, but it was too late to take it back. He could see in Kitteridge's eyes that he understood what he was thinking.

'I don't want it back,' he said forcefully. 'He wasn't working any case with me. I've got nothing on right now that is of any interest. Just estate stuff, not even a contested will. Poor old Drake. Didn't like him much — miserable soul, in my opinion — but I wouldn't wish that on anyone.'

Daniel stood up. 'I suppose I'd better go and tell Marcus.' It was not a question. He would like to have been relieved of that duty, but there was no honest way of achieving that.

'Want me to come?' Kitteridge asked, without moving.

'Do you know what might have happened?'

15

Daniel responded. 'Do you even know where he was going? The police think it happened about two o'clock in the morning.'

'Where?'

'Mile End, Whitechapel way.'

Kitteridge's face creased in puzzlement. 'What the devil was he doing at Mile End?'

'No idea in the world. Hardly be deposing a witness, especially not at that hour. I'll go tell Marcus . . . '

'I'll come with you, if you want me to?' Kitteridge offered again.

Daniel gave a brief smile. 'I know, but it might look as if I can't do it myself' He went out the door and closed it softly, then made his way along the corridor, meeting Impney halfway. He was carrying a tea tray. 'You'd better bring that with you for Mr fford Croft,' he suggested.

Impney turned around and followed him to the big office with Marcus fford Croft's name on the door.

Daniel knocked and, as soon as he heard the answer, went in ahead of Impney and held the door open for him. Marcus fford Croft was not a tall man, but he had a remarkable presence. His face was ordinary enough, at first glance, but he had a mane of white hair that had been auburn in his youth, and the unblemished fair skin that often went with such colouring. He wore a wine-red velvet waistcoat that strained its buttons to go around his middle, a pristine cream shirt and a meticulously tied cravat of a softer shade of plum than the waistcoat. He glanced at Impney as he set the tray down. The clerk gave a little inclination of his head and left the room without speaking.

'Well?' Marcus demanded of Daniel curiously.

'I'm sorry, sir, but I've got some very bad news,' Daniel said gravely, still standing upright and a little stiffly.

Marcus frowned. 'Bad news about what? You're not even on a case at the moment . . . '

'No, sir. I . . . ' Daniel stopped. He was getting ahead of himself. With an effort, he kept his voice level. 'Sir, I was called to the police morgue this morning to identify a body. The man had my card in his pocket. Well, in Kitteridge's coat pocket, actually — '

'Stop!' Marcus banged his hand on the pile of papers in front of him. 'You're talking nonsense! What is the bad news?'

Daniel straightened up a bit. 'Mr Drake is dead, sir.'

Marcus froze, his eyes wide. 'Our Mr Drake? Jonah? My God! Poor fellow. I didn't even know he was ill.'

'He wasn't ill, sir. He was stabbed. That's why he was in the police morgue. Wearing Kitteridge's coat. Which is why they came to see me, because my card was in the pocket, and apparently he wasn't carrying anything with his own name on — ' Daniel stopped, because he realised what he had just implied. 'He must have been robbed of his wallet, sir.'

Marcus looked pale, his face almost bloodless. He shook his head slowly. 'Poor fellow. How on earth did that happen? Are the streets getting so dangerous? I . . . ' He was lost for words. He

17

looked mystified, confused, and suddenly older and vulnerable.

Daniel bent forward and lifted the teapot, pouring a cup. Adding a dash of milk, he passed it to Marcus.

Marcus took it and drank at least half of it without looking up. It was a moment's respite.

'It happened in a bad part of Mile End, sir . . . ' Daniel spoke again. 'An alley just off Anthony Street.'

'Are there any good parts of Mile End?' Marcus asked. 'For the love of heaven, what was he doing there?'

'I don't know, sir. It appears he was robbed and any papers on him were taken.'

'We must see that he has a decent burial. I don't believe he had any close relations.' Marcus shook his head. 'But what on earth was he doing there?' he repeated. 'He has no cases that would require him to be in Mile End first thing in the morning.'

'It wasn't first thing, sir. More like two o'clock. I think he must have gone last night. Maybe there'll be a record in his office about what he was doing that might have taken him there.'

'Maybe. Yes, maybe.' Marcus drank the rest of his tea, then looked up at Daniel. 'Thank you. I must think about this. It is very sad. Very disturbing. What do the police say they think it was? A chance robbery?'

An idea ran through Daniel's head — a way to soften the blow — but then he realised he had no right to take away from Marcus the opportunity

18

to act with full knowledge of the facts. 'Quite possibly,' he answered. 'But it was a very vicious attack, sir, far more violent than was necessary to kill him. He . . . he was slashed several times with a very sharp blade, like a sword . . . '

Marcus stared at him. 'Are you quite sure? You're not being . . . melodramatic, are you?'

'No, sir, but you can always ask the police their opinion.'

'I shall. I shall. Do they have any idea which gang was responsible?'

'No, sir. In fact, they would be very glad of any assistance we can give them. They are bound to come here to look into whatever Mr Drake was working on. That seems the most likely explanation.'

Marcus stared at a point on the far wall. 'I suppose so. I will go and take a look at his desk. His files . . . '

'Kitteridge and I can do that, sir.'

'No, you can't! I'll go and see exactly what he was doing. Drake didn't always tell me what he was working on . . . not exactly.' He rose to his feet, a little stiffly. 'Poor fellow.'

Daniel tried to offer some comfort. 'The police said that he probably didn't suffer for more than a few moments, sir.'

Marcus looked very pale, even a little dazed. 'What?' He looked at Daniel uncomprehendingly.

'It was very quick,' Daniel explained.

'Oh. Yes. Thank you for that. At least there was some mercy to it.' Marcus shook his head. 'Get on with your own work, I'll handle this. He has

19

no family, poor man. I must speak to everyone in chambers, but I'll tell his clerk, Hobson, first. He must be properly told, not hear it casually. And, of course, I need to assign people to take over whatever he was working on.' He shook his head. 'Whatever took him to Mile End? Mile End, for God's sake! What on earth are we coming to? Thank you, Pitt. I . . . thank you.'

Marcus stepped out from behind his desk, skirting around Daniel and stumbling a little as he bumped into the door. Then he opened it wider and walked unsteadily along the corridor, leaving Daniel alone with the images in his mind of the terrible wounds inflicted on Drake's dead body, and a wave of anxiety for Marcus himself.

2

By nine o'clock in the evening, Daniel was exhausted, first by his fear for Kitteridge, then by the horror of seeing Drake's body so injured as to be almost unrecognisable. And yet on looking closer, it had been familiar enough to jar him with the reality of the death of someone he had known alive, full of sharp intelligence, opinions and probably emotions. Then there had been his duty to tell Marcus, and the anxiety of his very natural reaction.

It would have been easier if Marcus's daughter, Miriam, had been at home. The thought of her name brought her sharply into his mind: her bright auburn hair, the tilt of her chin, the swift changes of expression in her dark blue eyes. She would have looked after her father, been there to see that he did not indulge in too much brandy, forget how much he had drunk, and any number of other practical things. But she would have been there mostly just to share his grief, ease the shock of it, comfort him.

But she was in Holland studying. She already knew most of the things they would teach her about medicine, chemistry and forensic science in general. But England did not recognise women in the field of forensic medicine, so she was not accepted by the scholastic bodies required to give her professional standing. She could testify in court, and had done so on occasion, but only as a woman, and therefore considered an amateur. The Dutch were more enlightened, and Dr Evelyn Hall, perhaps the most brilliant forensic scientist in Britain, had advised Miriam to get her qualifications in Holland, where she had obtained her own. In spite of himself, Daniel smiled at the memory of Dr Hall's determination, her insight. To say she was eccentric was an understatement. When Miriam had agreed, Dr Eve — as she was called — had sponsored her.

Miriam could not afford to miss a single lecture, and particularly not examination papers. If Marcus were ill, of course, she would have come home immediately. Daniel had finally admitted he was glad she was following her dream and able, at last, to find a path to recognition, and the full use of her remarkable abilities. But he also admitted to himself that he missed her. He missed her dry humour, her insights, and her sudden, startling vulnerabilities, which he usually affected not to have seen, as he now realised she had turned an equally blind eye to some of his.

This evening he was grateful for the frequent invitations to go to his parents' home for dinner. He did not always take them up. Sometimes he ate with friends, or a particular young woman he might like, or other times he was simply tired and glad of an evening alone. Tonight, he was exhausted, and yet restless.

He arrived at Keppel Street, still the same house in which he had grown up, in spite of his father's knighthood and leadership of Special

Branch. This was the department outside the police that dealt with terrorism and violence against the state, focused especially on anarchists and bombers.

His mother answered the door herself, perhaps knowing it was Daniel, or hoping it was. She looked as she always had done — or so it seemed to him — but, of course, gradually she had changed over the years. She still stood straight, head high, and her mahogany-coloured hair had not lost its shine. She smiled with pleasure to see him, and her eyes were full of happiness. He went into the familiar hall quickly, closing the door behind him, and then turned to put his arms around her in a quick hug.

She returned his embrace, then pulled back and looked at his face. 'What is it?' she asked.

He was not yet ready to tell either of his parents what he realised was his deepest anxiety, but he did not want to lie either. A deliberate misdirection would destroy something between them. A straight-out refusal to speak would be better, and more honest. 'I'll tell you about it,' he answered, with an effort at a smile. 'But I think it's quite a long story. I'm hungry. At least, I think I am.'

'Then come in and sit down,' his mother offered, turning and leading the way to the sitting room.

The room had barely changed in as long as he could remember. It was actually two rooms knocked into one. It began with the bay windows on to the small front garden, and stretched all the way to the back of the house. There, French doors gave a view over the long garden, with a lawn and flower beds on either side. There was also a small sandpit where he and his sister Jemima had played as children. He smiled briefly, just for a moment, then he thought of the excuses they had made for not filling it in. Jemima was in America now, married and with two little girls of her own. And Daniel had finished at university and was a practising lawyer, living in a very comfortable boarding house. The sandpit was a memory from childhood, slightly incongruous, and infinitely comforting.

Charlotte came and stood immediately behind him.

His father was sitting in his favourite armchair, hair tousled as usual, now liberally sprinkled with grey. Years of leadership had forced a certain formality into his dress but, given the chance, he still had too much in his pockets, and he could not keep a tie straight. He rose as Daniel came in, his eyes searching Daniel's face, clearly understanding there was something wrong. It was both frightening and almost intrusive to be known so well and read so easily. But it was also a tangible reminder of being loved always by people who knew the worst of you, the vulnerabilities and the faults, the mistakes, and yet still believed in all your possibilities for good as well — perhaps more than you did yourself.

Daniel had intended to tell them the truth slowly, but his good intentions vanished when he felt his father's firm grip on his arm, leading him to sit down on the sofa. There were two armchairs, on opposite sides of the fireplace, even though at this time of the year it was warm enough to do without the fire itself. Thomas sensed his son's need to talk, and sat down with wordless enquiry, clearly waiting for him to speak.

'One of the senior lawyers in chambers was killed last night,' Daniel said bluntly. 'I was called to the police morgue to identify the body this morning. He had borrowed Kitteridge's coat and it had one of my cards in the pocket. That was all the identification he had on him.'

Pitt went straight to the point. 'An overcoat? Then he was outside, not at his home? And his wallet was gone.'

'In Mile End,' Daniel replied. 'And a bad part of it. An alley off Anthony Street.' He took a deep, rather shaky breath. 'He had been knifed . . . savagely. There was a lot of blood.'

Charlotte reached forward and put her hand on Daniel's arm, but she did not say anything.

'So, it was clearly murder,' Pitt concluded grimly. 'Senior partner, you said? Who?'

'Jonah Drake,' Daniel replied.

Something in Pitt's expression changed very slightly, as if a shadow had crossed his face. 'Do you know why he was in Mile End?' he asked.

'Not yet. He wasn't dealing with a case you would expect to end up there. But what else would he be doing in a neighbourhood like that? And at two in the morning?'

'Either following a case, or indulging a private taste,' Pitt replied, with a wry twist of his mouth.

He had begun his career as a constable on the beat and progressed upwards through the ranks, solving many murders, the majority of them in high society. Even, at times, the aristocracy. A professional enemy had driven him out of the police, and he had been immediately taken up by Special Branch. Now most of his work he could not discuss with anyone, not even his own family.

'How is Marcus doing?' Pitt asked. As Daniel was aware, he had known Marcus fford Croft for many years. They had each done favours for the other, as opportunity and necessity arose. In fact, Daniel himself owed his position at fford Croft and Gibson to one of those favours, and he was well aware of it, even though it was never referred to.

Pitt was waiting.

'I think he's pretty badly shaken,' Daniel replied. 'I . . . ' He did not know how to phrase what he had been going to say. In fact, he was not even sure whether he wanted to say it at all.

'Do you know what Drake was working on?' Pitt asked.

'Yes. Marcus said it was a pretty ordinary, if complicated, case of embezzlement,' Daniel replied. 'Nothing that would have taken him to Mile End. More like the opposite direction: Eaton Place, Park Lane, Mayfair. And not at two in the morning.'

'You haven't been given his cases, have you?' Charlotte asked, with concern in her face.

Daniel smiled. 'No, Mother. He was dealing with big, complicated cases in the field of

26

finance, and neither my mathematics nor my knowledge of banking stretch that far, never mind my reputation. One of the other senior partners will take over.'

'Then what is Marcus worried about?' Pitt asked, watching Daniel closely. 'He and Drake were close, at one time. Whether you liked him or not, Drake was an extremely clever lawyer. He brought in a big part of the chambers' income . . . '

'Thomas, even if you really don't like somebody at all, you are still devastated if they're stabbed to death in the back streets of Mile End!' Charlotte chided softly.

'You are grieved,' Pitt conceded, looking back at Daniel. 'But not unduly worried. And certainly not *afraid*.'

'I didn't say he was afraid,' Daniel pointed out, a little too quickly. 'I . . . I think that an unexpected blow like this has made him worry. We all are reminded how nothing should be taken for granted.' He tried to frame what he felt in words. 'We none of us liked Drake all that much, but we were used to him — and, honestly, we admired him. And now, suddenly, he's gone. That could happen to anyone, it seems. Of course, that has always been true, I suppose, but continual safety makes you forget it — '

Charlotte interrupted, glancing first at Pitt and then at Daniel. 'Do you find yourself at Mile End often, at two o'clock in the morning?'

'No, of course not! But . . . '

'Then what you really mean is that it has forced you to look at certain aspects of the people you work with a great deal more closely than you would have chosen to. You must reconsider your assumptions. And that includes Marcus fford Croft and — '

Pitt interrupted. 'Marcus is . . . ' he began.

Charlotte shook her head. 'Very charming, very likable,' she finished. 'But we all have faults, weaknesses, things we would rather other people didn't know about us. The more private they are, the more important it is to us that we keep some . . . secrets.'

Daniel looked at her in surprise.

'As you know, I first met your father when he was investigating the murder of my elder sister,' she said quietly. 'Of course, that was long before you were born. But I discovered then how little we know about other people, even members of our own family. The people we love most make their own mistakes as well. As do we ourselves, under pressure.' The colour crept up her cheeks, but she did not move her gaze from his face. 'We idealise those we love, and very often expect too much of them. As perhaps they do of us. In truth, real love takes account of our failings, and our weaknesses as well. You may discover a few things about Marcus, and about other people too, that you don't like. Isn't that what you are really afraid of?'

For several seconds, neither of them answered her.

Daniel's mind raced. He remembered now that there had been a third sister. There was his mother, and his Aunt Emily — and also Sarah, whose murder had brought together the young policeman Thomas Pitt and the much wealthier, and socially very acceptable, Charlotte Ellison. They seemed so natural together, so comfortable, that he forgot most of the time how different their beginnings had been. It seemed totally irrelevant to the life he knew.

And yes, that was the truth. He was afraid of the changes Drake's death would bring. Even sharper than the knowledge of that death was the awareness of how it would affect the chambers of fford Croft and Gibson, and Marcus himself. Daniel liked him, his personality, his eccentricities, at times his startling kindness and, lately, his vulnerability. In truth, he had become increasingly absent-minded, and occasionally forgetful of details.

Pitt glanced from Daniel to Charlotte, and then back again. 'It probably has to do with one of Drake's cases,' he observed. 'It would be a good idea if you investigated them again, before the police do. He's had some very prominent ones. Have you looked into them yet? You and Kitteridge, at least. You trust Kitteridge, don't you?' It was barely a question, more a restatement of fact.

'Yes.' That was acknowledged. 'Actually, we looked at the last half-dozen this afternoon.'

'Did Marcus tell you to?' Pitt asked curiously.

'No, not really. He told us to see what cases were outstanding and then take them to him so he could reassign them. Fortunately, there is only one major case. But it's big, and it involves embezzlement and fraud, both of them. A very great deal of money is involved. Not the sort of thing either of us does. It needs an understanding of economics and the law. We might have to pass the case on to other chambers. And that's bad, because we'll lose the client. But no lawyer is going to kill another lawyer in order to get a mess of a case like this one.'

'And the others?' Pitt asked. 'What else was he working on, or had been in the past? Or do you think it was part of his personal life? But who would ever go to Mile End, and alone? Was it a matter of revenge? An outstanding debt? Or perhaps he knew something that endangered someone. Blackmail?'

Daniel concentrated with all the attention he could muster. So many questions! And always in his mind was the image of the hideously slashed body of Jonah Drake lying on the morgue slab, naked under an anonymous white sheet, for decency's sake. But there was nothing decent about his wounds. And those repeated injuries had not been inflicted on him in the course of a casual robbery.

His mother was staring at him. Her face was his earliest memory, but how often did he really look at her carefully, and listen to her words — whether they were what he wanted to hear or not? 'Do you really want to talk about this?' she asked softly.

He weighed his reply. 'Thank you, but I'll be thinking about it, whether I talk or not. I see Drake's body in my head, no matter what I'm actually looking at. We've got to deal with it — and rather us than the police. If his death is connected to one of Drake's cases, we'd better find out about it before speculation ruins the reputation of the chambers.'

Pitt glanced at Charlotte, then turned to Daniel. 'Yes, you had better be the first to know. So, what cases of his did you find controversial?'

Daniel thought for a moment before answering.

Pitt waited.

'We went back a couple of years,' Daniel began slowly, recalling the pattern of the day as he and Kitteridge went through Drake's records, searching for cases that seemed in any way unresolved, or not to have ended with the outcome everyone had expected. Drake was clever, and he knew the law. He specialised in cases involving money, but every so often he defended in other trials as well. There were two that involved murder. Daniel repeated the details, as exactly as he could remember.

'The earlier trial was a man named Lionel Peterson.' He pictured the sheet of paper with Drake's own notes. 'He was accused of murdering the wife of one of his rivals in business. She was a woman of poor reputation, according to several eyewitnesses.'

'What kind of *poor*, Daniel?' Pitt asked. 'Be a bit more specific. There are many kinds. If you leave it unspecified, we will presume she was promiscuous.'

Daniel gave a twisted little smile. 'People are very circumspect in court. But Drake's notes said she was a high-class whore. I expect the truth was not quite so grubby, but definitely along those lines ... ' He remembered the curiously vivid little picture Drake had drawn beside his notes. It had depicted a woman's body, with the lower half a fish's tail. It was harsh, and funny, and probably accurate. He had not thought Drake so perceptive! Those few lines conveyed far more than a page of writing could ever have done.

'Would he know at first hand?' Pitt asked.

'I hadn't thought of that,' Daniel admitted. 'I don't know. I couldn't even imagine Drake . . .' He stopped. It was absurd. Drake was flesh and blood underneath the formal clothes of his profession. Why had Daniel not even thought of that? Because the last time he had seen Drake, the man had been a pathetic corpse lying utterly helpless, unable to defend his dignity, let alone act with any kind of appetite, or passion. 'I don't know,' he admitted aloud. 'Someone strangled her. Peterson was suspected, largely because he knew both the business rival and his wife socially, but also because some of the evidence suggested that he was more than just an acquaintance. That perhaps he and the man's wife were lovers. But even if that were true, Peterson was only one of many, and he surely knew what she was like. He would hardly have expected her to be exclusive.'

'The verdict?' Pitt asked.

'Hung jury,' Daniel replied. 'I think Peterson was damn lucky to get that. He avoided the rope, but his reputation never recovered, either professionally or personally. He blamed Drake for not getting him completely exonerated.'

'Did you think Drake was remiss in any way?'

'I thought he was brilliant to get him off at all,' Daniel admitted. 'I'm not sure anyone else could have done that. I confess, I took Drake a lot more seriously after reading as much as I could of the trial. We can go back and read it in detail if you wish.'

'Not yet.' Pitt shook his head. 'Was there a retrial? Or was anyone else charged?'

'No. Again, Drake must have done some pretty fancy footwork to get them not to retry the case. I'm beginning to see why Marcus respected him so much.' He felt the impact of that as he said it. No wonder Marcus looked so shattered. The loss to the chambers might be deeper than they could easily absorb.

Pitt was watching him, waiting.

'Peterson felt a lot of ill will towards Drake,' Daniel went on. 'At least, according to the letters in Drake's file.'

'Then you'd better follow it up,' Pitt advised. 'What else?'

Daniel hesitated. 'The issue of Peterson's guilt seems to have been a bone of contention between Marcus and Drake. As long as you don't know any different, you have to assume your client is innocent, if they tell you they are. It was a messy case, and Drake was very good — in fact, brilliant — at raising doubts you could not just disregard.'

'Then why was Marcus not convinced?' Pitt asked. 'You're missing something.'

'I know,' Daniel admitted. 'I'll ask him, when I can. At the moment, he's up to his neck in trying to find people to take over Drake's current cases.

I think it's pretty serious for the chambers to lose Drake so suddenly. Even if people didn't really like him very much, and sometimes didn't trust him. Marcus didn't say that! It's just a feeling I have. But we can't turn business away because someone *might* be guilty — after all, if there were no chance of them being convicted, they wouldn't have been charged. A lot of the financial cases needed Drake's special skills; such things are the backbone of our income.'

'Nobody wants to lose business,' Pitt said, with a small grimace. 'The chambers' reputation is good enough to survive this, as long as Drake's death is solved satisfactorily, and reasonably quickly. And, of course, assuming that he wasn't doing anything unprofessional.'

'I know,' Daniel replied. 'We have no choice, we've got to solve it, find out who it was, and why. If we don't, people will make up their own answers, and we've got enough rivals as it is . . . who will very politely cast suspicion on us.'

'Rivals who would murder Drake?' Charlotte asked in surprise. 'Is that really what worries you?'

'No, Mother, but certainly astute enough to take advantage of his death, and Marcus's weakness — ' He stopped abruptly. He had not meant to say that, but the words were out. 'I mean . . . vulnerability,' he corrected, but he was too late to hide it. Charlotte had seen that he was worried.

'Cover that up from other people, out of loyalty, but don't cover it up from yourself,' Pitt told him. 'Those who attack him are going to see the truth. You're not much use on a defence team if you don't face even the worst truths, however much you would rather not accept them. And with Miriam in Holland, you are the nearest thing he has to family. An advocate, in this or anything else, is no use if you don't see the harsh light of reality — especially if that is what's going to do the most harm.'

'I cannot see Marcus going to Mile End in the middle of the night and slashing Drake!' Daniel said, rather too loudly. 'He would do something far less violent, something more carefully planned . . .'

Pitt shook his head wearily. 'Of course he would,' he agreed. 'And this might have been the totally random act of a lunatic. But far more probably, it has roots in the past, and if so, it almost certainly has to do with a case.' He lowered his voice, the tone suddenly gentle. 'Real loyalty lies in facing the truth. And before you can do that, you need to find out the facts. But Daniel, don't go chasing shadows on your own around Mile End. Do you understand?'

'Yes, of course I do,' Daniel said miserably. 'If I go anywhere, I'll take Kitteridge. I want to know the truth, whatever it is. I have to know it — and make sure the world knows it, too.'

There was a moment's heavy silence. A log of wood collapsed in the fireplace with a fall of ash.

'You said two cases,' Pitt prompted. 'What was the other one?'

Daniel came to attention. 'Yes. It was more recent, less than two years ago. A young man, Evan Faber, was accused of beating to death a woman of thirty-five. Evan had been going out with her, even though she was at least ten years older than he.' He saw the anxiety in his father's face. 'What's wrong with that?' he said sharply, feeling the heat rise up his own cheeks. Miriam fford Croft was forty, yet he had never liked anyone so much. And he knew she was sensitive about her age, even though theirs was a friendship, nothing more. And yet, it was deep, and he valued it more than he was prepared to share with either of his parents.

Pitt looked puzzled. 'Young Faber was found not guilty, wasn't he? I seem to remember Drake was brilliant. I hadn't realised that he was part of Marcus's chambers.'

'Then you know the case,' Daniel concluded, shifting his position uncomfortably in the chair. 'Do you disagree with the verdict?'

'I don't have an opinion, except that it was like pulling a rabbit out of a hat to defend him successfully. There were reasons why it was an enormous feat. I'm not surprised Marcus is sick at losing a man who could do that. It won't be at all easy to find his equal. But that's not what concerns me. Do you know anything about Evan's father, Erasmus Faber?'

'No. Who is he?'

'Faber? Owner of the biggest shipbuilding company in Britain.'

Charlotte moved uncomfortably beside Daniel, but she refrained from interrupting.

'What has that to do with it?' Daniel asked. 'Drake got him off, and it looks as if he was innocent, so it was a just decision, reached after due process. Drake was brilliant. He left everyone feeling as if it were the right outcome, reached in the right way, after a hell of a struggle.'

Pitt's face was unreadable. 'Avoid Erasmus Faber if you can,' he warned.

'Why? Is he above the law?'

Pitt's face was bleak. 'No one is. At least, theoretically . . . ' 'But?'

'But . . . at the moment, he's a man very important to the government. And since you seem to be satisfied that Drake came to the right conclusion, in the right way, you don't need to question the verdict. Why did you even mention it, side by side with a case that wasn't satisfactorily concluded?'

'Because it was a hard-fought battle, and the police never found whoever did it,' Daniel answered, stiffening in his seat. 'But the jury were all satisfied that it wasn't Evan.'

'If there was no evidence pointing to Evan, why did the police arrest him?' Charlotte asked.

Pitt leaned forward and put another log of wood on the fire. It caught immediately, sending up a shower of sparks.

'There was evidence, but Drake explained it away,' Daniel answered. 'Evan did know her, but apparently quite a few other men did also. According to the description, she was very attractive, and not above spreading her favours pretty generously. Usually, she went for older men.' Daniel gave a sour smile. 'I think that was Drake's tactful, and less than oblique, way of saying *wealthier*. She might actually have liked

37

Evan. And he had no idea what kind of woman she was. The theory is that he discovered this accidentally, and the shock made him completely lose his head. He felt deceived and betrayed and, worst of all, that he'd been made a fool of. She was killed in a rage. And they didn't have any obvious suspects.'

'So why did the jury decide Evan Faber was innocent?' Charlotte asked. 'He couldn't have had any witnesses to prove he was elsewhere, or they wouldn't have charged him in the first place.'

'I haven't read the case in enough detail to know yet,' Daniel admitted. 'And it's not just a matter of having witnesses; you've got to have ones that the jury believes. But the case ended with a unanimous verdict. Evan was found not guilty, and no one else was subsequently tried for the murder.'

'So the real killer is still out there,' Pitt added. 'Did you look into the possibility of any form of corruption? Bribery? Threats?'

Daniel was surprised. 'Why, what makes you even think of that? Drake would do the best he could for his client, whatever he thought. And I think he was basically honest, or Marcus wouldn't have kept him on, however clever he was.'

Pitt thought for a few moments before he opened his mouth to answer.

Charlotte spoke before he could. 'Thomas, do you know something about it?'

He looked up in surprise. 'No! But I know Erasmus Faber is one of the richest men in London, and in many ways the most powerful.

He has a genius for shipbuilding, fast and yet completely thorough. Evan is his only son. In fact, his only child. His wife has been dead for some twenty years or more. He owns two of the biggest shipbuilding yards in England, and one of the biggest in Europe. We're a maritime nation. Without mastery of the seas, or at least the waters around our shores, we could be cut off by an enemy within a relatively short time, isolated and then starved into submission. Men like Erasmus Faber hold one of the keys to our prosperity, and he knows it.'

'Do you know something else about him, Thomas?' Charlotte, as usual, was direct.

He looked slightly surprised. 'No. But men don't get that kind of success without being clever, strong, and unwilling to dance to anyone's tune except their own.' He looked at Daniel. 'You have to find out everything you can about Drake's death, and the sooner the better, for Marcus's sake . . . and the sake of the chambers. But tread softly when it comes to looking at the Faber case again. Don't do it, as long as there is any other avenue open to you. Please.'

Without the *please* Daniel might have argued. He was grateful for the generous friendship he enjoyed with his father, how his father watched over him, giving advice even when it was not asked for. But Daniel's patience with his father's guidance, however well meant, was wearing very thin. He wanted Pitt to trust him more, and to let go of the idea that he needed advice in everything.

But the concern in his father's face — and the fact that he had asked it as a favour, rather than issuing it as an instruction — along with the sharp warning in Pitt's voice, softened his answer.

'Yes, I'll exhaust all the other possibilities first,' Daniel replied. He turned to his mother. 'Is dinner nearly ready? I don't think I've eaten since breakfast.'

3

Daniel slept badly. His night was full of dreams, mostly of a man lying crumpled up in a nameless alley in the dark and covered with blood. Daniel knew it was Drake. He was under a street lamp, and his face was grey, slashed open and smeared with congealed blood.

Daniel woke with his head thumping, temples sore, mouth dry. He was still tired, but he would rather be up than sink back into that dream.

Mrs Portiscale would be up. She rose early every morning and would be in the kitchen by now. She favoured him, he knew. He was the youngest of her three lodgers, and the only one who actually told her about his life, his job, and generally listened to her opinions. She spoiled him, and he appreciated it.

He washed, shaved and dressed, then went downstairs. She was in the kitchen, the shining pots and pans on their hooks on the wall, copper gleaming. Strings of onions hung from the ceiling, as if they grew there. A pot of parsley, bright with leaves, sat on the window ledge. As he had expected, she was bent over the fire in the stove, poking it to life. She heard his footsteps on the wooden floorboards and looked up.

'You're early.' She straightened her back with a little grimace and pushed stray wisps of hair off her face. 'My, you look bad. Didn't sleep? Hot cup of tea will help you wake up.' She reached

41

for the kettle and pulled it on to the hob. 'Take a few minutes, mind. Fire's a bit slow this morning.'

'That's all right,' he answered. 'I'll wait. Anything I can do to help while it's burning up? Do you need more coal?' He could see that the scuttle was almost empty. She insisted on getting it from the coal cellar herself, but it was all she could do to lift it.

'You just sit down and keep out of my way,' she said, with a smile.

He took the scuttle anyway, and went down the steps to the cellar door, opened it and went in. He picked up the shovel and began to work.

'You don't listen, do you!' she said when he brought it back. But she was grateful, and it did not need to be said between them. She looked him up and down. 'Black suit today? That's so you could shovel coal and no one would notice?'

He put the scuttle down carefully in its place and straightened up. She always knew when he was hiding something, and this time it was actually a relief to admit it. 'No, a senior member of our chambers died yesterday. Small hours of the morning.' He went to the sink and turned on the tap to wash his hands. 'He went to Mile End, we don't know why, and he was found before dawn. Looks as if he died about two in the morning. It was all very horrible. Someone slashed him several times with a long knife.'

'Mile End? That's no more than a slum. Near as bad as Whitechapel,' she said, seizing on the one thing that she was familiar with. 'Whatever for? Police tell you then?'

'No, actually he borrowed Kitteridge's coat, which had one of my cards in the pocket. They came to get me yesterday morning, to see if I could identify the body . . . '

She shook her head. 'The poor soul. No wonder you're wandering around looking like you lost sixpence and found nothing!'

'We've got to discover what happened,' he began.

She shook her head. 'No, you don't 'got to'! You just let the police take care of that. Sounds as if he were into something nasty. Don't you go meddling with it. You just do your job. The kettle will be boiling in a few minutes. Like your breakfast early, would you?' She set about making it without waiting for his answer. 'Bacon and eggs? Toast? Got this year's marmalade, made special.'

'Thank you, Mrs Portiscale. Your marmalade is always better than anyone else's.'

'That it is,' she agreed, appreciating the compliment. 'Now sit still and don't get under my feet.'

She went about fetching the ingredients from the pantry and setting them all out on the kitchen table. It was always the same: salt and pepper, although she often reminded Daniel that she had seasoned everything enough. How many times had he heard her telling off those who added salt without tasting the food first? The same large toast rack sat there every morning, the same blue and white milk jug, and three sets of knives and forks. The teapot remained on the hob.

She hummed a little to herself, but did not

speak again until she set the fried eggs and several rashers of bacon on a warm plate in front of him, and two freshly toasted slices of brown bread, with butter and the unopened jar of marmalade. She would leave him to unscrew it. She always put the lid on more tightly than she could undo. It was a ritual now that he should undo it for her, and take the first mouthful from the jar. Raspberry jam was made in the late summer, and plum jam. Marmalade was always made in January, with the ripe bitter oranges imported from Spain. Connoisseurs would accept only the bitter, Seville oranges. Nothing else gave the same fragrant sharpness.

He ate in silence, surprised by how much he enjoyed it. It was almost like being at home in his mother's kitchen when he was a child. Here, his landlady also had copper saucepans arranged on hooks on the wall, more ornamental than useful, with dried herbs hanging from nails almost too high to reach, and the Welsh dresser with plates on. These were white with blue rings. His mother's had been hand painted with wild flowers, no two alike. And, of course, there was the wooden rail winched up to the ceiling for sheets and towels, for their final airing before being put away. It was all so familiar . . . and safe.

Mrs Portiscale poured his tea for him in a large mug, and one for herself, then sat down opposite him. For a few minutes, she was silent. 'So, what are you going to do about it then?' she finally asked.

'We have to find out what happened to him,'

44

he said urgently. 'To Drake. It wasn't just an ordinary robbery. What was he doing in a slum like Mile End in the middle of the night anyway? Kitteridge will look into the cases Drake has been working on. He may even take them over, but I doubt it. It's terribly complicated and probably about money.'

'What about the police? Isn't that supposed to be their job?'

'Yes, but they don't seem to hold out much hope.'

He finished the last mouthful of bacon and took the first piece of toast. It was crisp, and done just as he liked it. He gave her a quick smile of appreciation as he spread the butter.

'That so?' she said, without moving her eyes from his face. 'Or are you afraid he was doing something as you'd rather the police didn't know about? Got a family around, has he, this present client?'

He took a spoonful of marmalade out of the jar and put it on the side of his plate. He thought of feigning innocence, but he knew exactly what she meant. She understood that they had guilty clients as well. He had explained very carefully, late one evening over several mugs of hot cocoa, why that was necessary, and fair. Nothing was ever precisely as it looked. There was always at least one other side to every case — if not more than one. And the guilty deserved a fair trial, too.

'Yes,' he admitted. 'And his young clerk, Hobson, helped us. He was terribly shaken, but he pulled himself together and gave us all the information. We owe it to the client to find out if it has something to do with the case. And, of course, we've got to find another lawyer to carry on with it, and pretty soon. They'll give us a few days to catch up, but that's all.'

She bit into the toast again before continuing. 'I see,' she answered. 'And what are you going to do?'

He had been hoping she would not ask that. He spread another piece of toast with butter, and then more marmalade.

He could see by her expression that she realised he was not going to answer, and would not press it. She stood up and began to lay out the ingredients for breakfast for the other lodgers.

'I'm going to go over his most critical cases,' Daniel said abruptly. 'We've got to know what happened.'

'To protect the chambers. I understand,' she answered, without looking at him. 'Do you want another cup of tea?'

'Thank you,' he accepted. It put off for another few minutes having to face the day.

★   ★   ★

When he got to chambers, half an hour later, Impney opened the door to him, his face grim. 'Good morning, sir. I hope you are well.' It was the usual greeting, only the tenor of his voice made it empty. He stood back and left the door wide open for Daniel.

Daniel went in, past Impney, and along to his own office. He looked at the papers lying on his

46

desk, all of them pertaining to the two cases most likely to have, one way or another, led to Drake's death. He should start with the more contentious of them: the one that had left unfinished the issue of guilt or innocence. What would he find? An error, a mistake, or something overlooked? Was that what he was afraid of, and Mrs Portiscale had seen it?

He read the papers for half an hour, then put them down and walked out into the corridor and along to Marcus's office. He knocked on the door and waited.

'Come.' Marcus's voice was flat, without interest or emotion.

Daniel went in and closed the door behind him.

Marcus was seated in his chair, a little slumped forward. As always, he was tidy, his waistcoat a plain dark green, his cravat an ordinary patterned foulard. What was out of character was his shock of white hair. It did not look well groomed. In fact, it looked lifeless, which was so unnatural for him.

A knot tightened inside Daniel's chest. 'Good morning, sir,' he said quietly. 'Would you like me to fetch you a cup of tea?'

'I would not,' Marcus replied. 'I'm drowning in it. Prick me and I should bleed tea!' He shook his head, then pushed his hand through his hair, which had fallen forward as usual. 'What was he doing, Daniel? What did I not know about Jonah that I should have? I wasn't paying attention. Or did I know it . . . and I forgot? Or is it that I chose to forget, because I wasn't willing to see

47

the ugly truth?' His face was creased, his eyes troubled.

How should Daniel answer truthfully? He wished to heaven that Miriam were here to care for her father, persuade him to be open about everything. Or was there really something to hide? Something relevant to Drake's death that Marcus had denied, until now?

Marcus nodded slowly. 'Find out for me, Daniel. I'd rather we did not poke into Jonah's life, but we have to. And you'll have to do it by yourself. I've got Kitteridge handling Jonah's present case. God knows, it's complicated. He's good on detail. Better than you are.' He gave a slight shrug. 'But you're a better judge of people. You must have that from your father. You're too young to have learned it yourself.'

There was a sustained silence, which Daniel finally filled. 'From my mother, sir.'

'What? Oh, yes. Your mother. Interesting woman. So, what about these cases, eh?'

Did he really want to know Daniel felt as if he were walking down an irregular series of steps, blindfolded, and with no idea where they led, only that it was downwards, and he was fumbling to find the next one. Was Marcus really unaware of what Drake had been doing? Marcus was head of chambers. There had never been a Gibson of fford Croft and Gibson. There was no one for Marcus to turn to, to lean on.

'I'm going to see Lionel Peterson today, sir. I've just looked at the file again,' Daniel said. He assumed that Marcus understood he was referring to one of Drake's cases.

48

'What?' Marcus asked sharply. 'Pitt, just . . . '
he stopped. He looked old and confused.

'It probably hasn't any connection, but if it
does, I'll find it,' Daniel said, and the instant
afterwards wished he had not. How could he live
up to such a promise? What if he found out that
Marcus knew all about it already? Had he told
Drake to win at all costs? Turned a blind eye
when he suspected that Drake, and therefore the
chambers, had crossed the line between advocate
and accomplice? And had taken the money for it.

'What is it?' Marcus repeated, now angry as
well, because he did not understand. 'For
heaven's sake, Pitt, how can I sort this out if you
won't tell me what you are talking about?'

There was nothing for it but to tell the truth,
or as much of it as would make sense. Daniel
was reluctant to burden Marcus with possibilities, especially ones that might turn out badly.
'Sorry, sir,' he apologised. 'I'm going to check on
the two outstanding cases that seemed the most
controversial, starting with Lionel Peterson.'

Marcus frowned. 'Peterson? Didn't Drake get
him off?'

'Hung jury, sir. Not guilty, but not cleared
either. But they aren't going to try him again.'

'Guilty,' Marcus said, pursing his lips, drawing
his own conclusion. 'If he'd been innocent,
Drake would have got him off!'

'That's what I would like to find out. If he
really is innocent, he might resent the fact that
Drake didn't clear him.'

Marcus's eyebrows shot up. 'So, he stabs him
to death in an alley in the slums of Mile End?'

49

'No,' Daniel admitted. 'And the other case worth looking at is one with a verdict of not guilty.'

'Also murder?' Marcus asked. 'Jonah did mostly fraud and embezzlement.'

'The alternative is that his murder has nothing to do with a case,' Daniel pointed out. 'At least, not in the last two years.'

Marcus looked down at his hands folded in front of him. 'I know. I know. But the only thing that's going to help is for us to find the truth, and . . . ' He raised his eyes and met Daniel's. 'And we've got to get to the bottom of this, Pitt. Not only for Drake, poor fellow, but for the chambers. If we can't show what happened to him, too many people will assume he was doing something illicit, and . . . I need to know. Why the devil would a reputable, middle-aged financial lawyer be in a place like Mile End at two in the morning? God! What a mess!' There was a sharp note of despair in his voice, and something else. Was it fear?

'Private business of some sort?' Daniel tried to suggest an answer.

'Nothing honest,' Marcus said quietly. 'Honest business is done in offices, in daylight. He must have been following a lead. I've got Kitteridge on it, with Hobson. I'm hoping he'll find something among all the money stuff. Even if we lose the case Drake was currently working on, the financial one. Very complicated, to do with embezzlement. Small price, compared with what else it could be . . . '

'But do you want me to look into the

50

murders?' Daniel asked. 'That will require a closer look — not only at Peterson, but also at Evan Faber.'

'Yes,' Marcus said wearily. 'Yes, look into both of them. Exclude them, if you can. And let me know. And for heaven's sake, tread lightly with the Faber case.'

'Yes, sir.'

Daniel left the office with a tightening knot of misery inside him. He spent the rest of the morning rereading the evidence against Lionel Peterson, and Drake's notes on all the witness statements. As he read, his admiration for Drake's skills increased. The man always kept to the right side of deception or collusion, but he had some ideas, questions — and even suggested answers — that came very close to the margins.

When Impney brought him a tray with tea at about half past noon, and asked if he would like sandwiches, or if he intended to go out, Daniel realised how tense he was. He had completely forgotten about such practical necessities as eating. He put the papers down reluctantly. 'I . . . can you please get me some sandwiches? I don't want to lose the thread of this.'

'Indeed, sir. Roast beef? Ham? Cheese?'

'Ham, thank you. I . . . ' He looked up. 'Impney? Can you tell me anything about Mr Drake, other than that he was a damn good lawyer . . . and that someone killed him, pretty horribly, both of which I already know?'

Impney considered the question seriously, looking not at Daniel but into the distance, at a landscape picture on the wall. 'He was a very clever man, sir, very good with money, but he didn't always care much for his clients,' he said, smiling. Quite clearly, someone in particular came to mind. 'He could see the deviousness in some of them, without understanding the path that led them to steal and then deny it, even to themselves.'

'You mean he had blind spots?' Daniel asked.

'Very well put, sir. Yes, he understood from the outside, as it were. Whereas some people understand from the inside. Occasionally, he misplaced his trust. Not everyone who pretends to serve the law really does so. If you know what I mean.' Impney brought his mild but curiously penetrating gaze back to Daniel, meeting his eyes.

'I think I do.' Daniel had a glimpse of something, but knew he had not seen all of it. 'If you think of anything that might help, please tell me. Mr Drake is beyond our help now, but Mr fford Croft is not.' He knew there was no need to explain it any further.

'Certainly, sir. The ham sandwiches are coming.'

'Thank you.' Daniel bent his head to the papers again.

The sandwiches were excellent; he ate them and then returned to work. By evening, he knew he would be ready to go and see Lionel Peterson the following day.

★ ★ ★

Peterson turned out to be a heavyset man, somewhere just over fifty, with thick grey hair

52

and a smile that did not reach his cold eyes. At twenty-five he must have been handsome, but at twice that age his character had worn lines into his face that were no longer flattering. He was dressed expensively, in a well-cut shirt and fine wool suiting. Daniel wondered for a moment if Mrs Peterson's clothes cost even half as much. Peterson's testimony in Drake's notes suggested a vanity that did not extend to his wife.

'I don't know what you want,' Peterson said irritably. 'And I don't appreciate your making a scene by coming to my place of business. Life has been difficult enough with that incompetent Drake failing to clear my name. I may not be in prison, but I'm still paying for another man's crime! I heard Drake's dead. Decency says I should grieve, but I'm not a hypocrite.' He stared belligerently at Daniel. 'I'll send a wreath to the funeral, but that's all: my wife wouldn't have me do that much.' He waited for Daniel to argue.

'I read that your wife was very angry on your behalf.' Daniel nodded slightly, as if he agreed.

'Yes, and Drake wouldn't call her to testify.' Peterson's voice rose sharply. 'She would have sworn to my presence at home all that night. That would have proved my innocence, not left the question of guilt hanging over me, threatening me. I couldn't possibly have murdered that poor woman but I can still see the suspicion in people's faces, in the things they don't say.' His voice was accusatory. 'That's a terrible thing to live with. It's totally unjust.'

Daniel sympathised, but he also remembered, as if the page were in front of him, Drake's notes on the subject. He had interviewed Mrs Peterson. She had promised to swear in court that she had been unwell, and up most of the night, and so observed everything there was to see. Her husband had been at home from early evening into the dawn. But Drake had not trusted her. She had a powerful hand in Peterson's defence, or alternatively, his conviction. Drake was certain that she knew it, and intended to use it in the future. He had made a little doodle at the side of the page, a dryly humorous sketch of a woman holding scales, with one long, sharp finger on the balance, and a smile on her face. It was only a few curved lines, but its meaning was clear. Actually, it was clever. It was Daniel's first moment of appreciation for a man who, before then, had shown no warmth, let alone humour. Daniel would read more of Drake's notes in the future and see if there were other revealing little doodles. Were they reminders to Drake? Explanations? Or a private sense of humour?

'Well?' Peterson demanded, interrupting his thoughts. 'Can you explain why she wasn't called?'

'Probably because he was trying to defend your wife, protect her from cruel questions . . . ' Daniel replied.

'Balderdash! She would have defended me!' Peterson snapped.

'She could well have been bullied, stripped of her dignity, and still not been believed,' Daniel pointed out.

'That's balderdash,' Peterson repeated, looking at Daniel with dislike. 'My wife is a very strong woman.'

'Assuredly,' Daniel agreed bleakly. 'But it is, in every way, in her interest that she should help prove you innocent.'

'I *am* innocent,' Peterson snarled.

Daniel drew in a deep breath. 'Think like a juror, Mr Peterson,' he said patiently. 'What sort of wife would see her husband convicted of murder — and the disloyalty to her that it implies, in this case — leaving her to be pitied, ridiculed, without means of support or income, an outcast from the society she had ruled, until this period? Wouldn't an intelligent, far-sighted wife prefer to protect both her husband's reputation and her own by lying?'

The blood drained from Peterson's face and he seemed to crumple in size. It was as if none of this had occurred to him at all.

'Mr Drake knew it was in your interest not to call her,' Daniel said quietly. 'What will any loyal wife say, except that her husband is innocent? Whatever the truth, she is fighting for her own survival.'

Peterson looked back at him with loathing. Had he really not thought of that before? Was this an act, because his wife had guarded her own interests, and they both knew it?

'Maybe the police will find whoever really did kill her. Wouldn't that end your difficulties?' Daniel suggested.

Peterson gave him a blank smile, and it was the first moment Daniel actually felt that the man might be innocent. It was a wretched situation, but definitely better than conviction, and possibly even the gallows. And he was satisfied that Peterson had not gone to Mile End and murdered Drake. If he had been tempted to carry out such a foul deed, it would have been immediately after the trial was over.

He would have to see if Drake did follow up the possibility of his client's innocence. So far, he had seen no evidence of that.

★ ★ ★

That evening, Daniel went through the notes — both the trial and Drake's — one more time, taking them home with him and sitting up long after dark. He found Drake's handwritten notes were useful and detailed where he had doubts, and he followed them all up. There were other quick little drawings, maybe just part of a face, but always expressive. They were far more powerful than words. There were some images with vivid, wide-open eyes, some with long lashes, a hand with fingers crossed, a man with a laugh, another with a sneer.

When Daniel finally fell asleep, one page was clutched in his hand and he had an acute sense of loss that he had not known Drake. He could have learned a lot from him. And he wished he had not seen the mutilated face. Jonah Drake had been so much more than that. The least Daniel could do was find out who had killed him so savagely.

Had it been fear, revenge, jealousy? Greed? Or something else?

★ ★ ★

In the morning, Daniel went straight to Marcus's office.

Marcus looked up from the papers he had been reading. His clothes were rumpled, as if he had been there all night, and he moved stiffly to readjust his position. 'Well? What have you found?' he asked, without preamble. There was hope in his eyes, which Daniel could not bear to see.

He explained to Marcus what Peterson had said. Then he offered him Drake's notes on his most recent cases.

Marcus held out his hand.

Daniel noticed that it was shaking very slightly. He leaned forward and gave the papers to him. 'Small mistakes, but we ought to know about them. They may mean more to you than I understand . . . '

'About Drake? Are there mistakes he made?' Marcus asked. There was an edge to his voice. Was it a very natural grief for a man he had known and worked with for years? Or a fear that Drake had been doing something Marcus did not know about — and even was afraid of.

'There are witnesses he didn't call,' Daniel answered. 'I think another lawyer would have.'

'Do you? Why?' Marcus frowned. 'What are you implying?'

'He would have had his reasons — some evidence he found compelling — and if he didn't, that was interesting in itself,' Daniel replied, beginning to think that he and Marcus could be talking at cross purposes.

'But do these 'small mistakes' suggest a motive

to murder him?' Marcus raised his eyebrows.

'No, I don't think so. But we should clear it up before anybody else finds them,' Daniel replied.

Marcus blinked. 'I want you to get to the bottom of these two cases, make sure there's nothing that we missed . . . nothing that will come back to bite us. There would be people glad enough to see that happen.' He shivered very slightly. He was only stating the obvious: fford Croft and Gibson had won a lot of cases. No chambers can have that much success without creating envy, at the very least, and Drake had been at the heart of many of these cases.

'Yes, sir . . . ' Daniel hesitated, and cleared his throat. 'Somebody killed Drake pretty violently. We can't afford to dismiss anything, even if it seems to be irrelevant. Or more than that, if the evidence points to something we would rather not have to look into. We can't afford that luxury.'

Marcus stiffened, as if he were going to argue, then his resistance crumbled. He put the papers down in the middle of his desk. 'What are you going to do now?' he asked, his voice soft and a little shaky. 'And for God's sake, don't tell. me you suspect he paid for perjury . . . or blackmail. The reputation of the chambers is on the line!' he added. 'Will it bear looking at?' He leaned forward, his hands shaking. 'We've got to be thorough. I have to know, Daniel, I must!' He shook his head. 'I was looking at Drake's present case. It's complicated, but not violent. And it's nowhere near the area around Mile End. Go and look at the papers, and then I suggest you see Hobson again.'

'Yes, sir . . . '

'Well, don't just stand there!' Marcus snapped.

Daniel bit back his intended response and turned to leave, closing the door quietly behind him.

★　★　★

Daniel and Kitteridge had already looked through the papers of Drake's current case. It was, as Marcus said, a tangled matter of embezzlement. He refreshed his memory on the main points, then went to find Drake's clerk, Hobson.

He finally discovered the young man in the chambers' library, studying a law book so thick it must have weighed several pounds and did not lie open easily.

'Morning, sir.' Hobson had to balance the book before he could stand up. He was fair-haired, and with skin so soft he barely grew a beard.

'Sit down, Hobson,' Daniel told him. 'I haven't come to give you a job to do.' He pulled up another of the easy chairs so he could talk without having to raise his voice. With luck, no one would interrupt them.

'Sir?' Hobson looked anxious.

Daniel chose his words carefully. This young man had just learned that his immediate superior had been suddenly and violently murdered, putting his own job in jeopardy.

Possibly he had knowledge — maybe suspicions, even fears — but to repeat what he knew might be, in his mind, some betrayal of a man who was dead and thus could not now defend himself.

'I'm sorry for your situation,' Daniel began. 'It must be very difficult for you.' He had never said that before, but it needed repeating.

Hobson looked overwhelmed. He smiled ruefully, but said nothing.

'But whoever takes Mr Drake's place,' Daniel went on, 'will be very grateful for your knowledge, both of the pending cases and of the chambers in general.'

'Mr fford Croft hasn't said that I'll be here to do that.' Hobson's voice was hoarse. He tried to control his nerves, but they were evident.

'They probably thought you knew. No one else could do your job,' Daniel assured him, hoping to heaven that he was correct. 'Added to which, we need you to help us find whoever killed Mr Drake.'

'Aren't the police going to do that?' It was not just a question; it was a plea.

'When I saw them, they didn't hold out much hope,' Daniel answered. It was honest, as far as it went. 'Mile End is a pretty rough area. Do you know why Mr Drake went there, and in the middle of the night?'

Hobson shifted uncomfortably in his seat. 'Not sure. I think he was going to question a moneylender . . . ' he said tentatively. 'There was a matter of money . . . '

'At two in the morning?' Daniel raised his eyebrows.

'He wouldn't want to be seen,' Hobson replied, twisting his hands together. 'And the moneylender wouldn't want it to get around that he was seeing a lawyer.'

Daniel kept his patience with difficulty. 'Do you know what he was seeing the moneylender for? Where they met? Or even the man's name? Address? Anything?'

Hobson looked up, meeting Daniel's eyes. 'No, sir, he didn't tell me. He said it was for my protection . . . '

Daniel felt a quickening pulse. Could it be this easy? Did Hobson hold the key, without realising it?

'Protection . . . from whom?'

'He didn't say, but I think it might have been related to a case I wasn't involved in. Somebody he knew from a while ago.' Hobson looked unhappy. 'Now I can't even help.'

'Maybe we could piece it together from what you do know, and what happened?' Daniel suggested.

'I can show you all the papers on the last case, and the one before, if you think it could help?' Hobson offered.

'I think there are things that need . . . better explanation? Mr Drake was . . . worried . . . ' He trailed off, not knowing what else to say.

'Good idea. And I'll need you nearby, so I can ask about things I don't understand.'

'Yes, sir. Mr Pitt . . . ' He hesitated, looking awkward, clearly trying to master a wave of

61

emotion. 'I learned a lot from Mr Drake. And, sir, he was very kind to me. He was patient and explained things so I really understood. He never talked down to me.'

Daniel was surprised. He had expected Hobson to say the exact opposite. He himself had seen Drake as a cold, calculating person, the least likely to have the patience to tutor a young man. But then, when he thought about it, Marcus said that Drake appeared to have no family at all, at least none that he was in touch with. Perhaps Hobson filled one of the gaps in his life. He might be the person to ask about Drake, and the things that were not written in his notes. Hobson might understand the little sketches that in a few lines offered a wit and perception that could not have been conveyed by a hundred words.

'Thank you,' Daniel said aloud. 'It's about the only thing we can do for him now. And, of course, for the chambers.'

⋆ ⋆ ⋆

Daniel spent the rest of the day going through Drake's last case, point by point. Then the next day, after Hobson's help led to concluding that investigation, they set out on the case before that.

Daniel learned that Drake was extremely thorough in his discovery, but there were things he deliberately avoided when the case came to court. Because they were irrelevant? Or damning? Drake's opinion of the police seemed to be low, evidenced by more than one sarcastic note written in the margin.

Perhaps there was more to this than there appeared? He hoped not.

Late in the afternoon, Daniel took his notes to Marcus and waited while he read them. He had considered summarising them, or to be more honest, concealing some of the worst offences, the tricks, the innuendos, revealing only the manner in which they had been concealed. But he realised, reluctantly, that this would only create trouble for the future. If what he found led to uncovering the identity of whoever had killed Drake, or had paid someone to do it, that might also implicate the chambers further.

Marcus listened to him without comment, his face growing paler and more tense, a tiny muscle in his cheek twitching as he clenched his teeth. He never once raised his eyes.

Daniel checked his notes again. He had said everything. Now he had to sit silently and wait for Marcus to respond.

It seemed like an age, but finally he did. 'I've been remiss, given him too much latitude?' He blinked quickly, several times. 'But he always got to the right answer, didn't he? There are no complaints. I mean . . . legal ones. Money that anyone could . . . ' His voice trailed off and he did not finish the sentence.

'You can't watch over us all, sir,' Daniel said quietly. He must guard not only his tongue, but his facial expression. Condescension would be the ultimate insult. What Marcus deserved or did not deserve was not for Daniel to judge. What mattered was that the final outcome must be something they could all live with. He must make that possible, and he had no idea how.

'Don't pander to me, Daniel,' Marcus said gravely.

'Ultimately, it is all my responsibility. Just as it's my name on the door.'

'There are a few things we need to do to put it right.' Daniel heard his own voice with disbelief. He sounded confident, as if he were promising something he knew he could accomplish. He saw Marcus's expression, how the muscle in his face stopped jumping. Daniel felt his own heart sink.

'Good,' Marcus said quietly. 'Leave your notes with me. The next thing I need you to do, as early as you can, is for you and Kitteridge to go to Drake's house and see if you can find any papers, notes, et cetera, that may be of use. Also, look for his will. We are executors, but we may not have the latest version. He said he was going to update it. If he did, we never received it.'

'Yes, sir.' That was partly an evasion, but for now it would suffice. The long, late-spring day was beginning to fade and Daniel was tired. 'I'll be on it first thing in the morning. Or at least as soon as Drake's housekeeper is likely to be awake.'

'Eight thirty, perhaps?' Marcus suggested.

Daniel rose to his feet. 'Yes, sir, I'll tell Kitteridge.'

★　★　★

Kitteridge had no choice but to come, although he did so reluctantly. 'What do you expect to find?' he asked, increasing his pace as he strode ahead of Daniel along the footpath. It was a crisp May morning, the sun already high, the dew gone from the leaves of bushes and from the odd strip of grass in the front gardens. Profusions of flowers were out, bright against the dark earth, and blossoms added colour to the delicate branches of trees.

Daniel took extra steps to keep up with the slightly taller man. 'Why are you in such a hurry? There's no point in getting there before the housekeeper's up.'

'To get it over with,' Kitteridge replied, without turning to look at Daniel. 'Just the idea of going through a dead man's private belongings. I think it's . . . repellent.'

'So do I. But who would you rather did it? Someone who didn't know him?'

'Yes,' Kitteridge said firmly. 'Someone he wouldn't care what they thought of him.'

'Do you suppose he cares now?' Daniel asked.

'You mean dead is gone?' Kitteridge did turn around this time, the sharp morning light showing the surprise in his face.

Daniel stopped abruptly so he wouldn't walk into Kitteridge. 'I don't believe the dead spend their time watching us,' he replied. 'If he was going to be upset, it would be about the way he died. And if you'd seen his body, you'd feel that way, too.' He could not get the vision of Drake's face out of his mind. It had haunted his sleep, reappearing in each nightmare.

Kitteridge gave him a pained look, but he did not argue. Instead, he continued walking, only this time markedly slower.

They went in silence the next couple of hundred yards, checked the address, then went up the path to the front door and knocked. They were answered within moments by a middle-aged woman with a strained faced, pinched and devoid of colour. She was wearing a plain black dress. Clearly, she had expected them, and took them through the hall to what was obviously Drake's study. It might originally have been the drawing room in the home of anyone else. It had high bay windows looking on to the front garden and then the street. At present, the curtains were pulled across, as was suitable for a house in mourning, but she drew them back to let in the light. Suddenly, there was colour in the dark Turkish carpet, and a sheen to the rich cherrywood of the desk, the bookcase and the small table.

'There you are, gentlemen. I can bring you tea at eleven o'clock, if you wish it. Perhaps I can find a biscuit or two?' she offered.

They both thanked her and, as soon as she had gone, stared around the room at the shelves and shelves of books, many of them leather bound, some even tooled in gold with the pages deckle-edged. There were very few pictures — all rather dark landscapes — and three marble busts. One was obviously Napoleon Bonaparte; the other two Daniel had to look at closely to read the names etched into their bases. The first was Dracon, the ancient Greek lawmaker who gave his name to the word *draconian*, the harshest of laws. The other was Justinian, the historic lawmaker from the Byzantine Empire. Suddenly, Drake seemed a thinker with more dimensions than Daniel had assumed. In addition to his sharp-edged, perceptive humour, he had also held a love for the history of law and its origins.

'What a marvellous collection,' Kitteridge said in some awe, standing before one of the bookshelves. 'Do you suppose he had read most of them?'

'Yes,' Daniel said, without hesitation. He noticed that the books were arranged by subject, not by size or colour to please the eye. Instead, they were ordered to please the mind, and put back carefully in the same order after having been removed. Daniel could not see a speck of dust on the books, suggesting they were handled, not ornamentation. He would have loved to have time to study them all. In a sense, the wealth of the world was there: history, laws, ideas, philosophies, but also drama from the Classical Greek to the present day, as well as Shakespeare, Marlowe, Shaw and a score of poets. This was a personal collection, Jonah Drake's preferences dictated by a love of literature.

'Come on,' Kitteridge said reluctantly, dragging Daniel's interest back to the matter in hand. 'We might not find anything, but we must look.'

They worked all morning, looking through the papers on the desk. They found the key to the safe and opened it, both of them disliking this intrusion into the life of a man helpless to prevent them. It turned out there was very little locked away, except for bank papers and statements, the deeds to the house, and the copy of his last will and testament, dated only one month ago. Daniel hesitated to open it. But rather than leave it to Marcus, he decided they had to know and there was no time to waste.

It was simple: the house and all its contents were left to the chambers of fford Croft and Gibson, with the exception of specific bequests of books, paintings and stationery to Charles J. Hobson, currently employed at the aforesaid chambers.

'What do you suppose the house is worth?' Kitteridge asked, looking confused, as if he had no idea.

'More than you and I earn in ten years,' Daniel replied. 'Not to mention the books and furniture. Heavens, he's got more books in this room than we have in the chambers' library. I don't know whether the pictures are worth anything. We'll have to get an expert to tell us. In fact, we'll need an assessment for all of it.'

Kitteridge looked grave. 'Did he really make enough money to afford all this? Do you think . . . ?'

'Maybe he inherited it?' Daniel gazed around. 'A lot of this furniture is very old. Old enough to be antique, and pretty good.'

'Do you suppose Hobson knows he inherited anything?'

'I doubt it.'

'And Marcus?'

'Maybe,' Daniel said again. 'But Drake was

worth more to the chambers alive. Let's look further.'

'Perhaps there are papers here about a case pending,' Kitteridge suggested. 'Drake seems to have known a lot about a lot of people,' he added pointedly. 'Could be it was a case that he intended to pursue but can't close now . . . '

'Not since getting slashed to pieces in Mile End in the middle of the night, you mean!' Daniel said sarcastically.

Kitteridge gave him a filthy look.

Daniel shrugged, but said no more.

They looked further, and by dusk they had made copious notes of the whole house and its contents, but could not give specific value to any of it. Standing back and thinking of it, Daniel considered they had documented a material record of a very private man of considerable means, someone who had earned both awe and respect from his peers, as well as fear from some of them . . . and envy. Young Hobson appeared to be the only person for whom Drake had any affection, yet there was no record to suggest they had known each other outside the office.

After their search was completed, they asked the housekeeper if she had ever seen Hobson, or heard Drake mention his name. She told them that she had not, which did not mean that Hobson had not been here. But if he had, it had been briefly. She offered the information that she had not cooked a meal for anyone but Drake, and no visitor had ever stayed overnight.

The two men left as dusk was falling. They walked out into the darkening street with feelings

69

of guilt, as if they had spied on someone, and sadness because they were sharply reminded of how mortal they all were. Daniel dwelt on this as they walked, considering how in less than one minute he could cease to be alive . . . and aware . . . and sentient, and then become only a memory in the minds of others.

4

Daniel was still undecided when he opened his eyes the next morning, his head heavy, having spent an uneasy night escaping one bad dream only to find himself in the middle of the next. In one way or another all were concerned with Miriam. He woke up thinking of her with intense relief. But of course she was not there, she was still in Holland, in what could be a turning point in her career.

He shaved, washed and dressed, then ate his breakfast in the kitchen, almost forgot, and had to come back from the hallway to thank an anxious Mrs Portiscale, before dashing outside into the mild late-spring day. He was hoping to be in the office before anyone else was there, except Impney, but in that he failed: Kitteridge had beaten him by nearly half an hour.

He went to Kitteridge's door and knocked, then opened it. Kitteridge was sitting at his desk, his jacket off and hung carelessly on one arm of the coat stand. His papers were spread out in front of him until there was no room to place another without hiding one of those already there. He did not even look up as Daniel closed the door.

'Just put it on the side table, thank you,' he said. 'I'll drink it when I'm ready.' He had taken Daniel to be Impney with his tea.

'Good idea,' Daniel replied, and before

Kitteridge could register his mistake, he sat down in the visitor's armchair. 'I hope he brings two cups.'

Kitteridge peered across at him. 'Where the hell did you come from? Don't creep around like that. It's ill mannered, at best. A man likes to assume privacy . . . '

'I did knock, and you answered,' Daniel replied. 'You must be stuck on something to be so acid this early in the morning. I need your help or, at the very least, your advice.' He rushed ahead, not giving Kitteridge the chance to respond. 'I'm supposed to be looking for any case of Drake's that could involve a passion for revenge. Peterson doesn't meet that. He's damned lucky not to be in prison, and he knows it.'

'What have you done so far?' Kitteridge asked with a sigh, putting his pen down.

'Exactly what Marcus told me to,' Daniel replied. 'Check on the cases that are most likely to have caused any difficulty or ill feeling. Drake wasn't robbed, or involved in a fight, you know. There were no defensive cuts or bruises. He was violently and very intentionally killed. Somebody knew how — '

'I know,' Kitteridge interrupted. 'I understand.'

'I've looked at Peterson, and he's lucky the jury was hung, and not him!'

'Hanged,' Kitteridge corrected him. 'Hanged when it's a man, hung if it's a jury. Or a picture. I don't know why they don't — '

'Kitteridge!'

Kitteridge pushed his fingers through his hair, making it look even thicker and wilder. 'What? I'm sorry! Damn whoever killed Drake. He was the only one who could make sense of these figures. No matter which way I look at them, there's a discrepancy.' There was apology in his tone, and a little embarrassment. He also sounded defeated. 'I don't know how the devil we're going to find anyone to replace him. It certainly won't be me.'

'Do you know enough to tell if what Drake was doing was all above board?' Daniel asked the question to which he dreaded hearing the answer.

Kitteridge stared at him. His expression was unreadable.

'If you don't know, say so!' Daniel demanded. 'We've got to get on top of it. The reputation of the chambers may be at stake. Marcus is . . . is scared about something.'

'I don't know,' Kitteridge admitted miserably. 'But I think Drake definitely cut a few corners financially. Moved things around, not great amounts individually, but when you add them all up, it comes to quite a lot. I mean thousands of pounds. Whether Marcus knew or not, I can only guess. I know he used to be extremely sharp. He could tell if there was any dishonesty even before he found it. But that was years ago, and before . . . well, he doesn't remember things the way he used to.' Kitteridge blushed as he said this, as if he had intruded on someone's privacy, found something embarrassing, and then broadcast it. 'I'm not sure if he realises it or not,' he added, as though that made it somehow better.

'But do you think there was an error on Drake's part?' Daniel pressed. Now that he had raised the subject, he was determined to get it all out in the open, and not have to say it again.

'I don't know,' Kitteridge repeated. 'I really don't. Money seems to have been moved from one account with the firm, to another, and then a third. Sometimes it's Drake, at other times it's Marcus. In the end, I don't know if the result is plus or minus. What troubles me is that there doesn't seem to be any point to it, except to confuse.' He swallowed hard.

'Why do it at all, unless it's to hide something?'

'Like what?' Daniel asked, afraid of the answer and yet more afraid of the silence that yawned before him.

Kitteridge looked wretched. 'Hiding how much the company is actually earning? Or overcharging certain clients? Undercharging others? Or even straight-out blackmail? Worst thing I can think of, bribing certain jurors, or witnesses . . . '

'Oh God!' Daniel gasped.

'I said that's the worst!' Kitteridge replied sharply. 'It could be no more than complicated bookkeeping that I don't understand.'

'Rubbish!' Daniel dismissed the idea. 'There's something wrong, even if it's only incompetence. We need to find out what, before someone else does. If they haven't already.'

'What has that to do with Drake's death?' Kitteridge asked.

'Whatever he was doing, someone found out,' Daniel replied. 'That's the first thing that comes to mind . . . '

'What do you mean?' Kitteridge asked.

'Heaven knows, Drake has beaten enough people in court. He was brilliant. Maybe that's where that nice house and all those first edition books come from?' Daniel suggested. 'A few jurors paid off? Or witnesses? I'm afraid of what I might find if I look too hard. It's all very well searching for the truth, but it's another matter when it's for people you care about who, in a way, frame your world. It's . . . ' Daniel trailed off, lost for words.

'If someone such as Peterson, for example, were guilty, and Drake knew and covered it up, and that came out,' Kitteridge filled in for him, 'it will ruin us. People who do something wrong don't always do it to suit themselves. Sometimes it's to save people they love, or need. It's all very complicated, like trying to remove a splinter without cutting your finger open. It's usually better to cut. Otherwise, you break the splinter and get the whole thing infected and — '

'End up amputating your hand,' Daniel finished for him.

'Don't exaggerate!'

'I'm not. Exaggerating would be to say you know you'll get blood poisoning and die! Toby, does any of this have anything to do with why Drake was killed? That's all that matters right now.'

'What are you going to do?' Kitteridge asked.

'What are we . . . ?'

'I don't know. I came to see if you've got anything. We . . . ' He did not know how to shape it. 'If there is a cover-up of something really serious, we've got to get there before anyone else does.'

'And do what?' Kitteridge's expression was one of confusion and anxiety. He looked utterly lost.

'I don't know that either,' Daniel admitted. 'Not until we see what it is. If it is a real crime and not carelessness. And if it involves Marcus, or not. If he really didn't know, or if he chose to look the other way.'

Kitteridge raised his eyebrows. 'And how do you propose we find out?'

If Kitteridge had said he knew how to find the truth, Daniel would have been intensely relieved. But since he had not, Daniel knew what he had to do next. 'Do you remember Roman Blackwell? And Mercy?'

Kitteridge closed his eyes, rather as if he was hoping that Daniel would be gone when he opened them. 'Yes, of course I do. But, Daniel . . . '

'I want him to look into Drake, but not through the ordinary channels. Through . . . other ways we can't use. Jonah Drake would want us to find out who did this to him. Somebody hated him, or was very much afraid of something they thought he was going to do, or *might* do. Roman can help.'

Kitteridge bit his lip. 'Are you sure about Blackwell? Do you even know what we're going to do if he finds out that Drake was cheating, stealing, or suborning juries and condoning perjury?' His voice was sharp with desperation. 'Or that Marcus knew? Or should have known, and chose not to question it?'

'You mean that he might have turned a blind eye, deliberately?' Daniel asked bitterly. 'Either way, we've got to know . . . '

Kitteridge gave him a long, steady stare. 'Yes.' Impney knocked on the door and came in with a tray of tea.

★   ★   ★

While it was still early and he had a chance of catching Roman Blackwell at home, Daniel went straight to the man's house. He knocked on the front door and stepped back, anxiously moving his weight from foot to foot. He was worried about being too late, and feared that Blackwell was already pursuing some of his various darker interests, in parts of the city where Daniel would never find him. Blackwell had been known to have a partiality to smuggling, for one thing.

He inhabited a shadowy area on the border of legitimacy, and his values were pliable, often on the side of his own personal sympathies, sometimes congruent with the law, at other times not. He had been caught years ago, and had served a term in prison. Far from reforming him, he had learned a great many skills inside, and made a variety of friends. After his release, he had remained on the right side of the law, even if by a narrow margin. He was highly imaginative, and loyal to a fault to those he regarded as friends, or felt indebted to, such as Daniel, who had won his first murder case defending Blackwell.

Blackwell's love of all the good things in life had increased with their threatened loss: good food, good wine, laughter, music, the company of friends. But also, things like a still morning on the river, a clear sky at dawn, scarlet clouds at sunset. And he loved a good puzzle, as much as a good quote with both wit and wisdom.

The door opened and Mercy Blackwell stood on the step. She was of an indeterminate age, but a short generation older than Roman, her only child. She was as dark-eyed and blackhaired as he was, except for the white blaze, from forehead up, winding round the thick coils of hair pinned at the back of her head. In her youth, she had been voluptuous, now she was magnificent.

'May I come in?' Daniel asked with a tentative smile.

'My dear, of course you may.' She smiled back at him and opened the door a little wider. 'Have you had breakfast?' Her initial gratitude for Daniel saving her son had mellowed to a definite fondness.

'Yes, a bit . . . ' He followed on her heels, down the hall with its mirrors, sunlight and optical illusions he was now used to. He knew which passages were real, and which merely reflections of each other, cleverly placed to repeat, and mislead the eye. 'But I could eat more,' he added hopefully.

She turned the corner into the kitchen where Roman was staring expectantly at the door.

The man's smile broadened as he saw Daniel. As usual, he was direct. 'What's wrong now? For heaven's sake, sit down. Tea? Toast? The marmalade's excellent. Sharp enough to clear your head.'

Daniel pulled up another chair and waited until Mercy was seated.

She poured a cup of tea for him, with milk and no sugar. He nodded his thanks and then told them about Drake's death.

'Is that all you know?' Blackwell asked when Daniel finally came to a stop. 'The police haven't said anything to Marcus, for example?'

'No,' Daniel replied. 'And Drake has no family that we could find. His will mentioned no one but his young clerk, Hobson, and the chambers.'

'Hobson?' Blackwell asked.

'Nice young man. He thought well of Drake, who was patient with him. From what he's told me, Drake was a good mentor.'

'Curious fellow, Drake.' Blackwell shook his head very slightly.

'You knew him?' asked Daniel.

'Famous in some quarters — deserves to be. Clever beggar, very. Odd-looking bloke. Mole on his cheek, right side of his nose. Not ugly, just odd. Great man with a pencil. Drew pictures with acute observation and sarcastic wit. Should have been a cartoonist. I've run into him, always found him straightforward. He's worked for fford Croft and Gibson for a long time . . . maybe thirty years. They are as much family as he has. He lives alone. Works alone. For the most part. Clever man. Can think sideways and then he

79

ends up behind you, when you think he's in front. Can wind a jury round his little finger, and you watch him at it, and still when you see it, you don't know how it happened.'

'You admired him,' Daniel observed.

'Yes, I did,' Blackwell agreed. 'And I liked him.'

'Straight?' Daniel asked. 'Financially, I mean? Would he steal from Marcus fford Croft?'

Blackwell shook his head. 'No. Winning mattered to him, but not money.'

'Enough to bribe a juror? Or a witness?' Daniel dreaded the answer. 'I need to know . . . '

'You always need to know.' Blackwell smiled. 'No, Drake was a lonely man, proud, but a win as a result of cheating wouldn't mean anything to him.'

Daniel nodded silently.

'So, who's bribing jurors?' Blackwell demanded.

'Perhaps no one.'

'Which one of his recent cases are you interested in? You're chasing motives for his murder, I presume?'

Daniel had been expecting Blackwell to ask this, and he had made a list of Drake's cases for the last two years. He passed it across the table and Blackwell took it. While he read it, Daniel sipped his tea. There was utter silence in the room, except for the ticking of the clock.

This was a list of clients, charges and verdicts, such as would be available to anyone prepared to look. Most were a matter of public record but, condensed on one sheet, they drew the pattern of Drake's professional life. The majority of cases were big ones, concerning many types of fraud and embezzlement. Huge sums of money were involved. Some of the verdicts had taken days of deliberation to decide.

What they all had in common was the large amount of money involved, whether it was stolen, embezzled or bequeathed. Also the high cost of the case, in court time, and the fee paid to fford Croft and Gibson in compensation for their efforts, whether successful or not. But very few of the cases failed. This much had struck Daniel immediately. He could see why Drake was so valuable to the chambers. He brought in almost three times as much money as anyone else.

There were lawyers who defended more noteworthy cases, those involving libel or slander, for example, and clients whose reputations were their most valued asset. Scandal always sold newspapers. And then there were young lawyers, like Daniel or Kitteridge, who had unintentionally taken on cases that caught the public eye, and looked impossible to win, but in the end, they did win them. They were avidly reported in the newspapers because they were unusual, and involved dramatic circumstances, or famous people. They made the chambers' name famous in the higher circles of society.

'Well?' Daniel demanded of Blackwell.

Finally, Blackwell looked up. 'That's pretty well his reputation. Very sharp,' he said, watching Daniel's face. 'Damn close to the edge, according to what I hear.' He held up the papers Daniel had given him. 'And as I said, clever bugger, Drake. Marcus will miss him. Could be a long time finding another as sharp. You're talking about the money? He knew what to charge, and when to do it for nothing, but gave the chambers a very good name.' As he said it, he was watching Daniel's face. 'You don't know anything about the business practices of the clients in these cases, do you?'

Daniel felt himself go cold. It started in the pit of his stomach, and spread slowly. 'You mean they were clever enough to stay on the right side of the law?'

'You deduced that?' Blackwell sounded surprised. 'I only know about it because I know the people on this list. How do you know?' He made no apology for asking.

'I don't. I'm guessing . . . '

He frowned. 'You mean you're afraid because you don't know whether Marcus was doing something a bit shady, on the side?' Blackwell challenged. 'That's what you're afraid of, isn't it? Either Marcus is losing his grip and doesn't examine these cases closely enough, or else he does, and deliberately looks the other way.'

And that was another thing: had anyone else known? Not Kitteridge, for sure. He had neither the art nor the desire to mislead. But there were at least a dozen other people in the chambers, counting all the juniors and clerks, as well as the practising lawyers. Did any of them know?

Blackwell was talking again. 'Do you think that all those people were innocent?' he asked, referring to the list of names and cases Daniel had given him. 'I don't wish to think that so many men had stood trial for things they didn't do! Or the police were so slipshod.'

'I don't know,' Daniel answered. 'I really don't. The cases I looked at were very complicated, and for the most part, I think Drake was a cleverer lawyer than the prosecutor. It only takes reasonable doubt to prevent a conviction. And I think that most jurors don't understand the details of the law. I read some of these trials. No matter what the charge, no decent juror will convict someone when they don't really understand the finer details of the case. A mistake could send a man to prison for years, even if he hadn't physically hurt anyone.'

'Very few violent crimes are on this list,' Blackwell remarked. 'But I notice there were two murders, and he got them both off.' His eyebrows raised.

'I'm looking at one closely,' Daniel answered. 'You're right that he got them both off. The case with the hung jury,' he said, pointing to the list, 'was not going back to trial, and nobody else has been charged in that case, so no innocent person was blamed. But who would be angry enough to kill Drake now?' he went on, settling more comfortably in his chair. 'Or at all, for that matter. You've got to have a lot at stake to follow a man to a place like Mile End and tackle him in the street, with a knife. And it's an even bigger risk to hire someone else to do it. You could end up paying them off for the rest of your life.'

Some of the light faded from Blackwell's face. 'Then it comes back to Drake himself. Nasty place, Mile End. Right next to Whitechapel, Jack the Ripper territory — that was twenty-eight years ago, you know. It hasn't changed that much.'

Daniel shrugged. It had been before he was born, but people still spoke of it. 'Hobson thinks he went there to see a moneylender,' Daniel went on, bringing the conversation back to what Drake had been doing the night he was killed. Daniel could still see the expression on Marcus's face, his horror and misery at the news of Drake's death, and the place and the manner of it. He tried to see it again in his mind's eye. Marcus had been quite clearly distressed, but was he surprised? Or had he known that such a thing was possible, even feared it? Why? There was one obvious answer: Drake had brought a huge amount of money into the chambers and Marcus had placed his trust in him. Had that amounted to giving Drake licence to go beyond the limits of the law?

Daniel refused to believe it. Marcus must have genuinely failed to grasp what was happening, to know where the money was coming from, or from whom. But did that make him at least partly responsible for Drake's death? The thought shook Daniel. He had trusted Marcus, had such faith in him.

Blackwell put his hands flat on the table and leaned forward earnestly. 'Daniel! You've got to get to the bottom of this. Because if you don't, it will follow you everywhere, and eventually trip you up. If anyone asked you now, you could say that you didn't know Drake was involved in anything shady. In six months, or even a year, that answer won't do. It's a case of deliberately avoiding seeing what you suspect exists. That is collusion, Daniel. And I know you won't lie, because you're no good at it, quite apart from the fact that you know it's wrong.'

Daniel did not reply.

'And,' Blackwell went on, 'what will you say to that young lady with the red hair who you like so much? That you watched her father walk into a disaster and you didn't do a damn thing about it?' He altered his voice to imitate Daniel's. '*I didn't like to face the facts, and maybe upset him.* Daniel, I can't even imagine her answer to that!'

Daniel knew that was true. It was inescapable: he must either do his best to find out the truth, and act on it, or face the fact that he might watch Marcus drown when it would be too late for anyone to help him. Whatever Marcus thought of him, Daniel cared more that he should be able to look Miriam in the eye and say, with absolute honesty, that he had done everything he could to help her father. Blackwell saw it in his face. 'Right! Then let's look at Marcus and Drake both. We know how long they've known each other, but what were the secrets they shared? Secrets that could stain their reputation? Bring your chambers to ruin? We need to know, and follow wherever the facts lead us.'

'How will you do that?' Daniel asked dubiously.

'Don't ask, unless you want to know,' Blackwell retorted. 'And you don't! Believe me, you are not a good enough liar to get away with it. Just do your part, and leave me to do mine. I'll find out the real history of Marcus fford Croft and Jonah Drake. There are people who know.'

Daniel glanced at Mercy, then back at Roman.

'And don't tell Miriam just yet,' Mercy said, speaking for the first time. 'She may not ever have to know. We all have things that are better left quiet.'

Daniel shook his head. 'I can't — '

'Lie to her?' she asked. 'Of course not! But you can protect her from the suspicion that her father watched Drake lie. Or steal. Or that he twisted the truth in any way . . . to his profit.' She shook her head. 'You don't know if he did. And if he did, you don't know why. You are not a child any more, my dear. You must take charge and find the truth, and then protect her, if you can. Without lying to her, of course. If you don't know how to do this, you'd better find out.'

There were no words to answer that, and he realised as he searched for them that she was right. He must find out the truth, or a version of it that would enable him to fight to protect Marcus. There was no escape from it. And the only people he could trust were Kitteridge and the Blackwells. Mercy's knowledge was encyclopaedic; he did not wish to know how she came by it, although he could have several guesses. She had been beautiful, funny and brave in her youth, and even now refused to give in to age, or anything else. The loyalty he had earned from both of them was lifelong: both a blessing and an obligation.

★ ★ ★

Daniel knew that Blackwell was right: he must learn the extent of Marcus's involvement, if any, in Drake's affairs and the events leading up to his death. He hated having to find out all he could without asking Marcus himself. It seemed so devious. But what if Marcus lied to him, to keep private some indiscretion — a few occasions on which he had drunk a little too much, or an affair which had gone further than he would like it to be known by others? Or mistakes he had made in cases — and everyone committed errors from time to time? No matter what, if he was dishonest with Daniel, it would be painful. On another occasion, Daniel would have said Marcus must be allowed his privacy, but now they could not afford the luxury of secrets. Concealing the past could lead to lies and deception, or at the very least, betrayals, disillusionment.

So, he needed to, as they say, bite the bullet and find out about Marcus. That way, if possible, he could protect him.

He would have to go back to the beginning.

Where did Drake go to school? Eton? That would be no surprise. Records said he hated sports, but was an outstanding scholar. That was no surprise either. When Daniel looked up his biography, however, Drake's school was not mentioned. Which naturally meant it was not

Eton! Everyone who went to Eton mentioned it.

The next step proved to be easy. Drake had been given a scholarship to Oxford to study law. He was top of his class.

Had Marcus been to Oxford? Yes! Ahead of Drake. Daniel's research turned up the fact that, three years later, Drake had caught up with him. So, they had known each other since their early twenties. Friends? Or just two people studying the same subject at the same place?

Who could confirm it? Would Impney know? Or should he just ask Marcus and be done with it? Did Drake have an intimate knowledge of Marcus's mistakes, early in his career? That way, Marcus would be in debt to Drake, and might have been persuaded to turn a blind eye to his later behaviour. Or were there indiscretions in Drake's past that Marcus knew of? If Marcus did not tell him voluntarily, Daniel could think of no way to dig up things that might well be painful. And, honestly, he did not want to know any sordid details.

Daniel would take it to Blackwell and let him find out. He had ways that were not available to Daniel.

Thank goodness Miriam was safely in Holland, her mind bent on her studies. She would hate this. Daniel wondered how he would handle knowing too much about his own father. It was like intruding on someone who had forgotten to lock the bathroom door. Only worse.

Perhaps asking Impney was not a bad idea; he might know a great deal. But he was discreet, fiercely loyal, and would consider it a betrayal to repeat what he had heard confidentially.

Stop being such a coward! Daniel chided himself. Would you rather Marcus were caught out, disgraced? Perhaps even the chambers ruined?

He found Impney in the small kitchen. The clerk was startled when Daniel spoke, turning round sharply at the intrusion.

'I'm sorry,' Daniel said, and closed the door behind him.

'Sir?' There was surprise and reproof in Impney's voice.

'I know this is difficult,' Daniel said, ignoring the reproof.

'But this is serious, and there is no time for approaching things slowly. I was the one who identified Mr Drake's body . . . '

'I know, sir. It must have been a dreadful experience.'

'It was. The attack was . . . very personal. I assume you don't know what Mr Drake was doing in Mile End? And please, Impney, this is no time for secrets. We have got to find out who killed him, and above all . . . why. Before the police do. Or before whoever did it takes their next step. Maybe it's not connected with the chambers at all, but we can't afford to suppose that, and look the other way.'

A dark shadow crossed Impney's face, as if he were just beginning to understand the seriousness of the situation. The mask of agreeable politeness vanished.

Daniel took a deep breath. 'It was personal,

Impney. Mr fford Croft may know about it, or he may not. We have to protect him, and we can't do it working blind. I know he and Mr Drake were at university together. If it dates as far back as that, and if they had secrets they wanted no one to know . . . well, we have to protect Mr fford Croft. I . . . '

'Yes, sir,' said Impney. His shoulders dropped just an inch or two, but it was noticeable. 'I understand.'

'Was Mr fford Croft aware of Mr Drake's penchant for cutting a few corners?'

'A nice way of putting it, Mr Pitt. He used to be, but lately his attention has not been as . . . as detailed as before. I . . . '

'I understand, but I need to know. Did Mr Drake cut legal corners? Enough to be in trouble with the Law Society, or the police? If you know anything . . . '

'Not as far as I am aware, sir, but he did come close,' Impney replied. 'He was . . . he was always on the right side, morally, I believe, but some people might not see it that way.'

'What do we need to be careful of?' Daniel knew Impney understood him.

Impney considered for several moments. Finally, he answered, slowly and carefully, his voice so low that anyone in the passage, even immediately on the other side of the door, would have had trouble hearing him. 'Many people lie to their lawyers, sir. Maybe about things they think are not relevant to the case. But you don't know what is and what isn't, until it's over. I would swear that Mr fford Croft didn't . . . lie,

90

that is. And Mr Kitteridge is an open book, if you'll pardon the expression. As you are yourself.'

'I shall have to learn,' Daniel said grimly.

'You develop your own style, sir. I'd stay with it, if I were you,' Impney replied, without hesitation.

Daniel had no answer, at least not immediately.

Impney took a deep breath. 'I know you are trying to protect Mr fford Croft. Believe me, Mr Pitt, I shall find the papers we need. However, there may be some I don't put my hand on. If it should come to that . . . '

'I need to know the truth,' Daniel began, knowing what Impney was implying.

'Begging your pardon, sir, but you don't. You need to know who killed Mr Drake, and why. That is not necessarily the same thing.'

Daniel stood still, looking at Impney's impassive face and the shadows in his eyes. 'I can't defend what I don't know . . . '

'Forgive me, sir, for contradicting you again, but you are mistaken. There are times when not knowing is the only defence. And the only way to protect the people who matter to you. A partial truth can distort things, make them two-dimensional instead of three. Mr fford Croft knows that. Would you like a cup of tea, sir? And perhaps a few biscuits?'

'No!' he took a breath. 'I mean . . . yes. Yes, please.'

'I have a nice ginger cake, sir?'

Daniel stared at him.

91

Impney gave him a sober look, then pulled the door open for him to leave. 'It'll be about ten minutes, sir.'

Daniel nodded and walked out.

5

Daniel was content, at least temporarily, to put aside the questions regarding money, fees and possible bribes, and what Marcus did, or did not know about them. He began enquiring into the second trial that Drake had fought, and also won, but which concerned violence and tragedy, and left a bad taste and unanswered questions behind it.

It was the Faber case, the one that Daniel's father had warned him not to look at if he could avoid it. But if he had to, then he must be very careful.

He was indeed careful, starting by going through Drake's papers and reading the formal charges, the notes on evidence and witnesses, and then Drake's own comments. They struck Daniel as sceptical at first, but as he became used to Drake's dry humour and his odd choice of literary references, the notes became much clearer. And, he was obliged to admit, he found that the funny little drawings and cartoons of people not only pleased him, they were more illustrative of the subtlety of character than any words. Most of them were sharp, revealing, but one or two were surprisingly gentle, even innocent. They were drawn by a man who concealed most of his feelings.

Finally, Daniel came to the specifics of the case his father had warned him to leave alone

— as if he could avoid it, or touch on it only lightly. The case against Even Faber, son of shipping tycoon Erasmus Faber. The murder victim was Marie Wesley. Drake had drawn her without sarcasm or any cruelty at all, but with perception, as a woman violated and alone. Daniel was curious as to why he had done that. Presumably, since he was brought in to defend her accused killer, he had never met her while she was alive. What had he learned of her that he had regarded her so . . . gently?

Daniel regretted not having known Drake better. That harsh crust he presented in public seemed to have hidden a man of immeasurably more depth. Now it was too late. What else did he miss, with eyes always looking only ahead of him?

The whole case was nasty and produced a lot of press commentary, because the victim was a thirty-five-year-old woman, very handsome indeed, with a mass of soft brown hair and a lush figure. She was of a very dubious reputation, but still managed to attend parties of the wealthy and well placed in society. Many gentlemen had known Marie Wesley, but when questioned by the police, they had been quick to say that the acquaintance was superficial.

Beneath the drawing of Marie, Drake had drawn a little cartoon of Tweedledee and Tweedledum, the identical brothers in Lewis Carroll's *Through the Looking — Glass*. Daniel thought he knew exactly what he meant! These characters always blamed each other and ended in actual physical battle. He touched the image with amusement.

Daniel read on about the people who had testified that they had seen Marie Wesley on several occasions with Evan Faber, the young man who had been accused of murdering her. Next to that, Drake had drawn a cartoon in red ink. It was a chess piece, the Red King, lying on its back, and a few notes. Daniel looked at the quote, 'We are all part of the Red King's dream.' There was also, 'Don't wake him up or we will all disappear.' What had Drake meant by that? A warning? Or did he mean that Evan had imagined a very different world — perhaps idealised? One that he knew was unreal, and could not last.

It seemed that Marie Wesley had been broad in her tastes, or perhaps in her need for money. She had, on several instances, also been seen with Evan's father, Erasmus Faber. No one could be exact about dates. Drake's cartoons in the margin of his notes were all sharp lines, teeth and whiskers, the ever-grinning Cheshire cat who kept appearing and disappearing. Once he sketched the whole head of the animal, once only half of the smile itself, just a row of teeth in the air.

Daniel sat looking for a while with Drake's notes in front of him. What did he mean by that smile? In Alice's adventures, the cat had been cryptic in its remarks, seeming to understand things other people didn't, but refusing to explain them. The animal would disappear, piece by piece, leaving only the grinning teeth in the air, melting away slowly, just as Drake had drawn it.

Did that mean that Drake did not know what was implied? Or that he did know — as we would know — where the rest of the cat must be, just could not see it?

The prosecutor's charge was that Evan was young and unworldly and had imagined that Marie Wesley was equally in love with him, and when he was forced to see that she was not, he had lost his temper, violently, and beaten her to death.

Drake had defended him, saying that there was no physical evidence to implicate Evan Faber, and Marie was a woman of such reputation that there could well be many men in Evan's position who had believed her commitment to them, and then found themselves profoundly mistaken. He had managed to create an innocent explanation for Evan's belongings being in her room. Yes, the young man had been there, but he did not try to deny it.

The more Daniel read of different people's testimonies, the more he found Evan believable. He wanted to think so, because Drake, and therefore the chambers, had defended him. But also because a pattern emerged of a likable young man, perhaps a little naïve, prone to see the good in people, and not the equally obvious spite, greed or weakness.

What about Evan's father, Erasmus Faber, a supremely wealthy shipbuilder? He was one of the mainstays of the British merchant fleet, and had now been given the task of building up the Royal Navy to match the expanding sea power of the Germans. Faber had the means to engage the best lawyers in London to defend his son. And apparently, he had considered Jonah Drake to be that. Daniel felt a sharp jolt of pride for the whole chambers, and for Marcus in particular. And Drake had lived up to it: Evan Faber had been acquitted.

But no one else had been charged. So, what did the police know? Who else had Marie Wesley been seen with? Did she have a secret lover? Or even a husband? What was she like? Daniel needed to find out more about her.

He wanted to meet Evan Faber himself and form an opinion of him. Was he charming or awkward? Was Marie Wesley likely to have preferred him to his rivals? And who did he blame for her death?

It was early evening when he went to Kitteridge's office and quite candidly put it all to him. 'Evan was definitely having an affair with Marie Wesley,' he started. 'But he never denied that. It seems she was a lot more than just pretty. She was fun, quick-witted, and a good dancer and a good listener. She was an enthusiast, and eager for adventure. And she wasn't greedy. She appears to have had a steady stream of money from somewhere . . . or someone — '

'Someone, you mean, who wasn't Evan Faber?' Kitteridge interrupted.

'Exactly,' Daniel agreed.

'So, Evan Faber was getting in on what someone else had paid for?' Kitteridge concluded.

'You can't buy a person,' Daniel said. 'You just have some of their time.' He shrugged. 'Although you might think you've bought her.'

'Isn't that what Drake suggested?' Kitteridge asked.

'Yes. But there are quite a few takers for that. And who would be indiscreet enough to mention their names? Or that Marie was dependent on their money? I get the feeling Drake rather admired Marie, for having fun, and for laughing at all of them.'

Kitteridge's face was acutely expressive of his mixture of emotions. 'Sounds like she lived rather dangerously.'

Daniel sighed. 'Yes. I saw a few newspaper photographs of her. She was beautiful in an odd, brave sort of way. A face you wouldn't easily forget.'

Kitteridge bit his lip and stared back with consternation in his eyes. 'What a hell of a shame! You need to look more closely into it. There's a lot of money changing hands in this case, and as far as I have seen, Drake ended up with a great deal of it himself.' He pushed his chair back a little and stretched his legs. 'Some was legitimate expenditure. The actual legal fees were huge. Probably the most any single client paid us for one trial. But he got the desired result, a clear verdict of not guilty.' He gave a slight shrug. 'I dream of being that good. Not for the money,' he added hastily, 'but to have that skill! And the satisfaction of clearing an innocent client's name and giving him back his life.'

'What did Drake do . . . exactly?' Daniel asked slowly, thinking aloud. 'Prove that Evan Faber was not guilty, without pointing out who was?

That compels me to ask, did he win justice, or did he buy it? Or something in between? It could be that Evan's father bought the best lawyer in the business. Is that also buying a verdict, or not?'

'Don't be an ass,' Kitteridge said flatly. 'That's our system, and you've known that from the beginning. The rich can always afford the best lawyers. The only way around that is to work for less than you could earn, in order to fight for the side you judge to be the more deserving. Then there's the plain, uncouth or awkward defendant — he must be terrified — who will appear guilty and will not get a fair trial.'

'I know,' Daniel agreed. 'It's an imperfect system, but it can tip too far on the side of money; the price of justice is too high.'

Kitteridge did not hesitate. 'For a not guilty verdict, free and clear? No, it isn't. And Drake's share of the money wasn't disproportionate, in any event. Any other lawyer that good would have asked for as much . . . or even more.'

How much had Marcus made out of the case? Was it profit? Or something to settle debts that had to be met? Daniel would face that only if he had to. He might not be able to avoid it, but even letting the thought cross his mind made him feel ashamed.

Kitteridge leaned back in his chair. 'What are you going to do now?'

'Go and see the police,' Daniel replied.

'What reason are you going to give them?'

'Drake is dead. I'm tidying up all the loose ends in his cases so I can put them to bed.'

'Isn't that done already?' Kitteridge asked reasonably.

'I'll say some of his notes are missing, or illegible. We want to be able to cover ourselves, explain everything if questions are asked.'

'Do we?' Kitteridge said uncertainly. 'Daniel, stop playing games. Was Drake in the wrong? I mean, did he lie to cover for Evan Faber? If you've discovered something unethical, then . . .'

'I haven't, but somebody killed Drake, and not cleanly or easily. He was slashed and stabbed and left in an alley in Mile End. Somebody was very angry indeed. I not only want to know who, but also why. I *need* to do this.'

Kitteridge's face was touched with real fear. 'Are you afraid we'll be next? Or Marcus?'

'I'll stay away from Mile End,' Daniel promised, neatly evading the answer. 'Especially after midnight.'

Kitteridge quite suddenly lost his temper. 'Don't be so stupid! This is serious! You could wind up dead. Daniel, use some damn sense.'

Daniel was very aware of the risk. It sat like a hard, cold stone in his chest. 'Can you think of a better idea?'

'If I could, I'd have told you. Just . . . just be careful. I don't want to explain to Miriam that I let you get yourself killed . . . and that Marcus is in prison.'

Daniel winced, and he felt the sudden reality settle harder and heavier inside him. 'I wouldn't leave you to do that, Toby. I'm only going to talk to the police. I'll be careful. I saw Drake's body. I have no wish to end up like that.'

Kitteridge did not speak.

'I'll be careful,' Daniel repeated, this time more gently.

'Good,' Kitteridge said, then looked down at the papers and began to read.

★   ★   ★

'Good morning, sir,' the desk sergeant said politely. He looked at Daniel warily. Had he remembered him from the morning after Drake's death?

'Good morning, Sergeant,' Daniel replied. 'As you may remember, you sent for me a few days ago to identify the body of one of the senior members of my law chambers?'

'Yes, sir. I'm very sorry it was your gentleman. But as far as I know, we are no nearer knowing exactly what happened, or who was responsible. I don't suppose you are any closer to finding out what he was doing in Mile End?' The man looked at him enquiringly. The question was mild, but it was very clear that he was going to fend off any criticism.

'I'm afraid not,' Daniel said politely. 'But we are going through all the cases Mr Drake dealt with in the last two or three years to see if any of them could have given rise to this murder. There are a few things you ought to know.'

'I think you mean Inspector Letterman, sir. He's in charge of the case.'

'Maybe I do. It might help us to clear up whatever could have contributed to causing Mr Drake's death?'

'Mr Pitt, we told you we would let you know if we had any further information.' This answer definitely held reproach in its tone.

'I realise that.' Daniel kept his voice level with an effort. 'But we need to give his cases to other lawyers, you understand?' 'Of course, but . . . '

'Anything you have found would help us to piece together what he was doing. Like who he may have been meeting at Mile End? You know the area, indeed, far better than we do.'

The sergeant gave a bleak smile. 'If you'd like to wait a while, sir, I'll see if Inspector Letterman can meet with you. Just take a seat on that bench.'

Daniel bit back his impatience and obeyed.

It was nearly half an hour, and it felt like twice as long, before the desk sergeant took him upstairs to the inspector's office. It was much like Daniel's father's office twenty years ago, when he was still in the police.

Daniel reminded himself that he must be polite, even respectful. He could barely remember Letterman from the morning of Drake's death. Their meeting had faded into the general nightmare of that time.

Letterman raised his head from the notes before him as Daniel appeared.

Daniel saw the man — neat, wiry, his face keen — and a memory of their meeting came back. There was a selfconscious authority in the way he held himself.

'Sit down, Mr Pitt, sit down.' He gestured to the chair in front of his desk.

Daniel appreciated the polite attention, but he

did not waste time leading up to the point, as he might have done with a jury. 'Mr Drake was killed very violently, Inspector,' he said gravely, meeting Letterman's eyes. 'More like a personal hatred than a robbery. If someone were taking revenge, or making sure to silence him, then it was personal. He was a very private man, and we can't find any relationships that were close, or anyone who would inherit from him.'

'Who does inherit?' Letterman asked, with no more than polite interest.

'The chambers of fford Croft and Gibson, with one separate personal bequest to his clerk.'

'A lot of money? I mean, a house free and clear? Valuable furniture?'

'Yes, the house was his. Not sure about the furniture, because I don't know if it is antique, or just old.'

'I see. You think it was a case he handled badly, or a current case he was perhaps handling too well?' Letterman asked.

'The current case hasn't reached trial yet, but his notes show no reason why he might have refused to handle it. If you look at his history, sir, he nearly always won his cases in court. He is a very large asset to the chambers. At least, he was. And we haven't found anyone to replace him yet.' Daniel was aware of the import of what he was saying, but he felt it more sharply as he put it into words. He also saw it register in Letterman's expression.

'Past cases, then?' Letterman said aloud. 'How is this my concern? Were any of them connected to Mile End?'

'I don't think so, but it's something we have to look at,' Daniel replied. 'I found two in particular, when he defended men for murder. He got one of them off, and the second was a hung jury and they didn't retry. So, effectively, that defendant got off as well. Though I spoke to the man, and he feels badly done by.'

'If he was guilty, then he was damn lucky. Would that be Lionel Peterson?'

'Yes,' Daniel agreed cautiously. So, Letterman had also taken the trouble to research Drake. Perhaps he had been involved in the Peterson case, possibly indirectly, and felt bad about it. 'You're familiar with the case? Do you think the jury got it wrong?'

Letterman thought for a moment, as if weighing in his mind what he was going to say next. 'Legally, no, but there was evidence that was disallowed,' he answered finally. 'The jury never got to hear it. They wouldn't have been undecided if they had. He was a very clever lawyer, your Mr Drake.' His expression was unreadable, as though he was deliberately concealing something.

'But on the right side of the law . . . ' Daniel made it more of a conclusion than a question.

'Oh, yes, he was far too careful to cross the line,' Letterman agreed dryly. 'He'll be a loss to you, no doubt about it. A very clever man . . . and one with contacts all over the place.'

'Including Mile End,' Daniel filled in. 'I saw no reference to the area in the papers on the Peterson case. I believe we need to find out more,' Daniel urged. 'Whoever killed Drake, that

104

was an extremely vivid way of being revenged. As if they somehow feared he could still harm them.'

'I take your point, Mr Pitt. We'd like to close the case of his murder. It's not exactly good for us, either.' He said that with total lack of expression, except for a faint gleam in his eye, which could have been a very black sense of humour, or just the light of the lamp on his desk reflecting for an instant.

Daniel nodded. 'If we opened any of his cases, who else would we suspect of the original crime? No one else was charged, that we know of.'

'We charged the right person in the Peterson case,' Letterman said. This time his expression was unmistakable. 'Just didn't make the case well enough. Then there's the case you haven't mentioned yet: Evan Faber. I think he really was innocent.'

He must have seen Daniel's look of surprise that the inspector even knew of the case. 'Drake's murder was on my patch, Mr Pitt. Did you not think I would look up his career, especially over the last two or three years, and not only the cases that were . . . controversial? Wouldn't you have done the same?'

There was a hint of emotion in his voice, but Daniel could not read what it was. 'Yes, of course I would . . . I did. Was there anyone else you suspected in the Faber case?'

'No.' Letterman shook his head. 'But there's no shadow hanging over Faber. He has been tried and found not guilty. And I agree with that. I think we had the wrong man there. Of course,

I don't know everything. Could Drake have been digging again?' This time his interest was unmistakable, just for a moment, a flare that disappeared instantly.

'I can't find anything in his notes that says so. The only thing — ' Daniel stopped, uncertain if he should raise such a dubious feeling.

'What? Spit it out, man!' Letterman snapped.

'I had the feeling that Drake was simply doing his job, defending most of the people he did. To quote him, 'We can't convict a man without a trial, and we can't have a trial without a lawyer for the defence. Litigate it, even if you can't get a man off.' But I think he really believed Evan Faber was innocent.'

'Then why not leave well enough alone?' Letterman's voice softened. 'Or did he discover something, perhaps by accident, that changed his mind?'

'Did you look at anybody else for it?' Daniel asked again, evading Letterman's question.

'Not seriously.' Letterman shrugged.

'The victim, Marie Wesley, what was she like? Apart from the newspapers' hyperbole?'

Letterman shrugged again. 'If you'd asked me before the whole thing happened, I'd have said a pretty woman, very pretty, but her looks were fading. She was full of life. But also funny, a lot of joy in all kinds of things: music, theatre, art, even science. Liked things such as the Royal Geographical Society, and stuff like that.' He smiled bleakly. 'But definitely on the make. Intended to use her looks well, while she had them. Invest for her middle age, as it were.' He

106

said this with an undertone of sadness, as if he could understand. 'If she didn't marry well, she'd end up on the street.'

Daniel was about to make a comment, then found he had nothing useful to say. Drake had covered these same interests in his notes, with the same conclusions. There was no reason to doubt Letterman. He seemed to understand the sense of loss and the waste of a life. 'Could she have known something about her killer, something he couldn't afford to have exposed?'

'Blackmail?' Letterman turned the thought over in his mind. 'We couldn't find any trace of it. But it did occur to us.'

'What trace would there be?' Daniel pressed.

'Not a lot.' Letterman leaned forward a little. 'She conducted most of her affairs in public. If she entertained married men, then their wives could have found out easily enough, if they wished to. Most of them don't. And she was too sharp-witted to have blackmailed a man she had a relationship with. That would have ended the affair, and a source of income. She got as many admirers as she did by never asking too much. She was fun, amusing and generous. Maybe she had loose morals, but she wasn't greedy, and she wasn't stupid.'

'You sound as if you liked her,' Daniel observed, then instantly thought he had gone too far.

Letterman's face darkened with sudden, real anger. 'I did. She made me laugh, as she did a lot of people, and there was nothing mean about her. Someone beat her to death, and I for one will be very pleased if the right man pays for it one day. To the last farthing! The evidence said it was Evan Faber, but I never believed that.'

'Same person who killed Drake?' Daniel asked after a moment or two.

Letterman concentrated for a moment, then he answered, his voice perfectly level.

'Doesn't look like it to me. No weapon used on her, except fists. Drake was slashed by a long, very sharp knife. If you ask me what I think, Marie was killed by someone in a blind, uncontrollable rage. Drake was killed by someone with the sort of blade you don't carry unless you mean to use it. But he hadn't a weapon, so he couldn't defend himself. Wish we could see what the other fellow looked like.'

Daniel did not reply. His mind was full of pictures he did not want to see, but he could not avoid them.

'I, for one, would appreciate it, if you could help us find the bastard,' Letterman went on. 'I'd love to take Drake off our unsolved list. But I would also be damn surprised if you can! We've done our best and, so far, got nowhere . . . ' He hesitated, then rose to his feet. 'Good luck,' he added, holding out his hand.

Daniel took it, and felt the inspector's grip firm and hard, tight for an instant, before he let go.

★ ★ ★

It took Daniel a little while to decide how best to approach Evan Faber. He dreaded the idea of trying to make it look as if it were by chance. It would almost certainly be seen through, and he would not only appear foolish, but also offensive. The only honest way of approaching him was to say that he had read the files, as a matter of duty, and since Drake had clearly taken the case very much to heart, he thought Evan might like to be informed of the funeral. There was still a comfortable amount of time in which to do this.

In his office, he read the file again, very carefully, and noted the address to which Drake had sent all post concerning the case. It was the place to begin.

It actually took him two evenings to succeed. He had to be open about who he was looking for, because he did not know Evan by sight. His manservant, resident at his London flat, recognised Drake's name, and was willing to suggest that Daniel try Evan's club. But since Daniel was not a member, and told him so, the man said a good alternative might be The Dog and Duck public house two streets away.

Daniel thanked him and walked to the pub. It was early in the evening, but it was already busy, full of young men released from the day's confinement in offices, doing what they wanted to, but still subordinate to rules and supervisors. Now they were free, thirsty, and full of stories to tell. There were a few older men among them, already heavier, a little better dressed.

Daniel went to the bar and spoke to the barman. 'I'm looking for Evan Faber,' he said, with an apologetic smile. 'I'm afraid I've got some bad news to tell him. A mutual friend died just the other week, and I thought he might not know, but he would want to attend the funeral. I don't know Evan by sight. If he's here, could you point him out to me? I'll take a pint of whatever he's drinking, if you please.' He put about twice what he thought it was worth on the counter. 'Keep the change,' he added.

The barman scooped up the money, put half of it in the till and the rest in his pocket, and proceeded to pull a pint of ale into a tankard, then gave it to Daniel. 'Thank you, sir. That'll be Mr Faber, over by the window, fellow with the striped tie. About your height, fair hair.'

'Thanks.' Daniel took the pint and walked over to the young man indicated. He had a pleasant face, intelligent, humorous, as if his interest were easily caught.

Daniel set the pint down on the nearest small table, with the handle turned towards the other man. 'Daniel Pitt,' he introduced himself. 'The barman tells me you are Evan Faber.' He raised his eyebrows enquiringly, making it a question.

'Yes, I am,' the young man answered. He looked to be in his late twenties. He picked up the tankard. 'Thank you, Daniel Pitt. To what do I owe this? Don't tell me you just happen to be interested in shipbuilding.'

'Not in the least,' Daniel replied, with a wide smile. 'I'm a lawyer.'

Evan looked slightly puzzled. 'I already have an excellent lawyer,' he began, his expression now slightly wary. Somewhere to the left of them there was a burst of laughter, and someone banged an empty tankard on the table, and there was a cheer.

'Jonah Drake?' Daniel asked when the noise subsided.

'Yes.' Evan was now troubled. The easy smile disappeared from his face. 'What concern is that of yours, Mr Pitt?' He was deliberately putting a distance between them.

Daniel did not have to pretend anything. 'From fford Croft and Gibson?' he said. 'I am with the same chambers. I'm terribly sorry, but I thought you might like to be informed that Mr Drake has been killed. I had to go through all his — ' He stopped. Evan Faber look distressed. His face had lost all its healthy colour. He put his tankard down on the table before it slipped out of his grasp.

'I'm sorry,' Daniel repeated. 'Since he is not representing you in anything at the moment, I thought you would not know. But he mentioned you with great feeling in the old case, and now and again since then. He obviously felt deeply about the injustice of your being accused, and I thought you would prefer to know before his funeral. Which is not planned just yet. We have to be sure that the police surgeon is through with the body.' He ignored the sorrow that filled Evan's expression. 'I hate to have to look you up for such a reason — '

'No. No. You are quite right,' Evan cut across him. 'What a terrible thing. I suppose you're telling me in a roundabout way that the man attacked and murdered in Mile End was Mr

Drake?' His voice was strained with obvious distress.

'Yes . . . ' Daniel answered quietly.

Evan shook his head, as if still clinging on to some idea that if he refused to accept it, it would go away.

'I'm sorry,' Daniel repeated gently. 'I was the one who . . . who identified his body. He looked . . . ' He struggled for the word. 'He looked different, *absent* in a way, but it was definitely him.'

'Do you know who did it?' Evan asked, with a lift of hope in his face.

'No, but I'm trying to find out,' Daniel replied. 'I'm hoping there will be something in one of the cases he was working on. It's the only thing to follow. He doesn't seem to have had any personal enemies. He was . . . ' He did not know how to finish the thought.

'He wouldn't,' Evan said, with a rueful half-smile. 'Have enemies, that is. He was a very lonely man, at least I thought so. He worked terribly hard, you know? At least, he did on my case, and I really appreciated that. Of course, it was my father's money that paid him, but he always treated me as if it were mine.'

'It was your life in the balance, not his,' Daniel pointed out, then wondered if he had gone too far, but it was too late to take it back.

Evan saw his awkwardness and smiled; it was sudden and charming. 'It's all right, it's perfectly true. But it wouldn't have done his reputation much good to have me found guilty, would it?'

He looked more closely at the young man sitting opposite him, and saw someone he could have been, in different circumstances, if his father had been one of the wealthy young gentlemen his mother had known in her youth, instead of a policeman. He had known men like Evan at university, sat up together all night, shared certain secrets, and kept others faithfully. Perhaps he and Evan had had similar university educations. What was certain, and even more telling, was they both had famous and powerful fathers. With Erasmus Faber it was immense wealth, with Thomas Pitt it was knowledge, connections to the police and government, and nearly forty years of increasing influence and reputation. And then there was the ultimate recognition by the Queen, after saving the reputation of the Prince of Wales, the man who had since become King. The new King, the old Queen's grandson, had not forgotten that service, either.

Daniel felt Evan watching him, waiting for him to answer.

Daniel smiled. 'Sorry. I was thinking of being expected to have the virtues my father has. It's a very long shadow.'

Evan laughed and some of the tension disappeared from his face. 'Stop trying to be tactful. The trial was horrible, a nightmare you can't wake up from.' He shook his head a little. 'You think you have, and then you realise it's still there. It was my father who paid the bill, and I don't suppose Drake would have done it otherwise, but he fought so hard for me, as he would have done for himself. He was very funny sometimes. And he made wonderful drawings with just a few strokes. He never lied to me or treated me as simply a case to be won or lost, a part of his own reputation. Do you know what I mean?' His face creased in an effort to find better words.

'Yes, I do,' Daniel answered quickly. 'We can get a bit lost in the effort to win, because we like to win. It's our success, at times, rather than the client's.' He shrugged. 'But a failure for us could mean ruin for the client, the loss of everything that matters, a loss of dignity and identity, or even death. It doesn't compare. For the lawyer, a failure in court is just a loss for one side and a victory for the other.' It sounded bitter as he said it, but it was the truth. It drained your courage to know what failure could represent, and that it would happen sometimes. Nobody could, or should, win all the time.

'And some men are guilty,' Evan put in, drawing Daniel's attention again. 'But I wasn't one of them. Drake even believed in me when I began to wonder myself if, perhaps, I were mad and didn't know what I was doing half the time.' He seemed self-conscious about the depth of his emotions. He looked away and blushed quickly.

'Thank you for telling me about Drake,' Daniel said after a moment or two. 'I don't think anyone in chambers saw that side of him. He was rather brusque with us.'

Evan looked back at Daniel. 'Perhaps you didn't need him, and he knew that.'

Daniel thought about that for a few moments. Was Drake not a cold man who wanted nobody, but a lonely one too proud to voice his needs? It had never occurred to him before. How blind of him!

'Are you going to find out who killed him?' Evan asked earnestly. 'If I can help you, please let me do so. I don't know how, but if it's someone from that time, I'll remember it. It's sort of indelible.'

'I will,' Daniel said soberly. 'But at the moment, I don't know where to look. Did he ever mention anything to you about Mile End? Informants? Moneylenders?'

Evan thought for a moment or two. 'He had some interesting information,' he said. 'I'll do my best to remember the names he mentioned. I've tried to forget all about that time, but perhaps I can bring back something. Where can I get in touch with you?'

Daniel fished in his inside pocket and gave Evan one of his cards.

Evan took it. 'Thank you. Now, will you join me for dinner? It's pretty good here.'

'Thank you,' Daniel said sincerely.

★   ★   ★

When Daniel went to visit his father the following evening, it was not so easy. They were in the drawing room alone for a few minutes while Charlotte went to the kitchen to inform the cook that there would be one more for dinner.

'I've discovered a lot more about Jonah Drake,' Daniel began, turning to his father. He wanted to get it all over with before his mother returned. Whatever he felt, Pitt would be circumspect in front of her. 'He had a completely different side to him,' Daniel went on. 'I told you before that he defended Evan Faber, and got him off.'

'And I told you to leave that alone, as much as was possible,' Pitt replied, his expression darkening a little.

'I did, *as much as possible*,' he repeated. 'But I met Evan Faber and had dinner with him.'

'Daniel . . . '

'I know!' he said quietly. 'And I wouldn't have, if I could have let it go, but I can't. It was a case Drake won conclusively, and no one else was tried after Evan was acquitted.'

'Is that all?' Pitt asked, his voice guarded, and his eyes never leaving Daniel's face.

Daniel drew a deep breath, and then let it go. 'No. He told me a lot about Drake. In chambers, we only saw him as a man who was brilliant . . . and cold. He never stopped to make conversation and seemed to have no life outside his work. Evan saw a completely different man. Drake worked around the clock, but not only that, he took time to explain things, and to encourage Evan. His father paid the bill, of course, but Evan said Drake treated him with kindness.'

'Go on,' Pitt said levelly, his face tense.

'I've also learned who Drake might have seen when he was in Mile End. Hobson, his clerk, said it might be a moneylender, one he needed to see secretly.' It sounded dubious, even as he tried to explain it. He took a breath, then went on. 'I know you said to leave Faber out of it, if I could. Well, I can't, I'm sorry.' He met his father's eyes and saw his anger dissolve. He felt guilty for causing this moment. He wanted to tell him that he liked Evan Faber, even felt a kinship with him. And that Evan understood the need to live up to a father he felt he would never even come close to. But he chose to keep these thoughts to himself.

Daniel understood his father's ire. He had disobeyed his warning. But to obey it, and turn his back on a possible avenue to the truth, was unacceptable, and Pitt would be the first to say that. 'I have to follow it up — '

'Do you?' Pitt interrupted. 'What about giving it to the police?'

'Not every policeman is like you,' Daniel replied instantly. 'And they've conspicuously failed to turn up anything yet.'

'Incompetence, or corruption?' Pitt asked, his voice expressionless but his face grave.

Daniel answered carefully. 'I don't know. It could be a mixture. It doesn't matter. They've still got nowhere . . . ' He tried to suppress the emotion rising inside, the sudden wave of regret for not having taken the time to know Drake, because he was older, and eccentric.

Pitt did not interrupt him.

'Evan might remember something about who Drake saw in Mile End,' Daniel went on. 'We've got no ideas now, and the police don't seem to be doing anything more than asking the obvious questions. And . . . ' he hesitated to say it, 'and I'd much rather we found the truth than the police. It might be . . . '

Pitt relaxed a little. 'All right, I take your point. But be careful, Daniel. You don't want Erasmus Faber as an enemy.'

Daniel's acknowledgement was cut off by Charlotte's return to announce that dinner would be in half an hour. He was grateful for the short relief. He smiled his thanks.

6

The next two days passed quickly. Daniel had dinner again with Evan Faber, which ultimately turned into an all-night pub crawl, something Daniel had not done since his days in Cambridge at university: Daniel at Caius, Evan at Trinity.

It was fun, and by midnight, or close to it, they were laughing at jokes, silly, irreverent and filled with memories softened by distance and affection. They laughed at the eccentricities of masters they had loved and hated, pranks that went right, or wrong, success and failure. They recalled people they no longer knew, but who never left the memory.

'He was such a clown,' Evan said, and the gentleness in his voice betrayed his emotions. He and Daniel were walking along the cobbled street a little above the dark tide of the Thames. They looked over at the strip of lights along the opposite shore, mirrored only a fraction less brightly in the water below them.

'Let's go over, and down a bit,' Evan went on with enthusiasm. 'I've always said I'd go down the river by night, one day.'

'One night,' Daniel corrected him, and they both laughed. 'Down the river to where? Not Gravesend. Too far. And too boring, through all that flat estuary land. Can't even see the birds in the dark.'

'I don't know. Get past the Isle of Dogs, and then the Royal Naval College. After that I believe there are marshes. Eerie. All that flat, sucking mud. Who knows what it has swallowed? Haunted by the ghosts of pirates . . . '

'What about Traitors' Gate?' Daniel suggested. 'That's the water gate off the river into the Tower of London, where they used to take in the people to have their heads chopped off. That's got to have the odd ghost! Queen Anne Boleyn. Sir Walter Raleigh!'

'Excellent!' Evan said happily, giving a dramatic shudder. 'This side of the river. Look at that!' He pointed towards the west, upriver, to where, were it earlier, the last of the sun would be spilling scarlet across the water.

'Tower Bridge,' Daniel suggested. 'Let's see if we can find a ferry still working, and go under the bridge. It's quite a spectacle.'

'Splendid idea,' Evan agreed.

They turned and worked their way across the cobbles and down the steps to the ferry pick-up spot.

Further down, the sound of waves was audible as the tide lapped against the steps. The wind was cool, but neither of them noticed. They swapped more memories of friends they had known, and lost touch with.

'Like a bouquet of flowers,' Evan said, narrowly avoiding slipping on the stones, made greasy by the tide. 'Memories,' he explained. 'So fragile. Perfect for a few days. But with care, they bloom again, and again. Need weeding, and a little rain . . . '

He had no idea why, but Daniel started to laugh at the idea. 'Lots of weeds in my memory,' he said cheerfully, and chuckled again. He would have a headache in the morning, and Drake would still be dead, and Marcus in danger, but tonight he did not care.

'Good times,' Evan said, picking his way over some broken cobbles. 'Life gets so complicated afterwards.'

Daniel glanced sideways at him, and saw in a moment's lamplight the gravity in Evan's face. 'Yes,' he agreed. 'You tend to put other matters aside when you're studying, no room for them in your mind. Understand what you're reading — not just the words, but what it all means. Remember . . . hold your own, but don't talk too much!' He looked sideways at Evan, but only saw the profile of his face in the dim light between one street lamp and the next.

'Life was so much simpler,' Evan said thoughtfully. 'Don't think I realised that at the time.'

'Can see that now, though,' Daniel answered. 'It can be good to let one thing crowd out everything else, and feel justified in letting it. Things you don't know how to deal with, you just put them aside. God, to study . . . ' He left the thought unfinished, at least half on purpose. He would never have a better chance than this to speak candidly to Evan. Then, when Evan did not speak, he suddenly went on. 'You can fall madly in love, but half of you knows it won't last. Everything's a dream, except study.'

'A good dream,' Evan said, with feeling. 'Even

121

heartbreak has an unreality to it . . . '

Daniel heard the pain in Evan's voice. The momentary dream could not last. 'Are you thinking of Marie Wesley?' he asked, and hated himself for it.

'I suppose everybody knows about that,' Evan said, his voice low and bitter.

'No,' Daniel answered. 'I do because, as I told you, the lawyer who proved you innocent worked in my chambers. And since he was murdered the other night, it's part of my job to read through his notes.'

'Is that why we're here?' The bitterness was gone from Evan's voice, only pain left.

'If you mean did I find you because of it?' Daniel answered. 'Yes, of course I did. Drake liked you, and believed you were innocent. I contacted you because I thought you should know he was dead. I've told you that . . . '

'Sorry,' Evan apologised. 'Of course I didn't kill her. I really liked her. I think you would have, too. She was a realist, you know? She knew what life was like, and that it wouldn't go on that way much longer, not for her. But she had no self-pity. She was generous and wise and funny. And I'm not entirely innocent of her death . . . '

Daniel felt as if the mist on the river was suddenly ice on his skin. He did not know what to say. He liked Evan, instinctively, without effort.

'I gave her nothing,' Evan went on, speaking now more to himself. 'I just liked her, liked being with her, and in an odd way, I trusted her. She didn't want anything from me except good company, and a little fun. And she was good in bed . . .'

'Then what do you blame yourself for?' Daniel asked.

'Being so damn stupid!' Evan replied. 'She was killed in a jealous rage, by someone who couldn't share her. I should have known there'd be someone like that. I didn't care enough . . .'

Daniel drew a deep breath. 'Do you know who it was?'

Evan sounded surprised. 'No, of course I don't, or I'd have told the police. Damn it, they could have hanged me! Would have, if it weren't for Drake.'

'Did he have any ideas?' Daniel could simply let the question go unasked, and unanswered, but he chose not to. He had to know.

'If he had, he'd have said,' Evan replied. 'But perhaps he was still looking? Maybe that was why he was killed? In a way, I'm responsible for that, too.'

'No, you're not!' Daniel told him sharply. 'Maybe she liked you better than she liked him, whoever he was, and he couldn't live with that. It was nothing to do with you. Sooner or later, she'd have found someone else, and he'd have reacted the same way. You think too much of yourself if you imagine you can control everybody else's jealousy.'

'I know,' Evan replied. 'Let's put our troubles aside, and go on down the river.'

It took them fifteen minutes to find a ferryman still awake. It was cold out on the water, but the soft sounds of the water slurping against the wooden sides of the boat, the easy rhythm of the oars, were infinitely pleasing. Who cared if they shivered now and then?

They talked of more distant memories. Evan could just remember his mother. That loss still hurt, and it was raw in his voice. He talked around it, without speaking of her directly, mentioning the things she'd loved: dewdrops on the heads of seeded grasses, the smell of pansies, skylarks too far above them to see, but their silver voices filling rhe air.

Daniel did not ask questions; silent companionship was better.

They drifted happily under the magnificent span of Tower Bridge and, on the far side, landed again. Evan insisted on paying the ferryman. They found a cheerful public house and had another beer, and then another. They sat and talked for a while, and then walked in companionable silence. It must have been three o'clock in the morning when they finally parted, Evan singing a song to himself as he walked away.

The differences between the two men were interesting, the similarities comfortable.

Daniel fell asleep on top of his bed, shoes off but fully dressed, and a smile on his face.

★　★　★

Thomas Pitt was fully engaged in uncovering what looked like an anarchist ring determined to blow up factories. These outbreaks of industrial violence were increasing all over Europe. Social unrest fuelled by political gatherings, arbitrary arrests, desperate poverty next to the glaring inequalities in power and wealth were all boiling over in open protests and sabotage, even bombings.

Pitt did not approve of the violence, but by heaven he could understand it. He just knew it would solve nothing. Those driven to despair would gain nothing from imprisonment — not until there was social change.

That evening, he and Charlotte went to dinner at the home of one of the leading members of the House of Lords. Pitt would much rather have stayed home, but this was an obligation of his role, a duty which he had learned to accept, even with some grace. Charlotte had schooled him in the manners of the social class to which she had been born, and he was finally more or less comfortable with it. He knew that this was where a great deal of the real power lay, as well as a lot of the secrets and information without which he could not do his job.

He was unsurprised when, after the excellent meal, with all the necessary civilities observed, Sir James MacPherson, of the Home Office, approached him, seemingly casually, except for the quiet word with the butler which Pitt knew was to see that they should be undisturbed for as long as Sir James intended. Charlotte was at the far side of the huge withdrawing room, dressed magnificently, in flame-coloured silk, talking to the Duchess of somewhere or other.

'How are you, Pitt?' MacPherson asked solicitously. Then he went on, before Pitt could answer him. 'Good job with that bank business in Grimsby. Could have done a lot of damage, if you hadn't caught the blighters.'

'Thank you.' Pitt accepted graciously. It had been a good job.

'Can't afford to let them blow up any of our shipyards,' MacPherson went on. 'God knows, we need every last one of them.'

Pitt sighed. It seemed as if it were going to be another lecture on the dire straits of the Navy again. Heaven knew, it was true. Britain had ridden on the astounding victory at Trafalgar, a century ago, for far too long. Nelson's brilliant figure had cast its protective shadow over the entire country, also for too long. That had been in the days of sailing ships! The great *Santissima Trinidad*, with three tiers of oars on either side, had been the terror of the seas. And Nelson, with his smaller, faster and more manoeuvrable ships, had won victory after victory, leaving Britain master of the world's oceans. But now it was just a glorious memory, and a current national delusion.

'The Kaiser of Germany fancies himself a great admiral, you know,' MacPherson said gravely.

'Yes, Sir James, I know that,' Pitt replied. He did know it. It was he who had told MacPherson, nearly ten years ago. 'That's why we are guarding our shipbuilding yards so carefully.'

'Yes, of course you know it,' MacPherson said, his mouth puckered with anxiety. 'But we have too many in government who don't know it.

Don't understand the seriousness of it. Ship-building is one of our major priorities. God knows, nothing short of a looming disaster would make me be civil to a man like Faber. Bloody outsider! But got to be civil to the man. And the scandal that nearly overtook him? It could happen to anyone.'

'I know a young woman was beaten to death,' Pitt agreed. 'But it was a regular police case. Nothing to do with Special Branch. And Evan Faber, the son, was found not guilty.'

'And then some bastard murdered the defence lawyer, and left his body in Mile End,' MacPherson went on, giving Pitt a narrow look. 'Don't tell me you don't know about that. Of course you do.'

A footman approached them with a tray of champagne glasses, saw the look on MacPherson's face, and changed direction.

Across the room someone laughed. He saw the silk of Charlotte's gown gleaming, as she moved a step or two.

'I know about Drake's murder,' Pitt agreed. 'Everyone does. But I have no idea who committed it, or why. But,' he went on, 'instead of repeating things we both know, why don't you say what you really mean?'

'You might be one of nature's gentlemen, in fact you are, but you're certainly not one of society's,' MacPherson said with a bitter-edged smile, as if he had swallowed something momentarily delicious, but with a sour aftertaste. 'What I really mean? Right! Erasmus Faber is a frightful man, straight out of the gutter, but he's also a genius at what he does. He can build the ships Britain might very well need in order to survive, if the Germans turn nasty, as they very well might. Europe is a social tinderbox at the moment. With luck, it will all die down again. There'll be a few more revolutions, like 1848, and it will all pass. But if we're unlucky, one bad act could escalate and we'll have violence. It seems the world is ready for it. Social change will come, and it seldom comes peaceably . . . '

'I know all that,' Pitt agreed. 'Believe me, I do!'

'Take that a little further!' MacPherson snapped. 'Britain has ruled the world's seas for a hundred years. We won't damned well continue if we don't radically update the Navy. And for that we need first-class ships, and a damned sight more than we currently have — '

'I know all that, too,' Pitt interrupted.

'And the price of it is people like Erasmus Faber,' MacPherson went on, as if Pitt had not spoken. 'Put up with the bastard. We all have to. He has pretensions to being a gentleman. I was even pressured to invite him this evening. Only just got out of it. But I won't for ever. The price of his hundred per cent cooperation is high . . . '

'Aren't we paying him enough?'

'Of course we are. At least, we're paying him all we can!' MacPherson's face creased in an expression of disgust. 'But he has his eyes set far higher than money. Use your imagination, Pitt, for pity's sake! He wants a title, and a seat in the House of Lords, and eventually power in the government. I should not be surprised if he even has delusions of marrying into the aristocracy. God help the poor woman! And he'll get what he wants. He may be a long way from a gentleman — in fact, I personally think he belongs in the farmyard — but he's a genius when it comes to shipbuilding.'

'If he doesn't sell his ships to us, then who will buy them?' Pitt asked, but a cold voice inside him knew the answer before MacPherson could say it aloud.

'The bloody Germans, of course!' MacPherson snapped. 'Have you been asleep for the last ten years? Half the damn royal family is German! Or didn't you notice? From Prince Albert onwards, good man as he was. The old King and the Kaiser were first cousins. Our present Queen was a German princess, before she married the King. They speak German at home, damn it! It's a narrow line, Pitt. Just don't go crusading for more justice for Marie Wesley. The woman's dead. Let her rest in peace. Be civil to Faber, even if it chokes you — just as the rest of us have to.'

Pitt wrestled with the idea. It revolted MacPherson to have to socialise with Faber, that was plain in his face. The thought of Faber one day being in the House of Lords, with the power that would give him — worse yet, more power in the actual government — was choking him. But Britain was an island. They could be blockaded. Napoleon had nearly succeeded. Indeed, so had the King of Spain, in the days of Elizabeth I and the Armada.

MacPherson was staring at him.

'Yes, I see,' Pitt said quietly. 'I don't think he'll sell to the Germans, but I'm as sure as you are that they'd buy. Thank heaven his son was cleared. At least poor Drake did a thorough job of that.'

'Yes,' MacPherson agreed. 'Poor devil.'

★　★　★

When the evening was over, Charlotte and Pitt rode home in a chauffeur-driven car. The frequent use of such a conveyance was part of the privilege of Pitt's position. It was very comfortable; it was also safe. He chose not to think of, or to mention, that aspect of it.

He glanced at Charlotte beside him. In the intermittent light from the street lamps, through the car windows, he thought she was the loveliest woman he had ever seen. Time had been kind to her. She said it had been happiness. He chose not to argue about that. It was a good thought. And after MacPherson's conversation, a good thought was a temporary refuge he very much appreciated.

They arrived home and went into the drawing room, where the embers of the fire were still warm. The clock on the mantelpiece said quarter to eleven, but Pitt was not yet relaxed enough to sleep. Perhaps sensing his need to talk, Charlotte sat down in her usual chair and leaned forward to poke the fire into life. She put a light piece of wood on to it, and it finally caught fire. She reached for another. 'Are you worried about something?' she said at last, satisfied that the fire

130

was burning up. She leaned back in her chair and looked at him.

'What are you talking about?' he asked, sitting down opposite her. And then he said, 'I don't know,' smiling in spite of himself. 'I hope I'm not as transparent to everyone else.'

'Probably not,' she agreed. 'If you can't tell me, just say so. And I'll worry without bothering you. As long as it's not about Daniel, and this wretched business of poor Drake. Is Marcus in trouble, Thomas?'

It was both comforting and disturbing to be known so well. If he evaded the issue, it would put a barrier between them he really did not want. There was already too much he could not share, the nature of his job prevented it. He did not lie, he just remained silent about many things. 'I don't know,' he replied. 'And that's not an evasion. His chambers dealt with a very ugly case a little while ago. Not Daniel, Jonah Drake . . . '

'The man who was murdered recently?' she asked.

'Yes . . . '

'Do they want you to take it up? Is it Special Branch?'

'Not yet. And no, they don't want me to take it up. They would rather his murder drew no attention at all.'

'Why? Who did it?'

Something in her had not changed a whit, in all the years they had known each other. 'I don't know,' he said honestly. 'They don't want to attract any attention to the case, because it might open up the issue of the young woman Faber's son was accused of killing.'

'Is he guilty, after all? Was Drake going to . . . to say so, somehow?' She frowned at the thought. 'How is Daniel involved?'

'He isn't, except that he knew Drake. They worked in the same chambers.'

'Stop it! Don't protect me, Thomas. There's a connection, otherwise MacPherson wouldn't be talking to you about it for half an hour.'

'Don't exaggerate — ' he began, then stopped. 'Faber has social ambitions, and very high political ones . . . eventually. We can't afford to offend him, because we need his genius at shipbuilding.'

'Or what will he do? Sell his ships somewhere else? Really?'

He hesitated.

'I see,' she said. 'Necessity and greed make strange bedfellows. What a disgusting thought!'

'It didn't take you long to work that out!' He was surprised.

'Darling, your roots are showing! And I love it in you, please don't change. But the aristocracy, even the minor gentry, have made accommodations to survive, for centuries.' She stopped. There was no sound in the familiar room except the rain pattering on the glass of the French doors, the crackle of the fire, and the soft whisper of a fall of ash as one of the new logs in the fire slid deeper into the flames.

'You and I married for love,' she went on. 'So did Jemima, and I hope Daniel will, one day. But the higher people rise in society, the less likely they are to get that chance. Not that that necessarily works out any better. But did you think a man like Faber would allow his son to make a disadvantageous marriage?'

'He doesn't need money,' he pointed out.

'Of course not. He needs class, position, breeding! And he has enough money to buy it. Especially if we are on the edge of conflict. Perhaps not anything as terrible as war, but unpleasantness, at least.'

He looked at her steadily. It was never her beauty that had held him, although he was charmed by it, nor was it really her intelligence. It was her courage. And although her candour terrified him, it was the very essence of her. Her emotional commitment was total.

'Yes,' he agreed. 'I think he's a very dangerous man. I wish we didn't need him. But, as MacPherson pointed out, and rather forcefully, we do.'

She hesitated only a moment. 'Is Daniel involved?'

'Dear heaven,' he sighed. 'I hope not.'

7

After a full day of work, and still tired from his outing with Evan Faber, Daniel went to bed early. He came to the surface of consciousness and opened his eyes reluctantly. His landlady, Mrs Portiscale, was standing beside his bed wearing a shabby blue dressing gown, which he could see only dimly in the light from the landing.

'What is it?' he asked, rubbing his eyes and blinking. 'Are you all right?'

'Yes, I'm as good as can be at this hour of the morning,' she answered. 'Lord help us, it isn't even daylight yet, and there's a gentleman here to see you. Said it's urgent.'

Daniel sat upright. 'Who is it? What has happened?' Now he was afraid. He threw the bedclothes off, regardless of modesty, and stood up. 'Who is it?' he repeated. 'Has something happened to my family?'

'No, Mr Pitt,' she assured him. 'It's a professional call, he says. His name is Dr Ottershaw. Says he knows you . . . '

Daniel felt a wave of relief. 'Oh. Yes, I know him. Give me a moment and I'll get dressed and be down. Please, go back to bed, Mrs Portiscale. I'm sorry you were disturbed.'

She ignored his remark with a slight shrug. 'I'll get you a cup of tea. It'll help you wake up. And a slice of toast,' she added, going out the door.

She left it open so he could see in the light from the landing, at least enough to turn up the gas in his own wall light.

He dressed quickly, not bothering to shave, only to wash his face and clean his teeth. He went down the dimly lit stairs as quietly as possible. Why would Octavius Ottershaw come at this ungodly hour? His profession was pathology; his passion was forensics. Daniel had met him because he was a friend of Miriam's, one who recognised her remarkable abilities and allowed her to work with him. Also, he was very fond of her.

He found Ottershaw sitting at the kitchen table eating toast, and with a cup of tea in his hand. He pointed to the tea and toast set on the other side of the table for Daniel. Mrs Portiscale was nowhere to be seen.

'She went back to bed,' Ottershaw said, with a bleak smile. 'Eat your toast. You'll maybe not have time for breakfast. And tea.' He took a sip. 'Good, and it's hot.

'What has happened?' Daniel demanded as he slid on to the seat opposite and reached for the butter and marmalade.

There were a few seconds of silence. He looked up and saw Ottershaw's face. He was a curious-looking man, his wild white hair and slightly hollow cheeks at first glance suggesting absent-mindedness and an overworked imagination. But Daniel knew him as a scientist, a lover of truth above everything else. Except kindness, always kindness. His present gravity was alarming. 'What is it?' he repeated, fear making his voice sharper than he meant.

Ottershaw sighed. 'I believe you are acquainted with young Evan Faber?'

'Yes. Only just. But how did you know that?'

A bleak smile touched Ottershaw's face, one utterly without pleasure. 'You blazed a very bright trail the other night, one way or another.'

Daniel flushed at the possible embarrassment to come. To tell the truth, he could remember little of the evening, at least in detail, only that he had enjoyed himself.

'What about him?' he asked.

'I'm afraid he was found dead, late last night,' Ottershaw replied. 'I was called to the case. I'm sorry.'

'Dead? He was fine when I last saw him,' Daniel protested, as if that were relevant.

Ottershaw held his hand slightly raised from the table, a very small gesture, but enough to silence Daniel. 'I'm sorry. The only good thing was that his death must have been almost instant. I dare say he didn't even have time to register it. No time for pain . . . '

'Surely it wasn't his heart? He looked — ' Daniel stopped talking. He was arguing, as if it could make a difference. He was only putting off the inevitable.

'A long knife through the heart,' Ottershaw said, the words spoken slowly and deliberately, as if making certain he would not have to say them again.

Daniel shook his head. 'You mean murder? No one has an accident like that!'

'Yes, I do mean murder,' Ottershaw agreed.

'And in the back streets of Mile End. At least, that was where they found him, but not where he died. He was moved, how far we don't know.'

'Moved?' Daniel blinked. 'How do you know?'

'No blood where he was found. Stains from a vegetable cart on his clothes. Unless that was gained during your . . . adventures?'

'No. No, of course not. Moved? Why?'

'We don't know.'

'How did you connect us?'

'He had one of your cards in his pocket.'

It was a nightmare, like Drake's death repeated. What was Evan doing in Mile End? Daniel was still arguing inside himself, as if the unlikeliness of Evan's death could make it someone else. And yet was it unlikely? Evan had still been upright, less tipsy than Daniel, when they parted. Had he gone to Mile End acting on Daniel's suggestion, almost a request, to find the person Jonah Drake had intended to see? Is that how Evan ended up being killed by a long knife, like Drake, but mercifully unaware of what was happening to him, without even trying to fight back? According to what Ottershaw said, it was almost merciful.

'You know something?' Ottershaw asked, his voice urgent now. 'It was the same place as your man Drake, but a different style of killing.' He leaned forward a little over the table. 'What is it, Daniel? What is the connection between Drake and young Faber?'

Daniel thought for a moment. 'Well, the obvious one is that when Evan was accused of

137

murder, and found not guilty, it was Drake who defended him.' He felt a wave of guilt wash over him, leaving his chest tight and a heat burning inside him. He looked down at the tablecloth, not at Ottershaw. 'I told Evan about Drake's death, ostensibly so he could attend the funeral, if he wished to. And he did. He felt strongly about it.' He raised his eyes. 'But really, I wanted to see if he could tell me what Drake was doing in Mile End.' He found the words difficult to say. Ottershaw was looking right into his soul. Could he see his foolishness, as if he were guilty of Evan's death? And perhaps he was.

'Did he know?' Ottershaw asked.

'He thought he could find out,' Daniel replied miserably. He looked down again at his plate and the toast on it. He could not eat it. His throat was tight with the strain of controlling his feelings, his grief, his guilt, and a raging anger that such a thing could happen. Evan had been so alive; he had felt so much, so intensely. How could he simply have ceased to be? Daniel could still hear his laughter, remember the softness in his voice when he spoke of the mother he barely remembered.

'Perhaps he did?' Ottershaw replied gently, breaking the spell.

But he said nothing comforting to Daniel about it not being his fault, and Daniel was glad of that. He did not want Ottershaw to be kind, as he would to a child who could not accept guilt or blame. 'He wouldn't have gone there if I hadn't told him about it,' Daniel said aloud.

'Possibly not,' Ottershaw agreed. 'But from

what you say, he owed Drake a lot. He might have wanted to find out who killed him as much as you do.'

'I didn't owe Drake anything, except decency,' Daniel replied. 'It was really Marcus I was thinking of.'

Ottershaw sat a little more upright. 'Marcus?'

'Drake worked for our chambers. I think we owe him our loyalty. Was his death linked to a case? Was it some unfinished business?' He would not say anything to Ottershaw about the unexplained movements of money.

'And was it?' Ottershaw pressed.

'I think so. I want to know why Drake was in Mile End. And if Evan was killed near there too, what did he find out that would make somebody want to kill him? It's difficult to believe it's coincidental.'

'Be careful,' Ottershaw warned. 'It's not in the newspapers that Evan Faber's body was found in Mile End. I think Faber will keep that quiet. He'll put it down to youthful lack of thought, strolling through London late at night. And if it comes out at all, it will be seen as the tragedy of a young man who was attacked on his way home, and could not defend himself. And don't mistake it, Daniel, Erasmus Faber has the clout to make that stick. There are hundreds, if not thousands, of workers in his employ. He'll have no trouble finding a dozen or so who will swear that Evan was somewhere else.'

'And the police will believe him?' Daniel could already see the doors closing everywhere he looked.

'No, but they'll pretend to,' Ottershaw opined.

Daniel was angry; it was so much easier to feel than pain. 'Then who killed him, and why?' he demanded. 'Did he owe money? Perhaps his father refused to pay?'

Ottershaw's eyes widened. 'A kidnap gone bad? I never thought of that. It's possible. If it was that, then Erasmus is going to move heaven and earth to find whoever did it, and kill him slowly and very painfully. And I suppose I care, but not a great deal. If they murdered that young man for money, they have a hard justice coming.'

Daniel looked down at the table, islanded in the pre-dawn darkness, with its comforting teapot, milk jug and blue-ringed china. His conversation with Evan was as sharp in his mind as if he had been sitting there with them. 'He was profoundly grateful to Drake, you know,' he said aloud.

'Evan was?'

'Yes. We've got to find out who killed him, and that begins with the motive.' Daniel said this as if it were obvious.

'Do we have any ideas about Drake? Or what he was looking for in Mile End?'

'Not much.' Daniel tried to recall exactly what Kitteridge had said. 'Moneylenders, brothels, that sort of thing. Opium dealers. Why does any decent man go to Mile End in the middle of the night? Information? But we don't know about what, or whom.' A darker thought occurred to him. 'Or possibly to collect money — or for blackmail, I suppose.'

140

'Did Drake own any property in Mile End?' Ottershaw asked. 'It should be possible to find out.'

'Well, if he did, there's no record of it either in his home or at chambers.' Daniel wanted to think of something more to say, but his mind was still trying to absorb the fact that Evan, whom he had liked so much, didn't exist any more. Just a few minutes, and he had ceased to be. Another corpse for the police to worry about.

'I'm sorry,' Ottershaw said again, more softly. 'I didn't want you to find out from reading it in the newspaper. Or not knowing, and going to look for him and hearing it from some gossip. When I found your business card . . . ' His voice trailed off.

Daniel looked up. 'Thank you. Is his father going to raise hell, turn the East End inside out, looking for whoever was responsible?'

Ottershaw's face puckered. 'I saw him briefly, at the morgue. Huge man. Evan must have taken after his mother. When he identified his son, he looked exhausted, poor man. As if he had just begun the worst day of his life. He asked the police to say as little as possible, especially about where the body was found. And he's right. His son, as you suggest, may have gone there to try and find out something about who killed Drake, but it wouldn't help anybody to make that public.' He sighed. 'People always put the worst interpretation on things, especially if it's someone young, good-looking and, above all, very rich indeed. Let him rest in peace. His father begged for that. And I admit, I felt sorry for him. I'd have given it to him, if it had been up to me.'

'Why did you come at this hour to tell me?' Daniel asked abruptly. He was angry, sad, confused and, he admitted it, a little frightened, not for himself, but for Marcus, and then for Miriam. He missed her courage, her humour, even her occasionally acerbic wit. Sometimes he understood her thoughts completely, as if she had plucked them straight from his mind. At other times, she was as alien as a different species.

He had discovered a lot more about her during the recent trials, when she had been so viciously attacked in court. She, too, was vulnerable, and she had made mistakes she was ashamed and embarrassed to admit at all, never mind in public, from the witness box, to be described by newspaper reporters and told to the world. At first, he had been shaken, then he had felt rage on her behalf, and closer to her than ever before. Not critical of her mistakes, but more protective of her emotions — her vulnerability, her foolish dreams about things and people — than he had imagined. But how was he going to tell her about this, and convey the reality of it, and how deep the emotions were, how much he cared? And how it frightened him because there was so much he did not know.

This brought him back to the fact that he must protect Marcus as far as was humanly possible, and he could do that only if he knew the truth. Who killed Drake? And, above all, why? Was Evan's death coincidental, or were these deaths connected? Maybe Erasmus Faber would solve the riddle of Evan's death, and perhaps avenge it. Or maybe he was wounded too deeply to think of that yet?

Had Evan gone to Mile End to look for evidence to give to Daniel, to help solve Drake's murder? That was a black shadow hanging over everything. Daniel could not dismiss the thought that if he had not gone to look for Evan, he might still be alive.

'Be careful,' Ottershaw said again.

'If you don't expect me to do anything,' said Daniel, 'then why are you here?' He could hear the edge to his voice and tried to soften it. This morning had a nightmare quality to it. Perhaps he would wake up and find it was only in his imagination? 'No need to answer that,' he quickly added. 'A second body has been found, knifed to death, and with one of my cards in his pocket.'

Ottershaw was staring at him. 'I told you so that you won't be caught out by the police asking you questions you can't answer,' he said gravely. 'Whether it's Drake's body turning up in Mile End or young Faber having your card, these are explainable. But you have to come up with the explanation immediately, if they ask: you know Evan because you went to tell him of Drake's death, the man who had saved his skin. You'll grieve for ever for Faber, whatever the outcome. But for Marcus's sake, I want this to get sorted out with the least damage possible to him and the reputation of fford Croft and Gibson. Grief can be dealt with. Suspicion is

143

entirely another matter. Unsolved cases leave a lot of pain behind them, fears and dark thoughts that breed like rats . . . '

Daniel listened, knowing it wasn't the pathologist speaking, but Miriam's close friend. He was protecting Miriam and her father, as well as Daniel.

Daniel shrugged at the image. Rats were dirty and dangerous. They had sharp teeth and, if cornered, they would attack. The idea that unchecked suspicions could hide and wait and breed, like rats, was too hideous to entertain in his imagination.

He looked up at Ottershaw and saw how pale he was, and how tired. 'Don't worry,' he said, almost like surrendering. 'It's too dangerous to rush into action without thought, I can see that. First Drake, and now Evan.' He put his head down and ran his fingers through his hair. 'Except that's not where it began, is it?'

'No,' Ottershaw agreed. 'Don't try looking for the beginning. It's probably too far away to find. Just get a thread you can follow. Drake was hacked to death; Evan was killed expertly. But it could have been with the same blade, as near as I can tell. Same shape and width, but the second wound was long, at the very least ten inches.' He shook his head as if overwhelmed by the thought. It seemed the pleasant kitchen table had disappeared for him. He was back in the morgue again. 'Probably longer,' he said. 'The first blade could have been anything over ten inches, used like a sword . . . but same shape entry wound.'

'Same person?' Daniel asked. It was a thought

as sharp and cold as the blade that had killed both victims. Who carried around such a thing? Or did they only use it when they had a victim already in their sights? 'We are in over our heads, aren't we?' he said quietly.

'Yes,' Ottershaw agreed. 'And I haven't any idea what it's really about. You need to find out everything you can about Drake, on the assumption that that is what Evan Faber was also looking for. And for heaven's sake, Daniel, keep out of Mile End,' he added sharply. 'You would be safer in a police cell than rattling around down there. And you are no use to anyone dead.'

'I know,' Daniel admitted. 'But I'm not going to sit this out and watch. I hope to find out whatever I can . . . ' He paused, and then added, 'Thank you for coming.'

Ottershaw sighed. 'You've got to face facts, Daniel. If Marcus is involved in this, intentionally or accidentally, tell me before you do anything. Give me your word, or I'll tell your father and he'll put an end to it. And possibly to your career as well.'

'You can't — ' Daniel began. Then he met Ottershaw's eyes and knew that he not only could, he would. 'What a mess,' he said, almost under his breath.

Ottershaw nodded his agreement. 'And it needs intelligence, not bravado, to get the best result. Another brave, idealistic person, bent on saving everyone else, going off at half-cock, will just be in the way. And worse than that, he'll need us to stop what we're doing and rescue him!'

Daniel started to laugh, then choked it off. It sounded hysterical, horribly inappropriate. 'I know. Noble intentions and no brains at all. A damn liability. I won't do anything rash. I give you my word.'

'Thank you, I accept it. Now, if you please, I could do with another cup of decent tea.'

Daniel leaned forward and picked up the teapot.

★　★　★

Daniel was in chambers soon after Impney had arrived.

'Good morning, sir,' Impney greeted him with surprise. 'If you don't mind my saying so, you look a little pale.'

'I don't mind your saying so.' Daniel smiled bleakly. 'There was another murder last night. Ottershaw came and told me at some ungodly time, a few hours ago. I lay awake thinking, and then left before anyone else came down for breakfast. I'll have to tell Mr fford Croft and Mr Kitteridge, but not before a good cup of tea, if you don't mind.'

Impney looked distressed. 'Another murder? In Mile End again?'

'Yes. I don't know what they're going to do about it, but they'll move heaven and earth to make it look better than it appears,' Daniel replied, without explaining that he meant Erasmus Faber, and whatever police or newspapermen he could pay.

'Accident, sir, so the early papers are saying.

146

That is, if you are referring to young Mr Faber.'
Without waiting for a reply, Impney turned and
left the entrance hall and went towards the small
kitchen to put on the kettle. Daniel followed
him. 'Perhaps you'd like a slice of toast also, sir?'
he asked over his shoulder. 'Difficult to do your
best thinking on an empty stomach.' He turned
the gas up and put the kettle on, and then looked
more closely at Daniel. 'And an aspirin tablet,
before your headache gets any worse. They are
very good, sir.'

'Thank you.' Daniel smiled as well as he could
manage. His headache was already throbbing. 'I
liked him, you know? Went out together on a pub
crawl that lasted most of the night. Felt as if I
knew him.' He took a deep breath. 'And in case
it had anything to do with Mr Drake's death, we
need to solve it ourselves, if we can.'

'Do you think it might have some connection,
sir?' Impney looked surprised. 'Why is that? We
weren't representing him, were we?'

'Not now. But I asked his help, because he
knew Mr Drake quite well, and thought a lot of
him. And he was killed very close to where Mr
Drake died.'

'Was he then? That's not what the newspaper
says.' Impney looked troubled. His hands moved
quite automatically, setting out the tea tray. He
did not need to look at it.

'Then Erasmus Faber must have spoken to
them already,' said Daniel. 'And he will have
persuaded the police as well, because Evan's
body was discovered only a street away from
where Mr Drake was found.'

147

'Most interesting. Poor young man.' Impney took the kettle off the gas ring and warmed the teapot. Then he put the tea leaves in it, and lastly the boiling water. 'If you like, sir, I'll bring this and a couple of slices of toast when they're done, and you can take it in your office. Would you like me to bring another cup when Mr Kitteridge arrives?'

Actually, Daniel would have liked to stay in the small kitchen where there were no problems, no one to get to him with any further news. But he realised the inappropriateness of it. 'Thank you. Yes, that would be a good idea.'

Kitteridge arrived three-quarters of an hour later and found Daniel sitting in his own office, but with the door wide open. He walked in, looking chilly but without the checked coat. It had lost its charm since Drake had borrowed it, even though the police had returned it to him. It might have been possible to mend it, but he did not want to. And Daniel did not blame him. It was not as if they imagined that Drake could be put back together. That was an absurd thought, and somehow trivialising his death, as if saying it could be undone, and everything was really the same.

'Impney said young Faber was killed last night. Is that true?' Kitteridge began.

Daniel looked at him. 'Sit down,' he requested, pointing to the hardback chair kept for clients. There was no room for a larger, more comfortable one. 'Yes, it's true. And they found him in Mile End. Although the papers didn't say so.'

'How do you know?' Kitteridge sat down awkwardly, knees and elbows at odd angles.

'Ottershaw came at about three o'clock this morning and told me. It's a pretty good mess.'

'It involves us?' Kitteridge saw the threat immediately. 'Does it go back to Drake?'

'I think so. I asked Evan to help. At least, I planted the idea in his mind. He wouldn't have been in danger if I hadn't told him about Drake, and asked him if he knew of any possible motive.'

'And did he?' Kitteridge pressed.

'I think it's possible,' Daniel admitted. 'And if not yet, then he was on the brink of finding it. If I'm right, Evan got too close for those responsible to let him go any further.' At last he put it into words.

Kitteridge's face was bleak. 'He wanted to help you? What was his interest in it?'

'Drake saved him from the gallows. Do you need anything more? Drake would have been paid, whether he won or not, but he worked all day and all night to get that verdict. And it wasn't just a *not guilty*, it was a judgment that really cleared Evan. The jurors left the court convinced that Evan was truly innocent. Even though no one else was ever charged. Because his name had been cleared, he was very grateful to Drake.' Daniel saw the image of Evan's face, sharp in his mind, the laughter, the regret, the gratitude. He found he needed a moment or two to get control of the profound sadness that welled up inside him.

Kitteridge lowered his gaze and waited.

149

'We've got to find out,' Daniel said at last. 'Why was Drake killed? And what does Marcus know about it? And what does someone else know that Marcus might have forgotten? We . . . ' he took a deep breath, 'we may have to protect him from something he can't defend himself over . . . because he doesn't remember all the facts.'

Kitteridge leaned forward to interrupt, and then leaned back, as if realising he didn't know what to say. His bewilderment was clear in his face.

'I wish we knew how deeply Marcus is involved,' Daniel went on. 'How much he really knows, or remembers . . . ' He bit his lip. 'Or what money Faber may have paid to Marcus, or directly to Drake, to win this case. To buy lies or . . . pay direct bribes to a juror.'

Kitteridge's face was bleak. 'Or how much he knew perfectly well at the time.' He looked wretched, but took a long breath and went on. 'If we find out that Marcus knew all about something Drake did that was wrong, will he plead old age, lack of memory and concentration, and therefore deny responsibility — ?'

'I understand,' Daniel cut him off. 'You don't have to explain.'

'We can't defend Marcus if we don't know how deeply he's involved . . . or, by extension, the chambers as a whole.'

'All right,' said Daniel. 'Then we need to find out everything we can about Jonah Drake.'

Kitteridge shifted in his chair, as if unable to get comfortable. 'I don't like to do this, but we need to go more deeply into his cases, his finances, even the chambers' accounts. And don't look like that! I fully expect to find nothing wrong, but I want to know it, not just assume. How did Drake get Evan Faber off the charge? Was he really innocent?' He bit his lip. 'Was there money that changed hands? I mean, money that shouldn't have.'

'Do you mean bribery of witnesses?' Daniel asked in a hoarse voice.

'I want to know there was nothing, rather than just trust and hope,' Kitteridge said. 'If we look into this, all the way, we've got to accept that we might find something ugly. Better we find it before the police do.'

'If we don't, and someone else does, we have no defence,' Daniel agreed. 'If it was Drake in the middle of some mess, he's dead and can't tell us anything, or defend himself. And we can't defend him, either. But that won't stop them. And if it's Marcus, there's no way to protect him unless we know the truth. We must, for everyone's sake.'

'In other words, there's no escape,' Kitteridge concluded. 'I'll hand some of my cases over, a few of the others can manage them. I know Marcus as well as anyone and — ' He stopped, unhappiness etched in his face.

'And you know the truth will come out, whatever it is,' Daniel finished for him. 'But do it quickly, Toby. We need to get there before anyone else does.' He stared miserably at Kitteridge and saw that he did not need to spell it out. 'I'm asking Roman Blackwell to dig more deeply.

151

He'll find things, if anybody can.'

'Do you trust him?' Kitteridge's head came up slowly.

'I'm going to have to,' Daniel replied. He did trust Blackwell, but he did not expect Kitteridge to. 'Let's hope we learn that Drake was killed needlessly, and it had nothing to do with any case he tried. He was visiting friends in Mile End, nothing more. God knows why, at that hour in the morning. And then Evan Faber went there asking about Drake, in Mile End, and just happened to be knifed to death while he was there. Nothing to do with us. And if you can get anyone else to believe that, you should be head of chambers, because I'm damn sure I couldn't!'

Kitteridge put his hand up to his brow and ran his fingers through his hair, making it look like a haystack after a high wind. 'Then go and find something we can all believe,' he said wearily. 'Something you can defend!'

⋆   ⋆   ⋆

Daniel went back to see Letterman again, to find out if there was any more information about Drake's murder. Actually, he wondered if the police were actively investigating it any more. They seemed to have reached a dead end. Or worse, uglier than that, what if they had never intended to pursue it? Did they actually know who had committed the deed and they were being well paid to leave it alone? He did not want even to entertain that idea! And he was determined to be polite, however hard it proved to be.

The bright sunlight made the street look even more drab, and yet somewhere out of sight he could hear children laughing in sheer joy, unselfconsciously. He found himself smiling along with them, even though he could not see them, nor they him.

He was in a better mood than he expected when he went into the police station. He asked the desk sergeant hopefully if he might speak with Inspector Letterman. This was not the same man he'd spoken to previously, so he had no awareness of Daniel or his position.

'If you don't mind waiting, sir,' the man replied. 'Just take a seat.'

'My name is Pitt,' Daniel told him. 'It's about the Drake murder.'

The sergeant's expression changed, and suddenly he found time to go and tell Letterman immediately. Five minutes later, he was back. 'The inspector will see you now,' he told Daniel, his eyes wide, as if he had surprised himself by what he said.

'Thank you.' Daniel stood up and followed the man into the main hallway and up the stairs to Letterman's room.

'There you are, sir,' said the desk sergeant, indicating a door. 'The inspector is in there.' And then he turned and went down the stairs at full speed.

Daniel knocked on the door, and when he heard the answer, went inside.

Letterman was sitting behind his large desk,

spread with papers. He looked tense, his mouth closed in a thin line, and his hands on the table, knuckles white.

'Good morning, sir,' Daniel said pleasantly. 'Thank you for seeing me at short notice.'

'Your father send you?' Letterman asked, an edge to his voice.

Daniel thought swiftly. 'We work together, occasionally.' He saw Letterman's face tighten, and just a shadow in the eyes.

'We've got nothing further,' Letterman said, his voice still tight. 'Your Mr Drake could have been here in Mile End for a dozen reasons, none of them illegal. Or he could have been here to pursue private pleasures. He was an . . . older man. Sometimes it's harder to find . . . ' He hesitated. Not as if he did not know what he meant, but because he was uncertain how to phrase it civilly.

Daniel was not going to help him. He remained quiet, looking interested.

'Could have been anything,' Letterman said tartly. 'A woman he didn't have to pay, for some fun, or pretend. Could have been opium. There's plenty of that around here, too, if you know where to look.'

'Or moneylenders.' Daniel made it only half a question.

'Them, too,' Letterman agreed. 'Or forgers, card sharps, you name it,' he finished. 'Though why a big-time lawyer would want any of them, I don't know.'

'Personal?' Daniel suggested. 'Rather than to do with any case he was working on.'

Letterman rose slowly. 'Don't hope for much,' he said. 'Looks to me like the man got into some quarrel. Perhaps he refused to pay.'

'Stupid thing to do,' Daniel said, aware that he was about to be shown out.

'Could have told him that!' Letterman said bitterly.

Daniel turned and left, closing the door softly behind him. He felt absolutely certain that Letterman was hiding something, but there was nothing to fasten on to, at least nothing to tell him what that might be. Perhaps the inspector was protecting one of the brothels — or to be more accurate, protecting the names of important men who would appreciate and reward his discretion, probably financially. Not many people would wish to have it known that they frequented such places. To suspect was one thing, to know for certain was quite another.

He went out of the police station and along the street, still in the sunshine. He had gone a few hundred yards when he saw a small tobacconist's shop. He remembered that Drake smoked long, black cheroots. Smelled awful. There was a nice selection of them in the shop window. Perhaps he had called in here. He might find out something. It was worth trying.

He went inside and the bell on the door rang, a surprisingly pleasant sound. There was a girl behind the counter. She was very slight and had a pretty, pixie face and blonde hair, cut short, with curls all over her head.

'Good mornin', sir.' She smiled widely. She had very white teeth and a fair complexion. 'Can

I get yer somethin'?'

Daniel smiled back. 'I'm sure I can think of something . . . '

'No doubt.' She put her head a little on one side and quite openly looked him up and down, still smiling. 'And not everything yer'd have to pay for . . . ' she added, quite brazenly teasing him.

He felt himself blushing a little, but he decided to take it as a compliment. 'Never paid before,' he said cheerfully.

If she had expected to embarrass him, her efforts fell flat. In an instant, she seemed to be taken aback, then she laughed. 'I'd lay money you 'aven't. Got the world on a string, eh?'

'Sometimes,' he agreed, smiling back. 'Other times, it feels like a load of coal on my back.'

She looked him up and down again. 'You ain't never lifted a load o' coal in your life! Wot you coming 'ere for anyway?'

'You have some nice cheroots in the window . . . '

Her eyes widened. 'Don't tell me you smoke them things! They're for old men. They smell something awful.'

'It was an old man I had in mind . . . ' 'Your father? Your grandpa?'

'My boss,' he said. 'Smokes them now and then. And you're right, they smell awful. But in his own office, not in mine.'

'Got on his wrong side, 'ave you then?' She was still smiling. She was curiously attractive, and she was well aware of it. It made the game more fun.

156

'Not yet, but I plan to,' he answered.

'Clever? I like a man who plans ahead.' She nodded approvingly. 'Any special kind?' She glanced at the pile of boxes stacked on the shelves behind her.

'I'm not sure. What do you recommend?'

Her eyebrows shot up. 'Come on! Didn't you look to see what he likes, then?'

Daniel could only picture Drake with the cheroot in his mouth. He had never noticed the box it came out of.

'Tall, dark hair, in his sixties. Got a dark mole on his cheek, just to the right side of his nose. I thought he might have bought them from you?' Had he pushed it too far? 'He came this way now and then,' he added.

'What? You expect me to remember 'im?' She met his eyes directly. Hers were startling, almost turquoise blue.

'If he bought those cheroots from you, I thought you might.' It was worth trying. If Drake had spoken to her, he might have given something away. And if he hadn't, he would be unusual. She wasn't just pretty, there was a vitality about her, a quick, sharp mind. 'What's your name?' he asked.

'Belinda May, but they call me Bella.' She looked at him curiously. 'What do they call you?'

'Daniel.'

'Well, Daniel-who-wants-to-please-his-boss-because-he's-about-to-do-something-as-he-shouldn't, I might have seen your boss. Miserable-looking old beggar who likes the black Dutch roots that smell like . . . nothing a lady would say. And I won't let

157

myself down in front of a nice gentleman like you by saying it. I know who you mean. And I got his favourites 'ere.' She picked a box off the shelf. 'Poor old sod, be nice to 'im. But not too nice, or he'll be suspicious. He was a nosy old thing. You going to be like that one day?'

'I wouldn't mind being as clever as he . . . ' He nearly said *was*, but finished with, ' . . . as he is.'

She stood absolutely still, frozen for a second. Did she really know Drake? And did she know he was dead?

Her eyes met his for an instant. They were clear, like tropical seas. Then she looked away. He knew in that instant that she had sold cheroots to Drake, and that she knew he was dead. Should he mention it? Or lie? She would know he was lying. He was caught.

She surprised him. 'Is that what you wanted to know then? Was he 'ere? Yeah, he was. Went along the street asking questions. Ain't wise. You look after yourself, Daniel-who's-going-to-upset-his-boss. You don't want those cheroots, believe me. You'll smell something awful.'

He pushed the box of cheroots back towards her. 'Thank you for your advice, Belinda May.'

She gave him a radiant smile.

He went out the door and into the street, smiling to himself.

8

It was about half past ten the same morning when Impney put his head around Daniel's door and told him that Mr fford Croft would like to see him.

'Oh, yes,' Daniel replied, rising reluctantly to his feet. 'Thank you.' He went straight away, partly out of obedience — Marcus was head of chambers, after all — but equally because, at the moment, he wanted to get it over with. He straightened his jacket and pushed his hair back as he reached Marcus's door and knocked.

'Come in, come in,' Marcus called from inside.

Daniel obeyed. 'Good morning, sir,' he said gravely. It was not a time to be cheerful. He had seldom had much to do with Drake when he was alive, but he felt his absence now, as if there were a chill in the building.

Marcus was sitting behind his desk which was, as usual, littered with papers. He looked sombre and somehow smaller. He wore a black velvet waistcoat and a white shirt beneath it, with a black tie. There was no bright colour about him, and he looked rather lost.

'Sit down,' he ordered. 'Tell me what you found. And shut the damn door!'

'Yes, sir,' Daniel obeyed, closing the door and then pulling the chair a little forward to face Marcus across the desk.

'Sorry about young Faber,' Marcus said. 'Damn shame. But not your fault.'

'My . . . fault?' Daniel felt as if he had trodden in quicksand and was sinking rapidly.

'Aren't we chasing down all of Drake's cases?' Marcus asked, eyebrows raised. 'That was his best. Never found out who killed the poor woman, but cleared Faber completely. Damn clever lawyer, Drake.' He shook his head. 'We'll never replace him, not really.'

There was nothing to do but agree. 'No, sir.'

'So, was there anything wrong with the whole thing? The case, I mean? Why would anyone kill him now? Was Drake looking into it again?'

'Nothing to suggest he was, sir,' Daniel answered.

'What the hell was Drake doing in Mile End anyway?' He stared at Daniel accusingly. Or was it fear? 'His work was mainly with financial cases, fraud, embezzlement, and so on. Nobody in Mile End has a ha'penny to bless themselves with, never mind to pay Drake's charges.' He looked utterly confused, as if he could barely understand what he was asking.

'That's what I was speaking to Evan Faber about,' Daniel replied. He hadn't meant to tell Marcus that, but neither would he lie, even by omission. Marcus might be a little forgetful, but he could read Daniel like a newspaper headline. At least, most of the time.

Marcus sat forward in his chair. 'You asked him?' he demanded.

'I guided the conversation in that direction. He had a great regard for Mr Drake,' Daniel

160

replied. 'He was not only grateful to him, he liked him.'

'And got himself killed,' Marcus replied grimly. 'I suppose you know who his father is?'

'Yes, sir. My father told me . . . '

'He would! Thomas will not be pleased about all this. You asked young Faber to check what Drake was doing in Mile End? Did Faber tell you then?' Marcus's voice was tight with anxiety.

Daniel saw it, and pretended he had not. 'Not exactly. Only how brilliantly Mr Drake had defended him.' He swallowed hard. This was as difficult as he had expected. 'I thought he might like to attend the funeral service. He said he would. Then he asked more about Drake's death, so I told him. Including where it happened, of course.'

'Just like your father.' Marcus shook his head. 'Can't leave a question unanswered! Dammit! But don't think you can pull the wool over my eyes, boy. Young Faber decided to find out what Drake was doing in Mile End because you wound him up like a clockwork toy, and pointed him in the right direction. Don't look so innocently at me! I'm getting on a bit, but I'm not a fool!'

Daniel swallowed. 'No, sir.'

Marcus stared at him steadily. He had very dark blue eyes, like Miriam's. 'I don't want to be telling your father your body was found in Mile End!' he said sharply.

It was a cold thought and it worked its way into Daniel's mind like sharpened steel. 'No one of us is going to go there alone, or after dark,'

161

Daniel stated with conviction. But his voice wavered, and he knew it.

'Then where the devil do you think you're going to find the answer?' Marcus said, white eyebrows raised.

Daniel was not ready to answer that, but he had no choice. Once Marcus thought he was being lied to, or sidelined, he would be defensive about everything else. It would be unforgivable to him that the young men he employed were working against him. Daniel tried to choose his words with care. 'We think Mr Drake was on to something, an old case, and it seems . . . '

'Don't waffle, boy,' Marcus said tartly.

'Sorry, sir. We think it likely that Mr Drake was working on the Faber case. I mean, the murder of Marie Wesley. Perhaps he even had an idea who actually was guilty. Or if not that, at least what it was really about.'

'You mean something other than a violent quarrel between a young man and his mistress, who had become bored with him?' Marcus sat motionless, rigid in his seat. He exuded anger and discomfort. Or was it the beginning of something much darker?

Put like that, the explanation sounded forced, and very unlikely. 'Yes, sir.' Daniel heard no conviction in his own voice. 'Kitteridge has been studying the business of the trial, and Drake was brilliant.' He went on, lifting his voice a little. 'He used everything he possibly could. Evan Faber was a very attractive witness. The prosecution tried to say his distress was guilt for his own part in Marie Wesley's death, but Mr

162

Drake turned everything upside down. I must admit, I hadn't appreciated how clever he was . . . ' He left the thought unfinished.

'Really?' Marcus feigned sarcastic surprise. 'I never noticed.'

'I'm sorry,' Daniel apologised. 'Of course he was. I just had to see it for myself . . . '

'I told you, don't waffle, boy. We are agreed that Jonah Drake was a damn good lawyer. Now find out for me who killed him, and why. I don't care who it was, even if it is someone in this office. Whatever we do with the knowledge, we need to know the truth. Otherwise, we'll trip over our own feet, and end up flat on our faces in the mud.'

Did Marcus realise what he was allowing, even inviting? Or had he forgotten the details?

'Well?' Marcus snapped. 'Get on with it then. And report to me regularly. If you discover something too late to tell me that day, then tell me first thing the next morning. Right?'

'Yes, sir.' There was nothing else Daniel could say, but he already knew what he was going to do. The truth: he must find it, whatever it was, and as soon as possible.

★ ★ ★

It was time Daniel caught up with Roman Blackwell and learned if he had found out anything at all of use. What had Drake been doing in Mile End? What had taken Evan Faber there? And why had his body been moved? Because the place where he had been killed

163

would implicate someone?

Daniel went to Blackwell's home, but he was not in, and he had to wait in a local café for Blackwell to return. He knew Roman would pass this place to reach his house, but wasn't certain when he would return. Sitting there gave Daniel time to get things in order in his mind. He drank coffee, then ate lunch, and afterwards took a long glass of ale in the early afternoon. He paid for each as the waitress brought it, in case he had to leave suddenly. He did not want Blackwell to arrive, and then go out again before he could catch him.

Was he really doing the right thing, trying to help Marcus? Or was he merely going behind his back?

He thought of the letter he had started to write to Miriam yesterday evening, but had left it unfinished. He could not tell her the truth. It would only worry her, interrupt her studies at a crucial time. But was lying by omission any less dishonest? No doubt she would say that she had the right to know what was going on, however muddled or tragic. Marcus was her father; she had the right to try and protect him. Daniel should not take that from her.

If it were Pitt who was losing his grip, or maybe worse — seriously implicated in a dishonest, perhaps criminal matter — would Daniel want to know? And if he were not told, wouldn't he feel cheated, dealt with as though he were a child? Of course he would, and he would hate whoever was responsible for keeping it from him. He would always think he could have helped, even if part of him knew he could not.

Then a thought struck him. When Daniel was at Cambridge studying, how many of his father's cases had been dangerous to his safety, his reputation, or his survival, and his mother had not told him of any of them? She had always protected him when she could. He was her child! So, would Marcus resent it if something were threatening his family, and Daniel had somehow heard about it, but did not tell him?

His parents had a right to protect him, up to a point. He had no such claim on Marcus.

Even as the thought came to him, he knew what he was going to do. There was another side to it: if it was not necessary to tell Marcus, he had no need ever to know.

Daniel was startled out of this train of thought by the sight of Roman Blackwell hurrying along the street, bent forward into the wind, his coat flapping around him. Daniel shot to his feet, left a tip on the table for the waitress, who had been unusually patient with him, and dashed out on to the pavement to race after the man.

He followed Blackwell along the street, caught up with him, and they entered his house before saying anything. In the hall, with its strange illusions created by the mirrors, Daniel finally spoke. 'I need your advice. It's all beginning to look pretty ugly.' What he meant was that he needed Blackwell's help, and they both understood that. But explanations must come first.

Blackwell swung around to face him, his coat half off and his hat still jammed on his head. 'Of course it is, and it will get worse,' he snapped.

'And I dare say you're going to find out a few things you'd rather not know. What's your alternative? I'll tell you: it's nothing you want, nothing you can live with.' He turned towards the kitchen. 'I'm cold and hungry.' He started to lead the way along the corridor. 'Bright, warm sun, sudden cold wind, rain that drenches you and leaves you shivering. And flowers all over the place.' With that he took his coat off, snatched his hat from his head and jammed it on to the coat stand. Then he led the way into the sitting room.

'Mother's out,' Blackwell went on. 'If you want tea, you'll have to make it.'

'No, thank you. I've drunk enough to float a ship.'

'Waiting for me? So, sit down and tell me what you know about this Drake fellow. You haven't come without an idea. Tell me all.'

'Drake . . . and Evan Faber,' Daniel answered, obeying the order and sitting in one of the armchairs. They all had velvet cushions in a wild variety of colours: rich plums, flamingo and shell pink, burgundy and crimson. It had been Mercy's choice, but Blackwell seemed comfortable enough with it.

Daniel told Blackwell about meeting Evan Faber, and liking him. He mentioned only a few of the things they had in common because Blackwell waved him on. Perhaps he could see how much it hurt. It was all so violent and so senseless.

'I'm sure he went to Mile End looking to see what Drake was doing there,' Daniel explained.

'Did you ask him to go?' Blackwell demanded, sitting forward a little in his chair.

'Yes,' Daniel admitted. 'Drake had saved his neck, literally. It was a brilliant defence. But it might have cost Drake his life, and Evan knew that. If Drake hadn't defended the case, he might still be alive.'

'Was Evan guilty?' Blackwell asked, with a note of curiosity, not open criticism.

'No,' Daniel replied.

'Because he said so?' Blackwell asked, with profound disbelief clear in his face.

Daniel avoided a direct answer. 'We didn't find who was, if that's what you mean.'

'I do . . . '

'I believed him,' Daniel asserted.

Blackwell gave a sudden, dazzling smile. 'Of course you did. It's your greatest charm, and I shall be sorry the day you grow out of it. Did any money change hands, other than the legal fees, which I imagine were handsome, and paid by his father?'

'I haven't found any evidence of that yet, but Kitteridge is going to look into it today,' Daniel told him. 'The chambers was executor of Drake's will, so we have access to all the papers.'

'Lived high on the hog, did he, this Drake?' Blackwell eased a scarlet pillow out of his chair, punched it two or three times till it was the shape he desired, then put it back.

'No, not at all,' Daniel told him. 'At least, not as far as we could see. Good house, good furniture, many books, but no expensive paintings or silver.' He did not know how to go

167

on. Drake's house suggested a man of some sensitivity, which Daniel had not expected. He was now far more aware of the man behind the dour exterior. He was touched by both guilt and regret that it was too late to do anything about it. A sense of loss filled him more than he would have thought possible just a couple of weeks ago.

'So, you told young Faber about Drake's death,' Blackwell went on. 'And Faber spoke well of him. And you asked him to help you find out what Drake was doing in Mile End? And he went there, and got killed, too.'

Put like that, it hurt, but it was correct. 'I did tell him to take care, and not to go alone,' Daniel told him, but had he really said anything like that? He could not remember now.

'And who was he supposed to take with him?' Blackwell enquired.

'He has money to burn,' Daniel said sharply. 'And, presumably, any number of friends. He's rich, nice looking and friendly. Or he could have taken a manservant. He must have at least one.'

'Or he got too close to someone or something,' Blackwell went on, his dark eyes staring at Daniel, as if trying to see beyond his words. 'You sure he wasn't guilty?'

'If my judgement of people is worth anything, yes, I am sure.'

'Right, then. He said something to somebody and it reached the wrong people. But if you want me to find out anything about Drake, which I presume is what you're looking for, you'll have to be prepared to have some of your pleasant illusions shattered. Are you ready for that?

Maybe he went there to satisfy some of his own tastes? You might not want to know that. We all need some illusions.'

'We can't afford them in this case,' Daniel replied, feeling himself clench inside at the ideas that filled his mind. 'We need to know.'

'And young Faber?' Blackwell asked. 'Am I looking into his tastes, debts and enemies, as well? Or don't you want to know?' This last question was touched with a bitter humour.

Blackwell's behaviour towards Daniel was full of affection. Nevertheless, Daniel knew that Blackwell considered him clever but naïve. 'I want everything you can dig up that has anything to do with either of them,' Daniel replied. 'Debts, favours, affections, appetites. And the police won't help you,' Daniel warned him. 'Evan's father is very rich, but more than that, he's powerful. He owns the biggest shipbuilding yards in Britain, and we are in dire need of expanding the Navy. I don't mean just the merchant side of it, I mean the Royal Navy, too.'

Blackwell let out his breath slowly. 'Ah! So, his father has friends in high places. And if he takes revenge for the death of his son . . . let's assume he won't be looking to the police to make a scandal out of it.'

'Faber is saying Evan's death was a dreadful accident of some sort.'

'He should take to writing fairy stories! He's good at it!' Blackwell said bitterly.

'I don't suppose anyone will believe him,' Daniel agreed. 'But they pretend they do. And no doubt will be rewarded for their tact.'

'All except you, of course,' Blackwell pointed out, taking another punch at the pillow.

'I liked Evan, and Drake was a member of our chambers. I want the truth.'

'And you wont let that go,' Blackwell added. 'It sounds as if this Drake might have been too clever by half! What does Marcus know about all this? Or am I a damn fool to ask?' His eyes widened. 'You don't know, do you? That's part of what this is all about. You're frightened for Marcus. What does he forget? Or what does he choose not to see? That's what you really want to know, but you're too mealy-mouthed to say so! Isn't that what you're really frightened of?'

Daniel could not afford to be defensive with Blackwell, and yet he could feel his muscles knotting in spite of himself. 'It's our practice to assume anyone is innocent until they're proved guilty. You know that. You rely on it enough . . . ' The instant the words were out of his mouth, he regretted it, but it would only make it worse to apologise. Blackwell knew what he had meant.

There was a second, two seconds, three of silence, then Blackwell let out a hearty laugh. 'Good for you, boy. I was beginning to think you'd gone soft. By all means, assume everyone is innocent until you have to change your mind. But keep your powder dry, just in case you do have to take a different view.' All humour vanished from his face. 'Don't do any such damn silly thing as getting a gun. You hear me? You'd only end up getting shot by it yourself. Use your brain. It's your best weapon. In fact, it's probably your only one.'

170

Daniel noted the advice, then changed the subject immediately. 'Drake was slashed to death by a long-bladed knife. Evan was stabbed in the heart with a single thrust. One killing was savage, even brutal; the other was almost merciful. But they could possibly have been the same blade.' He felt his stomach churn as he said it, and Drake's white face, the flesh torn open, came back to his mind — as if he had seen it only yesterday. 'I'm not going to look away, just because it's going to be uncomfortable,' he said aloud.

Blackwell sighed. 'No, of course you're not! Damn it! I'm coming with you. I owe you that. And I might need you again.' He gave a sunny smile.

'Well, put it off for a bit, will you?' Daniel returned the smile. 'Right now, I'm busy.'

★ ★ ★

Daniel went back to the chambers and worked on a few small current matters he had to deal with. Meeting with Blackwell had taken the edge off his worry. Just knowing his friend would provide his expertise helped.

An hour or so later, Kitteridge knocked on his door and came straight in, without waiting for an answer. He had an armful of papers. He dumped them on Daniel's desk, closed the door, then sat down in the single visitor's chair.

'Well?' Daniel asked.

'I don't know,' Kitteridge admitted. 'Been to the bank and got these.' He nodded at the

171

papers. 'There seems to be a lot of money that I can't account for, money moved around from one account to another. What I do know is that Erasmus Faber paid Drake very well indeed to defend his son, and he earned it. That's easy enough to see. He surprised everyone, because we never thought of Drake as a dramatic performer in court. No pulling rabbits out of hats.' He shook his head, as if to get rid of all the old misconceptions. 'In our minds, he was diligent, thorough, and rather boring. Really good at finding one or two provable facts, and we took it for granted that he knew what he was doing . . . and we would've been right.'

'So, boring but successful. How does that help?' Daniel asked, his hopes rising.

'It doesn't.' Kitteridge shook his head. 'Because it's one-sided and not a fair summary of the facts. He and Marcus had known each other since university; they were at Oxford at the same time. Drake started when Marcus had already been there for three years. They hit it off straight away, according to the people I spoke to. They came from similar backgrounds, professional families, but provincial. Drake from Shropshire and Marcus from County Durham. Which makes both of them outsiders, in a way, and — '

'Does that make a difference?' Daniel interrupted, hoping to hear something helpful.

'Yes.' Kitteridge's face changed, as if a shadow had passed over it. 'It's damn hard being an outsider at university. You wouldn't know, being a Londoner, Home Counties and so on. But I

172

do.' His face tightened, as if a memory hurt for a brief moment. 'I always felt an outsider, provincial, about as sophisticated as a farmhand, compared with the gentry, let alone the sons of aristocrats.'

Daniel felt a twinge of guilt as he remembered how he had treated the scholarship boys from the industrial Midlands and the coal mining north exactly that way. Perhaps it was because he felt just such an outsider himself. His father was a policeman, and his grandfather had been the gamekeeper on a rich man's estate, transported to Australia for poaching. Nobody had heard from him since that day. But, of course, no one else knew that.

Had Drake felt like that, too? Or even Marcus? Daniel had always assumed that Marcus had inherited his confidence, that success was his birthright, and security was something he had never been without. What a superficial judgement.

Kitteridge was still talking. 'I could find no trace of Drake gambling,' he went on. 'And I know some of the people to ask. But he invested pretty cleverly in stocks and shares, and never seems to have lost.' He shook his head. 'I've looked, and I can't find anything that is illegal, or even shady. Drake had far more money than most lawyers, but he seems to have handled some pretty big cases. The thing is, he gave a lot of it to charity, one way or another. He paid the university costs for scholarship boys from his hometown in Shropshire, but he kept it private, almost secret.' He stared at Daniel.

'It shows that we don't know each other as well as we think. Was Marcus aware of that?'

'I'm not sure. Possibly not.'

'We're not sure of much, are we?' said Daniel.

Kitteridge sighed and shifted his position slightly. 'Not yet . . . '

'Then get all the accounts, anything from his desk, and bank, and see if you can trace anything back to the source,' Daniel suggested. 'And see if there's any more property we don't know about. Shares . . . anything.'

★ ★ ★

Daniel was tired by six o'clock. His vision blurred when he looked at a page of paper. But far more than tired, he was confused. There seemed to be no common thread that made any sense. And the more he looked, the less he was able to form any coherent pattern. The harder he looked, the more complicated it seemed. Had Marcus been careless, or deliberately neglectful? Was it a lack of understanding, or had he missed things here and there? Everybody was forgetful now and then, so perhaps Marcus was merely forgetful? But he used not to be careless. Was Daniel seeing faults where there were none . . . or trying not to see them at all?

He gave up for the evening and decided to go home to Keppel Street for dinner. Perhaps if he told his father, who had spent his adult life untangling such mysteries, he would see a thread that made sense. And Daniel would follow it, even if it did implicate Marcus. Daniel knew that

174

refusing to accept an explanation, and the bitter disillusion and grief that went with it, was like putting a plaster on a boil. The only way to deal with such an infection was to lance it. Leaving the poison inside inevitably made it worse.

He indulged in the extravagance of a taxi from chambers to Keppel Street. While the driver fought with the traffic, he sat back and engaged his thoughts.

Marcus had said very little about Drake. What had he really thought of him? Suspected of him, but preferred not to see? He had known him most of his adult life, so he had to have an opinion. With Drake being only a couple of years younger, Marcus would have understood much about the younger man. Their personal lives had followed very different courses, but that was irrelevant. He forced his mind back on to the subject. Drake had enjoyed none of the comforts that Marcus had acquired, at least the outward ones of family and prestige. Did he envy Marcus? Like him or dislike him? Marcus was charming and gregarious; Drake was clever, but hard to like, solitary, showing only a rare and sharp humour. What had held them together, other than the law? Drake seemed to be at the centre of all this violence. He had defended Evan brilliantly, preserving not only his freedom and his reputation, but his standing in the community, and without blaming anyone else. Did he actually know who had killed Marie Wesley? Or had he discovered this since the trial ended? That was a new thought, dangerous and possibly painful. Could he have told Marcus, and been ordered to leave it alone?

Why had Drake gone to Mile End on the night of his death? Was he killed before he made his intended rendezvous, or after? That could be important, for several reasons. If he was looking for information, and he found it, perhaps it was too dangerous to let him share it. Or did he go to tell someone something? Or to learn something? Had he succeeded, and whom did it threaten?

It seemed to Daniel that the police were slow in seeking Drake's killer; they had little to show for their work, if indeed they were working on it at all. And if his murder had some connection with Marie's death, which had been over a year ago, what was holding them back? What had changed?

Again, it came back to Mile End, and whatever Drake had been doing there. Perhaps he had been following up on who killed Marie. But why? What had woken his curiosity again?

Daniel wondered if Erasmus Faber might have asked Drake to investigate. But that made no sense. Unless . . . was someone blackmailing Erasmus with a piece of evidence that would reopen the case? But nothing changed the fact that Evan had been tried and found not guilty, and he could not be tried a second time, even if he admitted to the crime. It would have to be something new . . . but what?

The taxi jerked to a stop and Daniel realised with surprise that he was at the front door of the house in which he had spent most of his life. He paid the driver with a handsome tip and stepped out on to the kerb. The lights were on inside and he was relieved. He had not called ahead to see if it was convenient. If his parents had been out somewhere, he would have waited for them. Cook would always find him something to eat, although it would hardly be the same.

★ ★ ★

Charlotte had not been expecting Daniel, but she was always pleased to see him, and greeted him with pleasure. She noticed the anxiety in his eyes, but affected not to.

'Come in,' she said, smiling and stepping back to allow him to enter. He looked tired. There was no spring in his step. 'You're just in time for dinner. I suppose that's not by accident?'

He turned and smiled at her. 'Oh? That's fortunate. Thanks, Mother.' He walked past her into the long-familiar room. 'Hello, Father. How are you?'

Pitt made the usual reply. It was not the words that mattered, it was the inflection of the voice, the look in the eyes, the smile.

Daniel took his usual seat and stretched out his legs. There was an immediate ease in him. Charlotte noticed it and relaxed a fraction. He would tell them, if he wanted to, what it was that lay so heavily on his shoulders.

The three of them made general conversation until the meal was served: thick slices of ham, freshly cooked, and lots of spring vegetables. There were winter-stored apples, sweet and tart, in a crusty pie. And, of course, cream.

177

Conversation was light, and about trivial, pleasant matters, news of people they all knew, especially of Jemima in America.

'Well?' Pitt said when the last plates had been cleared away and they had retired to the drawing room. 'Have you got any further with the case?' It was a question, but there was no lift of enquiry in his tone. Charlotte knew he would not press for an answer. 'Do you want to talk about it?' Pitt asked.

Charlotte made no move to excuse herself. This was her home and she had every intention of being part of the conversation. Other than being told secrets of Special Branch, she had been a part of many of Pitt's cases, ever since the terrible case when they had first met. That was now nearly thirty years ago. Long-buried memories stretched back, some heavy, some of ugliness and tragedy, but they were all bound together, making the close pattern of their lives.

Pitt was waiting. 'Give us the pieces,' he said, with the thread of impatience in his voice.

Charlotte bit back her instinct to tell him to be patient. Daniel was looking for exactly the right words. He did not want an argument. She decided not to add to the tension.

'There is a definite link between Evan Faber and Drake,' Daniel began. 'More than just a successful defence. I have wondered if, in some way, the murder of Marie Wesley is at the root of all this present violence. No one was ever charged, so in a sense the case is still open.' He looked up at his father.

'Not with the police, apparently,' Pitt pointed

178

out. 'Someone knows what happened, even if it is only the person who killed her.' He was concentrating on Daniel, as if Charlotte were not there. She knew that he would ask her opinion after Daniel had gone. 'Do you think Drake knew who that was?' he asked. 'Or perhaps Erasmus Faber was paying someone to keep quiet, and he suddenly stopped? Something precipitated a crisis. Did Drake actually discover something new? Or was he about to? Or maybe he was a victim of bad timing, misfortune?'

Daniel was momentarily lost, and it showed in his face. Were they looking in the wrong direction?

Again, Charlotte had to restrain herself from interrupting. It would not help, in the long run. She had learned that lesson the hardest way, sometimes with hurt feelings.

'I don't know,' Daniel admitted frankly. 'I can't believe it was just a series of accidents. Why would they kill Drake, unless he was on the brink of discovering something? And still more, why kill Evan? That's just . . . vile. And it doesn't make any sense.'

He was clearly angry, and Charlotte understood why. It was so much easier to admit to rage than let the full tide of hurt rise inside you. To acknowledge his grief would make it harder to control, like giving it permission to overwhelm him.

'If there was a blackmailer, he could have given his information to the police, or to the newspapers,' he reasoned aloud.

'Or could it be someone else?' Charlotte

suggested. 'Someone you had not previously thought of?'

'Maybe Drake was in on that?' Pitt asked. 'Or he was brokering the deal?'

Daniel looked down at the floor. 'Are you thinking of Marcus?' he asked.

Charlotte hesitated for a moment before putting it into words. She looked from Daniel to Pitt, and back again. 'What is it you're afraid Marcus could have done? You've been skirting around it, but not yet named it.'

There was a moment of silence. Neither Daniel nor Pitt looked at the other. It was Pitt who spoke. 'I think it all comes down to money, or preserving the reputation and success of the chambers. Which, in a way, is still money . . . '

Daniel's head jerked up as if in protest, then he realised that he had been thinking the same thing, but had not admitted it even to himself. Money, continued business, reputation.

Charlotte looked at him. She did not need to put her question into words.

'It's all part of the same thing, one way or the other . . . ' Daniel began.

'You don't know,' Charlotte concluded. She turned to Pitt. 'You've known Marcus for years. You must have some idea of his strengths . . . and weaknesses? Can't you help, Thomas?'

'They are the same.' Pitt gave a faint, wry smile. 'They are with any of us. Generosity to the point of extravagance. Generosity of judgement to the degree of not seeing another's faults. Charm that gains him friends, and dependents

180

whom he then feels obliged to protect, no matter the cost. A dislike of unpleasantness, and ultimately the evasion of conflict. And discipline. A lot of virtues, carried to excess, become faults. That's not unique to Marcus. Leadership is a lonely business.'

Daniel did not speak.

Charlotte thought for a few moments, weighing what her husband had said. He understood loneliness, but he had not realised that it weighed just as heavily on the leader who was admired and respected, obeyed, as the junior in the office, the one who has yet to gain any influence or power.

Pitt still said nothing, but the uncertainty in his face was plain.

Charlotte stared at him, her expression pinched with pain at the ugliness of the thought, but she gave no denial of it. Pitt spoke at last. 'I was actually thinking that Marcus might have been trying to help Drake get out of the situation, if there was a blackmailer, and if that blackmailer had threatened him. It is possible that Drake's death and Evan's are not connected, except that Evan was also asking questions. I suspect it goes back further than that. We are missing whatever started this train of events.'

'Could it be something other than Drake's defence of Evan at trial?' Charlotte's mind was racing. 'Could Evan have had an idea who killed this poor woman? No one argues that he didn't know her quite well, and probably many of the others who knew her also. Perhaps he was close

181

to discovering who killed her — or somebody thought he was.'

Daniel sat more upright. 'I suppose that's possible. He said he was very fond of her, attracted to her. Apparently, she was happy, and she made people laugh.' He shook his head. 'It was a lot more than just being pretty. I suppose she might have told him something? She knew a wide range of people . . . ' His voice trailed off, as though he were seeing Evan's vulnerability to blackmail, deep debt, a drunken accident, all the various disasters that any man in society could fall into, with music too loud, too much wine, and an attractive woman with too little to lose.

'Oh dear!' Charlotte felt suddenly, overwhelmingly sad. 'There's a pretty well endless range of possibilities, isn't there?' She turned to Daniel. 'Did he really like her? Evan, I mean?'

'You mean was he in love with her? A little, I think. She was fun, and she didn't care about how rich his father was . . . '

Pitt's face reflected his disbelief.

'It's possible she was clever enough not to focus on the old man's money,' Charlotte pointed out. 'She might have set her sights a lot higher than a single necklace, or bracelet . . . '

Pitt looked at her sharply.

She gave a little shrug. 'Or perhaps she just liked him. Daniel, did you ask Evan that? Did he think of marrying her?'

'Erasmus Faber is very rich,' Daniel said ruefully. 'But Evan's grandfather was self-made, scrap metal, or something of that sort. Married up. Evan's mother was minor gentry, or so he

182

said. She sounded very nice. But she died when he was young, ten or eleven. Anyway, Erasmus was hell-bent on Evan marrying at least an earl's daughter, if not a duke's.'

'Poor soul,' Charlotte said, with feeling.

'Who?' Pitt asked, with a bleak smile. 'Evan, marrying for position rather than love, or the duke's daughter, being married off for money?'

'Really, Thomas,' she sighed. 'Both of them, of course! The duke's daughter will probably have expected as much, but Evan sounds like a nice young man.' She turned to Daniel again. 'Anyway, he wouldn't have been allowed to marry Marie Wesley, even if he had wanted to. And believe me, she would know that.' She smiled briefly. 'All the money in the world wouldn't make me want to marry Evan and get Erasmus Faber as a father-in-law!'

'It would take a lot of money to make you want to cross him, if he were your father,' Pitt observed, with a downward twist of a smile. 'If money could make you do anything at all, of course.'

'Not for money,' Charlotte agreed. 'But there are other pressures.' She looked at Daniel. 'Perhaps you might consider other people who cared for Marie Wesley — people who would have been affected by her life or death? Perhaps there is someone who didn't let the case drop, and really believed Evan was guilty. It's likely Drake dug up something that mattered, and might open up the case again.'

Pitt leaned forward earnestly. 'Why did Faber want his son's death put down as an accident?

Has money passed between Faber and the police to put a lid on it? I think if I were investigating this, I would look for any movement of money that isn't easily explained.'

'Drake was the man to do that,' Daniel assured him. 'If Evan had been killed, and Drake were investigating it, and then he was killed, it might well make sense. But that wasn't what happened. It happened the other way around.'

'Do you know yet what Drake was doing in Mile End?' Pitt asked.

Charlotte had a sudden idea. 'A catspaw,' she blurted.

'What?' Daniel and Pitt asked at the same moment.

'A catspaw,' she repeated. 'Someone who does the dirty work for someone else, because they don't want to get dirty themselves. Or worse, burned.'

'A catspaw used to kill Drake? Or do you mean to kill Marie Wesley?' Pitt asked.

'To do anything dirty and dangerous for someone who can pay them,' she replied, a little impatiently. 'You just need someone with money and motive, but not necessarily prepared or able to do it themselves . . . starting with getting rid of Marie Wesley.'

Pitt gave a bleak smile, but his eyes were soft. 'You've just made it ten times worse,' he said ruefully. 'And I'll make it even worse than that. Why are the police calling Evan's death an accident? They know damned well it wasn't. People don't get a clean sword thrust through the heart by accident. And why would anyone who might have corroborated it leave the scene without a trace?'

Charlotte stared at him. 'You've been following it up, haven't you!' she said, with a sudden realisation. Although she did not entirely blame him. In his place, she would have done the same thing. He knew that, too.

'Of course I have,' Pitt agreed. 'If someone did that to one of my friends, I would dig into anything and everything to prove who was responsible. And if it happened in a place like Mile End, I'd try to explain their presence there . . . unless I had a damn good reason not to!'

'A reason like what?' she asked. 'Guilt, because it was actually murder? Or something else?'

Pitt nodded. 'Exactly,' he agreed. 'Guilt, or something close to it.'

Charlotte felt Daniel's eyes on her. She said nothing, but her mind was racing.

9

Later on, when both Cook and the young housemaid Minnie Maude had gone for the night, Pitt again picked up the conversation about Evan's murder.

'The police have accepted the story that it was an accident. Young men fooling around, playing at fighting. Someone's foot slips and the next thing you know, the knife has gone deep into someone, and you can't stop the bleeding. The police can't cover up that there's a dead body,' Pitt argued, 'so they say he died on Martha Street. But there was no blood around his body and the debris on his clothes didn't come from there. Mile End is in Letterman's area, isn't it?' He looked at Daniel.

Daniel nodded. 'The most important question is: why was he moved?'

'Perhaps they don't want any attention focused on where he actually was killed?' Charlotte suggested. 'Who were the other young men who were supposedly involved? No one mentioned their names . . . '

'Possibly they've got families who can pay to keep it quiet?' Daniel surmised.

'Or perhaps they don't exist?' Charlotte said grimly.

'We can't wait to see,' Pitt said, as the reality sank deeper into his mind. 'If we knew the location of his death, it might lead us to something quite different. Another person, perhaps.'

'Or reveal what he was doing there,' Charlotte said, with a small gesture of distaste. 'Mile End,' she said quietly. 'Such a seedy place.'

'How do you know what's there?' Daniel turned towards her. 'I mean, in Mile End.'

Charlotte looked a little confused, and a slight blush crept up her cheeks.

Pitt tried to hide his amusement, and failed. 'Your mother is not as ignorant of the seamier side of life as she would have you believe . . . ' he said to Daniel.

'Thomas!' She gave him a black look that in any other time might have silenced him.

Daniel's discomfort was plain.

Pitt needed to rescue the situation. 'It would be so much easier to avoid this altogether, but we can't afford to. And *you* can't, because a member of your chambers was very violently murdered. We have to assume it was because Drake learned, or was involved in, something very dark indeed, and with a strong connection in Mile End. We don't know if it had anything to do with the death of Marie Wesley . . . at least, not yet.' He paused. 'And now we have Evan. A young man you liked, whom Drake saved from the gallows, also murdered. Probably with the same weapon, and possibly in exactly the same location, and then moved to hide that fact. And we don't yet know by whom, or why. That raises several questions.' He looked from one to the other of them, but no one spoke.

'And the possibility, much as we may desire not to think it: did *he* have anything to do with

Drake's death, or the death of Marie Wesley?'

'Wasn't she beaten to death?' Charlotte said, sadness filling her face. 'And in the West End, the other side of the city, nowhere near Mile End?'

'Yes,' Pitt responded. 'And Evan was accused of the crime, and tried for it. No one has suggested any connection between Drake and Marie Wesley, except through Evan.' He turned to Daniel. 'Have you looked any further into that case? What evidence did the police have? It must have been good, or they wouldn't have prosecuted him. In fact, it must have been overwhelming evidence for them to have gone ahead.'

Daniel was silent for a moment or two.

Pitt waited, refusing to soften the question.

Charlotte glanced at Pitt, then waited also.

'It was a private house in Chelsea,' Daniel said at last. 'At a party of over a hundred people. Marie Wesley was beaten. There was no weapon. Evan had been seeking her company quite a lot. Everyone assumed he was one of her lovers, and he didn't deny it. Some men were jealous of him, with good reason. Drake managed to find witnesses who had seen at least two young admirers near her at the time, just before she died. Sorry.' He looked from Pitt to Charlotte. 'I'm talking around it. She was savagely beaten.' His face was filled with misery at the thought.

'It was a huge house,' he went on. 'Where a rather . . . self-indulgent party was taking place. Many members of high society were there, all of whom wanted their names withheld. Drake managed to catch out a few of them in lies, and suggested that they didn't want to be associated with the whole thing. But at least three of them had gone to the effort of embroidering the truth when they spoke to the police. Evan was one of the few who was honest. The police surgeon could find no old scars or abrasions on her. Also, there was some evidence suggesting it was a man much heavier than Evan who had beaten her, someone with the physical power to lift her bodily and slam her down . . . '

Pitt frowned. 'Not exactly conclusive . . . '

'No, but Evan was terribly upset about it. I . . . I think he really loved her.' Daniel lifted his eyes to meet his father's. 'I believed him, and so did the jury.'

'But they never charged anyone else?' Pitt reaffirmed.

Daniel nodded. 'Probably because there were two or three other suspects, all with titles, which are worth more than money.'

As if reluctantly, Charlotte agreed with Daniel. 'To some people, it sets them apart, every time you mention their name.'

'And there was nothing to suggest any of them specifically,' Daniel continued. 'It seems they all lied to cover for each other. What they said couldn't be true, because it was full of contradictions, but the police didn't think they were guilty, and certainly didn't want to make enemies of their families. Honestly, it began to look as if Evan were the outsider. He had new money, and was not aristocracy, so they chose to place the blame on him. Drake played it that way, and the jury believed him.'

'Do you?' Pitt asked.

'I don't believe it was Evan, and I think Drake proved that.'

Pitt could see it vividly. Society protecting its own, blaming the outsider, who had the effrontery to actually have more money than most of them. How many times had he observed that? Even more, felt himself the outsider? More often than he wanted his son to know. Or even Charlotte, for that matter, although in the past she had burned with rage for him, and suffered pain at his rejection. But he did not want Daniel to know that. No man could bear being humiliated in front of his child.

'I see,' he said aloud. His opinion of Drake went up. Perhaps Drake, a rough-hewn northerner living in the south, could understand that himself? 'Daniel, you've read Drake's notes. Do you know from them if he believed Evan to be innocent? Or was it a very clever, even dubious, piece of lawyering? It can't hurt either of them now, so please tell me. If you know the answer, but you can't betray the implicit trust of having read Drake's papers, then say so.' He stared at Daniel, waiting.

Daniel looked back at him, clear-eyed. 'I didn't know Drake well enough to say whether he would have defended a guilty man, and been prepared to use whatever legal trickery was required, but he didn't on this occasion.' He held his father's gaze unwaveringly.

'Therefore, someone else is guilty,' Pitt concluded. 'Presumably, one of the other young men suspected.' He stopped for a moment, as if to reconsider. 'But not necessarily. Miss Wesley may have had a . . . ' He wanted to avoid using the word *pimp*. It would offend Charlotte, but more important than that, it would hurt Daniel, and give him the idea that Pitt judged the victim, when he did not. He knew the wounds of poverty far better than did his son or his wife, but he preferred they be spared the knowledge. Assuming was one thing, seeing was another.

'But they are connected, surely?' Daniel said, frowning. 'Drake discovered something that associated Marie Wesley's murder with Mile End, even though she died on the other side of the city.'

'Not proving a thing true isn't the same thing as proving it untrue,' Charlotte argued. 'He could have gone there on another case, and been killed for an entirely different reason.'

'But Evan believed there was a connection,' Daniel insisted. 'And he must have found it, or he wouldn't have been killed.'

'Then we have to find it, too,' she replied, glancing at Pitt, then back again at her son. 'I assume you've been through all Drake's notes? Then why did he go there, of all places? You don't just wander into Mile End alone, in the middle of the night!'

'Perhaps he went for one thing,' Pitt answered, 'and found another? Who knows what he expected, or what he actually stumbled on? The Home Office warned me off having anything to do with Faber, any sort of investigation or blame, because of the country's need for his shipbuilding skills, which are apparently unique.'

191

Charlotte turned. 'You think they'd look the other way? From murder?' There was disbelief in her eyes.

'More likely just scandal,' Pitt said, quite honestly. 'Something someone wanted to keep secret.'

'And Evan was murdered because he found it?' Daniel's face was bleak but hopeful.

'Or a debt that he wouldn't ask his father to pay?' Pitt surmised. 'The place is riddled with moneylenders. It's easy to make a mistake, especially if you're young. You think you can buy anything. Discretion . . . silence.'

'Silence? For how long? Isn't that a bit short-sighted?' Charlotte asked.

'What? Are you talking about protecting Erasmus Faber? We need him and his shipbuilding. In his own way, he has a sort of genius.' Pitt resented having to say that, but it was the truth.

'Enough to let him get away with murder?' Charlotte asked.

'He didn't kill anyone, Charlotte. He was merely twisting the truth a little to protect his son.'

Charlotte looked down and bit her lip. 'Would that include allowing a murder to go unsolved, just turning your back because it involves someone you love? Doesn't that open the door to just about anything . . . eventually?'

'Decisions are easy when all the odds are stacked on one side,' Pitt answered. 'There's usually a cost. Sometimes it turns out to be higher than you can see at the time. If you pay someone to do it for you, then you've made yourself a debtor, for life. Or . . . you kill them in turn. But that's the police's job. There's one more thing,' he said, his voice dropping. 'What I told you about the Home Office, and warning me away from Erasmus Faber.' He turned and faced Daniel. 'That was confidential, but I thought you should know.'

When Charlotte changed the subject, Pitt knew they had taken this conversation as far as it was going to go. At least, for now.

She read to them the latest letter from Jemima, in America, including news about her little girls, Cassie and Sophie. It seemed that having a younger sister had made Cassie suddenly very grown up. She couldn't be the baby any more — Sophie had usurped her place — so she would take charge instead. According to Jemima, it was funny, sweet, and also exasperating.

★ ★ ★

The following morning, Thomas Pitt went to see Marcus fford Croft, not at the chambers in Lincoln's Inn Fields, where Daniel would be bound to see him, but in Marcus's home, catching him before he left for the day.

The butler let him in, courteously but with obvious surprise. It took him a moment or two before he even recognised the visitor's face. 'Good morning, Sir Thomas.' There was reproof in his tone for such an early call. It was full of respect, but Marcus was his first loyalty, always. 'I hope nothing is wrong, sir?' It was another way

193

of reminding him that this was a very uncivil hour to call, particularly without any warning. Or did he, too, worry about Marcus's memory, his judgement? He would be bound to notice the occasional lapses of memory. The instructions that made no sense? Appointments broken, people's names forgotten? Perhaps bills ignored until they became demands. Wearing unsuitable clothes for an occasion. A manservant notices lots of things, and possibly he had not told anyone, because it would seem to him a disloyalty.

'Good morning,' Pitt replied. 'Nothing major is wrong, just the usual problems of one sort and another. I wish to see Mr fford Croft a little more privately than in his chambers, where my son is one of his junior lawyers.'

'I see, sir.' The man nodded sympathetically. 'I will advise him that you are here. Perhaps you'd like to wait in the morning room? Would you care for tea, or coffee?'

'No, thank you, but I appreciate the offer.'

'Yes, sir.'

Pitt was shown into the morning room. It had long windows looking on to the back garden and the sunlight was streaming in. It was still cool inside, but the light was clear and soft on the pale yellow walls, and he was amazed at the powerful suggestion of warmth the colour gave. Marcus's idea, or Miriam's?

He walked over and stared at the garden, losing himself in the pleasure of imagining what it would be like to sit there, daydreaming, in a few more weeks, when it was high summer.

Marcus came in quietly. All that Pitt heard was the click as the door latch closed.

'Morning, Thomas. What can I do for you this early?'

Pitt turned around. 'Good morning, Marcus, how are you?' It was a question of manners. Marcus looked pale. He was too robust to have lines on his face, even at his age, but there was an inescapable tiredness in him. 'I was very sorry to hear about Drake,' Pitt added.

'A very bad business,' Marcus agreed, shaking his head sadly. 'Horrible. Poor man. There were times when I could have wished him far away, but I was honestly grateful to have him. Tell me, Thomas — ' And then he was suddenly irritated. 'For God's sake, sit down! Is this Special Branch business? Was Drake doing something wrong in Mile End, something that you care about?' He searched Pitt's face, all suggestion of a smile gone. He was worried, even frightened.

Pitt would have liked to reassure him, but the man needed to admit the truth, and he needed Marcus to press him for it. Comfort would not last long, and for all his affability, Marcus was not a fool, nor had he ever looked for the easy answer to anything. 'I don't know,' he replied. 'What did he say he was doing there?'

Marcus looked helpless. He sank backwards into one of the soft chairs, shaking his head. 'If he told me, I have forgotten . . . ' He looked up at Pitt, fear in his eyes. But was his confusion affected, or genuine?

Pitt sat down in the chair nearest to Marcus. The man had dispensed with courteous and meaningless phrases. Now, Pitt was obliged to be equally frank, or else he would appear devious, which would be cruel. 'Was he right in the Evan Faber case?' he asked. 'I mean, was Faber innocent?'

'Yes,' said Marcus, without hesitation, then he looked away. 'It wasn't just the money, Thomas. Although we certainly were glad of that — not all the work we do is paid. I lose track sometimes of how much we take on that is pro bono. Good thing to do. Morally, I mean. But we need a few wealthy clients to support the chambers.' He shook his head again and looked down at the carpet. 'But I forget such things sometimes. Don't do the bookkeeping myself, you know . . . '

'Is the chambers in trouble?' Pitt asked gently. He did not want to hear the answer, but he knew he had to have it. 'Or are you?'

Marcus looked up at him, wide-eyed. 'Good God, no! At least . . . ' He breathed in and out several times. 'I don't think so.' He stared into the distance. 'Drake would have told me. He kept his eye on that sort of thing. Should have been fford Croft and Drake. There never was a Gibson, you know?' He smiled, as if the thought pleased him, perhaps a reminder of less uncertain times.

'And Drake gave you no hint that you needed to bring in a bit more . . . paying business?'

Marcus blinked. 'Do you think that's what he was doing in Mile End, looking for grubby but well-paying work? He wouldn't do that without telling me . . . would he?' A shadow crossed his face. 'Oh, you think that he did tell me . . . and I forgot. Well, I didn't agree to it, I know that much.' He stared at Pitt, as if expecting an answer.

Pitt had an overwhelming feeling that Marcus was answering the question directly and honestly, because he was avoiding something else, something fast slipping out of his control. It hovered, like a dark presence in the room.

'No,' continued the older man. 'I think it was more likely that he went to Mile End because it had something to do with the Evan Faber case.'

'Think hard, Marcus,' Pitt urged. 'You've known Drake a long time. Can you remember anything he said that would suggest what he was doing there?'

Marcus shut his eyes. 'I have been trying to.' He spoke so quietly that Pitt barely heard him. 'He was worried about something, an old case. One that he still wasn't finished with, at least in his own mind. But he wouldn't tell me.' He opened his eyes and frowned. 'Do you think I could possibly have forgotten that, if he'd told me?'

'No,' Pitt answered, then had to moderate the criticism in his tone. 'Unless you didn't believe it . . .'

'That he was going to . . . what? Or the reason . . . ' Marcus asked, totally confused. 'Pitt, I don't know!'

'The reason,' Pitt said gently. 'You don't want to feel that, if you'd stopped him, he would still be alive. No one would want that.'

'You damned well don't mince words, do you!' Marcus looked at him accusingly. 'Drake was no fool, you know. He knew that I . . . I forget things sometimes. But he didn't condescend to me! Treat me like a halfwit.'

Pitt felt the sting of the reproach. 'Of course I don't think you're a fool, Marcus, but you've lost one of your best men — '

'My very best man,' Marcus corrected him. 'Got good ones coming up, but they've a long way to go to match Jonah Drake!'

'And a long way before they bring in anything like the money he did,' Pitt added. He knew the reference to 'good ones coming up' meant men like Daniel. Personally, he was glad to see Marcus with a little fight left. 'So, why do you think, or even imagine, that Drake went to Mile End?'

Marcus jerked upright. 'I remember,' he said, his eyes suddenly more alert. 'Blackmail!' He pronounced the word as if it were filthy in his mouth. 'He told me that there was someone there dealing in opium. Dreadful stuff. He saw it was related to a case . . . some time ago.' He shook his head sharply, as if to get rid of insects in the air. 'But either he didn't tell me who it was, or I forgot.'

'Marie Wesley?' Pitt asked, almost hoping he would say no.

Marcus's hands were in his lap and curled into fists. He stared at Pitt. 'I . . . I think so, but I don't — '

Pitt interrupted him. 'She wasn't a client, Marcus. She was the woman Evan Faber was accused of beating to death.'

Marcus went sheet-white. 'Oh! Do you mean

he was guilty after all, and we got him off?' He sounded appalled, as if it had caught him off guard.

'Did Drake act without your knowledge, Marcus?' Pitt asked gently. 'Or did he tell you only part of the story?'

'No,' Marcus shook his head. 'At least, I don't think so. I believe Drake did a good and fair job . . . I don't know. No one else was charged . . . ' Marcus's face creased in anxiety. 'Are you saying Drake lied to me — to us?'

Pitt smiled. 'Don't worry, Marcus, you're not losing your memory, just a few details here and there. The Home Secretary's office told me not to meddle in it . . . '

'And are you?' Marcus's eyebrows shot up, his eyes wide and frightened. 'Meddling in it?'

Pitt hesitated. 'No, no I'm not. At least . . . ' He saw Marcus begin to smile. 'Not officially,' he amended. 'But I know Daniel, and he won't let it go. And in his position, I wouldn't either.'

'No,' Marcus said slowly. 'Neither would I, and . . . I couldn't face Miriam if I did.' His smile turned rueful. 'But I don't know what to do. I . . . I might just make things worse.'

Pitt thought rapidly. He must answer. 'See if one of your people can follow the money,' he suggested. 'No one will notice, because you can simply explain that you need to know the chambers is sound financially. You've lost one of your leading partners. Now you need to determine how you're going to replace him. No one would suspect anything.' He paused for a moment, as if thinking this through. 'Yes,' he said. 'Follow the money. If someone is paying or receiving blackmail money, there will be a trace of it somewhere.'

'Do you believe that?' Marcus winced, and his face was even a little paler. 'About Drake?' he added.

'No, actually, I don't. I don't know any more than you do, and I'm not certain that the police are really trying to solve his death. No one seems to know where to begin. Or possibly they know, but they can't prosecute.'

'Or they're corrupt?' Marcus added.

'Yes, or corrupt,' Pitt repeated the word slowly. 'Talking about money, there is a lot of business in Mile End, of all sorts: brothels, of course, and moneylenders, opium dens, forgers, pretty well every vice. And there's more profit to be made than the simple price of it, if you are prepared to blackmail.' He saw Marcus grimace. 'And that can bring you a variety of things, as you know: the price of a continued supply of opium, or the price of silence about your weakness, whatever it is. It could be introducing more customers, or it could be payment in kind, depending on what is your particular taste.'

'In kind?' Marcus said, clearing his throat nervously.

'Don't pretend,' Pitt said quietly. He did not want to do this; he did not want to know of Marcus's weakness, if one were really there. He did not even want to know the weaknesses of Marcus's friends or clients either, but he needed to. He felt like a surgeon with a scalpel in his hand, and no certainty as to what he was about to cut into. 'Many people turn a blind eye to all sorts of things, when they have little or no choice,' he went on. 'That is, for themselves or for those they love. Or, I suppose, those they owe. It's a way out of debt, or a way to gain power, or to be free of pain . . . of one kind or another.'

'All right!' said Marcus. 'I take your point. I have no client, that I am aware of, who is being pressed about any of their weaknesses. Not that I would tell you if I had. But I wouldn't lie, Pitt, I would simply tell you to go to hell!' He smiled bleakly.

Pitt knew that there was a part of Marcus that savoured the taste of that, and he respected him for it. He smiled back. 'Then I had better look elsewhere. Perhaps I shall begin with Letterman, at the police station.'

Marcus sat rigid. He swallowed as if there were something stuck in his throat. 'Letterman?' he asked. 'What would he know?'

Pitt felt a sudden chill in the room, as if he had accidentally opened a door into a storm. How should he answer?

Marcus was waiting. There was total silence in the house.

Pitt waited also.

'Be careful of him,' Marcus said abruptly. Every word seemed louder, more distinct than usual. 'He's . . . a sly one . . . '

Pitt had a sudden certainty that Marcus was deeply afraid, and of something specific, and he had no doubt that it involved Letterman. The coldness was not only around him, it settled deep inside him, touching everything.

Marcus was still staring at him.

Pitt cleared his throat. 'Have you any advice about approaching Letterman? If you know him, or have had any experience to offer, I'd be grateful for it.'

'No . . . ' Marcus struggled for words, and failed to find any.

Pitt hated this. It was as real as subjecting Marcus to physical torture. He wanted to put a stop to it, but then he would only have to start again. There was no way to avoid it.

'No, not really,' Marcus added. 'Just . . . don't take anything he says without getting confirmation. I can't be more specific. It's just, sadly . . . well, I suppose it's a collection of impressions. Lot of clients, you know. A bit here, a bit there.'

He was lying, and Pitt knew it.

Pitt stood up. 'Thank you. I'll not take anything he says as truth unless I can confirm it myself. Thank you . . . '

Marcus cleared his throat again, started to say something, and then changed his mind.

Pitt left feeling not as if he were walking out into a spring day, but into a rapidly darkening evening.

$\star$　$\star$　$\star$

He did not go straight to the police station to confront Letterman. Instead, he walked some distance from the underground railway, thinking about what he would say. First, he must gain

Letterman's attention, and there would be no point in doing so without having a plan. He had to be certain as to what he was going to do . . . and exactly what he wanted.

Marcus's warning crowded his mind and made everything sadder, and more difficult. He couldn't hide his identity: Letterman might know him by sight. Any subterfuge at all would make him look ridiculous. He must give a reason for being there, and a good one. It was not the norm for the head of Special Branch to drop in on the regular police, whether it was in Mile End or not. He would have to stay as close to the truth as possible. And it must appear important.

He could not mention Marcus yet. So, what was his strategy? An idea began to take shape in his mind, and it bore strong elements of the truth. By the time he reached the station, he had it clear in his mind. It was, obliquely, true. It was Special Branch's duty to care for someone as powerful in shipbuilding as Erasmus Faber. Britain's survival might one day depend upon the Navy.

'Good morning, Sergeant,' he said, with a very slight smile. 'Sir Thomas Pitt, of Special Branch. A recent matter has become urgent, and I need to speak to Inspector Letterman.' He did not add *please*. He wanted it understood as an order, even if one courteously phrased.

'Yes, yes, sir!' The desk sergeant stood a little straighter. He called a constable over to take his place and hurried off, his leather boots loud on the wooden floor.

Five minutes later, Pitt was upstairs and seated

203

in the chair opposite Letterman's desk and facing the man. Letterman appeared exactly as he had imagined him: neat, well groomed and composed. His face was bland, his clothes plain, but Pitt was aware of their quality by the ease with which they fitted.

'What can we do for you, Sir Thomas?' Letterman asked smoothly.

'The matter is one we need to keep discreet.' Pitt smiled, so slightly it was barely there at all. 'It concerns the recent murder of Jonah Drake, which happened on your patch.'

Letterman's expression darkened, but he remained silent, assuming an air of concern.

'I realise you may not be able to find out exactly who committed the crime,' Pitt continued. 'Mile End is a complicated place; I am well aware of that. But I know a little more about Drake now than I used to. He handled some . . . very interesting cases.' He watched Letterman's face for any sign at all that he understood the specific meaning behind the words. The increase of tension was so small, he was not sure if it was more than a trick of the light.

'I take it you mean interesting to Special Branch,' said Letterman, not moving his direct stare from Pitt's face.

'Yes,' Pitt lied. 'There are matters that affect many people not connected with Mile End. Gentlemen of means . . . and influence.' He tried to disguise how intently he was watching the man, every shadow on his face, each tiny movement of the eyes.

'I understand,' Letterman granted, as if it were

a favour, not a duty to respond.

'Of course you do,' Pitt agreed, without expression. 'We know that you have dealt . . . discreetly . . . with certain issues.' Let him interpret that as he liked! Even a compliment, if he so wished.

This time the reaction was plainer. Letterman's expression remained the same, but his right hand, which lay on top of the papers on the desk, clenched and shook very slightly. 'I understand,' he repeated. 'Discretion is important.'

'We cannot protect people from danger we ourselves do not see.' Pitt was trying out various approaches, without mentioning that Drake worked for Marcus. He decided to make the major play. 'There are certain people who are important, even vital, to the national well-being.' Should he be direct? Or did Letterman already know to whom he was referring? No, he needed to be clearer. 'Just over a year ago, Drake defended young Evan Faber in a most unpleasant matter,' he continued. 'Of course, he was innocent.' He relaxed a little, not quite smiling, and waited to see if Letterman understood him.

Letterman nodded. 'Quite.'

The silence hung heavily for a moment, then two.

Pitt waited, his attention complete, as if he were waiting for Letterman to finish his thought.

'It was impossible to avoid.' Letterman looked uncomfortable. 'We had evidence against young Faber,' he said unhappily. 'Couldn't avoid it . . .'

Pitt let the ghost of a smile bring a curve to his mouth. 'I understand. Better to face it, if you have to. Fortunately, they had Drake, and he proved himself completely up to the job.'

'Quite,' Letterman said again. Why was he being so careful before committing himself? Interesting, if he wanted to ascertain which side Pitt was on. The side of the government. Or perhaps of rearmament?

'We believe Drake was still enquiring into who actually was guilty, when he was killed,' Pitt continued. 'I don't know why, but I have several guesses. Chief among them is blackmail . . . ' He hesitated.

Letterman winced but did not interrupt. However, there was definitely a sharper interest in his face.

Pitt did not know the cause of this interest, and it worried him. Could it be that Letterman knew some of the answers, but not that particular one? Or was he concerned about how much Pitt knew, and if he was going to present a problem?

'We tried everything we could,' Letterman said, as if uncertain for the first time, even defensive.

So, he didn't have all the answers!

'Something has changed.' Pitt tried a different tack. 'Perhaps Evan Faber was killed because he knew too much, even if he didn't intend to do anything about it. But Drake was a threat, so he had to be the first to be got rid of — ' He stopped. He had seen a flash of understanding in Letterman's face, something indicating that this had meant something to him.

Letterman was silent, waiting.

'If anything occurs to you, Inspector, please let Special Branch know.' Pitt handed Letterman one of his cards. 'Just tell me if you have something. Whatever it is, I will decide if anyone else should be included in the information. I fear there is a lot of corruption going on, and at the highest level. This would be one way of finding out who is involved.' He actually smiled, as if imparting a confidence to an ally. He hoped it appeared more sincere than it was.

Letterman took a long breath. The parameters of battle had suddenly altered, widened. There was no longer certainty, whereas only minutes ago he had not entertained any doubts. 'Yes, yes, Sir Thomas,' he said, clearing his throat and going on. 'Of course.'

Pitt wondered if Letterman was attempting to establish his innocence, thinking how to blame someone else, if it all fell apart. Or could he be genuinely surprised? Pitt was certain in his own mind it was the former. He judged Letterman to be someone who was always on the winner's side, once he had ascertained who the winner would be.

Pitt stood up. 'Thank you, Inspector. And I am sorry to have disturbed your morning. However, this whole thing could be coming to a head soon, and then we can clear it up. Good day.'

Letterman found his voice and rose also. 'Good day, sir.' Pitt went out into the May sunshine, feeling as if he had lit the fuse of a bomb that could very well cause an explosion.

His mind was already made up as to what he must do next. He no longer had the freedom to avoid it.

★　★　★

Pitt knew that Faber was very recently bereaved of his only son — in fact, apparently, his only relative. His wife had died many years ago, and there were no other children. Pitt could not even imagine how the man must be feeling. In any other circumstances he would not have troubled him, but this issue was too serious to observe even the normal decencies. It would be natural for him to refuse the request for an interview, so Pitt must forewarn him, and explain why he was making so tactless a request.

When he extended the request for a meeting, he phrased it politely but did not attempt to obscure the issue. Faber was a practical man, as was Pitt himself. He asked for Faber's help and it was granted, without evasion or delay.

Pitt went immediately, taking only the driver of the car with him. Faber was in his huge dockside offices, where Pitt was shown in as soon as he arrived. There was no officious attempt to delay the interview, with the pretence of business Faber had to finish.

Faber himself met Pitt at the doorway to his suite of offices. He was a big man, Pitt's height, but much more heavily built. He was barrel-chested, muscled like a wrestler, but he moved easily, although he must have been well over fifty. His red-brown hair was thick, not yet greying, but his face was haggard. He made no attempt to hide his grief. He was sombre in manner and dressed in black.

'Good morning, Pitt.' He made no concession to office, not even using Pitt's title. He led him into his own office with its huge main window overlooking the dockyard, and beyond it the Pool of London. He indicated a chair for Pitt to be seated, then hesitated a moment before sitting down himself. He did not offer any refreshment, nor had Pitt expected it. This was far from a social visit.

'What can I do for you?' Faber asked. He had no time nor was he in the mood to waste precious minutes on niceties.

Pitt had already decided how to approach the question, depending on how Faber phrased it. Clearly, he wished to be direct. 'You are aware of Jonah Drake's death in Mile End,' he began.

'Of course,' Faber responded. His clear, light blue eyes were studying Pitt's face. 'What has it to do with Special Branch?'

'In itself, nothing.' Pitt realised how careful he must be with this man. This was no polite exchange, no leading up to a question. 'Except that Drake was an unusually good lawyer, as you know.'

'Because he defended my son?' There was an edge to Faber's voice. He was guarded and angry, and he was in no mood to accept sympathy.

'Obliquely, yes,' Pitt granted, keeping his voice perfectly level. 'I cannot imagine you would use anyone but the best for such a task.'

Faber took a deep breath and let it out slowly. 'For example,' he conceded. 'But why does that concern you?'

Pitt had expected that. 'My son, Daniel, works at the same legal chambers. He knew that Drake not only defended your son, but personally believed him to be innocent. That is not always the case. The guilty have to be defended also. And Daniel liked your son . . . '

A shadow of grief crossed Faber's face, deep pain. And then he mastered it. 'Come to the point, man, I do not need you to tell me that my son was a likable person. You haven't come here to commiserate with me. Your son is still alive and well. You want something. What is it?'

Faber was no duellist. There was no leading up to the subject, no parrying, no dance with an epee. His approach was more like slashing with a broadsword, one blow of which would take off a man's head.

But it did make Pitt's job easier, knowing that even one slash would end it. 'Drake was certain Evan was not guilty. Therefore, someone else must be . . . '

Faber's face tightened. It was almost imperceptible, little more than a changing of the light on his jaw.

'Of course,' Faber agreed. 'It was not conceivable that it was an accident. But women like that live dangerously. What is it to Special Branch?'

'Marie Wesley herself is of no interest to Special Branch, Mr Faber, but your safety and well-being definitely are.'

210

Faber moved almost indefinably, but his shoulders eased a little. It was more than a trick of the light. 'I am in no danger, Sir Thomas.'

'I assume not,' Pitt agreed, taking note of the *sir*. 'But then, I did not know Drake was. Nor did I foresee it for your son. In both cases, we were wrong.' He stopped because he saw the sudden blaze of anger in Faber's eyes, perhaps the one feature he could not control.

'And what are you offering me?' Faber said in a hard, tight voice. 'Protection? Sympathy? Advice? Warning?' His smile hovered on the edge of a sneer.

'What do you want?' Pitt asked.

Faber drew in breath to speak, then changed his mind.

'Someone killed Drake, and your son, and perhaps others we don't know about,' Pitt went on. 'If you want Special Branch protection . . . '

'And have you following me around?' Faber asked. 'For how long? The rest of my life?'

'A warning would be preferable,' Pitt answered.

'Such as I stay away from Mile End?'

'Do you need such a warning?'

Faber changed his mind and tried to smile instead. 'Consider it given. But I shall please myself where I go, what company I keep, and when.' He stared steadily at Pitt.

There was a silent moment which probably seemed to Pitt much longer than it was. He could hear a clock ticking somewhere as its second hand moved around its face.

'I appreciate it,' Faber said at last. 'I am

grateful to you for taking my well-being so seriously. Although, of course, it is your job.' His face relaxed into a very slight smile. 'Ships, yes? Your eyes, your mind, your thoughts are on ships. You do not want to be disturbed by . . . lesser matters.'

He had been evasive, using euphemisms, but meeting his eyes, and Pitt knew exactly what he meant. It was Pitt's job to swallow his criticisms, turn a blind eye where necessary. His opinion did not matter. He served the state, and the state's well-being rested on Faber's skills. His own morality was irrelevant.

'We serve the same cause, Mr Faber,' Pitt replied. 'I am very concerned for your safety.'

'I'm comforted by that, Sir Thomas. I know that I shall be better, safer, for your personal concern . . . ' He met Pitt's eyes, and this time he was definitely smiling.

10

Daniel felt the urgency to forge ahead. He went through Drake's notes one more time, adding his own comments on the points that, to him, were the most important, and writing question marks everywhere he felt needed further explanation. It was after lunch when he met with Kitteridge, who was also taking a break from those past cases that needed small issues cleared up. Marcus had told both of them to concentrate on that, and so Daniel had given his current case to someone else.

'What have you found?' Daniel asked, stepping into the office before Kitteridge answered his knock. He closed the door behind him. The sun was bright on the window and shone in elongated patterns on the woven carpet. The books stacked two-deep on the shelves were old, but immaculate. Like the books in Drake's study, they were read too often to collect dust.

Kitteridge looked up from his desk, scattered with papers, but none of them had to do with a current case. They were lying half on top of each other, but he always knew where everything was, as long as nobody attempted to tidy them.

'I see you're doing the same thing as I am,' Daniel observed, sitting in the visitor's chair. 'Find anything?'

'Come in,' Kitteridge said unnecessarily, a touch of sarcasm in his voice. 'All roads lead to

Mile End. That is, all roads that are definitely not leading to somewhere else.'

'That's a nonsensical observation,' Daniel replied. 'But I know what you mean. Every loose end I found more or less leads there, too, or a nameless place somewhere near Whitechapel, which has to be either the Isle of Dogs or Mile End.' He leaned forward a bit, resting his elbows on Kitteridge's desk. 'My mind keeps coming back to the location of Evan Faber's killing. Do you think it might have been Erasmus Faber who had the body moved?'

Kitteridge looked puzzled. 'Who else would care enough to lie about where Evan was killed?' He frowned. 'But it doesn't make any sense.'

'Whoever is guilty clearly didn't care about Evan, but he would care about himself,' Daniel pointed out. 'Maybe Faber has some kind of connection to Mile End that we don't know about? Or to Drake's murder?'

'Like what?' Kitteridge said. 'Are you thinking that young Faber really was guilty? And Drake was on the brink of finding that out? It wouldn't make any difference. The case is closed. Can't open it again.'

'What a mess,' Daniel observed. 'You mean Drake got him off, believing him innocent, then discovered his mistake, and was killed to keep him from . . . what? Telling everyone? Would he do that? Drake certainly didn't kill Evan . . . he was already dead himself! A random killing?' He shook his head, as if ridding himself of the idea.

'That's all rubbish!' Kitteridge said bitterly. 'If

214

the killer didn't know who Drake was, why kill him? That was hatred, Daniel. Personal. And don't forget that Drake still had his money on him, and a decent coat. That coat was worth a bit.' A momentary flicker of annoyance crossed Kitteridge's face. Daniel knew that he still felt a need to defend his taste. It was as if, by arguing, Kitteridge could reverse it all: the death, the blood, the waste.

'But I agree,' Daniel said. 'It was definitely personal, which is worth remembering. So, are you saying it had to do with the one thing Drake and Evan had in common, which is the Marie Wesley case?'

Kitteridge blinked. 'Don't you think so?'

'Yes. Either that case itself, or something that sprang from it,' Daniel agreed.

'Like what?' Kitteridge asked, running his hands through his hair which, as always, left it sticking out in all directions.

'That's what we need to find out,' Daniel answered. 'It could have been a misunderstanding. They assumed Drake went back there because it had to do with Evan, but possibly it was something else.'

'Like what?'

'A moneylender. That's what Hobson thought.'

'Why not something to do with Marie Wesley?' Kitteridge argued. 'Nobody was ever held to account for her death, and it doesn't seem to matter. Someone beat her terribly. Maybe that's where we should start?' Kitteridge insisted.

'I looked again at Drake's notes on Marie's death,' Daniel said. 'But he doesn't seem to have

215

other suspects who stand out. It was a pretty disreputable sort of party, and several people were drunk. All the police got was *I don't know, but it wasn't me!'* His disgust rang in his voice. 'Nobody can remember where they were, or where anyone else was either. Certainly nothing that would stand up in court.'

'You mean they're suggesting that an outsider broke in?' Kitteridge said incredulously.

'No.' Daniel felt suddenly as if hope were draining away. 'I'm quite sure it was someone who knew her, but I don't believe it was Evan.'

Kitteridge rolled his eyes. 'Not even if Evan was so drunk, so out of his mind, that he didn't remember it?'

'Nobody said he was so very drunk,' Daniel argued. 'And if it is someone else who doesn't remember — or whose friends are willing, for whatever reason, to lie for them — it goes nowhere. So, what was Drake after? And why does it matter? And above all, to whom does it matter? We don't even know that.'

'All right,' Kitteridge said. 'Where do we begin?'

'If I knew, I'd be out there after them,' Daniel said sharply.

'Not alone, you wouldn't!' Kitteridge snapped. 'If you're going, I'm coming with you.'

Daniel wanted to be equally terse, but he found himself smiling. Kitteridge was a good friend, always. 'Thank you, Toby.'

'I suppose that's what you wanted all along,' Kitteridge said, a trifle tartly. 'So, what do you propose?'

Daniel had known he would ask that, but he still had no answer. He leaned back a little in his chair. 'I can't find anything certain in Drake's papers. Will you — ?'

'No,' Kitteridge said flatly. 'I've been through them twice. The man thinks sideways, and in circles, and then draws pictures nobody understands. I wonder if he deliberately didn't want anyone to understand them — except, presumably, himself. I even tried his clerk, Hobson, but he wasn't much help, although he wanted to be. I'm glad he's got a place here, at least for a while.' He stared at Daniel. 'Where do you want to begin?'

Daniel had thought hard about this. 'There are some things we need to know, if we can find them out. Does everything start with Marie Wesley's death?'

'Yes,' Kitteridge answered. 'I think we're agreed on that. If it starts anywhere else, we don't know where, or with whom. If anyone does know, they're not telling us.'

'Are there a lot of loyalties concerned? Which ones are the strongest?'

'Faber to his son, agreed, but that's to be expected,' Kitteridge said.

'Evan to any of his friends, and perhaps to Marie,' added Daniel. 'Who else was involved? The truth would have hurt her reputation, or someone she loved. We don't know anything about her, not really. She could have had parents, or brothers and sisters.'

'That's true,' Kitteridge agreed. 'I never thought of it, but yes, it could all be traced back

217

to Marie Wesley in a way we hadn't thought of. Go on . . . '

'Did Evan know the truth of something, and was killed to keep him silent?'

'Which brings us back to asking who knew anything,' observed Kitteridge.

'Evan . . . I think,' Daniel replied. 'Although we know for certain that Drake was there asking questions. We know he didn't go there only on the night he was killed. We ought to ask more questions, like when did he go there? And who did he see?'

'The tobacconist? When you spoke to her, did you think she really knew anything, except who bought those disgusting cheroots she sold?'

'Belinda May? Bella? I have no idea,' Daniel admitted. 'But I know she had more information than she was letting on. She remembered Drake, but pretended she didn't know he was dead. I'm going to ask Blackwell to look a bit further. He'll fit in better in a place like Mile End, and with the likes of Bella. I'll stick out like a sore thumb, and they'll never tell me anything.'

Kitteridge plainly bit back the response that came to his mind. 'Good,' was all he said.

★　★　★

Daniel spent two days of anxious digging, revealing more small pieces of Drake's past cases; scraps of information that added up to no new information.

Roman Blackwell came to see him at the end of the next day. They were sitting quietly in Mrs

218

Portiscale's kitchen, with a pot of tea on the table. They could hear the murmur of voices beyond the door, and now and then a gust of wind blowing rain against the window. There was a vague aroma of something cooking in the oven. Daniel was waiting for Blackwell to tell him what he had learned. From the expression on Blackwell's face, he did not expect it to be much.

'The place he went to was just what you'd expect,' Blackwell said quietly. 'A big brothel with a lot of clients who would rather not have their names known. Some of them had bizarre tastes that I'm pretty sure their wives would rather they took elsewhere . . . if they knew about them at all. And an extra item on the side, just a few steps across the alley: an opium den.' His lip was curled with a mixture of pity and contempt for those addicted to what he regarded as poison. 'Drake seems to have found out quite a bit. Not certain that I could prove it. He was definitely looking around there, but for what, I don't know . . . yet. He was an odd-looking duck, so he stays in people's memory. From what I can see, he was unravelling something, piece by piece. Might have been the identity of some of the patrons, but who cares? That's the question. Maybe even some of his own clients, or a client's wife? Get a wonderful divorce settlement out of that piece of knowledge.' He pulled his face into an expression of revulsion. 'Or possibly something a little more tasteful, like a large financial settlement, enough to allow her to set up a separate establishment for herself, without the scandal of a divorce. It's happened often enough.'

'Not as scandalous as it used to be,' Daniel agreed. 'You think that was why Drake was killed? His client was a disaffected wife, and he was looking for enough proof for her to use?'

'It's possible.' Blackwell shrugged, and huddled a little deeper into his jacket, although the kitchen was warm.

Daniel knew that Mrs Portiscale would be back soon, to check on whatever was in the oven. It was beginning to smell good.

'But you don't think so?' Daniel asked.

'What would Marcus think about Drake taking on that sort of work?' Blackwell asked. 'Maybe it's not quite blackmail; some might prefer to call it leverage . . . '

Daniel had a sudden thought. Was it possible that this was the scenario that had made Marcus so unhappy? Was the chambers desperate enough to take on that kind of work? He could have told Drake to keep it to himself, mark it as something different in the books. It was a grubby piece of work, even if some husband had thoroughly deserved it.

Or was he being naïve? Was it possible to sustain a legal chambers that was never prepared to lend its hand to divorce cases? Weren't many cases sordid, one way or another? Theft, embezzlement, violence, fraud, forgery, deceit about property, and occasionally murder? The least objectionable of them were arguments over wills and inheritances, with slander and deceit close behind. And infidelity. And yet, no one

220

sought out criminal defence lawyers unless it involved a crime. The job was to see that innocent people were not convicted and that, if the client was guilty, the sentence was as lenient as possible.

If this was about a domestic situation, was Drake representing the husband or the wife? Or was it that kind of case at all? From the look on Roman Blackwell's face, there was more to it than he had so far revealed.

'And?' Daniel prompted. 'Who killed Drake then? Please don't tell me Drake was using his information for his own benefit.'

'No,' Blackwell said firmly. 'And I got most of the important bits from Mercy. She went and found people from the old days. The nineties were . . . ' He smiled. 'You should've seen her then! I have to say, she was the most remarkable woman, even if she is my own mother. Hair black as ink, down to her waist; a face designed for laughter and a figure that made every other woman look skinny, only half alive.'

Daniel smiled, in spite of his weariness and impatience. He could imagine Mercy Blackwell fifteen or twenty years ago. She must have been spectacular, ready to take on the world. He returned to the present reluctantly. 'Then we've got to find out who Drake's client was. If he was in the books, he was well disguised. Presumably, it was he who killed Drake, but why? And if the same man killed Evan Faber, why?'

'If it was a woman who hired him — ' Blackwell stopped. 'Not the killer; I'm referring to Drake.'

221

'What do you mean?' Daniel asked.

'If it was a woman, where did she get the money to pay him?' Blackwell explained. 'Not from her husband's account, or we'd be looking for her corpse. Easiest way to stop a scandal,' Blackwell pointed out. 'No, there's something wrong with our story. Don't know what.' He banged his open hand on the table. 'Come on, you must have known Drake a little bit! You've been here for over two years. Do you walk around with your eyes shut? There's something important that you're missing.'

★ ★ ★

Daniel soon discovered what that was. He awakened the next day when Mrs Portiscale knocked on his bedroom door. When he turned over and mumbled something, she came in with a hot cup of tea.

'Morning, Mr Pitt.' She seldom addressed him formally, preferring to use his given name, and certainly not at this hour in the morning. In May, dawn came very early. The next month was the summer solstice, although at this hour it felt chilly and very far from a summer's day.

Daniel sat up slowly. 'Is it time to get up?' He blinked at her uncertainly.

'No, it isn't.' Her voice was indignant. 'But you've got a visitor. It's that doctor again, Otter-something.'

Suddenly he was fully awake. 'Ottershaw?'

'That's right,' she replied. 'Large as life. I said to give you time to put your clothes on. You can have some breakfast before you leave, if you like. I can get bacon and eggs and toast ready for you. And for him, if he wants,' she added grudgingly.

Daniel pushed his hair off his face and rubbed his eyes. 'Oh hell! Who's dead now? Yes, I'd better have breakfast, thank you. I expect there will be nothing much else today. Thank you, Mrs Portiscale.'

'Somebody's got to look after you! I didn't know that the law was so full of dead bodies.'

'It isn't . . . usually.' He sat up and swung his legs out of bed, then took a long drink of the tea she had put on the bedside table. 'Thank you,' he said again. 'I'll be down in about five minutes.'

'Whoever's dead in't in no hurry,' she said as she went out of the door and closed it with a sharp click of the latch. Her retreating footsteps were almost silent on the landing carpet.

Breakfast was on the table when he went into the kitchen, and Ottershaw had clearly just finished his and put the knife and fork together on his empty plate. He looked up at Daniel as he crossed the floor, pulled out the other chair, and sat down. 'Eat,' Ottershaw said. 'It's going to be a busy day.' He shook his head and his hair flopped forward. He had had no time to shave, and there were shadows beneath his eyes.

Daniel took a mouthful of bacon and egg and glared at him.

'Found a couple of hours ago,' Ottershaw said, as if Daniel knew what he was talking about. He shook his head again slowly. 'At least, reported then.'

Daniel finished his mouthful. 'What? Or is it a who?' He fought down the horror that was rising inside him. Please heaven it was not someone he knew. To have to identify Drake was bad enough. It was ridiculous to think it was Kitteridge, or Marcus himself. 'Who?' he said sharply.

'Don't know her name yet. Young woman, but Mrs Blackwell found her during the night. Remarkable woman, that Mrs Blackwell.'

'Mercy Blackwell identified her?' Daniel stared at him. 'That makes no sense. How? Where?' Then as his mind cleared, he stared at Ottershaw. 'It's something to do with the Drake case, isn't it?'

'Yes.' Ottershaw looked beaten, and undeniably tired. 'It looks as if this girl has something to do with it. She was killed in much the same way, and with the same sort of blade. From the shape of the wound, it could be the exact same long knife. More rightly . . . a sword.'

'A prostitute?' Daniel asked.

Ottershaw shook his head. 'No, she . . . she was a virgin.' He looked away, as if to hide the emotion that was welling up inside him.

'Oh . . . hell!' Daniel said miserably. 'What does she have to do with it? Did she see something? Know something? And this bastard, whoever he is, killed her to keep her quiet?'

Ottershaw cleared his throat and said, 'Possibly.'

'How did Mercy find her?'

'Mercy?'

'Mercy Blackwell!' Daniel did not mean to snap, but the emotion welled up inside him and threatened to overtake his self-control. 'Mercedes.'

'Seems she was looking for her. No idea why.'

'Is she anybody we know?'

'I don't think so. Belinda May Blades. Her grandmother confirmed it. She lives in one of the rambling houses nearby. A brothel.'

Daniel stared at him. His heart was beating so violently, so high in his throat, he felt as if it were shaking his whole body. 'Belinda May Blades?' He swallowed. 'Slender, pretty, with short blonde hair, all curls?' He felt sick as he asked. She had been so alive, so full of energy and laughter.

'You know her?' Ottershaw asked quietly.

'I met her.' Daniel took a deep breath. 'She keeps a tobacconist's shop in Mile End. Anthony Street. Who'd want to kill her?'

Ottershaw said nothing.

'Who'd want to kill her?' Daniel asked again, raising his voice considerably.

'They called her Bella,' Ottershaw began, then stopped.

'What?' Daniel demanded, glaring at him now. 'Yes, yes, I know: Bella.'

'I'm sorry, Daniel, we don't know who killed her, but it was her own knife they used.'

'Her own knife? What on earth would she want a knife for? I mean, one that would inflict such injury?'

Ottershaw was staring at him, his face contorted with grief. 'To kill people with, Daniel. Her grandmother said it was her knife, and that she was a professional assassin . . . '

It was nonsense. It could not be true. It was a

225

nightmare. The room was spinning and he was losing his balance. He gripped the table. His voice was stressed, choking. 'And why would her grandmother admit such a thing? It's absurd! Don't be ridiculous!'

'I'm not,' Ottershaw said quietly. 'Who'd suspect a young girl, pretty as you like, of carrying a knife, a sword of sorts, that could kill you? Her grandmother was proud of it — ' He broke off. 'Put your head down, take a deep breath. There's nothing we can do to her now, anyway. It looks as if one of her intended victims got the better of her.'

Daniel wanted to argue. How could he accept this? 'You're saying she killed Drake and Evan Faber? That it wasn't a man at all . . . it was a girl? Is that what you're saying? That she was a clever . . . assassin? But this other person, whoever killed her, was quicker? Better?'

'Yes,' Ottershaw replied. 'So it seems.'

'Then how did she let someone creep up on her, take her knife, and kill her with it?' Daniel demanded. He was grasping after a fact, any fact, that would make the whole story collapse, and therefore be untrue.

'Only one answer to that,' Ottershaw said, his face pulled tight with distaste. 'It was someone she knew . . . and trusted.'

Daniel said nothing. He was seeing her in his mind's eye, standing in front of the boxes of cheroots, smiling at him, laughing inside, flirting with him. How could she be just . . . gone? And . . . a killer?

Ottershaw continued. 'Apparently, she's been

doing this for a while. She must be good at it. She was a paid assassin, Daniel. I doubt a stranger could get the better of her, take her completely by surprise.'

It was a moment before Daniel could find his voice. 'Where do we begin?' Perhaps it was useless, this investigation, except as a brief ease from the stunned pain inside him. He had only met her once, and now it seemed she had killed Drake. And more than that, Evan Faber too. He should hate her. Part of him did. But another part remembered only the girl who had laughed at him, with him, so intensely alive. He felt confused, cheated . . . and he grieved. 'Who did she work for?' he said aloud.

'Unfortunately, she can't tell us,' Ottershaw said quietly.

'Is that what you came for?' Daniel asked. He heard the anger in his own voice. It was unfair, but he was losing control of it.

Ottershaw hesitated only for a moment. 'I came because you care about all this. I know you do. And the police don't. She was nothing to them, just another unsolved crime in an area full of them. And they don't want to be reminded of Drake, because that's one they didn't solve either.' His face was solemn, full of pain, and self-mockery, yet infinitely serious. 'We have to look at this, Daniel, or at least try! No one else will. I wish Miriam were here. She'd insist. But . . . We can try . . . '

'I am trying,' Daniel said, with a note of desperation. 'I . . . I don't know where to try next. Do you?'

'No.' Ottershaw had better mastery of his anger, or whatever emotion so obviously filled him. 'One way we might get answers is to work out who paid her to kill Evan Faber. Does the whole thing go back to the murder of Marie Wesley? She ties into this somewhere.'

Daniel put his head in his hands. 'Yes. Yes, I'll try to find out, but I don't even know where to begin. Their lives should cross somewhere, whatever it looks like!'

'Do you mean Marie Wesley and this Belinda . . . Bella? Are you sure?' Ottershaw asked. 'Worlds can meet where we don't even notice. The lady of nobility and the maid from some village fifty miles away, and yet they sleep under the same roof and meet every day.'

'What does that mean?' Daniel snapped.

Ottershaw sighed. 'Marie Wesley was a young woman of great charm, who used it to make her living. Belinda May Blades, Bella, was a young woman who lived on the edge of the same world, and knew many of the same men . . .'

'I suppose so,' Daniel conceded. He looked at his unfinished breakfast and pushed the plate away.

11

It was a warm day. There was a chatter of birds in the branches of the roadside trees, and gardens were brimming with colour. It would not be long before the first flush of roses burst their heavy buds. Here and there the early yellow roses around doorways were beginning to show. A whiff of hyacinth perfume drifted in the air. Charlotte smiled without even realising why.

Two men walked along the footpath towards her and she smiled briefly. She did not know them as residents she had seen before. One of them stood aside to make way for her; the other remained on the outside of the path, next to the kerb. She did not realise this was a little odd until it was too late. The men moved in unison, closing in on her and taking both her arms tightly. It pinched her flesh and she tried to pull away, but they gripped even harder.

'Don't cry out,' said one of them, having moved so close he was speaking into her ear. 'There's nobody near, and we could hurt you before anyone got here. We don't want to hurt you, not if we don't have to.'

'What do you think you're doing?' she demanded furiously, almost choking on her own words. 'Let go of me!'

They answered by tightening their grip until pain shot through her arms.

Despite it being a lovely day, the street was

deserted. She realised with dismay that there was no one to help her. 'There will be people coming by, any minute,' she protested. 'Let go of me!' She tried to snatch her arm back and succeeded only in wrenching her wrist painfully. When she attempted to bring them to a stop, they dragged her forward, scraping the toes of her shoes and twisting her ankle.

The bigger of the two men jerked her arm even more forcefully. 'Look, you! We 'ave to keep you alive, that's what the boss said. You're no use to us dead. But there's nothing says we can't 'urt yer, if you give us enough trouble. Bones break easy. If you're older . . . and you are! Twenty-one? They can heal in a month or two. But fifty? Not nearly so good. So watch yerself! I don't mind if I 'ave ter carry yer! But broken bones 'urt something dreadful, and I know what I'm talkin' about. So straighten up and shut up. You 'ear me?'

'Yes,' she said, having to force her voice out. Her throat was dry and she was finding it hard to breathe. Who were these men? And what did they want her for? Who was the boss? There was no point in asking. Perhaps she did not want to know. Because once she knew, it might make it impossible for them to let her go. Or let her live.

They were still walking along the pavement, Charlotte squeezed between the two men so that she could not possibly break free. Home seemed miles away, although it was no more than half a mile.

They came to Tottenham Court Road, the main street. One of the new black cabs slowed as it passed them . . . and then stopped. The taller of the two men grasped the door handle and yanked it open.

Charlotte was pushed from behind, banging her twisted ankle on the steps of the cab. She lost her balance and pain shot up her leg. The other man hoisted her by her hips and shoved her inside, climbing in after her. He pulled down the extra seat that faced backwards, shouting something at the driver. His partner moved rapidly to the far side and pulled that door open, sliding on to the seat.

Charlotte was trapped.

The cab lurched forward. A moment later they were a very ordinary part of the traffic, and Charlotte feared that no one had noticed anything, except perhaps a rather clumsy woman being assisted by two men.

They followed the traffic towards the river for a few hundred yards, then turned left and headed east. Neither of the men spoke, not to her, not to each other. Charlotte tried to think clearly, but it was difficult to ignore the pain in her ankle, as well as in her hip, caused when she had twisted her body getting into the cab. Were they doing this for money? She and Thomas were comfortable, at least by the standards of most people, but there was not much money to spare, making her far from a good candidate for collecting a ransom. Did these men know that?

She rubbed her ankle, which was beginning to swell. They had said they were doing this on someone else's orders, so it did not matter to them if she was rich or poor. Someone who wanted her alive. But for what? She tried to think of reasons, but nothing came to mind.

And then it struck her. Of course! She knew nothing, but Thomas knew all kinds of things, about all kinds of people, and at the highest levels of government and society. If somebody needed him to stop an investigation, and knew he was too ethical to do so, then what better way than by kidnapping his wife? She was suddenly overwhelmed with gratitude that it had not been tried earlier, when her children were home and could have become the victims. A sick feeling overcame her. It could have been Jemima, when she was younger and living here in England — or Daniel, at any time. But that also included the present. He might be harder to snatch now, but how difficult would it have been for these two men to overcome him?

If they had taken her in order to silence Thomas regarding some case he was on, then she was worth an immeasurable amount if she were kept alive, especially if she became their bargaining chip in some negotiation. But who was in charge? A person of prominence in industry or society? Someone important on the international scene? A foreign government? Who would put a price on one woman's life to attain a goal?

But if she were damaged badly — not just the odd broken bone or sprained wrist or ankle, a wrenched hip, a few bruises — she would be worth very little. However, the vengeance for killing her would be terrible. She hoped they realised that. If they were caught, they could face the gallows. How could she use that to her advantage? There must be a way to make them see that with her alive, and relatively unharmed, they could walk away. Whereas if she were dead, they would be hunted down until they, too, were dead. Thomas would see to that! And then she told herself to be careful. *Think this through!* Her life depended on not saying the wrong thing.

She looked out of the window. Where were they? She did not recognise the street. Judging by the angle of the sunlight, they were going east, away from the wealthier area and towards the slums. Like Mile End, Whitechapel, and the Isle of Dogs. Or perhaps across the river, at the same point, to the south bank. From there, the taxi cab could take them anywhere.

She tried to think of something to say, something to bargain with, but her mind was in turmoil. She had to concentrate to stop her hands from shaking. Better to be silent than to speak and give away her thoughts. Then another thing struck her: if she could identify them, they would have to kill her! Kidnapping was a very serious crime indeed. For the second time in only a few minutes, she thought of the gallows. And what if they did not kill her? That could mean a long sentence for holding her against her will, and served in one of the worst prisons, like Coldbath Fields. Thomas had told her about these places. Even if you got out alive, in your dreams you never left. The first touch of sleep carried you back to the grim, damp cell. No matter where you were, if you woke up cold, or in the dark, it was as if you were still there; freedom was just an illusion. She hoped these men had not thought of such things. But even if they weren't thinking of it now, they would at some time, which made it imperative for her to escape, at whatever cost. She sat back and kept silent as they moved at a good speed along the riverbank, always travelling eastward.

It was not long before they were in Mile End. The taxi slowed and came to a complete stop just off Anthony Street. She had seen the road sign as they turned the corner: Anthony Street! It was in an alley just off this place that the body of Jonah Drake had been found, horribly slashed and left to die. Maybe it was not Thomas they wanted to silence, but Daniel!

'Come on, get out,' the bigger man ordered. 'Move yourself.'

She obeyed, tripping on her skirl, and was only saved from falling when the larger man caught her roughly by the arm.

'No one's going to care if you break your toe or your ankle, you clumsy mare!'

She knew that was the truth. There was no point in arguing. She followed him obediently, aware of the other man a few steps behind her.

They went into a house, then through a reasonably pleasant series of hallways and rooms towards the back. It was warm here and smelled musty, as if it were never cleaned properly with soap and water.

'Grandma!' the big man shouted. 'It's Jacko! Where are yer?' He stopped, staring around. There were a couple of tables and plenty of chairs, some of them hard-backed, but mostly soft, plus sofas and a few tables. Nothing matched, but they appeared reasonably comfortable, even lush. 'Come on, yer old mare!' he called out, his voice sharper. 'Got a job for yer!'

There was a noise behind one of the three doors that led out of the room. It opened slowly and an old woman appeared. She was a little over five feet tall and could have been any age between seventy and ninety. Her shoulders sagged and her face was blotched. She was red-eyed, as if she had been weeping. She did not look at either of them but at Charlotte, who was standing between them, her weight all on one side to ease the pain in her hip. The old woman's mouth pulled into a bitter line and she looked at all three of them with contempt. A black and white dog stopped beside her, his lip curled into a snarl.

'So, what yer got there, yer great fool?' she asked, in a surprisingly strong voice.

'A job for yer,' Jacko repeated. 'Look after this ladyship fer the boss, and 'e'll go on looking after you. No damage to 'er, mind you, she's valuable. At least for a time. You 'ear me? Or the boss'll sling you out of 'ere into the gutter. Take care of 'er, till yer told not to.'

'I run this place, yer great fool!' She turned from Jacko and looked Charlotte up and down through red-rimmed eyes. 'Oo are yer then?'

'My name is Charlotte. Who are you?'

'Grandma Blades,' the old woman replied, straightening up a little. 'And this here's Patch.' She indicated the dog. 'Won't bite yer, if yer treat him decent. Good ratter, 'e is. But 'e'll go after you if you provoke 'im.'

'And what would provoke him?' Charlotte asked. She tried to keep her voice level, as if she were not afraid. The dog would sense fear and attack her. But not if she made some kind of connection with the old woman. That was the only way of survival. Don't be obvious.

'If yer upset me,' the old woman was saying to her. 'In't that right, Jacko?' She looked at the big man, and gave a gurgle in her throat which, in better times, might well have been laughter.

Jacko made a low, growling noise in his throat, but he said nothing.

The lighter, thinner man with the scrawny neck looked at the old woman and nodded, then turned on his heel and went out. Jacko followed after him.

'Don't just stand there,' Grandma Blades ordered. 'Yer sit down in that chair. No! That one be'ind yer, with the wooden arms. I'm going to shackle yer to it. If yer be'ave yourself, I'll let yer move around. If yer play silly beggars, move up on me like, the dog'll get yer. Yer should see 'im kill a rat. Yer wouldn't want him to do that to yer. Yer do as I tell yer, and we'll get on.' She gave a sharp sniff. 'If not, I'll set Patch on yer.' As she was speaking, she picked up a heavy set of manacles. ''Ands out!' she ordered, and when Charlotte obeyed, she locked the heavy chain bracelets on her wrists. She had to move slowly, or they hurt.

'Won't your boss be annoyed?' Charlotte tried to force a smile, as if she were not shaking inside with terror. Deliberately, she did not look at the dog. 'I'm not worth anything to you dead.'

The woman looked at her with rage, then suddenly her eyes filled with tears and they spilled over and ran down her cheeks.

For an instant, Charlotte was sorry for her. What on earth could hurt her so much? Her first guess would be the loss of the dog. But the dog was there, and bright eyed, and someone had obviously brushed his thick coat with care. She wondered if showing sympathy would help, perhaps make the old lady care about her as well, identify with her prisoner's well-being. But she sensed that would only make her angry. 'How long am I going to stay here?' she asked. 'Until someone pays you for me? Or . . . not?'

'Huh,' the old woman grunted. 'Worked it out, 'ave yer? Well, some of us don't wait for ever. Yer thought of that? I got more ter do than look after you night and day. Better 'ope yer old man comes up wi' whatever they want.'

Charlotte had thought of it, but it had only danced at the edge of her mind. Of course the old woman was right, they would grow impatient — and more likely sooner, rather than later — and they would get rid of her, probably into the river. She preferred to find an explanation that made more sense, such as they wanted Thomas to do something . . .

Then another thought came to her. She had seen their faces. She did not know exactly where she was, but she knew within a few streets. She had tried to remember the journey here. She had been too frightened to think clearly, but she remembered only too well the sign for Anthony Street, shortly before she'd been bundled out of the cab and into the house where she was now held prisoner.

It was not an enormous area, but densely populated. In this neighbourhood, there were thousands of people packed into a few streets, sometimes a whole family in one room. And a lot of the area was occupied by pawn shops, small businesses such as tobacconists, newspaper shops with resident petty forgers, brothels, opium dens, as well as merchants of every kind. She was quite sure that she was in a building that housed a brothel. The entrance was intended for public use, to impress, and yet in many ways it was both lush and vulgar. She had passed more than a dozen bedrooms, some with doors open. From the outside, the building could easily resemble a milliner's, a dress shop, or anything else. How would anyone find her, looking at the building from the street? How would Thomas ever know, even if he came here?

She looked around this room and was certain it was used regularly. But by whom? It was full of the sort of belongings that are permanent. There was a good stove, which warmed the whole area. Only two scuttles of coke sat open in the corner, so there must be a coal cellar somewhere beneath it. It was probably down the steps and behind one of the doors she had passed on the way in. As much as she looked, she saw no means of escape.

She looked further around. There was a dresser stacked with dishes, not expensive, but not cracked or chipped either. There was an airing rail hanging from the ceiling on pulley ropes, and storage bins for dry supplies, like flour, beans, rice or oats. And she thought that the door in the far corner might lead to a pantry. People lived here, cooked food, ate, slept. There would be rooms for sleeping, as well as for the women and their clients. It was either a very large house, or more likely, several together, with a rats' nest of passages between them.

She looked back at the old woman whose face reflected some terrible grief, her expression far away from the practicalities of daily life, cooking, laundry. She seemed, at least for the moment, entirely unaware of Charlotte, who was now only a few feet away from her and chained to the chair.

Only the dog seemed to notice Charlotte. His eyes never moved away from her. That alone was enough to keep her glued to the chair.

Should she try to engage the old woman? Force her to regard Charlotte as a person, not something inert and without feelings? Or would that make any difference? Perhaps the woman was afraid of the boss? Or depended on him?

She swallowed down her fear. She ought to try her best to learn something while she was here, not just sit like a sack of potatoes. The more she learned, the more she increased her chance of escape!

Then another thought found its way into her mind. If she knew nothing, her safe return was simply the price for Pitt's silence. But if she knew something important — or they even suspected that she did — then possibly they could not afford to give her back, or let her go at all! She would have to disappear altogether. If they got what they demanded, did that mean they would not let her live? It made grim sense, and it was so frightening she almost choked on her own panicked intake of breath. She gasped and coughed, trying to breathe normally again.

The old woman started into wakefulness and glared at her. 'What's the matter with you, then?'

'Sorry, I swallowed the wrong way,' Charlotte answered. Why was she apologising? Who was this woman? And why was she weeping? 'Who are you?' Charlotte asked again. Then, the moment after, she realised that she did not want to know. She could not afford to know! She drew in her breath to say so, but the old woman was already answering her.

'You 'eard 'im! I'm Grandma Blades,' she answered. 'Except I'm nobody's grandma — ' She choked on the words, as if the tears rose from inside her chest.

Charlotte made a guess that came from pity, not any intelligence. 'Someone you love has died . . . your grandchild?'

The old woman jerked around and stared at her, her expression venomous even through the tears. 'What do you know about that, Miss Oh-So-Proper? You tell me. Or . . . ' She stopped, as if suddenly realising she had no power except to taunt with words.

It took Charlotte all the strength she had to look calm and stop her body from shaking. 'It was what you said, that you were nobody's grandmother. I have two granddaughters.' That was safe to say. They were in America, thousands of miles away, so could not be vulnerable or at risk. Sophie had been only a tiny baby, but Cassie had been very much an active child when they visited. Charlotte could not help but see her bright little face in her mind's eye, and hear her voice. The little girl had been fascinated with Daniel, because he argued for a living, whereas she did it for the fun of it. It was second nature to her to question everything.

She forced her mind back to the present and the old woman. 'You lost your granddaughter?' No wonder she was weeping. Charlotte could not even imagine how she would feel if anything happened to Cassie or Sophie. Jemima's letters were so full of the baby, she felt as if she knew her, too. The concerns, the trust, the eagerness for life were so precious, even the thought of them being hurt was unbearable. She ached for the old woman, even as she knew the pain was bone deep and unending.

'I didn't say it was a girl!' Grandma Blades' face hardened. 'How do you know? You in it some'ow, then?'

'No.' Charlotte kept her voice level with difficulty. 'But mine are both girls, so it just came naturally. Their names are Cassie and Sophie. They live in America. I know Cassie because they came to visit when she was three. She's four now. Always it was questions: why, how, what for? All the time!'

The old woman's eyes misted over with memory. 'That's little girls, in't it? Bella was

241

always asking, always trying to find out how things worked.'

'Bella?' Charlotte asked tentatively.

'Yeah. Her name was Belinda May, but we called her Bella.'

'Bella?' Somehow the name meant something. Where had she heard it?

'That's right, why?' The old woman's voice was sharper now, her face distorted with suspicion. 'You heard it before, then?'

She must be careful how she answered. Daniel had mentioned Bella, but she must not share this with the old woman. 'No, I don't think so. How old was she?' It did not matter, as long as the old woman understood that they shared something precious. She knew that she must build on it. It might make the difference between whether she lived or not. Perhaps this woman needed to talk about her granddaughter. Charlotte knew that people were often embarrassed speaking of the dead, afraid they would upset others, or reveal too much about their emotional frailties and not know what to do about it. So, they skirt around it, as if that person never existed. It had been a bit like that with Sarah, Charlotte's elder sister who had been murdered so many years ago. It was still indelicate to mention her, and no one seemed to know what to say, so they had removed her from the conversation, and in its own way, that hurt Charlotte even more. 'What was she like?' she said aloud.

The old woman's face hardened. 'Why do you want to know? She weren't nothing to you.'

She must keep talking, build this frail bridge.

Also, it was instinctive. She was sorry for this old woman, in spite of her cruelty. 'I had a sister who was murdered,' she answered, 'and people stopped saying her name, as if it would upset us, or it would be embarrassing. Or we might get emotional and they wouldn't know how to deal with it . . . ' The old woman relaxed. Even Patch, lying at her feet, put his head down on his paws, as if Charlotte did not need to be watched any longer.

'Bella were murdered, too,' she said quietly, her voice nearly swallowed up by the room. 'Cut with one of 'er own knives, she were. Quick, one slice. Like she would have done herself . . . '

Charlotte felt as if all the air had been sucked out of the room. Bella. Drake had been taken by surprise and slashed to pieces, so Thomas had said. But Evan Faber had been stabbed skilfully, directly into the heart. By Bella? And now she was being told that Bella herself had been stabbed . . . and with her own knife. She knew that she must keep talking. When she spoke, her voice was husky, tight in her throat. 'You mean she was murdered, too, like my sister, Sarah? Only with a knife? Sarah was strangled — or should I say garrotted? — with a cheese wire around the throat.' She could hardly believe she was saying such a thing aloud to this bitter old woman. No one in the family had ever mentioned it like this . . . and with such brutality.

The old woman looked at her with more interest. 'Didn't know ladies went around having that sort o' thing done to them. Thought it were

243

just us common folk!' She said the words with bitterness. 'Was your sister pretty?'

'Yes,' she said quietly, and with feeling. She could not even picture Sarah's face in her mind any more, not clearly. How quickly memory blurs. How long ago? Thirty years? Sarah would have been nearly sixty by now.

'So were Bella. Yellow curls on her head, and a pretty face. Little, she were. Almost like a boy. Not like you!' She regarded Charlotte's handsome figure with something like disapproval.

'Sarah was fair haired, too. So is my other sister,' Charlotte told her.

'Huh. You the odd one out, then?' The old woman seemed amused. Perhaps she felt herself the odd one out, too, in some way.

'Yes,' Charlotte replied. 'They married well,' she added. 'I married a man I loved, and still do, but he had no money.' She smiled as she said it. That view of things was so out of date now. It had been a long time since Sarah's death. Her other sister, Emily, had been widowed and remarried. Charlotte and Thomas had been happy and had prospered. She had had more than her share of good fortune and real, profound happiness. She no longer enjoyed the social position she had grown up with, or the money, but unlike many of the women she knew, she was never bored. She had involved herself in many of Thomas's cases, in spite of everyone's disapproval. That was because she had been both brave and clever, but also unwise and foolish. No, she was never bored — and never a butterfly, resting nowhere.

She sat there thinking how, while sharing Thomas's work, she had learned about all walks of life, and had made friendships that were the richest blessings one could have. And she had seen enough poverty and experienced enough danger to remind her of the abundance she enjoyed.

The old woman smiled bitterly, showing yellow teeth. 'And 'ere you are now, sitting in chains in a Mile End brothel, talking to an old woman and a dog. And likely no one will ever know where you are, or what 'appened to yer!'

Charlotte felt the chill, as if someone had opened a door and let in an icy wind that snuffed out all the lights. She took a deep breath. 'If you kill me, the police all over England will be looking for me, and they'll probably start around here.'

The old woman stiffened. 'And why should they? We never 'eard o' yer before!'

Charlotte tried to stop her voice from trembling. 'But you killed Jonah Drake around here. Do you think the police won't connect it?'

The old woman gave a snort of derision. 'Letterman? 'E's got more sense than to look 'ere!'

'Seems to me a very sensible place to look,' Charlotte reasoned. 'Evan Faber was also killed somewhere around here . . . ' She realised with another, deeper chill that the police had agreed to lie about that. Why? To please Erasmus Faber? Were they corrupt, and part of this? Did Thomas know that?

'Yer worked that out, did yer?' Grandma

245

Blades was watching her closely now, her suspicions awakened. 'All on Letterman's patch, eh? Aren't you the clever one!'

Charlotte had said too much; she knew it instantly, but it couldn't be taken back. Would they let her go now? Could they afford to? If Letterman had turned a blind eye to these murders, was that why Daniel had received no help?

The old woman smiled. 'Not so clever now, are you?'

'Are you ever going to let me go?' Charlotte asked.

'Per'aps. Per'aps not! Not up to me. And I don't care, anyway. We got nothing 'ere, 'ave we, Patch.' It was not a question, it was a blank, emotionless statement of despair.

Charlotte could see that this woman did not care what they did with her, because she had no control over it. In her own mind, it seemed, she felt no responsibility. 'If you kill me, the police will not give up until they have you all,' she said. It was meant to be a brave statement, but it sounded uncertain, and afraid.

The old woman looked at her derisively. 'The police don't give a sod about any of it, yer stupid cow. They're paid not to.'

Charlotte's heart was beating so violently that she was certain Grandma Blades could see. 'Not about Jonah Drake, maybe,' she agreed. 'Or about Evan Faber. But I'm a different matter.' This was the time to show her hand and shake up this bitter old woman. 'Did I mention that my husband is head of Special Branch?'

246

The old woman's face was blank. 'Yeah? And wot's that when it's at 'ome?'

Charlotte tried to understand what the woman meant. At home? She leaned forward, but was brought up sharply when the chains stopped her.

Patch raised his head and gave a warning growl.

Charlotte took a deep breath. 'Special Branch is above the police, a secret agency that fights against bombers and anarchists, anything that threatens the country.'

The woman waved away the explanation. 'Yeah? Well, we don't threaten the country,' she replied. 'Nobody knows about us . . . or gives a damn.'

Charlotte hesitated. She wasn't winning, and she could feel it. The old woman's moment of empathy was almost gone. 'Do you hate whoever killed your granddaughter?' she asked. 'I would, if it were my family . . . ' There was no need to finish the thought. The old woman's eyes blazed with hatred so vividly that Charlotte half expected her glance to scorch everything she looked at.

'So would I,' she said, as if the woman had replied. 'And my husband would do that to whoever killed me. Forcing me to come here could be forgotten, if I'm not hurt. That means I can go home and pretend it never happened. But if you kill me, there will be no end to it until each of you stands beside the gallows and watches the hangman put the rope around your neck and pull the trapdoor.'

The old woman laughed bitterly, her voice cracking as she gasped to draw breath. 'You'll never get us to trial, 'specially not 'im. And never mind the rope! Yer don't know what yer talking about . . . '

'I don't know your boss, that's true,' Charlotte retaliated. 'And you don't know my husband . . . ' She waited a moment. When the woman didn't respond, she said, 'I believe your boss had your granddaughter killed . . . for his own safety.' She took a deep breath and saw the old woman wince. Tears filled her eyes again and ran down her withered cheeks. 'Do you want to get revenge for Bella?' Charlotte went on, although she knew the answer.

'I'd die to get it,' the old woman said between her clenched teeth.

'Then let me go, and — '

Grandma Blades gave a dry, sour laugh. 'Yeah? What? Yer'll forget me the moment yer foot's out o' the door. Why not? I'm nothing ter you!'

Charlotte's mind struggled to think of an answer the old woman would believe. What would Charlotte herself believe, if they traded places? She could hear the desperation in her own voice as clearly as Grandma Blades could hear it. What could she say? She had seconds to think, and they were bleeding away.

'If I lie to you,' she began, 'then I'll be afraid for the rest of my life. You took me from my own street this time. What's to stop you doing it again? And again?'

Grandma Blades thought for a moment.

There was a clock somewhere ticking so loudly it seemed to echo round the room.

Charlotte moved restlessly. Her legs were stiff

and her back ached where she had wrenched it being pushed into the car. She tried to sit straighter to ease the pain.

Patch rose also, lip curled to show his teeth, a low, singing growl in his throat.

Charlotte began to shudder with both fear and determination. She must try now, or she would fail for sure. Finally, she broke the silence. 'Was Bella your daughter's child, or your son's? Where are they? What would they want?'

The old woman's face was wet with tears. 'Why? Wot's it to yer?'

'Just wondered if you were the one who raised her,' Charlotte replied. She could almost see the emotional knife she was twisting as Grandma Blades' face registered a new depth of pain.

'Me daughter's. Jenny died, I raised Bella . . . ' Her voice choked and she stopped.

Charlotte felt her own eyes prickle and her throat was tight, waiting.

'I will,' the old woman repeated at last. 'Whatever it costs me. You'll see. You'll eat your words.'

'Happily,' Charlotte agreed. 'Now let me go. And I'll see that whoever killed Bella hangs for it. I can do that. You can't, or he'd be dead already.'

'Why should I believe you?' Grandma Blades demanded, but her voice was shaking now, and there was a lift of hope in it.

'Because you know where I live. And you'll know if I get it done. And if I don't, you can come back any time and make me pay double for lying to you.'

'Mebbe,' the old woman nodded. 'I'll think about it.'

12

Pitt arrived early at fford Croft and Gibson.

'Good morning, Sir Thomas,' Impney said, with what Pitt would describe as well-hidden dismay. He opened the door to Pitt and invited him in. 'Is Mr fford Croft expecting you, sir?'

'Thank you,' Pitt accepted as he stepped inside. There was no time to admire the discreet, classical decor, although he was aware of the formal furnishings, the pictures of great figures from the history of jurisprudence, and the soft, neutral tones of the walls. 'I expect he knew it was inevitable at some time. But he was not expecting me this morning, specifically,' he replied.

'Then I shall go and inform him that you are here,' Impney replied, standing back for Pitt to pass him. 'Would you care for a cup of tea, sir? It would be no trouble, and take only a couple of minutes.' He looked hopeful, as if it would be something useful to do. His normally mild, unreadable face was tight with concern.

Pitt understood that this man knew both too much and too little about the misfortunes that had struck the chambers: the shocking death of Jonah Drake, the struggle to reassign his work, which required very specialised skills, and most of all the difficulty of coming to terms with the fact that it seemed the violence was not over. As for the duties carried out by Drake, Impney would naturally worry that there was now no one to perform them. Drake's expertise had been unique. Nothing regarding the business of the chambers was unknown to Impney. Was he worried that the very rewarding side of the practice that Drake managed would now slip away to other chambers eager for it?

All this was clear to Pitt. 'Thank you,' he said, accepting Impney's offer. 'If I may take tea with Mr fford Croft, that might be the best arrangement.'

'Yes, sir. If you would give me a moment, I shall tell him you are here?' It was not really a question, although it was posed as one, and Impney did not wait for an answer. He departed, leaving Pitt alone in the silent waiting room.

In less than five minutes, Impney was back and invited Pitt to follow him to Marcus's office. Pitt entered and closed the door quietly behind him.

Marcus looked rumpled and sad. He still wore a black bow tie. After all, it was not so long since Drake's death. But Pitt missed the colour in other things. Marcus's jacket was a soft grey, relatively drab without the usual purple cravat he wore with it, and somehow he looked unfinished, as if he had come unprepared for the day.

They exchanged greetings, but this time the formal words seemed just that. They could have been strangers, not friends who had known each other for over three decades. They exchanged polite phrases that had no meaning for either of them, merely filling the silence.

Impney brought in the tea and left the room.

251

Marcus poured it and passed Pitt a cup, then finally met his gaze.

'I assume you are here about the Drake business?' Now he was meeting Pitt's eyes fully, his face a pasty white.

Pitt took the cup and put it on the edge of the desk. 'I can't avoid it any longer, Marcus,' he admitted. 'The Home Office has told me, more or less ordered me, not to look into it. Why is that? What is there that Drake found out that they are so afraid of? And don't tell me that you don't know. You may be forgetting the odd dates here and there. You may be absent-minded. You will certainly have forgotten many of the people you used to know, because they're not part of your life any more. But you won't forget the things that matter.'

'How do you know that?' Marcus said. 'I'm twenty years older than you.'

'More like fifteen,' Pitt corrected him. 'And don't try to evade the point. I'm staying here until I know as much about Drake as you do.'

'Stay and finish your tea, at least,' Marcus said, with a hint of his old smile. 'Which will take far longer. It's hot. Don't scald yourself.'

Pitt smiled back. 'What was Drake doing in Mile End?'

'I don't know . . . '

'You can guess, Marcus. Don't tell me you haven't thought about it. Of course you have. Was it moneylenders, as Hobson was told?'

Marcus lifted his head a little and looked straight at him. 'What has it to do with you, Thomas? Hardly Special Branch stuff, the brothels and opium dens of the East End? Or moneylenders. Your job is spies and anarchists, traitors. Drake wasn't after traitors, and he certainly wasn't one himself.'

'What about corrupt policemen turning a blind eye for a suitable payment?' Pitt suggested. This was painful, but it was also impossible to avoid any longer.

Marcus froze. 'Are you suggesting that Drake was making such payments on behalf of one of the chambers' clients?'

'No. I assume I already know the answer to that,' Pitt replied, without raising his voice. 'I think he was investigating something that he feared might be of that nature. Or worse . . . '

'Worse? Such as . . . what, for heaven's sake?' But Marcus's face was white as he said it.

'Such as bribing witnesses,' Pitt answered. He hated saying it, but it was suspended in the prickling silence, whether he said it or not. 'Or probably even worse, bribing jurors.'

Marcus's eyes widened a little. 'On whose behalf? And with what?' His voice was harsh.

'I don't know, but that might answer a lot of questions about some of the brilliant victories that Drake had in court.'

'He was a brilliant lawyer,' Marcus said slowly.

'We have been investigating his cases from the present day backwards, as far as we can. Which hasn't led us anywhere conclusive. Why did Drake — a lawyer renowned for his expertise in fraud and embezzlement, not homicide — defend Evan Faber? It was an excellent case for you, and certainly you could all but name your own price. But why did Faber ask you? Or did he go directly to Drake? And if so, why? It doesn't add up, Marcus, unless there's something at the heart of this that we don't understand.'

Marcus stared at him unwaveringly now. 'I assumed it was because Drake was the best they could find, in the circumstances.' He was defensive. The tone of his voice had changed. 'Are you saying young Faber was guilty? He wouldn't be the first guilty man we've represented. Everyone is entitled to the best defence they can afford, Thomas.'

Pitt hesitated for a moment. This was more adversarial than he had intended. 'Are you thinking Drake found out afterwards that young Faber was actually guilty?' he asked.

Marcus shook his head. 'He could have been wrong. But I think he actually liked the boy.'

'Do you think young Faber killed Marie Wesley?' Pitt pressed. 'And Drake knew that he was guilty?'

Marcus's face screwed up in revulsion. 'That's ridiculous. I don't know why you're even suggesting it.' After a moment, he added crossly, 'What have you really come here for?'

Pitt waited a moment before responding. He needed to shift the tone before Marcus became so frustrated or angry that he threw Pitt out of his office! 'I was wondering if Drake was still following the Wesley case,' Pitt finally said. 'And then, in his scrutiny of it, realised who killed her. Considering the guest list of that party, it could have been someone with a great deal of money and influence. Enough to get rid of Drake, and then young Faber, by paying Bella Blades to do it and wipe away all traces. And then get rid of her, too.'

'Damn it to hell!' Marcus exclaimed. 'If you're talking about Erasmus Faber, that's nonsense. You're treading on hazardous ground, Thomas. He's a very dangerous man.' He had an expression of disgust. 'Leave him alone, and let the police prosecute this, if they have the evidence. Which I doubt.'

Pitt leaned forward a little across the desk. 'The police are very unlikely to do it. I have no proof that Letterman is corrupt. But if he's in this person's pay, he would warn him . . . or worse. And I think you know that. That would be a good reason why these crimes are happening on his patch. Haven't you wondered about that, too?'

'Have you spoken to Erasmus Faber about this?' Marcus sidestepped the question.

'I've seen him. A very powerful man,' Pitt answered. 'And dangerous, I agree. I've been told by the Home Office not to dig too deeply. Not to disturb him. And I have a strong feeling they also don't wish me to find anything that could indicate his guilt.'

Marcus did not actually move, but he seemed to shrink in his seat. 'Is all this an oblique way of warning me that if I've got anything to hide, I had better get it out of the way first?' A new and terrible thought was clearly dawning in his mind.

'Yes,' Pitt answered. 'If you are involved in any way, other than as Drake's senior partner, it's time to get everything settled that you can. I can't leave you out of this one, Marcus, and you know that. This time, it's the murder of a young woman, then of Drake, then Evan Faber, and probably of this girl, Bella Blades. Whoever is responsible appears to have a licence to do anything he wants. It sets him above the law.'

Marcus shook his head slowly. 'That's appalling. But you have no proof of it. I'm not even sure I understand . . . ' He leaned back in his chair, as if defeated. 'Are you saying I should look through all the notes again? I really didn't think Drake was crooked, or greedy, for that matter. He was an odd man, a bit sharp sometimes, but I understood him. Known him since university. I really did think he was honest. And I still do. I used to be a good judge of character, Thomas.'

'I think you still are.'

'Don't patronise me!' A flash of temper crossed Marcus's face.

'I'm not!' Pitt denied. 'Your judgement of people is fine. Or should I say, your judgement of men. I'm not so certain about your judgement of women. I think you underestimate them, which is odd because your daughter is one of the brightest and bravest people I've ever seen.'

'You don't even know her!' Marcus snapped.

'No, but Daniel does,' Pitt pointed out.

Marcus's face relaxed into a smile. 'Ha! Yes.'

Pitt drank most of his tea, then put his cup down and started again. 'Do you think Drake could have found out who really killed Marie Wesley, and paid for that with his life?'

Marcus brightened a little. 'Yes, I do. But he

didn't tell me, and I can't find any mention of it in his papers, and neither can Daniel or Kitteridge. And believe me, they've looked.'

'Would Drake have told Erasmus Faber, perhaps? Even sold him the information?'

Marcus remained silent for several minutes.

Pitt waited, without interrupting the man's thoughts.

Finally, Marcus raised his eyes. 'Yes, I think he might have meant to, but was killed before he could.' He hesitated, looking more and more unhappy.

Pitt felt a deep well of pity for him. They had known each other a long time, and the affection was deep, also the respect. But this was something he could not let go. And if Marcus or his chambers were involved, the only way Pitt could help was by uncovering the truth.

'You think Letterman is in the pay of whoever this man is?' Marcus asked. 'And Erasmus Faber may have been party to Drake's enquiries into the man's identity?'

'It's possible,' Pitt agreed.

'Then don't go to see Faber alone, Thomas. Take someone with you.'

'It's hardly the sort of thing I want my juniors to know,' Pitt told him. 'If Drake was going to tell Faber, so that he could exact his own justice, the man — whoever he is — has already killed Faber's son. Who knows what he will do next?'

Marcus was right. But Pitt wanted the man. He wanted to follow the trail, because this man had paid someone to kill, several times, and without hesitation. First Marie Wesley, then

257

Jonah Drake, then almost certainly Evan Faber, and maybe the girl Bella. Had he committed that last murder because, in some way, she had threatened him? She must have known something, perhaps could even identify him as the origin of all the crimes. If only they could unlock the puzzle, he was certain they would find all of these murders tied together.

'I'll go publicly, and in broad daylight,' Pitt continued. 'I'm going to stop this . . . creature. I don't care if his father is a belted earl! He'll kill again, if somebody crosses him. And sooner or later, someone is bound to.'

'I suppose you're right,' Marcus said grudgingly. 'But be careful, Thomas! Wish I could come with you, but I'd be a liability.' There was a great sorrow in his voice, even pain.

'I promise I'll take someone,' Pitt replied, and he met Marcus's eyes long enough for him to know that he meant it. He started to rise to his feet.

'Thomas!' Marcus said abruptly.

Pitt sat back in the chair. 'What?'

'I find that there are . . . discrepancies . . . in the books. I'm trying to sort it out, but I'm not good at it. I've got copies of everything. Took me a long time to make them, but this way, nobody can change the records. Now young Hobson's looking into it. Clever with figures, and knew Drake's mind and the way it worked. If it is . . . if it is as it looks, and somebody has been moving stuff around to hide missing money, payments to juries or witnesses, or anybody else, I'll . . . well, I don't know what I'll do.' His voice caught in his throat and for a moment or two he could not control it. 'It'll end the chambers,' he whispered. '*I'll* end it. There's nothing else I can do! But I didn't do it, I swear to you! It's . . . ' He could not go on, but sat staring at the sheet of blotting paper in front of him, tears running down his cheeks.

Pitt longed for something to say to comfort him, but the words eluded him. Finally, he asked, 'This young Hobson, would he tell you the truth?' There was no comfort in asking, but he had to.

Marcus looked up. 'Oh, yes,' he said, with conviction. 'His entire future in the law depends on it, not to mention his inheritance from Drake . . . ' He paused a moment. 'I still can't believe Drake was crooked, Thomas. He didn't care about money, he cared about the law, and winning the right way, using the law, not cheating. He despised a cheat. But I'll get Kitteridge to check. And don't worry, I'll not cheat. I won't leave Miriam that legacy, I promise you.'

'You don't need to promise me, Marcus, I believe you,' Pitt said quietly, hoping to heaven it was true.

★　★　★

Pitt's plans to see Faber were prevented by a summons to report to MacPherson at the Home Office. It was delivered by a uniformed chauffeur, who had the car waiting for him. He had passed it on the way in, without taking any

259

notice, too much absorbed in his own thoughts to observe.

'If you please, sir,' the man said politely. 'It is important that you come as soon as possible.' He did not explain himself any further. That it was a summons from Sir James MacPherson was sufficient.

Pitt obeyed. He had no choice. He should have expected it — indeed, he had — but not so soon.

He rode in silence. As soon as he arrived, he alighted, thanked the driver, and went straight inside the familiar building. MacPherson saw him almost immediately. He wondered if this was intended to create the delusion of importance. He smiled grimly to himself, but made certain his demeanour was appropriately reserved when he was shown into MacPherson's office.

The head of the Home Office dispensed with all formalities. He was standing, not as if he were receiving a junior, but an equal. And from the cast of his expression, not a friend. 'Good morning, Pitt. Except that it's not. I thought I made it quite plain to you that you were to leave Faber alone. What was it about that instruction that you did not understand? You're not a fool. Good God, man, we are in a very dangerous position. You see enough anarchists, bombers, spies around. They're not all damn Fenians wanting Irish secession. A good many of them are European socialists wanting general anarchy. But behind it all is the threat of naval war! Can't you add two and two, and get four, man? What's

260

the matter with you?' There was not only anger in his voice, but an edge, if not of fear, at the very least of deep anxiety.

Pitt smothered his own anger with difficulty. He could not afford to lose his temper with a man who was his superior, even if indirectly. That would mean he had lost control of himself, and of the argument.

'We are dealing with four murders, sir,' he said, slowly and distinctly. 'We must — '

MacPherson cut across him. 'The man has lost his only son. He wants to grieve in peace, get lost in his work! Which is our work, and don't you forget that! Do you really think that poking around in his private life is going to do anything but expose him to gossip — ?'

'Sir, I . . . ' Pitt began.

'Don't interrupt me, damn it!' MacPherson's face was growing redder. 'Do you have the faintest idea who the murderer was? No, of course you haven't. Some street robber, or maybe two. Have you no sense of proportion? You are ripping the man's reputation apart to further a case you'll never finish. Bury the poor young man in peace and walk away from this.'

'Is that an order, sir?' Pitt asked.

'Yes, it is! I can't make it any plainer.'

'Do I let one murder go, or two, or three?'

'Are you trying to be offensive, Pitt.'

'We have four murders now,' Pitt replied. 'Tell me what number is too many?'

'The two female victims were little better than street women, for God's sake! Are you really suggesting that we endanger the country's safety

261

over the murder of a couple of whores?'

'Of course not,' Pitt said sarcastically. 'We've got plenty to spare. But fewer really good lawyers, like Drake. And Faber had only the one son . . .'

MacPherson's face was red with frustration. 'Exactly. Let him mourn the boy in decency. He says the boy wasn't killed in Mile End. Leave it at that.'

'And the police accommodated him in that lie, for his reputation's sake,' Pitt went on. 'Is that acceptable, too?'

MacPherson stood motionless. His hands tightened into fists at his sides. 'Yes, it is, Pitt. For heaven's sake, get a sense of proportion!'

Pitt knew it was a dangerous, foolish thing to say, but the words were out before he regained control of himself. 'Proportion? Between one murder and four? Or between whose death matters, and whose doesn't?'

MacPherson breathed in and out slowly, his hands still shaking.

Pitt went on while he still could. He needed to say it all. He might never have another chance. 'Or perhaps, more importantly, ignoring the line between when we can still stop it, or when it gets too far, and we can't. As long as Faber is building ships we want so badly, we'll cover up murder for him? Or when we've done that, and he asks for a peerage, a seat in the House of Lords, or maybe a position in the government? Or in the cabinet? At what point do you say no? I'm interested in your opinion on that. Mine is that you bring him to a halt while you still can.'

MacPherson started to speak, then stopped.

'When he has his seat in the government, that will be too late,' Pitt said. 'I surmise it might already be too late. Four murders, and we're being polite, because we think they are people who don't matter, who are dispensable.'

MacPherson's eyebrows shot up. 'Are you suggesting Faber was responsible for the death of his own son? That he was 'dispensable'? You've taken leave of your senses!'

'I don't know. But you're going to make sure I don't find out, in case it proves to be someone paid by him. Are you going to let him take his own revenge? I imagine he will. Don't you?'

'No, I do not!' MacPherson snapped.

'You think he'll let it go?' Pitt said incredulously. 'Would you?'

'My son's got nothing to do with this!' MacPherson said angrily.

'And that would make all the difference, of course.' Pitt knew it was too late to hold his tongue now. 'Your son being a young man who doesn't attend parties where a little too much is drunk, and there are women of pleasure, or . . . '

'My son knows where to draw the line,' MacPherson said, and then perhaps realised that such a statement was absurd and pinched his lips together.

'Most young men don't even know where the line is,' Pitt finished for him. 'But men our age ought to. My line is at one murder.'

'Young Faber didn't kill the woman,' MacPherson responded.

'No, I don't believe he did. I think Drake

263

proved that. And he might well have been on the trail of whoever did. It cost him his life. Isn't that enough?'

'You are out of order, Pitt. You're in Narraway's mould, aren't you! He had your job before you and lost it. You are heading the same way.'

'He ended in the House of Lords,' Pitt pointed out. 'And did a lot of good there. Perhaps because he was innocent of the things he was accused of, and you know it. Or, on the other hand, because he knew a great deal of secrets about a lot of people, and kept them.'

MacPherson looked at him with intense dislike. 'Is that a threat, Pitt?'

'It's a warning, Sir James. I know nothing to your discredit, nor would I repeat it if I did. But as we both know, Faber is a dangerous man. If you give him a hold over you, he will use it if it suits him. And I can't help you, neither can anyone else. And I won't protect him, if I discover anything about him that is relevant to these murders.'

'Brave words, Pitt. But you're a fool. Be careful. I can't and won't help you. Now get out.'

'Yes, Sir James. Good morning.' Pitt turned and walked out of the room. In spite of his defiant words, he was shaking when he reached the corridor and started down the marble balustraded staircase.

13

Daniel stood in Kitteridge's office, too tense to be able to sit down. The murder of Belinda May Blades, Bella, had shaken him badly.

'Why?' he demanded, as if Kitteridge could come up with an answer. He did not seriously believe that he could, but he was frightened. Everything seemed to be closing in, not from one direction, but from all sides. What was the connection? What did all the deaths have in common? Marie Wesley, then Drake, Evan Faber, and lastly Bella. Marie was beaten. All the others were knifed. 'What's the thread?' he demanded of Kitteridge. 'What makes sense . . . ?'

'The relationship of Marie to Evan is obvious,' Kitteridge replied, his patience stretched thin. He was pale, and there was a rough edge to his voice. He sat in his chair behind his desk, but there was no comfort in the angles of his limbs. He looked up at Daniel. 'And between Evan Faber and Drake — that's obvious, too. It seems as if Drake continued with the case after the verdict. Either that, or he took it up again — '

'Why?' Daniel interrupted. 'Why did he take it up again? What changed? Who discovered something new? What was he on the brink of learning?'

Kitteridge pursed his lips, and then said, 'Drake discovered new information. We need to find out what it was. But I admit, I don't know where to look . . . '

'Was he looking for something in particular?' Daniel stopped moving restlessly from one foot to the other and sat down in the chair opposite Kitteridge. He was desperate, and he knew he was putting unfair pressure on his friend, but he had nowhere else to turn. 'Or did it come to him, either by some person, or accidentally.' He leaned on the edge of the desk. 'Did he connect things that he hadn't before? He didn't just wake up one morning with nothing to do and suddenly decide to dig into Marie's death all over again. He'd won his case. Why should he care about it?'

Kitteridge looked puzzled. His tie was working loose, his shirt was crumpled and his jacket was hanging on the chairback behind him.

Daniel needed someone else to balance his own thoughts, to think of the things he had missed, misunderstood, forgotten. Kitteridge was always slow to believe things. Daniel knew he rushed in, while Kitteridge asked questions, pondered, and took his time. It was this balance that made them a good team.

Then, suddenly, Daniel's mind was brimming with ideas. 'It mattered to him,' he said urgently. 'He wouldn't have gone to Mile End in the small hours of the morning if it weren't urgent. Wouldn't he rather have turned over and gone back to sleep? It's May, but it's cold and dark at midnight. He went after something special. His death was . . . ' He hated saying it, but it was inescapable. 'It was vicious. He wasn't robbed by

266

chance, and then killed because he fought back.'

'Can you be sure?' pressed Kitteridge.

'Yes,' he said. 'I saw Drake's body, when I thought at first it was you. I saw that damn coat on the hanger, and I really thought it had to be — '

'Well, it wasn't, thank God!' Kitteridge interrupted. 'But it's no less a crime, all the same. And we knew Drake. He was a funny old bird, but I've learned about another side of him from reading his papers. When he got a clue, he was like a terrier at a rabbit hole. And he had one — a clue, that is — when he went back to Mile End in the middle of the night. He knew something about the Faber case, and he wasn't going to be shaken from it till he'd unravelled the whole lot of it, to the very last knot.'

'And was the last knot of it a noose?' Daniel asked, with a bitter note.

Kitteridge took a deep breath and let it out in a sigh. 'Did he know the truth of who killed Marie Wesley? Or perhaps the real reason why? What did she know, or what was she going to do, that was unbearable to someone? Perhaps destructive to . . . what? Money? Reputation? Life?'

Daniel stared into the distance. 'I don't think I understood it at all, in the beginning,' he said. 'Could I have been wrong about Evan? Was he guilty? He seemed so . . . ' He remembered their trip down the Thames. They had been a trifle tipsy, but not really drunk. Evan had seemed so . . . open, and in a way almost naïve. Daniel had honestly liked him. And he understood what it

267

was to have a father you believed you could never live up to. Thomas Pitt was, in his own way, one of the most powerful men in London, or even all of England. It had nothing to do with money, and it was probable that very few people knew who he really was, and what it meant to be in his position. But he knew the secrets of the most influential people in the country — their land, their money, their mistakes. It was part of his job. And that meant he had enemies. Perhaps the only thing that kept him safe was that his successor would know exactly the same secrets, inherited from Pitt, just as Pitt had inherited them years ago from Victor Narraway.

Evan Faber understood what that was like, the length of the shadow cast by such a father. He would never live up to Erasmus Faber, just as Daniel would never live up to Thomas Pitt. Could Toby Kitteridge understand that? Or was his heritage too different?

Now Evan was dead. 'He seemed so innocent,' Daniel finished the thought aloud. 'I believed him.' He found his throat choked with the effort not to let the overwhelming sense of loss get out of control. First for Drake. Then Evan. And now Bella, who had laughed so easily.

'So did Drake,' Kitteridge responded. 'He believed him, too. But when I was going through his papers, I couldn't find what it was that took him to Mile End.' He looked suddenly very alone, sitting crumpled in his chair, arms and legs too long to know where to put them.

'There's got to be a clue,' Daniel insisted. 'Let's look at his notes from the day before. Is that when he decided to go to Mile End? That day? Or in the middle of the night? He found something, someone said something, and this changed his mind. We need to know what that was.'

Kitteridge frowned, sitting up a little straighter. 'Perhaps we're on the wrong track. Maybe Drake wasn't actually looking for it, but stumbled across whatever it was.'

'Such as . . . what?' Daniel tried to concentrate, but his mind was suddenly filled with the memory of Bella's face, her laughter. Then the thought struck him. 'You mean a connection that didn't make sense? Or one that suddenly did? Pointing to who might have really killed Marie Wesley? The police didn't seem to look very far into that, did they?'

'Lots of powerful people,' Kitteridge replied. 'But it didn't deter them from picking on Erasmus Faber's son! He's got money to burn. Far more than most aristocrats, I should think.'

Daniel gave a slight smile. 'It isn't about money. All sorts of people can get money, earn it, steal it, make it. But it's birth that counts. Better to pick on Faber's son than the son of some earl or marquess. Or higher still, some duke's son.'

'Would the police cover up the involvement of a titled family?' Kitteridge frowned. 'No love lost there, for most of them.'

'It isn't love, Toby, it's money — 'old' money that brings with it influence and status. Knowing on which side your bread is buttered. Underneath, we are all the same, but put the right clothes on and it makes all the difference, believe me!'

'So, someone fitted up Evan Faber?' Kitteridge said thoughtfully. 'And maybe Drake found evidence of it? Let's go through all his papers again, carefully. Unless you've got a better idea.'

'I haven't,' Daniel admitted. 'We'll start from the day Drake died and go backwards. The clue must be shortly before that.' He leaned forward again, trying to find somewhere comfortable to put his knees. 'We'll get Hobson to help. I don't care what else he's doing; it will have to wait. We should only have to dedicate a few days. Come on.' Daniel stood up a little awkwardly and went straight to the door, certain that Kitteridge would follow him.

'It might not be anything to do with Mile End,' Kitteridge pointed out as soon as they sat down again, now in Drake's old office.

They had sent for Hobson, and he soon joined them, looking cold and unhappy. This mixture of emotions was clear in his face. 'What would someone like Evan Faber have to do with that part of the city, sir?' he asked respectfully, looking at Daniel.

'We don't know,' Daniel admitted. 'Only that he was killed somewhere else and then moved there. But for now, we are looking for whatever took Drake to Anthony Street, whoever it connects with. Why did he go there, and in the middle of the night? It had something to do with whoever killed Marie Wesley. We've got no answers. At least, not yet.'

The three men passed considerable time going through Drake's files. Every paper was checked, including scraps with notes scrawled on them. They did this in silence, all of them fully focused on discovering something, anything.

It was nearly an hour before anyone spoke, and it was Hobson. He held up two pieces of paper. 'Could this mean something?' he asked tentatively. 'They were mixed in with the financial papers.'

Daniel took the smaller item from him. It was a scruffy piece of paper, creased, as if it had been crumpled up to throw away and then rescued and straightened out again. On it was a very detailed and deftly drawn picture of a locket set with precious stones.

'What is it?' Kitteridge asked. 'Why would Drake keep it?'

Daniel looked at it more closely. He turned it over and saw the printing. 'It looks like a pawnbroker's ticket of some sort. So the locket is old. I mean, it has belonged to someone already.'

'Stolen jewellery? So how does that help us?' Kitteridge could not hide his disappointment, and he was too weary to try. 'It could be anything! And clearly Drake threw it away, and then rescued it.'

'The chain is broken,' Daniel observed, studying the drawing. It was so well crafted that even the smallest elements of the necklace were revealed. 'I mean, really broken, snapped. You can see where one of the gold links in the chain was wrenched so hard it lost its shape. And the one at the other end is broken altogether.' A very ugly pattern was forming in his head. 'Maybe it was torn from somebody's neck.'

Kitteridge frowned. 'It would leave a devil of a scar. Gold is soft, compared with some metals, but it's still damned hard compared with human skin.'

'So . . . taken violently,' Daniel concluded. 'The biggest question is, why did Drake have this picture? Who brought it to him?' He turned to Hobson. 'Is this Drake's drawing, do you think? Could he draw this well? This precisely? It's not a cartoon, it's an exact copy. And why would he? Around this time, did he have a case concerning stolen jewellery?'

'I'm sure that drawing of the necklace belongs to the Marie Wesley case,' said Hobson. He pointed to the corner of the picture. 'And that squiggly little mark there,' said Hobson, clearly nervous at his own temerity. 'That's his signature for drawings, handwritten notes, and so on. He was clever with the pencil.'

Daniel put the drawing on the desk, picked up the second one, and studied it closely.

'What is it?' Kitteridge asked.

'Maybe a man stabbing a woman in the neck? I'm not sure . . . '

Upon peering at it more closely, he changed his mind. 'No, wait.'

The lines of the weapon were sharply tapered at the woman's neck, and then broadening as the blade extended towards the hand of the attacker. But no one would hold a knife in that fashion. Examined more closely, it was not a knife at all. The large man was gripping a chain of some sort, a chain that was round the neck of the woman on the floor. And the drawing of that man ripping off the necklace had been done by Drake.

Daniel looked at Hobson, and then Kitteridge. 'This necklace was torn off the neck of Marie Wesley? Is that what Drake thought, or at least considered? And the pawnbroker would be able to tell him who brought it to him?'

'The man who killed Marie Wesley?' Kitteridge asked. 'It's a bit of a stretch.'

Daniel studied the drawing. 'It's an unusual necklace,' he said. 'It could be identified. It only takes a little legwork: the pawnbroker, the necklace, and who owned it. If it was Marie Wesley, we've got our first solid clue. If it wasn't, why did Drake care about it?' Daniel turned to Hobson. 'You've got a good eye,' he said. 'I never thought to look in those papers. Drake was so meticulous, it never occurred to me that documents might have been misplaced.'

Hobson was clearly pleased.

Kitteridge looked from Daniel to Hobson, and back again.

'We have to grant that these drawings probably had to do with Marie's death.'

'Maybe the police followed this lead, and it was what led them to Evan Faber,' Daniel suggested, tapping the drawing of the necklace. 'If this is real, it's an expensive piece of jewellery. We've got to follow it. We need to be certain. We're looking for someone who saw Marie quite often, even knew she was wearing it that night. If they recognise it, we'll be taking a major step forward.' He looked at Kitteridge, then at Hobson. He was not as sure of himself as he had been. There was too much that had gone badly wrong. Three people he had known, even if only slightly, had been murdered: Drake, who had worked in the same offices, day after day, even year after year; Evan, with whom he had shared all kinds of private dreams, and old memories; and Bella Blades, with whom he had joked and laughed only days before she was killed. And still he had very little idea who had done it, or even why. It left him painfully hollow inside.

'Robbery?' Hobson said, clearly. 'Is it that valuable? To beat a woman to death for it?' He looked profoundly unhappy.

'I don't know,' Kitteridge admitted. 'But I don't think robbery was necessarily the motive. Would it mean so much to her that she would sacrifice her life to keep it?'

'If not robbery, then what?' Hobson asked.

'She was beaten to death,' Daniel said very quietly. His whole body ached as his imagination drew it for him: the pain, the fear, the hatred that was beyond reason. Perhaps the murderer took it because, in a way, it identified him somehow. 'It's an unusual piece, and expensive. Not the gift of a poor man, unless it was stolen.' He looked at Kitteridge. 'Can we find out?'

'Probably,' Kitteridge said, nodding his head. 'But it won't prove much.'

Daniel looked at the drawing again, then back at Kitteridge. 'Can we find out if she wore it that night? And then if it was found on her body . . . or not.'

'Prove it was stolen?' Hobson said, frowning. 'I mean, when she was killed?'

'It would help,' Daniel said.

'Would you get anything like its value, when it's tied to a famous murder?'

'Probably not,' Kitteridge agreed. 'He took it because it could identify him.' He winced. 'Or perhaps it was some kind of ghoulish trophy?'

'That sounds like somebody who kills with premeditation, and more than once,' Hobson said, and then blushed selfconsciously for his impertinence.

Daniel was racing through so many thoughts as he spoke. 'She was killed in a rage. He tore it off her neck after he beat her to death. There is more ungoverned passion than we thought in this.'

'What a damnable mess,' Kitteridge said quietly. 'We can't afford to ignore this. I'll take care of it.'

'There's another thing,' Daniel said in a low voice. 'Who killed Evan? And was he killed because he knew who gave Marie that necklace, or might have guessed who did? Maybe his death had nothing to do with Mile End?'

'Why didn't the police deal with that?' Hobson asked. 'Aren't we just following in their footsteps?' He looked worried and unhappy.

'Yes, we are,' Daniel admitted. 'But that's the only way we can find out if they extracted every piece of evidence that was possible. They arrested and charged the wrong man, for a start.'

Hobson looked miserable. 'Are we sure of that, sir?'

'I'm honestly not. But what would you rather do? What else is there to follow up?' Daniel asked.

'I don't know, sir. I really would like to catch whoever killed Mr Drake.' The young man lifted his chin a bit higher. 'He was a trifle odd, sometimes, but he was a good man.' Hobson's voice was thick with tears. 'It's not right that he was slashed so viciously — ' He stopped abruptly, as if overcome by the horror of it.

Daniel put his hand lightly on Hobson's shoulder. 'No, it's not right,' he agreed.

Hobson nodded. It seemed to Daniel that he wanted to say something, but that his throat was too tight to speak.

14

It was still broad daylight when Thomas Pitt reached home, although it was six o'clock in the evening. It would be the first day of June tomorrow, and summer would officially begin.

He walked up the short path to the front door, hardly aware of the flowers in bloom. The blues and yellows of spring were over and now it was mostly brilliant splashy freesias. He put his key in the door and pushed it open.

Charlotte would hear it and come out to meet him. She always did. Perhaps that was what coming home really meant? Not the long-familiar house, but Charlotte coming to meet him.

'Hello,' he called out.

There was a momentary pause, then footsteps in the hall: rapid, not Charlotte's step. Minnie Maude came hurrying in, her face filled with consternation.

'Sir, it's you . . . ' she gasped.

'What's wrong?' he asked, touched by a sudden, absurd fear. 'Has something happened?'

She was flushed and clearly frightened.

'I don't know, sir. But Lady Pitt went out for a walk this morning and I ain't seen her since. I don't like to call Miss Emily and see if she's there. It in't really my place, but it in't like her to go without telling Cook and me . . . ' She stopped, as if afraid she had overstepped her authority.

'This morning?' he asked, puzzled. 'And she didn't say when she'd be back?'

'No, sir . . .'

'She said . . . nothing?'

Minnie Maude shook her head. 'No, sir . . .' She spoke as if she were already afraid she had done something wrong.

Pitt thought he must tell Charlotte to make sure she informed at least one of the staff if she meant to change her plans. If she called, would they answer the telephone? He glanced at the instrument on its hook on the wall. 'Anyone call?'

'No, sir . . .'

'I'll call Mrs Radley,' he said, referring to Charlotte's sister.

'Yes, sir.' But she did not leave. It seemed to Pitt that she was really more worried than she had said.

He picked up the instrument and waited to give Emily's number to the woman at the exchange. After a few moments, it rang. One of Emily's servants picked it up and took the message. Emily was quick to respond. 'Thomas? Are you all right?'

'Is Charlotte with you?' he asked. 'She went out this morning but forgot to tell anyone where she was going, and the servants are concerned.'

'No,' Emily replied. 'I haven't seen her for . . . oh . . . ten days? Is something wrong, Thomas?'

'She isn't home. She went out for a walk and

278

hasn't returned. The servants don't know where she is . . . '

'That's unlike her . . . ' Emily seemed at a loss for the appropriate words. Already she sounded anxious.

Pitt's assurances to Minnie Maude no longer worked to allay his own concern. Where could Charlotte be at this hour? Could she have gone to see Daniel? Why would she, during his own working hours? She had not been there when he had seen Marcus, only a few hours ago.

He would call fford Croft and Gibson. Impney might still be there. Perhaps he could tell Pitt something.

'Certainly, sir,' Impney replied. 'Mister Pitt is still here. Would you like to speak to him, sir?'

'Yes, please,' Pitt replied.

A few moments later, Daniel was on the other end of the telephone. 'Yes? Are you all right?'

'Have you seen your mother today?' Pitt asked, trying to keep his voice level.

'No . . . what's wrong?' Daniel's voice had changed, as if he had picked up his father's anxiety. As if he could see him and read it in his eyes.

'Nothing,' Pitt lied. 'She's just gone out and forgotten to tell anyone where.'

'Oh. You're not worried, are you?'

'No. I just wasn't going to start dinner without her.'

'I see . . . '

'Don't worry. She's just a bit late . . . that's all.' Pitt hung up the telephone, determined not to frighten Daniel unnecessarily. Part of him

279

expected Charlotte to walk through the door at any moment. Or telephone him, at least. Another part of him pictured her lying in a hospital, unconscious or not able to tell them who she was. He refused to acknowledge the tiny sliver of imagination that things were worse than that. Blood, body lying somewhere like Mile End, where it would barely be noticed. Except that the quality of her clothes would mark her as different from the local residents, even at a glance.

He felt so helpless! He was head of Special Branch. His wife was late home for dinner, and he was already panicking inside, imagining all sorts of things. He would look absurd if he called the local police station. That would be awkward for her, particularly if she were visiting a friend, perhaps someone who was in distress of some sort, and she could help. If he started calling around, asking people if they had seen her, she would be embarrassed. He was being hysterical.

He told Minnie Maude to hold dinner till Charlotte came home. He had been hungry, but that had vanished. In fact, his stomach felt like a hard knot under his ribs.

He decided to sit and read, but after going over the words of a paragraph four times and finding his mind unable to absorb them, he gave up. Where had she gone? Why had she not at least contacted him? Was she unable to contact him? Or did she not want to? He tried to think of the last thing she had said to him. Was she angry? Worried? Had she said something he had not heard, not understood?

The telephone rang once. He lunged for it, but it was only Emily to ask if Charlotte had returned yet.

The silence grew heavy. It was still daylight, but then it probably would be until at least nine o'clock.

As time went on, Pitt wavered between images of all the terrible things that could have happened to Charlotte and telling himself he was being ridiculous. Here he was, sitting comfortably by his own hearth, even though the fire was unlit, and panicking inside. He wracked his brains for some forgotten detail that might explain his wife's absence, but nothing seemed out of the ordinary. How easy it was to take happiness for granted.

The front doorbell rang. Before he could stand up to answer it, he heard Minnie Maude's feet clattering along the hall as she ran to open the door.

There were voices, and a moment later Daniel came into the sitting room. He looked a little dishevelled. His hair had fallen over his forehead, as it so often did, but he had not bothered to push it back, and his face was flushed. 'Is she not back yet?' The question was not necessary. Daniel read his father's face immediately. 'Have you heard anything? Who have you asked?'

'Only you and Emily,' Pitt replied. Was he sitting here, paralysed, while Charlotte was helpless somewhere, hurt? Or worse? He saw the answering fear in Daniel's face. He should have expected it. Daniel had seen the bloody bodies of people he had known, too many of them in the

281

last two weeks. But this was different. Daniel had known his mother's love and depended on the certainty of it for the whole of his life. As for Pitt, he had not been without Charlotte's love for as far back as he could remember. They had had their disagreements, of course. Everyone did, if they were honest. But had he been so absorbed in his work that he had missed something that really mattered? Had he taken her for granted? Wouldn't she have said something? She must know how much he cared . . . loved her . . . how she was the centre of everything in his life that was good, generous, funny, wise.

Pitt made an effort to calm his voice, even to smile. 'She'll be all right,' he said hoarsely, and cleared his throat. 'She's probably helping someone who's in distress, and never realised we would worry.'

Daniel relaxed a little. 'I expect so. Someone who hasn't got a phone, which is just about everyone. Let's . . . No, I don't . . . '

'What?' Pitt asked, too quickly. And then the alarm on his face intensified. 'Daniel, we need to act. I'll stay here, in case your mother calls, or . . . ' He nearly added *the police*, or *a hospital*, but even saying those words might make it come true. 'You need to look for her! Check along the streets, knock on neighbours' doors! No side streets. The main ones, especially those leading to the avenues. Maybe she fell!' Before Daniel could speak one word, he added, 'Now! Go!' He watched as Daniel rushed out of the house and then stood on the pavement. He looked up and down the street, as if trying to decide which direction his mother would have taken.

Pitt sat near the phone, begging for it to ring.

★ ★ ★

He had no idea of the passage of time. When the front door opened, he rushed into the foyer. It was Daniel, exhausted, breathing hard, despair etched in his face.

His footsteps brought Minnie Maude running from the kitchen.

'Anything?' asked Pitt.

When Daniel shook his head, all signs of hope disappeared from Pitt's face.

Minnie Maude turned and walked slowly towards the kitchen, leaving behind the sound of hushed sobbing. In a short moment, she turned and said, 'You need ter eat. I'll toast bread.'

Before the men could protest, she was gone.

'Tell me,' said Pitt. Did he want to know? Yes! His entire life was about collecting information and then using it to solve a problem. A crime. God, make this anything but a crime.

'I covered four streets,' Daniel explained. 'The ones leading to the avenues. I stopped every time there was a place where someone could fall and not be seen.'

'Alleyways, too?'

'Would Mother even go down an alleyway?' He pushed that question away with a brusque gesture. 'Then I came back to Keppel Street and knocked on doors, at least two dozen. No one has seen her.'

Pitt nodded. There were no words.

'Mother will hate this,' said Daniel. 'Informing all the neighbours that she's missing. A few of them showed real concern; others looked at me as if I were crazy.' A sardonic expression crossed his face. 'You'd think wives and mothers go missing every day around here.'

Minnie Maude called them into the kitchen. This was no time to use the dining room and make a pretence of sitting down for a normal meal.

Pitt and Daniel drew up chairs to the kitchen table and stared at the toast. They glanced at each other. The thought of eating made them both feel ill; not eating might increase the consternation of poor Minnie Maude.

They nibbled at the toast. Pitt hoped that his eating would encourage Daniel to eat. He needed something in his stomach, and he might see his father's appetite as proof that Charlotte was safe and his father wasn't terrified. She was late home. It was inconsiderate, but no worse than that. Despite his intentions, it was clear that both father and son were forcing down the food.

Pitt knew that he looked awful. Fear does that. He had glanced at his face in the hallway mirror. He looked hollow, skin grey around the eyes and mouth. With all the vitality drained from him, he looked nearer sixty than fifty. He wanted to stay strong for his son, but he was holding on to his composure by a thread.

Daniel was about to say something, but remained silent.

'What?' asked Pitt.

'Empty words,' he said. 'We both know they're

empty: *It will be all right, she will be here any moment now, she's always been all right . . . and she will be this time, too.*'

'I just don't . . . understand,' said Pitt.

Daniel nodded. 'You know Mother. If she were angry about something, or upset, she would have said so. She never keeps her feelings concealed for long.'

A little smile played on Pitt's face. 'It's infuriating, but I wouldn't change it, even if I could.' What more could he say? A chill ran through him. 'You've had enough violence . . . ' he added.

Daniel ran his father's words through his head. Violence. Yes, more in the past few weeks than perhaps in years. People did get killed, God knew. He thought of that awful day, not so long ago, when he had stood in the morgue and had seen Kitteridge's coat hanging on a peg, and then seen Drake's slashed body on the table.

Then Evan Faber, who had been so alive just a couple of nights before.

And Bella, so pretty, so eccentric, so full of ideas and decisions. He imagined her lying on a slab, her bright hair still as shining as when she had been alive. He still struggled with thoughts of that lively young woman being a killer.

He looked down at his plate and then up at his father's eyes. Was he thinking much the same thoughts, haunted by hideous possibilities? Death was as quick and as sudden as that. It could happen to anyone, any day.

The fear was growing inside him, like a hollow of coldness swelling, eating him from the inside.

'Father, we need to call the police.'

Pitt remained silent, and then said, 'I did, Daniel, and two local hospitals. And then the local police stations.'

Daniel said nothing for a long moment, and then he spoke. 'If anybody knew anything, they would have called here. She's not just anybody — she's the wife of the head of Special Branch.' Daniel knew that every police station in London knew of Pitt, even if they had not actually met him.

He looked at his father's eyes, and then away.

He could not sit still any more. He stood up. 'Didn't she say anything this morning? Anyone ill, in trouble? Was she angry about something?'

'No,' Pitt stood also. 'I've been trying to think, but she was just the same as usual. I . . . ' He stopped when Minnie Maude asked if they would like coffee. She, too, looked bewildered.

'In the drawing room, please,' Pitt told her.

They went into the drawing room and sat down. Minnie Maude brought coffee and Pitt thanked her. They drank it without tasting it.

Daniel wanted to say something, but what? He had to will himself not to keep glancing at the clock on the mantelpiece. When the front doorbell rang he jumped up and raced to the foyer, his father close behind him.

Minnie Maude was already there, flinging open the door. No one was in sight. Before she could close it, Daniel moved her aside and picked up a folded note left on the step.

'What does it say?' Pitt demanded.

Daniel opened it. 'It says, *Stop your*

286

investigation or your wife dies.'

Minnie Maude pressed her hand over her mouth, her eyes wide with fear.

Pitt walked to the phone and placed a call. His head was down as he spoke. When he was done, he made a second call, also speaking in low tones. Before Daniel could ask, he said, 'My people at Special Branch, and then one of my best men.' He walked back into the morning room, sat down hard, and buried his head in his hands.

'This must be connected with Drake's death,' Daniel said as he closed the door. 'Do you have any idea who is behind it?' He watched his father's face closely. He saw something in his eyes change colour, a shadow. 'You do,' he answered himself. 'Who?'

'Letterman,' Pitt replied slowly. 'He's rotten . . . taking bribes. I'm going to see him.'

'But you just said . . . '

'He may be dirty, but he'll do his job. He doesn't know that we know . . . '

'Bribes? Who from, in particular?'

'Probably lots of people. The commissioner is looking into it. I couldn't stop it now, even if I wanted to. And I don't.' The words were said without conviction.

'We have to do something!' Daniel found himself almost shouting. 'Face it! Someone has her!' He took a deep breath. 'The note didn't ask for money, so whatever it is they want, they think you know about it. Do you?' he demanded. 'Tell me! Never mind secrets, this is Mother's life! Are you willing to pay that price?'

Pitt met his eyes and the pain in his face was terrible. 'No,' he said quietly, 'I'm not. I think I know which case it is, and we are both involved. It's Drake . . . and I think it may be Erasmus Faber behind it. The Home Office warned me to leave it alone — at least, to leave Faber alone. And I didn't.'

'Drake?' Daniel said incredulously. 'But Bella killed Drake, and she's dead, too.'

'But who paid her to do it?' Pitt asked. 'That's the man we're after, and he knows it. I think this is a message to me — to both of us — to leave the matter unsolved. MacPherson warned me, obliquely, but it was quite clear. I told him there were four murders, and asked how many there must be before we act.' He ran his palm across his eyes. 'I . . . more or less dared him.'

Daniel felt as if he had been battered by a giant wave that had always been on the horizon, he just had not thought it would ever reach him.

'You mean Erasmus Faber took her? To stop you looking into Drake's murder, and Evan's? Why? I mean, why would he do that? What could you find out?' He struggled for an answer that made sense. 'Doesn't he want to know who killed Drake? Or if he doesn't care about him, at least who killed Evan. If someone killed me, wouldn't you move heaven and earth to find them?' He gave a sharp little shrug. 'Faber's wife and son are both dead. What could anyone possibly threaten him with?' He needed to be sharp and clear minded, but he was too frightened to think clearly. 'It makes no sense! It's got to be something else.'

'With Evan dead, he has nothing else to lose . . . ' Pitt agreed in a flat, steady voice, as if nothing mattered. Or perhaps because everything mattered, more than he could bear.

'Do you know who is behind it all?' Daniel asked.

'No,' said Pitt. 'But I think Letterman does.' His face looked grey. 'I've already told the Police Commissioner. He didn't want to believe me, and without proof, he won't.'

'You would tell me if anyone had asked a price for her, wouldn't you?'

'Of course. What they want is my silence. They don't have to spell it out any clearer.'

'Can we find a way . . . ' Daniel had been going to say to undo their investigation and what they'd set in motion, but he realised how desperate that was. Could Pitt manage to be believable, quite apart from forcing himself to construct a credible lie? But how would they get Charlotte back, otherwise? And then another, more dreadful thought struck his mind. Could the people who took her afford to let her go, if she knew who they were? Please heaven, she had enough sense to pretend she was compliant, frightened enough not to think, not to work out who they were and why she had been taken prisoner. What if she could not hide her intelligence? They would know that as soon as they let her go free, she would turn on them.

He looked at his father's face and hoped he had not considered that. But he was a policeman at heart, no matter how elevated his rank . . . that would be the first thing on his mind.

And in the same moment another thought entered his mind, and he knew that it entered his father's as well. 'If we can't do anything, who can?' he asked aloud. 'Who do we have that we can go to, to tell them? Is it Letterman who has Mother?'

'I don't know,' Pitt admitted. 'I don't think he would do it himself, even if he is in Faber's pay. And I'm not sure he is, only that he's for sale, job by job. It all goes back to Marie Wesley, and then the Drake case.'

'We've got to think. We've got to solve this.' Daniel controlled his voice with difficulty. He was going to have to take over. Pitt did not have the knowledge of the case that Daniel had. And, quite honestly, he was emotionally so wounded he could hardly think. If anything did happen to Charlotte . . . No, he was lying to himself, by evasion. If they killed his mother, his father would be so stunned that it would be impossible to guess what he might do, or even if he could do anything. Could Daniel himself? Perhaps not. He had never tasted such grief, such a sense of guilt, of complete failure. He could barely imagine . . . 'We must solve it,' he insisted aloud. 'Tonight. I've been working on it all week. We — Toby and I — we've been working backwards to the very beginning.' He looked at his father, who seemed worlds away. 'Are you listening to me?'

'Yes,' said Pitt. 'Go on.' He looked hard at Daniel, as if having to force himself to concentrate. 'Go on,' he repeated.

'It began with Marie Wesley. Someone killed

her in a rage, probably in a fit of jealousy.'

'A quarrel between Marie and a former lover?' Pitt asked. 'The present lover being Evan Faber?'

'Yes.'

'Do we have any idea who the former lover is?'

'The glimmer of an idea,' said Daniel, remembering the necklace. 'We have a piece of very good jewellery. It must have cost a lot. And according to the pawn shop owner from whom we retrieved it earlier today, who's pretty knowledgeable about jewellery, it's handmade.'

'So, have you traced it?' Pitt was interested, as if focused for the first time.

'We're working on it. Toby's been trying jewellers' workshops — '

'Then give it to me,' Pitt interrupted. 'I'll wake somebody up. We'll go to your office, or wherever the necklace is, and find out. Get Kitteridge up. Tell him what's happened, and perhaps we can learn who gave it to Marie. It's a start!'

'And you get one of your men, or all of them,' Daniel answered. 'We need help . . . '

Pitt was already on his feet and opening the door into the hall. Daniel heard his voice on the telephone, but could not make out the words.

He was gone several minutes, and when he came back he looked white-faced, but the light was back in his eyes, and there was firmness in his step. 'I spoke to Kitteridge. He'll work with my men. We'll find that necklace and who made it, if he's still alive and anywhere near London. He should be able to tell us for whom. We already know that whoever purchased it gave it to Marie Wesley.'

'It's the middle of the night!' Daniel pointed out.

'I'm Special Branch,' Pitt replied. 'Middle of the night doesn't make any difference. What else did you find? Was Evan Faber guilty? I don't care why — just was he, or was it somebody else? And if so, who?'

'I don't think it was Evan. I really don't.'

'Then why was he killed? Because he knew who did it? If so, following his actions may lead us to discover whatever he found out.'

'I don't know of any other reason,' Daniel replied. 'But I have a lot of things I don't know the answer to. And a lot of it is deduction . . . and guesswork.'

'Then we're probably looking at something from the wrong angle,' Pitt stated.

'Something important,' Daniel said, with difficulty. 'Bella was a professional killer. Three of the people connected with this were knifed: Drake, then Evan, and then Bella herself. Marie was beaten to death; that couldn't have been Bella's work.'

'Marie was first,' Pitt pointed out. 'Let's suppose that all the rest sprang from her death, and they were all done by Bella. If so, who killed her? The man who paid her? Why? To silence her?'

'Or because she rebelled,' Daniel replied.

'So, it all depends on who killed Marie Wesley. And we believe that Drake was right and that it was not Evan Faber. It was a jealous lover whom Evan replaced. At least, is that the most reasonable assumption we have? Did Drake actually discover this person's identity, and that's why he was killed? Somehow it ties in to Mile End.'

Daniel thought hard. 'Marie was discreet, according to Drake's notes, and he was very thorough. She flirted openly with many people. But, as to whose mistress she was . . . well, she kept that to herself.' He recalled the pages, and how intrusive he had felt when reading a dead man's thoughts. 'He had an odd sense of humour,' he went on. 'I have a strong feeling that there was something specific in his notes, if only I could understand them. It's like doing a jigsaw puzzle when you don't have a picture of what it's supposed to look like. In fact, worse than that, I don't know which pieces belong in the picture, and which don't.'

He tried to recall Drake's drawings precisely. There were several of them, many featuring a large figure always dominating the smaller. 'In two of the pictures,' he said, 'there was a figure that seemed literally to consume the design. I'm guessing a man, and powerful.' There was something in them that was frightening, but he kept that to himself. It was clear that Drake was conveying a message about his conclusions. Daniel looked at his father. Pitt seemed confused and desperately weary. They were both groping after some meaning to all of this, as if they knew it could be important, but couldn't quite reach it.

'Erasmus Faber?' said Pitt.

Daniel tipped his head. 'What about him?'

'He's so damned important to shipbuilding,

the Home Office won't touch him. But what if
. . . he was Marie's lover?'

'You're confusing him with Evan,' said Daniel.
He knew his father was exhausted, but he hadn't
expected confusion.

'No,' insisted Pitt, bitterness in his voice. 'I can
see the argument for protecting him from
charges of theft, or even corruption . . . but not
murder. I don't care who he is. What the hell are
we fighting for, if we condone murder
committed by a person wealthy enough, or clever
enough, to get away with it? As long as the
victim's not my family? Well, it is my family!'

'We have no proof!' Daniel said quickly,
grasping his father's arm as he began to get to
his feet. 'We can't arrest him on the basis of a
drawing made by a dead man! And there's no
point in telling the Home Office,' Daniel went
on. 'They won't believe you. You haven't got
anything but my word for it. Which won't carry
any weight at all.'

Pitt snatched his arm away from Daniel's
grasp. 'If what you say is true — and the more I
think about it, the more I think you could be
right — then these people can't afford to let your
mother go. Ever. She'll put it together . . . And if
we're wrong, there'll be hell to pay.'

The words struck Daniel like a physical blow.
It all seemed so dreadfully clear. At least it made
sense. The threat was desperately real, no room
for argument. The truth held the two of them
motionless, as if caught in a vice. 'Do you want
to go looking for her now? But where? Mile
End?'

'I don't know who's holding her,' Pitt said, his voice shaking. 'But I think I know where she is . . . ' He looked like a man about to collapse. 'We must be cautious, plan it exactly right. No slips, none at all, or they'll kill her.'

Daniel wanted to argue, but there was nothing to say. He crossed the two steps between them and put his arms round his father, and within a moment he felt the answering hug.

15

Without his wife beside him, Pitt thought nothing could make him sleep, but nightmare-filled exhaustion overcame him for at least a couple of hours. When he awoke, for the first few moments, he felt relief at casting aside the turmoil of the dream. Then he turned in the bed and saw the other half empty and rumpled, and he remembered the reality of the day, and the chaos of the troubled dreams seemed a better place than reality.

It was broad daylight, even though the bedside clock said it was six thirty. His head ached and his mouth was dry. It was too early for any of the staff to be up, but he would dress and go down to the kitchen and make himself a cup of tea, perhaps a slice of toast. He felt stiff, awkward, and unseasonably cold.

He washed, shaved and dressed automatically. He needed to look better than he felt. No one, least of all Letterman, must see his weakness. He was desperate, but he must not show it. It would be a battle of wills, and he must win. Not for the case, but for Charlotte's life. He wanted to go back to bed, wake up in a different day, but it was impossible. For Charlotte, and for Daniel, he must face it, fight, make the right judgements . . . all of them. Even one mistake could cost Charlotte's life. He could not even consider the alternative — that he would fail, no matter what he did.

He found the kitchen bare and cold, but he knew it was only in his mind. Actually, the oven was warm, the ashes inside it still smouldering from the night before. He cleaned out the old ashes and carried up the coal from the cellar to start the stove again. It gave him a brief sense of serving some purpose.

He had just relit the oven when Daniel came down. He looked like a lost and crumpled child, and the thought forced itself into Pitt's emotions: how like Charlotte he was. He had her colouring, her soft hair with the hint of auburn in it. 'Did you sleep?' he asked.

'Not much,' Daniel replied. 'Did you?' He looked worried.

Pitt realised how much Daniel still depended on family. He was twenty-five. Pitt himself had been so young at that age, so unsophisticated. He ached from the fear inside him. He must win. The alternative was unbearable. He straightened up and closed the oven door.

'Fill the kettle, please,' he asked. 'We'll have breakfast. And not leave a mess for Minnie Maude when she comes down.'

Actually, it was only twenty minutes before Minnie Maude walked into the kitchen. She knew, before asking either of them, that Charlotte had not come home. She wiped her hand across her cheek, then looked around, saw the remains of breakfast on the table: milk jug, butter, marmalade, used plates. She sniffed hard and began to clear it away. She did not ask any questions.

Pitt and Daniel both went back upstairs and prepared for the day. Daniel was going into chambers. It had been agreed that he and Kitteridge would go on working on the issues they had already begun. Pitt was going to Mile End to face Letterman.

★ ★ ★

The journey to Mile End seemed to stretch out, street after street, and yet Pitt was still there too soon. He stepped out of the car.

'Stay with the car,' he ordered the driver. He crossed the footpath and went into the police station. The desk sergeant's face froze at the sight of him.

'Good morning, sir. How can I help you?'

'I'd like to speak to Inspector Letterman — it's urgent.'

'Yes, sir. I'll see if he's available,' the sergeant replied, without moving.

'Now, please.' Pitt's voice cracked and he cursed himself for letting his tension show so easily.

'Yes, sir. I'll go and see if I can find him.' The sergeant smiled and turned away, walking easily, slowly, towards the passageway.

Pitt thought of sitting down, but he could not rest. He could almost feel the panic rising inside him.

The sergeant came back, smiling. 'He'll let me know as soon as he's free, sir.'

'And when will that be?' Pitt asked, unable to keep the edge out of his voice.

'About half an hour, sir. If you'd like to take a seat?'

Pitt sat for perhaps one minute and then started up from the bench. In a flash he was heading upstairs, his feet pounding against each wooden step and sending a rhythmic echo throughout the building.

'Sir!' the desk sergeant called out.

Pitt ignored him. Did the man really think he would wait half an hour . . . or two minutes? Charlotte's life was in jeopardy!

He reached Letterman's office and slammed the door open. The policeman was sitting behind the desk, with nothing in front of him but two sheets of paper and a pen, a pencil and a pad of blotting paper.

'Good morning, Sir Thomas,' he said, with a very slight smile. 'Sorry to keep you waiting. Busy morning.'

It was a lie, and Pitt knew the inspector intended him to know it, but he was in no state to play games, and he realised that there was no choice but to go along with whatever pace Letterman chose to set. At the moment, Letterman controlled all the moves, and it was clear he knew this. But what really threw Pitt was that Charlotte wasn't mentioned in Letterman's first words. Why? Was he toying with him, knowing he must be frantic and enjoying the power? Or was he afraid of bringing up the kidnapping — which by now every policeman in Greater London knew about — for fear he would show his hand?

'I imagine it's a difficult patch,' Pitt remarked,

keeping his voice absolutely level, when all he wanted to do was reach across the desk and grab the man by the throat.

Calm was not what Letterman had been expecting, and it showed for an instant in his face, before it was covered over with a polite polish of disinterest. 'Indeed. What can I do for you, Sir Thomas?'

Pitt hesitated only a second, or perhaps two. If he was going to bring up Charlotte's abduction, it had to be now. If only he understood this man! 'I am driven to the conclusion that our interests intersect, Inspector.' He said this unblinkingly. It was a risk, but it was fast approaching the time when any risk was worth it.

'You surprise me.' Letterman was playing for time. Indeed, he was surprised, and he needed a moment to realign his thoughts. 'In what way? What case of yours could concern Mile End? Your authority certainly exceeds mine.' He smiled.

So, the evasion would continue. Pitt was certain that this odd balance of power amused Letterman. Pitt was far superior in rank. Letterman was head man in his area, true, but Pitt was the head of Special Branch, for the entire country. As for jurisdiction, Letterman was police, while Pitt's power was very elastic and could be stretched in every direction. What united them today? Pitt was the hostage to fortune, and Letterman knew it. As painful as it was, he pushed the thought of Charlotte away and proceeded.

'I believe someone may be planning to gain

power over Erasmus Faber, the shipbuilding magnate,' said Pitt. 'And thus, over the future of shipping for the nation.' He saw something like surprise in Letterman's eyes, and at the same time a warm glow of satisfaction — brief, but quite definite. 'I'm sure you appreciate how serious that would be?' He was making it up as he went along, but he had Letterman's attention, and they both knew it.

'Of course,' Letterman nodded, the good humour entirely disappearing from his face. The careful look came back into his eyes. 'I don't know what makes you think so, but I am sure you must have indisputable grounds for such an opinion.'

'Blackmail to begin with, Inspector Letterman,' Pitt said gravely. Part of him was terrified for Charlotte's life, another part relished the play and counter play of lies, inventions and irony. 'Escalating all the way to murder. We all have things we care about, people . . .' He stared hard at Letterman, smiling very slightly. He could see that the man's mind was working furiously. He was fighting his way towards understanding, and being able to regain the mastery that he had been so sure of only a few moments ago. He was wise enough not to speak yet.

'I'm not precisely sure what the blackmail was about,' Pitt went on. 'There were many possibilities, but when you try to pressure a powerful man, when you insult him enough, anger him enough, the results are possibly out of proportion to the actual threat.'

'I have no idea what you are talking about,'

Letterman said, as if hoping to call his bluff. 'You will have to be a good deal more precise. Who is blackmailing Mr Faber? And what about, for heaven's sake? Why doesn't he just pay up? He has an enormous amount of money. He must be one of the richest men in England.' Letterman managed to look puzzled.

'Blackmail is a never-ending crime,' Pitt answered. 'Once you feed it, as soon as it's hungry again, it's on your back, licking its lips for more blood.'

Letterman shifted his position in the chair, sitting a little more upright. 'You paint a vivid picture, Sir Thomas. I see you are on to something very real, very . . . immediate. I understand, possibly far better than you know . . . ' He left the sentence, and all its weight of suggestion, hanging in the air, unfinished.

Pitt's mind raced. What did Letterman mean? He could not afford the slightest mistake. It was a battle of wits, suggestions, misunderstandings, concealed enmity.

Letterman was watching him, waiting. Any misstep now could cost Pitt everything.

'Do you?' Pitt asked. Then, before Letterman could answer, he continued. 'Are we speaking of the same people? The same issue?'

'I doubt it,' Letterman replied, not taking his eyes away from Pitt's. 'I believe you are not aware of the issue I'm referring to. I sincerely hope that that is so. I'd rather not think you are corrupt, although I have to grant the possibility. It's the most unpleasant part of my job.' He started to smile; it turned into a mere baring of the teeth. Finally, he gave up altogether.

There was no way for Pitt to evade the next question. 'Who is being blackmailed?' he asked with mild interest, as if nothing of importance rested in the answer.

'I am,' Letterman answered.

Pitt drew in a breath to ask if he were serious, then let it out without speaking. He was here to find his wife, but he was absolutely certain that bringing her into this conversation could endanger her. He must not give even the smallest indication that he believed Letterman to be involved in the abduction. The abduction, the cover-ups, everything.

Letterman waited, his eyes bright.

'And do you know by whom you are being blackmailed?' Pitt asked. 'I take it there is no doubt about over what . . . or the price?'

Letterman genuinely smiled this time. 'Not police procedure. Nothing as . . . open as corruption, forgetting evidence, blaming the wrong person. It was a severe lapse of judgement on my part, but personal, not professional. My wife was . . . distant . . . for some time. I found solace elsewhere. An unfortunate choice. My blackmailer knew and took advantage of it. Adultery is not a crime, but it is not . . . something one wants commonly known, joked about among one's men.' He inhaled and then paused. 'It began as something very small. At first, I thought that was all it would be.' He shrugged his shoulders as if he were at ease, rueful, self-deprecating. But his left hand resting on the top of his desk was rigid, his fingers so straight they would have broken before they bent.

'But of course it wasn't,' Pitt answered for him. Letterman was leading this conversation, this duel of words. Pitt would rather have had command of it, but if he were honest, he had never had the upper hand. Letterman had always been in control. It was absurd to imagine otherwise.

Letterman's smile was a drawing back of the lips from his teeth.

Pitt thought of a hungry wolf. There was no humour in this smile, none at all. But there was satisfaction.

'Of course, I never knew when the demands were coming,' Letterman added. 'Only that they would, as long as he lived. It was very carefully done, small amounts, and at irregular intervals. Only one thing was certain, that another demand would come. Maybe just for fifty pounds. But the threat was there. And I suppose the fact that I had paid before was in itself an admission of guilt. I realised that too late.' There was bitterness in Letterman's voice, but he was watching Pitt as a frog watches flies. It was all in the timing: a flick of the tongue and he would be eaten.

'You have said how much,' Pitt observed, 'but not by whom. I presume from what you have said that you know who it was.'

'Oh, yes,' Letterman said. 'I even considered bringing the proof to someone: my seniors, perhaps.' He looked down at his desk for a moment, and then up at Pitt, meeting his eyes with a brilliant victory stare. 'But I always put it off. You have given me the chance to expose him, and the desire to . . . ' He waited.

'Why to me?' The minute the words were out of his mouth, Pitt could see that this was exactly what Letterman wanted him to say. He had followed, like a dog responding to his master's voice. He could have kicked himself. But he must play the cards as he had chosen. He waited now for the answer.

'Because you can act,' Letterman replied. 'And you will; you have to.'

Was this it? Was this when Letterman would bring up Charlotte, and what Pitt would have to do, in order to get her safely home? He waited.

A flicker of anger crossed Letterman's face that he was being forced to divulge the information at Pitt's silent command, instead of delivering it up reluctantly, at the man's begging. 'Marcus fford Croft,' he said between his teeth.

Pitt tried to keep the shock out of his face, and knew he had failed. Could it be true? Was that what Drake had found out, and Marcus had feared? Had Drake been killed for that?

He knew Letterman was watching him, but he was still absorbing the horror of it. Had Marcus really been bleeding Letterman slowly over the years . . . because he could? One act of weakness, the betrayal of his wife, and Marcus had seen the opening and inserted a wedge that he had been pushing for years. It was an act of greed and cruelty he would not have believed Marcus capable of performing.

The thought and the emotions must have been

reflected in his face, because Letterman said, 'You know that I'm right?' His lip curled in contempt. 'Of course you do! But you want a neat line between black and white! The guilty and the innocent. No shades of grey. God knows how you survived all those years in the police force — never mind now, in Special Branch. You are — '

Pitt interrupted him. 'Human,' he provided the word for him. 'I like some people, and trust them, until forced not to. I like Marcus fford Croft.'

'And your son works in his chambers, so you have to protect him, too!' Letterman sneered.

'Would *like* to protect him,' Pitt corrected him. He was keeping his temper with great difficulty. His body ached with the knotting of his muscles, but always right at the centre of all his thoughts was the knowledge that this man sitting opposite him, with the smirk on his face, might hold the key to saving Charlotte's life . . . while it was still a possibility. They had taken her in order to ensure Pitt's silence, his inactivity. The note had spelled it out. His wife's safety, her life, depended on his silence. If she were freed, nothing they could do would stop him from taking every vengeance he could. They must know that. It was a balancing act, and he must tread warily.

'Leaving Marcus fford Croft alive and well, in charge of his own company, would be one option,' Pitt said aloud. 'But there are others, less pleasant — ' He stopped because he saw the change in Letterman's face. He could see the man's muscles knot with tension. In the silence, somewhere a clock was ticking, consuming the seconds. 'Such as ripping this whole blackmail business wide open, and — '

'That would ruin fford Croft,' Letterman interrupted, but there was doubt in his face and, for the first time, a whisper of fear.

'It would,' Pitt agreed. 'And you, too. You paid the money. You felt it was a secret worth paying to keep quiet.' He forced a bleak smile he did not feel. 'Which makes me wonder if there is a great deal more to it than just a rather sordid affair. If it becomes public, your juniors might not mind very much. It would paint you as a more interesting man than you seem. But your seniors would find it a weakness. And more than that, it would convince them that you made a catastrophic error of judgement, and ended by putting yourself in the power of someone else.' His mind was racing. 'They would be obliged to look into many of your old cases. A policeman who can be blackmailed is a liability to the whole force . . . '

Letterman's face was blotched with red. 'Don't be so damn naïve! Everybody has weaknesses . . . of some kind!'

'Of course,' Pitt agreed. 'But not everybody pays a blackmailer!'

'You can't prove that I did!'

'No, but I'll wager Marcus fford Croft could.' Did that explain the odd amounts of money that Marcus moved from one account to another? He profoundly hoped not, but right now all that mattered was Charlotte, and getting her back.

'Not without admitting his own involvement,' Letterman countered. 'A blackmailing head of chambers? How many people have told him their deepest secrets, even admitted their guilt, because they trusted their lawyer?'

'If he had done that to anyone at all, then he should be put out of business,' Pitt replied. The fact that Marcus would blackmail anyone, for his own private financial gain, was hard for Pitt to believe. He felt sick at even the possibility. It was not a mere weakness: everybody failed at one thing or another, at some time, but blackmail for money was a vice of choice, not chance. And if it were true — and he was certain it could not be — was this the only instance? A lawyer's opportunities to blackmail must be legion. That thought alone was sickening.

Letterman must have seen it in Pitt's face. Indeed, the same thought must have run through his mind; his next words proved it. 'It would not be my finest moment, but it would be the end of fford Croft's career,' Letterman said. There was a faint gleam of relish in his face. 'And, of course, the end of the chambers. The stain of it would mark everyone associated with him, don't you think? Including your son? Not to say he was guilty himself, or had any idea of it, but who's going to believe that? Who would take the chance of employing him, when there are so many other young lawyers eager for a place?'

The balance of power had shifted again, back to Letterman, and the knowledge was clear in his face.

Pitt's mind raced. 'I'm surprised you had not

thought of this before,' he continued. 'Why on earth are you still paying him? Tell him to go to hell! He's in it deep enough to see that. If what you're saying is true — '

'It's true,' Letterman cut in, but his voice did not hold the exhilaration it had before. Pitt sensed that he was afraid, and angrier because of it. 'I'll show you the proof, and then you will see how deep he's in this. And I'll wager I'm not the only victim.'

Pitt found the idea sickening, but it had to be faced. 'Of course that's a possibility,' he replied, as levelly as he could.

Letterman appeared to be thinking, weighing his words carefully. 'And how, exactly, does this concern Mr Faber? Do you fear that the death of his son is somehow involved in this? His death probably occurred outside my area, although the body was moved to Mile End. I don't know how you think I can help.'

Pitt sensed that Letterman was gaining confidence again. It was in his voice and the angle of his head as he stared back.

'I know where he was found,' Pitt said, as calmly as he could. 'And I know that it was not where he was killed. I can understand well enough why Evan's body was moved. It obscures the motive and hampers the police investigation.'

'Quite,' Letterman replied. 'But it still begs the question, was he killed in another part of London? Which takes it out of my jurisdiction.' He gave a small, tight smile.

Pitt hesitated.

'I think you will learn far more from asking

Mr fford Croft about his blackmail efforts.' Letterman smiled again. 'I'm glad to be of assistance, Sir Thomas.'

Pitt left because there was nothing to gain by staying. Letterman knew who had taken Charlotte and why, he was certain of that. He also believed that, saying nothing, and therefore making no allegations, might help to save her life.

He walked to his car and told the driver to take him to fford Croft and Gibson, then he sat back and tried to imagine how he was going to face Marcus. Had it been anything other than Charlotte's safety — no, that was a ridiculous evasion, it was Charlotte's *life* that was at stake — he would have found a way around it, tried to reach the truth in some other fashion. He occupied his mind with all the embarrassment, the awkwardness and the tragedy of it, because it was easier. Anything was easier than thinking of Charlotte — where she was, what she was doing, if she was terrified, or fighting. Was she hurt? The words *is she alive?* were being formed in his mind but he pushed them violently away. It kept the horror and grief from rising inside him and overcoming him completely.

★ ★ ★

It was still relatively early in the morning when he reached Lincoln's Inn Fields, but into the normal working day. Impney met him at the door and immediately saw the anxiety in his face. He was used to that: few clients called at a

310

lawyer's office without some burden of anxiety.

'Good morning, Sir Thomas,' he said gravely. 'Whom do you wish to see?'

'Mr fford Croft, thank you,' Pitt replied. 'And will you see that we are not interrupted?' It was more of a demand than a question.

'Yes, sir, of course.' Impney knew better than to argue or ask for reasons. He went immediately and in three or four minutes returned to conduct Pitt into Marcus's office.

Pitt felt guilty instantly. Marcus looked tired and pale, except for a slight flush on his cheeks. He stood up a little uncertainly.

'Good morning, Thomas,' he said. 'Please sit down. What can I do for you?'

'Good morning, Marcus,' Pitt replied, sitting in the chair opposite him. 'I am sorry for interrupting you, but this cannot wait.'

'I haven't seen Daniel this morning,' Marcus said. 'Is he ill? You look very . . . concerned.'

'No.' Pitt had been undecided whether to tell Marcus the truth of the situation or not. This was the perfect opportunity. 'I am more than concerned. A case I'm investigating has blown up in my face. They have kidnapped Charlotte, sometime yesterday morning, and the price of her life is that I do not investigate it, other than as directed.'

Marcus looked ashen. 'Dear God! How appalling! What can I do to help? Anything . . . '

Pitt felt guilt carve out a hole inside him. It was as bad as he had expected; indeed, it was worse. He did not know whether to meet Marcus's eyes or not. How cowardly! He looked directly at him. 'This case got my attention. First Drake's death, and then Evan Faber's, and now the girl who was paid to kill them . . . and all three of them are dead.' He saw Marcus's face drawn tight with horror. Perhaps he had not known about Bella? 'All the bodies were found in Mile End,' Pitt went on. 'All in Letterman's area. Someone, presumably Erasmus Faber, paid to have his own son's death declared an accident, which is balderdash. The deaths are almost certainly connected.'

Marcus nodded stiffly, but he did not interrupt.

'I went to see Letterman this morning,' Pitt continued.

Marcus sat absolutely motionless. He had not moved at all, and yet there was something different in his attitude. He made as if to speak and then changed his mind.

'Letterman fought back.' Pitt suddenly wanted to end this quickly. 'He told me that he had had an affair with a woman, quite a long time ago. He said you knew about it and that you required payment in order not to tell anybody else.'

'What? Payment? You mean . . . money?' Marcus gasped.

'He said he had bank records. Please tell me the truth, Marcus. Charlotte's life is the price of this. What am I dealing with?'

Marcus started to speak, but his voice slurred. He gave a strangled cry and tried to tear his cravat off, fingers groping frantically. And then he slumped forward over his desk.

For a couple of seconds, Pitt was paralysed.

Then he shot to his feet and flung the door open. 'Impney!' he shouted. 'Impney! Come here, now!' And then, without waiting for him, he turned back into the room and lifted Marcus up very gently. His face was ashen pale, but he appeared to be breathing. Pitt loosened the cravat at Marcus's throat, then stared at the limp body and the grey-white face.

Impney came into the room, with Toby Kitteridge on his heels.

Impney took one look at Marcus. 'Kitteridge, call an ambulance immediately,' he ordered. 'Tell them it's an emergency. I believe Mr fford Croft has had a heart attack. Every second matters!' He turned back to Pitt. 'I've been afraid of this. This whole business has been too much for him, but he wouldn't be told! Can you help me lift him? He's heavy. You take his shoulders . . . be careful.'

Pitt did as he was directed, and very carefully they lifted Marcus on to the couch. He could hear directions being given in the hallway, an authoritarian voice telling everyone to get on with their work, keep out of the way. They would be informed when there was any news.

Impney disappeared to direct other staff, and to receive the ambulance as soon as it arrived with a stretcher.

Pitt sat alone with Marcus while the nightmare went on around him. Had he caused this? Or had Marcus been building up to it for weeks, perhaps months? He wanted to think the latter. If Marcus were innocent, surely it would not have resulted in a heart attack? There would be bewilderment, wouldn't there? Even anger? But not this!

It seemed like an age that he sat alone with a man he had known for decades, and liked. Letterman had seemed so sure of himself. He had said he had proof; he would get records which showed irregular payments, but many of them, over a span of years. Marcus was not Letterman's lawyer. Had he been, the payments would have been to fford Croft and Gibson, not to Marcus personally. It would not be difficult to track these down.

The minutes ticked by, but they felt to Pitt as if they were passing in slow motion. Marcus was still breathing, but unconscious. He heard feet clattering in the hallway, hurrying, but no one came in. Suddenly, Marcus stopped breathing . . . and then started again. What could Pitt do for him? Nothing. He was as useless as the inanimate objects in the room.

Then, at last, the door opened and a man stood there. He glanced at Pitt, then beyond him to Marcus lying on the couch. 'This the gentleman who's been taken ill, then, sir?'

Pitt looked up. 'Yes, Mr fford Croft.'

'Can you tell me what happened, sir? Mister . . . ?' He crossed to the sofa.

'Pitt. Yes, we were talking about a case . . . '

'He your lawyer, then?' The man kept talking while he felt for Marcus's pulse, and listened to his heart, touched his skin and generally examined him.

'No, he's a long-time friend . . . ' Why was the man asking such questions? It hardly mattered.

314

Perhaps he was hoping to keep Pitt calm and concentrated, in case he panicked, and the man ended up with two patients. Very professional.

'I'm with Special Branch,' said Pitt. 'I was informing him of a case that affects us both. The death of one of his senior partners.'

'Was he upset?'

'Yes.' He could say that honestly. 'I'm afraid the partner was murdered, very savagely, in Mile End. I was telling him about a further development . . . ' That was true, as far as it went.

The man went to the door and gestured for two other men to come in and lift Marcus on to a litter. Very carefully, they carried him out through the deserted passageway and across the pavement to the waiting ambulance. Pitt followed.

'Do you know his wife, or someone in the family, sir?' the man asked him.

'He's a widower,' Pitt answered. 'And his only daughter is in Holland at the moment, but I can get hold of her, if you think it advisable . . . '

'Live there, does she?'

'No, she is studying there. She's brilliant, and about to take several medical and forensic exams.' Pitt realised he was talking too much. It gave him the illusion of doing something.

'I suggest you do that, sir, if it's necessary. Let's just see how he is first.'

'Can I accompany you to the hospital in a car?'

'You can, by all means, sir. But behind us, thank you, sir.'

The nearest hospital was St Barts. It was as huge, anonymous and busy, as all such places were. When they arrived, Pitt went with the ambulance men who carried Marcus to the area where he was to be treated by a doctor.

Pitt sat outside the examination room and waited for what seemed like hours, staring at the other frightened and worried people who were similarly waiting for news of a member of their family or a close friend. Some spoke to others, trying to give or receive any kind of comfort. Most, like Pitt, stared into the distance, or even paced the floor. Pitt worried about Marcus because it was not only the decent thing to do, but it helped prevent his mind becoming filled with paralysing terror for Charlotte. It was a long battle. He was flooded with memories, painfully precious. Might these memories be all he would have left of her, whatever he did? Could the kidnappers ever afford to let her go? Would she fight them? She had never known when to fight and when to give in to the inevitable. Would she panic, and they would have to silence her? Temporarily? Or for ever? He felt a sudden urge to rush out of the hospital and go to Mile End. He strongly suspected she was being held there! Just as he was about to get up, he became dimly aware of someone standing next to him, speaking to him.

'Mr fford Croft is conscious now, sir,' the doctor told him. 'I think he would like to see you. If you come with me? He's going to be all right, but he's pretty weak. Just a few minutes, sir.'

'Yes,' Pitt agreed, rising to his feet. 'Yes, of course.' He followed the man down the corridor and into a small private room. Marcus was sitting slightly raised against the stack of pillows behind him. He still looked very pale, but his eyes were open and there was the faintest flush of colour in his cheeks. He was dressed in a hospital gown, anonymous looking, without dignity, a matter only of decency.

'I'm sorry,' Pitt said immediately, then wondered what he was apologising for. He could not avoid mentioning the subject, and allowing Marcus to defend himself. His only fault had been not to realise how fragile Marcus was.

'Not your fault, my dear chap,' Marcus replied, but his voice was weak. He knew he had a fight ahead of him, possibly the greatest of his life.

'Wasn't it?' Pitt asked. He meant it. 'I touched a very important subject.'

'Not really,' Marcus replied. 'I know Letterman, have known him for years. Too proud to accept that I made a bad mistake with him.' He stopped for a moment, breathing in and out slowly, as if he needed to take care not to disturb his chest and the heart that was beating so uncertainly inside it.

Pitt waited. He could not place the pieces together yet, or see where they fitted into the whole picture he needed in order to get Charlotte back . . . and connect all the people involved, so his family did not walk in fear all the rest of their lives. A step at a time. Get her back first. Without that, he could see no light ahead. Nothing but deepening shadows for the rest of his life.

'What mistake?' he asked aloud.

'Trusted him,' Marcus said weakly, one syllable at a time. 'He got himself into a pickle, financially. Lent him money. I was doing well. Very well. I could afford it, and he promised to pay me back. And he is still doing that. A bit at a time, over the years, whenever he can afford it. No interest. It was a favour to a man I trusted. Not a business deal. No profit in it. I never asked for a favour, or received one. Just a plain loan. You can find records of it in my accounts . . . ' He stopped, his breathing light and shallow.

Pitt was engulfed by a wave of relief. He grasped Marcus's hand where it was lying on top of the bedclothes.

Marcus moved slightly. It was not anything as definite as a grip. 'Promise me you'll do that,' Marcus asked.

'Look over your records? Of course I will,' Pitt answered him. 'If the repayment amounts are shown to be subtracted from the original loan . . . '

'Of course they are . . . but I don't greatly care. Coming in dribs and drabs, the money's hardly worth anything, except to Letterman, as a matter of honour. How can I use such a word now in connection with him? Pity, he used to be a good man — at least, I really thought he was.'

'Do you want me to tell Miriam — ?' Pitt began, gesturing towards the hospital room. The consternation in Marcus's face stopped him from finishing the sentence.

'No! No, thank you, but no need. I can't remember when her exams are, but not long now. She needs to study; this is her life, Thomas. Her dream. That's one thing I can do for her, not worry her now. Promise me?'

There was only one possible answer. 'I promise,' Pitt said quietly.

Marcus closed his eyes and smiled. 'Thank you.'

16

Daniel spent a wretched day doing all he could to work back to the case of Marie Wesley. He decided to spend the morning at his parents' home reading Drake's notes again to see if the lawyer had any ideas of his own, either in the beginning, or even after the trial and acquittal, as to who might really have been guilty. Was there any evidence that might have led to a different interpretation?

Concentration was difficult. He kept imagining he could hear Charlotte's footsteps in the hall. After twice getting up and going to the door to find it was only Minnie Maude looking at him apologetically and with tears in her eyes, he let it pass and went back to reading. Parts of the notes were so familiar he could have recited them. Was this only to keep his mind at least partially occupied? Or did he really think he would find something of value in them?

Then a new thought occurred to him. Where had Marie Wesley come from? She might have had a nice flat in a better area of London, but where was her original home? Was it possible her roots, her family, were in Mile End? Was this to do with a private act of vengeance, by someone who felt the law had let them down?

His mind went back to that necklace. There was no word about it yet. Were people still asking about it, or had they let it go, as if it did not matter? A dead woman's necklace. Possibly stolen, anyway. Charlotte would have liked it. It had character, and it was quite heavy. A good bit of gold in it. Simple in shape, on a heavy gold chain. A bit old fashioned. Wait, wasn't Kitteridge following that up? Where was his memory!

Minnie Maude was crossing the hall again and going upstairs. The eleventh stair creaked a bit. He wished she would keep still. Her step was like Charlotte's. They were about the same height, and Charlotte still walked very upright, like a girl.

He felt a moment's panic, and tears welled up inside him. He must get control of his emotions. What use was he, if all he did was grieve? Nothing had happened yet! Or at least nothing they knew of.

He forced himself to refocus, but it was not easy. Could anybody know for certain who had given the necklace to Marie? Had they even asked? Who had taken it to the pawnbroker? Whoever had killed her, of course. Or ripped it off her throat. Was that the same man? Probably. Someone knew who he was, but it was too dangerous to let him be identified.

What was the reason for taking the necklace? It wasn't to sell it, because the sort of man Marie kept company with would hardly stoop to take a pretty thing. What could provoke a man to beat a woman as savagely as Marie had been beaten? According to the reports, she had been hit a great many times. Really beaten to death. What had provoked such a blind rage? Some sort of betrayal, most likely. The most obvious thought was a lover, usurped by someone perhaps younger, and very likely better looking . . . as was Evan Faber. Or was his father right, and the lover might have been Erasmus Faber?

Daniel tried to decide what he could do that would be useful and not further endanger his mother. His first thought was to go to Jonah Drake's house and see what he could find.

He walked along Keppel Street, intending to take the bus. That would give him time to think things through. When he saw an available taxi, he flagged it down. The more time spent searching through Drake's effects, the better chance of finding something useful.

He found the spare key where he had left it a few days earlier, let himself in and went directly to Drake's study. No one would ever know he was doing this. Drake had a telephone. Daniel picked up the receiver: dead. That made sense. He counted himself lucky that the electricity was still connected. But it meant that if someone needed to contact him, they could not.

He should have left a note on the kitchen table, and another on the mantelpiece in the drawing room, telling Pitt where he was going, and why. What if his father needed to contact him? What if his mother had been released?

'Get control of yourself,' he mumbled, settling back into Drake's desk chair and opening the first file, the one on top of a rather large stack.

And then another thought: would Kitteridge or Impney be concerned? Would Marcus need him for something? He pushed those thoughts away as well. What he needed to do was conduct a meticulous search through these papers yet again, perhaps find something they had missed before, or didn't understand. Perhaps they had not looked hard enough.

There were blocks of unused paper. He riffled through them. All clean. There were other loose sheets, clean ones too. And under them, scribbled on even more sheets, addresses, names, a few telephone numbers, all mixed up with doodles Drake had made, presumably while talking on the telephone. Daniel had only glanced at these during the last visit to this room. This time, he looked at them one by one. No names. Were they worth bothering with? Old clients? He turned them over. There were more doodles on some of them.

Daniel tried to imagine himself back in time, more than a year ago, when Evan was on trial. But these were Drake's private notes, not from the trial. A few were in outline form, as if Drake had attempted to plot the relationship of various elements. Marie Wesley had been the first victim. The start of it. Her murder was not a planned crime. It had sprung from rage, jealousy, injured vanity, a man who felt himself doubly betrayed. *Doubly?* Why had the lawyer written that?

Drake had drawn a picture of a man whose shadow held a knife! Drake's mind worked with a dark, oblique humour. Was the betrayal by the man's inner self? Or by someone close to him?

Daniel sat back. He had been reading for more than an hour and his eyes were already burning.

Marie was the first victim, yes, and Drake was the second. He knew something, either dangerous or humiliating. He had gone to Mile End to discover more. Had he found it? The knot at the core of it all was in Mile End. It must be. So, what had Drake learned there? Whatever it was, it was lethal to somebody. It had certainly turned out to be lethal to Drake.

Daniel took out a piece of paper and began his own outline. He noted the details of Marie's case, followed by the questions and information related to Drake. Now for Evan.

Evan Faber was the third victim, killed elsewhere but moved to Mile End, to Anthony Street, to draw attention to Letterman's patch. But why? Daniel stared at his notes, made a few changes, and then added one more question: is Erasmus Faber at the heart of this?

His thoughts went to Bella. She, too, was killed in Mile End. There had to be a thread connecting them all. Yes, of course there was! But what on earth connected Evan and Bella? Evan found his excitement, romance, whatever one liked to call it, in the fashionable west of the city, certainly not the East End. At the beginning of this tragedy was Marie Wesley. Her murder was violent, committed out of jealousy, a beating by fists, heavy and hard, not a knife like the one used to kill Drake and Evan. And Bella.

Bella had killed because she was paid to. That was still difficult to take into his mind, much less accept the connection! Who would pay a young woman to kill?

He looked at the drawings on the back of

Drake's notes again. They were very small; he needed a magnifying glass to see them clearly. Some of the little drawings were very clever, some angry, but some gentle, almost beautiful. When this was all over, he would ask Marcus if he could have some of them.

This one was lovely. It looked very like Bella. In fact, the more he stared at it, the more he could see that it had to be her. The way her hair grew was individual, with those arresting curls. But there was one on the next page almost like it. Same angle, same profile, just a little stronger, more masculine.

Were the sketches of two different people, or one person, but seen from different views? The longer he stared at them, the more he was fascinated and knew that an important element was eluding him.

He was parched for a cup of tea and something to eat. He checked the time. No wonder he was hungry, it was already close to noon. He studied the two drawings again. Then he turned over more sheets, and found others, not recognisable except through the magnifying glass.

'What do you make of that?' he asked himself. The answer shot through his head, a bolt of recognition that sped away before he could grasp it. He bent over the drawings, switching from one to the other, back and forth. They could be the same person, but it could also be two people who closely resembled each other. There were slight differences, especially about the hair. After all the time he had spent poring over Drake's drawings, he knew they were never made unless they had meaning.

He needed aspirin, and more than one.

Was it someone in a clever disguise, playing two roles? Or two different people? They could be, certainly. The more he thought of the possibility, the more it engaged his mind. He gathered the documents and the magnifying glass, locked the door behind him, and looked for the nearest café. Tea and sandwiches, that's what he needed.

As he chewed on his sandwich, he pulled out the two drawings and stared at them through the magnifying glass. Of course, how could they all have missed it? Was that it? Was that what Drake had found out? That Evan Faber and Bella Blades were brother and sister? He pictured them in his mind: the golden amber colouring, the angle of nose and jaw, the setting of the eyes. Yes, half-brother and half-sister. Evan was the son of Faber's wife, and Bella must have resulted from some affair in Mile End. But why did it matter so much? A love child, to use the euphemism. Was that a reason for people dying?

Daniel mulled over this. It was not something that Faber would want to become known, that his daughter was a paid assassin. Possibly Faber himself did not even know of her. But it was still something to explore. And had this been the reason Drake had gone to Mile End, where Bella lived, and in the small hours of the night? And if Evan knew about Bella, maybe that was why he had to be killed? And Bella? Enough in itself! Or was there far more, underneath the surface?

He replaced the two pictures in the folder, paid his bill, and left the café. By the time he arrived at Keppel Street he was fighting to stay awake. He went directly to his old room, stretched out on the bed, and fell into a deep sleep.

★ ★ ★

It was mid afternoon when Pitt came back home. Daniel was at the kitchen table, but he shot to his feet at the sound of the familiar footsteps and met his father just as he reached the door. He looked exhausted and almost bloodlessly pale.

Daniel's heart skipped a beat. It was bad news. It had to be. He tried to ask what, but when he opened his mouth he made no sound.

'No,' Pitt said, as if he knew the fear that made Daniel almost sick. 'It's Marcus.'

'What!' Daniel was confused. 'Marcus . . . what?'

Pitt walked over to the kitchen table and sat on one of the hard-backed chairs. 'He had a heart attack,' he replied, pushing his hair off his forehead in a gesture that was almost an exact imitation of Daniel's. Except, of course, that Daniel had inherited it from his father. 'It was a hell of a fright,' he went on. 'But I think he's going to recover. I called here, but Minnie Maude had no idea where you were, and you never did come to chambers.' He took a slow, deep breath. 'I told him something that upset him deeply.'

'Father, people don't have heart attacks

327

because of what someone says, unless they are going to have one anyway.' Daniel did not know if this was true, but he did not want his father to blame himself, whether it was his fault or not. He had enough to deal with. He looked older than Daniel had realised. It was not the grey in his thick hair, it was the exhaustion in his body, his white knuckles, the lifelessness in his face. 'Do you think he's going to be all right? Did they let him come home?'

'Not yet,' Pitt replied.

'What did you say to him? Did you . . . ' He was going to mention Charlotte, then changed his mind. 'Did you blame him for any of this case?'

Pitt avoided his eyes. 'I went to see Letterman first. He told me Marcus was blackmailing him over an affair with some woman, threatening to tell his wife and colleagues. He's got bank books and so on to prove it.'

'I don't believe it,' Daniel said instantly. 'I don't care what he's got!'

Pitt gave a faint smile. 'I asked Marcus about it. He said Letterman made the payments all right, but he was repaying a loan made ages ago, when Marcus was doing very well and Letterman wasn't. He was paying it back over a number of years.'

'Legitimate?' Daniel asked, adding *please heaven* in his mind.

'It will be easy enough to check,' Pitt replied, then he looked up at Daniel. 'Why do you ask?'

'I know he's worried. Drake is going to be very hard to replace.'

Pitt nodded, but remained silent.

'I thought Drake was a miserable old fossil when I first knew him,' said Daniel. 'I dare say he thought I was a privileged upstart. But, actually, he had a very dry sense of humour which came out in his notes. He did little cartoons that were horribly perceptive.' He thought about it with regret, an opportunity missed. 'They were very clever and funny. He could say more about a person in half a dozen lines than most people could write on a whole page.' He stared into the distance. 'I found a couple in particular which might tell us why he went to Mile End . . . '

'What, in heaven's name?'

Daniel retrieved the file from his room and returned, opened the envelope and took out the drawings and the magnifying glass. He showed them to Pitt, who stared at them intensely, his brow furrowed. Then he looked up. 'Who are they?'

'I don't know for certain, but having seen them both, I think they're Bella Blades . . . and Evan Faber.'

'Related?' Pitt said slowly, looking at Daniel curiously.

'I think so,' Daniel replied. 'It looks as if Erasmus Faber might be the father of both of them.'

Pitt's eyes widened. 'That's why Drake went to Mile End?'

'It's possible.'

'To meet whom?'

'That I don't know. Perhaps Letterman?'

Pitt thought for a moment or two. 'I think Erasmus Faber has his eyes on a lot more than building ships and making money. I think he has ambitions for a bigger role in government . . . a very big role.'

'Running for Parliament?' Daniel said slowly.

'Nothing so pedestrian. A seat in the House of Lords, an appointment to the cabinet.' He stopped. From Daniel's expression, it was clear that he understood. 'That's from MacPherson at the Home Office. No wonder Drake was disturbed . . . '

Daniel nodded. 'Is Marcus going to be all right?'

'Yes, I think so.'

'Should I tell Miriam?' He had already made up his mind, even as he asked.

'Marcus said not to,' Pitt explained. 'She's got important , exams . . . '

It was in Daniel's mind to tell Pitt that if Marcus died, Miriam would regret not being told for ever. Then he tried to think of the last thing he had said to his mother, and it eluded him completely. Whatever it had been, he hoped at the very least it had been something kind . . .

'Daniel!' Pitt repeated.

'Yes? What? I'm sorry, I didn't hear you.'

'Do you think we should tell Miriam anyway?'

'Yes, we have to give her the choice. It's wrong to decide for her. I've got her address. If she wants to come, I'll meet her at the station and take her to the hospital. Toby can manage the office work for both of us for a little while. Major decisions, if there are any, can be referred to

Marcus, if he's all right.' He really meant *if he's alive*.

Pitt looked at him steadily. 'Yes, of course you're right. We must let Miriam decide for herself. I can't say definitely that her father will recover.'

★   ★   ★

Daniel went immediately to the post office and sent a telegram to Miriam in Holland. Although telegrams were delivered promptly, he marked it as urgent and willingly paid the extra fee. He had asked Pitt what to say of Marcus's condition, so that what he told her was accurate, but would not panic her.

> *Marcus had mild heart attack this morning stop recovering in hospital stop if you choose to come home I will meet you at station Daniel*

It was rather a lot of words, but he did not want her to be more frightened than necessary, or to underplay it, so she would think it was less serious than it was.

He went home and back to the papers he had been reading. He could barely remember what they had said. How could he concentrate with his mother missing and his mentor possibly fighting for his life? He pushed those thoughts away. There were still so many questions unanswered, and they might lead him to his mother and the men who had kidnapped her.

No one had seen the necklace that Marie Wesley had worn in the drawing. The doctor who had examined her body reported that there were marks around her neck, as if some kind of chain had been ripped off, cutting into her flesh as a chain would do. Had it been that necklace, or another? And why would anyone take it after beating her to death? Out of hate? The wish to keep it in memory of . . . what? Love? Revenge? The most logical reason would be that the murderer meant to destroy it because it could identify him. Was that the real, practical reason why he had taken it?

According to Toby, the necklace had most likely been pawned because it would have been too dangerous to keep. And too exquisite to simply throw away. Who had commissioned it was the most important question to answer.

He found his father about to leave the house. Pitt seemed to have found renewed energy.

'I can't sit here and do nothing,' he explained, looking through the window to determine the weather. He removed the heavy coat and hung it on the rack. He was pale-faced and exhausted.

Daniel wanted to ask if there had been any word of his mother, but there was no use. Had his father heard something, he would have said. At the same time, his silence was worse than any of their nightmares, because in a sense it made every fear a possibility.

Daniel brought up the subject of the necklace. 'If we found out who gave it to her . . . ' he started.

'Yes, I see,' Pitt replied. 'Good.' He made no

attempt at a smile. 'I'll get my men on it right away. You're right, Daniel. If we know who gave it to her, we are almost certainly closer to her killer.' He sighed. 'Although, if it's Erasmus Faber, I don't know what we can do about it.'

Daniel did not reply. Perhaps he had deluded himself into thinking that if they knew the truth, and could prove it, it would make Faber release Charlotte — if it was Faber who was responsible for her kidnap. But the bitter truth was that he could not afford to let her go, and all they were talking about was vengeance. He tried hard to think of something hopeful to say. He wanted to comfort his father, just as his father was trying to comfort him.

'Where are you going?' asked Daniel.

Pitt looked confused, and then nodded. 'I was thinking of going to Drake's house . . . or his office . . . or . . . I'm not sure.'

Daniel placed his hand on his father's shoulder. 'Stay here, please,' he said, leaving no doubt that it was a request built on his own need to have his father close.

★ ★ ★

Several hours later, the doorbell rang and Daniel stumbled to his feet and went to answer it. He thanked the boy who handed him a telegram, and gave him a shilling. He tore it open, his hands shaking.

Will come stop arrive tomorrow morning 8 am Saint Pancras stop Miriam

He breathed in and out slowly. She was going to come. He would go to the station and meet her, of course, and take her to the hospital. Please God, Marcus would continue to recover.

He walked back to the drawing room and showed the telegram to Pitt, who nodded a silent acknowledgement.

Daniel wished he could think of something positive to say, but it all sounded false. They knew that the longer his mother was missing, the more chance there was of a tragedy, or some new incident to force their hands. Was there any proof that she was still alive?

Perhaps they both had the same thoughts. If she was dead, they would both be staring into a long-drawn-out nightmare that ended with a bereaved and darkened life. How could they help each other? How would he tell Jemima?

★ ★ ★

Daniel slept badly, as he had expected, and rose early with a pounding headache. He forced himself to eat breakfast, which Minnie Maude prepared for him, moving silently around the kitchen, afraid to speak, obviously wanting to, but not knowing what to say.

'Thank you,' Daniel said as he stood up.

She took in a breath, and then let it out again without speaking.

'We're doing everything we can,' he assured her. 'No one has given up. This could still end with her coming home.'

'Do you think so?' Her eyes filled with tears.

'Or are you just being kind to me?'

'Kind to both of us,' he replied, and then hesitated for an instant. 'I'm going to meet Miss fford Croft at the station. Please try and make Sir Thomas eat something.'

She nodded, unable to speak.

He was early at the station. He walked up and down the platform because he was unable to stand still. He carried a pocket watch, and pulled it out again and again, although he was within sight of the station clock. He rehearsed what he was going to say to Miriam, to be both accurate and helpful, but whatever he came up with, it never sounded right. And all the while, his mind was full of his own fear for his mother . . .

Then, at last, the train came, and he could not see Miriam among the crowd of passengers getting off. What was he looking for? A hat? Her bright hair? Had she missed the train? Was he on the wrong platform? In the matter of forty-eight hours all his old certainties had slipped away. He looked for them, but they were not there.

There was a tug on his arm, light but definite. He turned to face the person, and shake himself loose from their grasp. He met Miriam's dark blue eyes. A wave of relief swept over him and, without thinking, he put his arms around her and held her tightly. For a moment, she did not resist, but then she pushed him away and looked directly into his face.

'Is he . . . still alive?'

'Yes,' he said decisively. 'I called the hospital earlier this morning and he slept well, but he's very weak. I didn't tell him you were coming, in case something held you up. Have you got a suitcase?'

'Just a small one.' She indicated it close to her feet.

He bent and picked it up. 'The car's this way.'

Wordlessly, she followed him through the crowd, outside, and across the street towards the waiting car, where Marcus's driver was sitting at the wheel. He climbed out and held the door open for Miriam and Daniel to get in, then resumed his own seat and pulled the car out into the stream of traffic.

'To the hospital, miss?' he asked, his face showing signs of worry. Daniel had no idea how long this man had worked for Marcus, but even one day was enough to grow a fondness for the old man.

'Yes, please,' she said, and then leaned forward and touched his shoulder. 'Thank you.'

She glanced sideways at Daniel, smiled, but said nothing.

For a few moments he tried to think of something to reassure her, and yet not lie. He had forgotten what it was like to be with her, how honest they had always been with each other, no pretences. There was nothing to say now. First, she must find out how Marcus was. There was time to tell her about Charlotte later.

He looked at her, and the long time since they had last met telescoped into itself and disappeared. He wanted to say something to her, a promise that Marcus would be all right, but he could not, he did not know. And there was more than the heart attack, so much more. If these accusations were correct, what would become of the chambers? Jonah Drake was dead, and they were still reeling from the horror of that. With the loss of his skills, the whole company might be in jeopardy. There was nothing to say that was reassuring. Anything else was either a lie, or would lead to questions he could not answer yet. He wanted desperately to tell her about his mother, and the fear that was tearing away at him. But was this the right time? She was on her way to see her father, with her own deep fears. No, best to wait.

Daniel wanted to divert her from this fear, but she would not want that. He put his hand down on the seat between them. A minute passed by, then two, then three. She slid her hand down and touched his, the warmth of skin, no more.

They reached the hospital and Daniel asked the driver to wait for her. He walked inside, beside her. When they reached Marcus's room, he turned and said, 'Would you like me to wait for you?'

She hesitated, as if she had not foreseen the question.

'I'd like to know how he is myself,' he said. 'And if he's well enough, ask him if there is anything he would like me to do.'

'Oh.' She gave her head a small shake. 'I'm sorry. Yes, I . . . would you please come in with me?' She looked awkward and very alone.

He did not bother to answer with words, but took her arm and knocked on the door. There was no answer. He tried the handle and went in.

They walked over to the bed. Marcus was

sitting up, still very pale, but his eyes were open and he was quite clearly wide awake. His face lit up with pleasure as Miriam came towards him, with Daniel following a couple of feet behind her.

'I told his father not to tell you!' he said immediately to Miriam, but he was unable to hide the delight that filled his face. 'Don't you Pitts listen to anything I say?' That last remark was directed at Daniel, but his eyes stayed on him only a moment. 'You shouldn't have come,' he said to Miriam. 'It's nothing serious, just a bit of a shock. We lost a member of chambers and haven't been able to replace him yet. How are you, girl? How's the studying? When are your exams?' Then his face darkened. 'You're not missing them . . . '

'No!' she said, in a tone which forbade any useless questioning. 'I'm missing an afternoon picnic, that's all. Who's gone from chambers? Not Toby Kitteridge, I hope.'

'Jonah Drake. I don't think you knew him . . . '

'Of course I did. Did he decide to retire? He could have given you better notice! Can't he — ?' Then she saw the darkness in his face. 'What?' she demanded. When Marcus did not answer her straight away, she swivelled around and looked at Daniel.

'He died,' he answered. 'Unexpectedly.'

She stayed looking at him for another moment, trying to judge the meaning behind the words he was saying. Was it true? Half true? Was he hiding it from Marcus for some reason? She

338

looked back at her father. 'Another heart attack?' she asked gently, but her voice was tight with new anxiety.

Marcus hesitated. He understood her fear.

Before Marcus could reply with the best lie he could think of, Daniel chose the truth. He had never lied to Miriam, partly because he did not want to place dishonesty between them, but also because he knew he would not do it well. 'No,' he answered. 'For a reason we don't know, he went to Mile End late at night. He was attacked and killed.'

She crumpled a little, her shoulders sagging. She had been travelling all night by train, and ferry, and then train again. Daniel could see that she was anxious and frightened. Now there was a new horror on top of that.

Marcus glared at Daniel.

'She doesn't need lying to,' Daniel answered, speaking to Marcus. 'If we lie about that, how can she believe anything we say about you being all right? She'd have to stay, because she wouldn't trust us to tell her the truth.'

Marcus replied, 'All right!' He turned back to Miriam. 'We know who actually did it, but not who paid them. Everyone's working on it, and I'm getting better all the time. Got to stay here for a day or two, but I'll be home soon. Plenty of people there to look after me. Don't worry. Daniel and Kitteridge will keep things going, and Impney, of course. And then there are other lawyers to keep us in business.' He smiled. 'It does me good to see you, but go back tomorrow, don't miss your lectures. And above all, don't miss an exam. Or be too tired or worried to perform well. I want your promise on that . . . '

She did not hesitate. 'I promise. Now, is there anything I can do for you?'

Daniel wondered if she could help with these questions around Letterman's payments. It would relieve Pitt of a small part of the problem. It might even help to find Charlotte. The words were out of his mouth before he thought any further. 'Yes,' he said urgently, directing this at Marcus. 'Before she goes back to Holland, she could sort out the payments from Letterman. Get the bank to prove it. If we caught him in a lie . . . ' He saw the confusion in Marcus's face, the struggle to remember.

Miriam swivelled round where she was sitting on the bed and looked at Daniel again. 'Letterman? Who is that? And can't it wait?'

'No,' Daniel replied decisively, knowing he was about to upset Marcus. 'Someone has accused your father of blackmail. We can prove he is innocent, but we need access to his bank accounts. If he gives you permission, then we can legally look through them. My father has offered to do this, but it's far better for your family reputation if Special Branch isn't involved.'

She looked at Marcus, her eyes wide. It was so much to take in. First the heart attack, and now this. 'May I, Father? Give me permission; I'll only look at what is relevant.'

'Would you?' Marcus said earnestly. 'I don't remember everything Thomas said, but I do know that this needs to be handled quickly.'

'I'll do it straight away,' she promised. 'Might

as well be useful while I'm here.'

'But your exams!' he protested, looking worried and confused again.

Daniel felt a sadness move through him. She had explained about her exams only minutes earlier. He gave a silent wish that this lapse was due to the heart attack . . . and nothing more.

She put her hand over his where it lay on the coverlet. 'I'm not going until I'm sure you are all right.'

He drew in a breath to speak.

'Unless the doctor tells me,' she finished.

He relaxed. 'Look after Daniel,' he said, almost under his breath.

She kissed his cheek, then walked, stiffly upright, to the door and out of the room.

Daniel followed her silently. Before the door was closed, Marcus was almost asleep.

Miriam was waiting in the passageway. She was pale and controlling herself with an effort. She attempted to smile. 'Thank you for telling me. I suppose he told you not to?'

'Yes . . . '

'What else is wrong, Daniel? And don't lie to me. You're not good at it. Is the chambers in trouble?'

'Losing Drake was bad, but as far as I know, we are managing,' he answered, and that was the truth. 'We'll find someone to take his place, but whether they will be as good remains to be seen. It was all pretty horrible. They called me to identify the body, because he had one of my cards in his pocket. At least . . . he had borrowed Kitteridge's coat and it had one of my cards. But that doesn't matter now.'

'Whatever it is, will the truth about the money in my father's bank account sort it out? Is it even anything to do with Drake's death? And don't make me pull your teeth out one by one to get an answer! For heaven's sake, tell me!'

'Can we go and have a cup of tea somewhere?' he asked. 'I don't even remember if I had breakfast . . . '

'You do look pretty awful . . . ' Her face was tired and full of sorrow. 'I could use a cup of tea myself.'

She allowed him to take her arm and together they went out of the hospital and along the pavement to the nearest café. They found a table and ordered.

'Tell me,' Miriam said. 'And don't dance around it!'

Daniel finished his tea and toast, thinking how to tell her, what to omit, but when he started, all his plans disappeared. He told her about Drake's murder, and then he added Evan Faber's death. And then, finally, Bella's. Once or twice he had to stop to regain his composure, but he felt he had told her the bones of it. The most dramatic and painful part, however, was trapped somewhere in his throat.

'I'm so sorry,' she said quietly. 'I knew Jonah Drake. He used to draw pictures for me, when I was a lot younger.' She looked away and blinked rapidly. It was a moment or two before she could find her handkerchief and stop the tears rolling down her cheeks.

He waited.

'We go on!' she said when the silence had stretched out too long. 'Was Evan Faber guilty of whatever he was charged with?'

'Oh . . . he was found not guilty.'

'You already said that. It's not the same thing!'

'I believe so. It was the murder,' he saw her wince, 'of a young woman who was of what they call *dubious morals*. I really don't believe he did it . . . '

'Who did?'

'Maybe that's the key to all of it. We don't know.' He told her all that they knew. The waitress brought them sandwiches and a new pot of tea, and took away the used dishes.

'You are avoiding something,' she said, after a moment's hesitation. 'I know you are. Does it concern my father? Did he make a serious mistake about something? I can't help if I don't know.' She did not add how deep her fear was, but it was there in her face.

'No.' He looked away from her, struggling to keep his composure. He did not want to crumble to pieces, especially in front of Miriam. 'He makes the odd mistake; we all do. And he forgets people's names now and then.'

'Then what is it? It's serious, I can see that.'

'The police in Mile End are corrupt. That's where it's all centred.' He took a shaky breath and swallowed. 'And someone has kidnapped my mother.'

A look of pale shock crossed Miriam's face and Daniel feared for her.

'My God, Daniel! How? And . . . why are you here? Where do you find the . . . ' She grabbed his hand and squeezed it, gratitude for his presence in her eyes. 'When . . . ?' she finally said.

Daniel felt both grief and release from holding back such powerful emotions. This was Miriam; he could speak his fears. 'I think it was two days ago. Time seems to be a bit hazy. She went out for the morning and just . . . disappeared. When she didn't come back in the afternoon, or the evening . . . or all night . . . ' He swallowed hard and felt tears prickle in his eyes. 'By the next day, we knew . . . there was a note left at our door. Someone wants to keep my father from investigating these deaths any further. Erasmus Faber is at the heart of this. He's very powerful, a brilliant shipbuilder, and God knows, we need ships. I suppose it's a matter of the price we're willing to pay for them.'

He saw the puzzled look on her face. 'Morally, not financially. He wants a place in the government, the higher up the better. Cabinet, the House of Lords. Father won't do it. And the price — ' He stopped.

His hand was on the table. She took hold of it, very gently.

For seconds he did not move or speak. He felt the tears running down his cheeks. Then he had to take back his hand to reach into his pocket for a handkerchief. He wiped his cheeks and blew his nose.

'What can I do?' she asked.

'Look into those bank accounts. It will disprove the charge by Letterman that your father was blackmailing him. If we can prove that

that is a lie, then Marcus is safe, and Letterman is finished.' He saw the look on her face. 'I believe your father, but that isn't enough to arrest Letterman, and he's one of the chief players in this whole thing. He's head of police in the Mile End area. If we can arrest him, that would be the beginning of the end for Faber . . . '

'What's the connection between Letterman and Faber?' she asked.

'I thought at first that Letterman was using Faber, possibly blackmailing him. I think he still imagines he's doing that. But Faber is the one pulling the strings. He's using Letterman, and he'll cut him off the moment it suits him. At least, I think he will. Faber has the money. With Letterman's access to information about crimes committed, and the people charged with committing them, he's a useful tool.'

'Of course I'll do it,' she said firmly. 'When I have the documents, who do I go to?'

'Toby Kitteridge. Tell him, and then he can tell the police.' Daniel's face became suddenly dark, angry. 'Miriam, we've got to get him. Once Faber knows Letterman's gone, arrested, he'll be much more vulnerable. We have a chance. And we've got to get Mother before . . . '

Her hand tightened over his. 'I know, you don't have to say it. I'll start right away. We'll do it. I'll find the loan, and the record of those repayments.'

He wanted hope. He didn't want to be realistic and face the truth that it might all be too late to save his mother. 'I know,' he said. When she smiled at him, he knew she was keeping up the pretence. Her hand tightened over his again and he felt hopeful.

17

Charlotte had fallen asleep still chained to the chair. She had been allowed, twice, to get up and use the toilet facilities, such as they were. But the chains were fastened again as soon as she returned, forcing her to sit uncomfortably in the armchair, able to stretch only a few inches. The half-promise of escape drifted into the past. After this last trip she dozed, and then finally slept.

She woke with a start, for a moment bewildered. Then she saw Grandma Blades' face a couple of feet away from her own. She drew in a breath to speak.

'Shush!' the old woman hissed. 'Time to get dressed.'

Charlotte glanced down at herself. 'I am dressed.'

'Not like that, you stupid creature! You look like you wandered off one o' them papers' society pages. You gotta look like you belong in a brothel.' The old woman swept her eyes up and down Charlotte's figure. 'Bit past yer best, but ye're not bad, fer all that.' She looked at Charlotte's bosom. 'At least you got somethin' for a man to get 'old of. Dress yer different and yer'll pass.'

Charlotte opened her mouth to protest, but she saw the old woman's eyes and realised that something was afoot. Was she about to be set free? Why else must she pass as a whore, if not to escape this brothel? Wearing her own clothes could draw attention to both of them, and possibly cost them their lives. Or at best a humiliating return to ever harsher restrictions.

The old woman must have seen in Charlotte's face that she understood. 'Good,' she said. 'Now take that off, it's the wrong shape, and it's quality. We may not 'ave class, but we know it when we see it. I'll fetch yer something else.' She turned to the dog. 'Come on, Patch. Got to find something that'll fit 'er. She's gotta look like one of us, or she'll finish us all, God 'elp 'er.' She left the room, the dog on her heels.

She came back without a sound, about ten minutes later, carrying a bundle of clothes in her arms. She dropped them on the floor, then put aside some underclothes and a petticoat. She unlocked the chains around Charlotte's wrist. 'Come on, come on, girl. We don't got all night! It'll be light in less than an hour, and we gotta be out of 'ere. Now shift yerself.'

There was no time for modesty. Charlotte moved as she was told. These clothes were nothing like she was used to wearing. They felt uncomfortable, and they were immodest in the extreme. On the other hand, by the time she had the dress on, she looked like a very buxom tart. If she had not been so frightened, she would have laughed. But right now, she would have choked at the absurdity of it.

'Well, come on, then!' the old woman snapped. 'And don't trip over that skirt. I 'aven't time to pick yer up off the floor.' She turned and

348

walked surprisingly swiftly out of the room, with Patch at her heels.

Charlotte picked up her skirts as told and followed after her.

They passed through narrow, crooked passages, upstairs and down, until Charlotte had no idea where they were; she was only relieved that they had not been challenged. They finally emerged through a small door and into a narrow alley that smelled of sewage. Patch growled softly.

Grandma Blades held up her hand and glared at Charlotte. It was an unmistakable warning to be silent . . . and careful.

Charlotte nodded, and tried not to breathe in the smell through her nose. Not that breathing in through her mouth was much better. She felt as if the taste permeated all parts of her. The path felt slippery under her feet. She dared not look down to see what she was stepping in. The air was cold on those parts of her skin that she was unused to exposing. She felt not only cold but indecent, and vulnerable.

They made it as far as the corner, where the passage opened on to another alley that led to the street, before they ran into anyone. It was a man leaning against the stained back wall and smoking a cigarette. The old woman hesitated. Charlotte saw her hand go to her waist, then her hip. The dim light from a street lamp thirty feet away caught the reflection of the flat blade of a knife in her hand.

For an instant, Charlotte froze. Then she realised that any response at all would only draw attention to her, which was the last thing she could afford. She wished she were completely invisible.

The old woman said something unintelligible. The man wavered.

Patch was no more than a shadow beside her, pressing against her legs.

Grandma Blades moved forward and Charlotte remembered to pick up her skirts before following her.

They came level with the man and he noticed them for the first time. He was startled, and swore at them. Grandma Blades swore right back at him, and grasped Charlotte's arm, half pulling her off her feet. She stumbled before regaining her balance.

The man called out something obscene, and both women ignored him. Charlotte thought Grandma knew him, then realised that she didn't, and that she, too, was afraid.

He shouted after them, and Grandma increased their pace. Charlotte also realised that he was hurling obscenities at them because he thought they were whores, and they had no business walking away from him.

They hurried out along the alley and then turned sharply, went a few hundred yards, and then crossed a main street and dropped back into the shadows again.

At one place they were stopped by three drunk men who turned aggressive very quickly. Charlotte was both angry and frightened, and she was grateful for the old woman's confidence; Grandma Blades walked past them without looking at them or speaking. She felt better when they were a good hundred yards past them. She was also relieved to have Patch nearby.

Dawn was breaking and the slight breeze was cold as it turned into a slicing wind. Charlotte was shivering uncontrollably.

The old woman grabbed her arm and began to pull her sharply forward. 'Come on! We've got to hurry. They'll know we're gone by now. They'll be after us.'

'Why? What did you say to them?' Charlotte demanded. 'Nobody's going to pay a ransom for me.'

'Course not, yer silly cow! But as long as we got yer, yer 'usband's going to keep silent. They ain't gonna let you go now! You seen too much. You can swear all you like that you won't tell anyone, but they ain't stupid. Once yer safe, yer man's gonna crucify the lot o' them. From what I've seen, that's 'is job.'

Charlotte knew, all along, that underneath the surface of her thoughts lay one she could not bear to look at. They were never going to let her go — they dared not. Now the street seemed long, cold, dirty and dangerous. The dress she was wearing fitted badly, but there was nothing she could pull around her shoulders and over the exposed part of her bosom.

They walked even more quickly, staying close to the walls of the buildings they passed, and half ran across the open streets, Patch never leaving their side. They were almost clear of the area around Anthony Street when they saw two men on the narrow footpath ahead of them. The old woman swivelled around, dragging Charlotte after her, but there were two other men coming from the opposite direction as well.

That was the moment when Charlotte realised they were after her, to silence her and prevent Thomas from pursuing the truth about Drake's death. They could not afford to let her go, or even to let her live. If they killed her, they could hide her body and keep him believing, hoping desperately, that she was still alive. He would discover the truth only when they wanted him to — if they wanted him to!

Grandma Blades pulled Charlotte to a stop, with their backs to the wall. The men moved closer.

Patch growled and his hackles rose.

Grandma Blades had her hand on her knife, but Charlotte had no weapon at all and she felt helpless.

The four men were approaching from both sides. They were less than twenty yards away.

The sun rose above the horizon in cold, pale light.

Then, suddenly, the men's arms were swinging. Charlotte ducked and felt a blow land hard on her shoulder. There was a loud scream as Patch's teeth sunk into the flesh of one man's leg.

Charlotte swung around and hit the nearest man as hard as she could, across the face. She felt the jolt of his teeth and smelled the sweetness of blood. Someone hit her hard and she staggered forward, only just saving herself from falling by grabbing on to the man in front of her and knocking him off balance. He raised his arm, his blow aimed at the old woman. There was a flash of light on the blade for an instant, and then blood everywhere.

Charlotte had very little idea of what was happening. It was four men against two women and a dog. Charlotte was hit several times. It hurt. It knocked the breath out of her and she was pushed with great force to the ground. She sought to regain her feet. Then she heard one of the men scream. He fell against her and she narrowly escaped being crushed by his body. Another man fell over him. Before he could regain his footing, Patch tore into his throat. Blood spurted from the wound and splattered across the pavement.

It was chaos. Cold, grey, terrifying chaos.

One of the men ran away, shouting. The one on the pavement lay still. He was either unconscious or dead. Charlotte could not tell which.

The old woman lay in a heap, blood running from wounds that seemed to cover most of her body.

The last of the men looked around him, the scene bloody and chaotic. Without a word, he fled.

Charlotte knelt beside the old woman. She began to realise that much of the blood was not from the men, but from Grandma Blades herself. Her face was grey and her eyes cloudy, with a faraway look.

'Yer can't 'elp me,' she told Charlotte, her voice barely a whisper.

Charlotte cradled her in her arms. This dirty, miserable old woman who had loved her granddaughter, and saved Charlotte's life.

'What can I do?' Charlotte was weeping, stroking the old woman's face.

For a moment there was silence, except for the wheezing of breath, then a whispered word she could not make out.

'Yes?' Charlotte asked, leaning closer. 'What?'

'Take Patch, will yer? Promise me yer'll look after 'im?'

'Of course I will, if he'll come with me. Stop talking and — '

'Yer can't 'elp me, yer daft creature. Just get out of 'ere. Go west.' Her breath grated, caught in her throat. 'Yer can tell east from west, can't yer? Away from the sunrise. That don't take no brains. Get on! Get that bastard that killed my girl. Promise . . . '

'Who?' Charlotte asked urgently. 'Who killed her?'

'Faber, yer silly cow.' Her eyes glazed over. She did not take another breath.

Charlotte ignored the tears running down her cheeks. She started to pull her skirts out of the way, and stood up. The dog was pressed against the old woman, her blood smeared on his fur. There was blood around his muzzle. He gave a low, mournful whine.

'She's gone, Patch,' Charlotte said softly. 'We can't help her any more.'

The dog looked at her and stood up.

'Will you come with me?' she asked. 'We need to see if you're hurt. You seem all right, but . . . '

The dog looked at her and slowly sat down.

'What does that mean?' Charlotte asked. 'That you're listening to me? Or that you're not?'

His tail moved a little.

'We can't stay here,' she told him. The dog was listening to her, but would he leave the old woman? Did he understand that she was dead?

'Patch! I can't wait here. Be reasonable. You can't help her now. But maybe you can help me? Come on!'

She started to walk away. Patch gave a long, mournful howl, and then he stood up and followed her along the street and westward into the light.

18

Daniel and Pitt had finished their plans and made all the decisions necessary before trying to sleep. If they were lucky, they might get in two or three hours. After a fraction of that time, they gave up. Now, sitting in the warmth of the kitchen, with cups of tea and a plate of biscuits before them, their conversation focused not on Charlotte — it would serve no purpose to express their fears, their nightmares — but on those things over which they had some control. At least for now.

'We'll not take my men,' Pitt said gravely. 'We don't need force. And more than that, I've been warned to leave Faber alone. If I'm dismissed from Special Branch, as I may well be, then the structure of it still has to survive, with the men who are in it now, and know what is going on. If they are completely ignorant of this, then their positions are safe. A political coup would get them dismissed. Thank God, I don't think we are anywhere near that.'

'Do you think we are near war?' Daniel asked. 'Honestly? Or is it political posturing, because of the social unrest in Europe?'

Pitt thought for a moment or two before replying. 'I think we'll be lucky if there isn't some sort of unpleasantness, but it may be like 1848, each country separately, and all put down within a year.'

'With his shipbuilding empire, could Faber actually want a war?'

'Please God, I hope not! No. He's greedy, hungry for power, but I don't think even he would want it at that cost. But we might just be idiotic enough to get into it sideways, by not looking where we are going.' He gave a bitter smile. 'Most train crashes are accidental.'

'Can't our government see that?' Daniel asked.

'Some, of course. But people have an amazing capacity to see what they want to. If enough of them believe it, it becomes a sort of mass delusion.'

'Even in the Home Office?'

'You do know that I have been specifically ordered by MacPherson in the Home Office to leave Faber alone. I considered waking the Home Secretary himself, at two o'clock in the morning, to explain what we believe of Faber. But if I failed to convince him, which I certainly would — because we have no proof, only our own reasoning — then he would have me arrested. And if he had any sense at all, he'd send men to arrest you, too. We're in this alone, Daniel. The least I can do for my men is keep them out of it.'

Daniel thought his father looked a little self-conscious. He took his duties very seriously indeed. Daniel knew that as surely as he knew anything at all. But Pitt was not a man to speak in superlatives. That much of his background would always be with him. It had become his nature. Sometimes it seemed an impediment, but Daniel did not want to change him, even if he could.

'I've studied the notes Drake left,' Pitt went on. 'And your observations on the tobacconist's shop where Bella worked. From that we can deduce where the brothel is that Drake visited. We may have to search a few, but we'd best do it quietly.'

'And if we don't find her?' Daniel felt compelled to ask.

'There's no use threatening anyone.'

Daniel sighed loudly. 'Faber won't care what we do to any of the people connected with this.'

'No, I dare say not. But they will care,' Pitt replied. 'I can make life very unpleasant for them . . . and I will, if I have to.'

Daniel believed him. He hated it, but what choice was there?

'Are you all right to come?' Pitt asked.

All sorts of replies flashed through Daniel's mind. In the end, the only one was simple. 'No, I'll just let you go alone!' he said, and then stood up quickly. 'Come on!'

They would take a car, that much Pitt had conceded. The driver was not party to where they were going in advance. He could not be blamed. They slipped quickly and with very little noise through the shadowed streets, with Pitt giving directions to Mile End. It was the place to start. Drake's body had been found here, and Evan Faber's body had been moved here, because Letterman could be relied upon to stall the investigation and rebuff any awkward questions. Bella Blades' body had been found here as well, which was natural enough. She had lived and worked here. It was the seat of Erasmus Faber's dark power.

Their plan, insofar as they had one, was to identify the brothels and then take each one by surprise. The establishments had been doing business most of the night, so they would be closed and the women asleep at dawn. Pitt and Daniel would find the place, then demand to see the books — the ones kept day by day — and say that they intended to expose all of the men in them, even though their names might well be in code, unless the person who ran the premises promised to give Pitt a cut of the profits. Not enough to drive them out of business, but sufficient to give Pitt a very nice income. They were used to Letterman taking his dues, so they would not find this hard to believe. Whether Pitt would do any part of it, if they did not comply, he had not considered. He would have to make the threat severe enough that, for the brothel owners, giving up Charlotte was the easier choice. If they did not have her, they might well know where she was. Neither he nor Daniel had considered the possibility of complete failure; there was no obvious next step.

It was the first time Daniel had seen his father visibly rattled. How many other times had there been when Pitt had successfully hidden it? He had no idea. Right now, it did not matter.

They were going eastwards, into the dawn. The cold, early light showed grey streets and only the stirrings of life. One or two people huddled in doorways, having slept there most of the night. A cat, little more than a moving shadow, crossed the narrow pavement and caught something in its jaws, probably a rat.

'We're getting close to Anthony Street.' Daniel spoke for the first time since he had left home.

'Look out!' Pitt said sharply to the driver. 'Dog in the road.'

The driver swerved and pulled up, with a sharp screech of brakes.

Daniel turned to see if they had hit the animal, and saw a woman bending down to look at the dog, which seemed to be all right. She was obviously a street woman, judging from her clothes. She must be freezing. Perhaps she had nowhere to go.

Pitt was opening the car door and getting out.

'Father?' Daniel watched Pitt walk towards the woman.

The woman stared at him.

Pitt kept walking, faster now, stumbling a little.

The dog snarled at him, showing his teeth.

The woman put her hand on the dog's head, reassuring him. Daniel could hear her words quite clearly. 'It's all right, Patch. It's all right.'

He stared at the woman, dressed like a street whore. 'Mother!' He scrambled out of the car, leaving the door wide open, and ran towards her.

His father was holding her fiercely, ignoring the dog and mumbling something into her hair.

'Mother?' Daniel repeated, almost choked with relief. 'Are you all right?' He saw the blood on her clothing. 'Oh, God, you're ... you look ... '

'Terrible,' she replied through tears of relief. 'The blood isn't mine.' She glanced down at her red dress, the blood on it visible only as dark stains. 'It's Grandma Blades'. She's . . . gone . . . they killed her.'

'But you're all right? Are you? Really?' Pitt demanded, his voice rough-edged with emotion.

Charlotte nodded, clinging to him. 'Yes, but Thomas, it's Erasmus Faber . . . he's behind it all.'

'I know.'

Charlotte looked startled 'Do you?'

'Yes, but I haven't proof. Charlotte — '

'He's not here,' she interrupted. 'And please, we need to get out of Mile End. They're still . . . '

Her words were unnecessary. Daniel turned and could see black shapes moving far down the street, coming towards them. 'Get back in the car!' he shouted. 'Come on!'

As one, they turned and ran towards the car, Patch with them.

Pitt pushed Charlotte inside. 'The dog . . . '

'He's with me,' Charlotte replied. 'Come on, Patch, inside.'

The dog obeyed.

Daniel went round to the other side and almost fell in, slamming the door behind them as Pitt did the same. The driver hit the accelerator and the car lurched forward. He moved the gears and put the pedal down. They passed the men on the street, who scattered, realising the car would hit them if they stayed in its path. A few minutes later, the driver eased up on the speed.

The men were already half a mile behind them. Pitt was holding Charlotte tightly against him.

'Where to, sir?' the driver enquired, his voice hardly wavering at all.

'Keppel Street,' Pitt told him.

'No,' Charlotte argued urgently. 'They know that I've escaped, and that Grandma Blades must have told me things. I know too much. They took me to scare you off, but they didn't intend to let me go . . . ever. They'll warn Faber that I got away.'

Pitt hesitated for only a moment, then leaned forward and gave the driver Faber's home address. It took a further twenty minutes to get there. The streets were becoming busier, with early workers and delivery men, loads of fruit and vegetables coming into the city for the morning markets.

'Stay here,' Pitt ordered, and got out of the car and went to the front door. Daniel and Charlotte sat close together in the back seat. Pitt came back in a few minutes. 'He's already gone to the shipyard,' he told them, then got into the car and closed the door. 'The Faber shipyard,' he told the driver, who obeyed instantly, as if he knew the way well.

'Is that where he's gone?' Daniel asked. 'Are you sure?'

'No,' Pitt replied. 'But it's too early for anywhere else. No one will be at the Home Office at this hour. I don't think the people in Mile End have had time to tell anyone that Charlotte has escaped. We've got to hurry . . . '

'What are we going to do?' Daniel asked.

'Please, let me confront him. I've read all of Drake's notes. You're the head of Special Branch. You've got no interest in this, now that Mother's safe. I have a legitimate interest. Faber ordered the death of Jonah Drake, a senior partner in my company. Now that I know the truth, I can prove it through Drake's notes.'

'Can you?' Pitt turned his face to look at him more closely. 'Are you certain?'

'No, but Faber doesn't know that!'

'Daniel!'

'We've got Mother and she's safe. He doesn't know what she could testify to. Added to which, the Home Office hasn't given me any orders to let Faber go.'

Charlotte looked steadily for a moment at Daniel, then turned to Pitt. 'He's right, Thomas, and it's time to let him do it.'

Pitt hesitated. The battle was clear in his face: he wanted to protect his son, and also to take Charlotte somewhere warm and safe. And perhaps there was a small part of him that simply wanted to retain control.

Finally, Pitt let go. 'Be careful,' was all he said.

No one spoke for a time, until Charlotte turned to her husband. 'Thomas?' Her voice was low, almost beseeching.

Pitt looked into her eyes.

'I need you to do something for me.'

A sweet look came into his face. 'Anything.'

'Someone has to go back and find Grandma Blades. She's in the street. I don't want her to be collected . . . like garbage. She . . . she saved my life.'

'Of course,' he promised.

'And there's one more thing.'

This time, he said nothing, but waited for her to speak.

'A funeral,' said Charlotte softly. 'She must have one, a proper one. And we must pay for it. Even if we're the only ones there . . . ' When Pitt nodded, her face relaxed into calmness for the first time since her abduction.

After that, no one spoke.

* * *

Kitteridge woke up with a start. It was early daylight, about five or six in the morning. Someone was knocking at his bedroom door. The first thought that came to his mind was that Daniel had found his mother. He was up and grasping his dressing gown to open the door before he realised how unlikely that was. He slipped his gown on and tied the belt, then went to the door.

Miriam fford Croft was standing just outside on the landing. 'I'm sorry, I know this is early, but I've found all the banking details to prove that my father lent money to Letterman, and that Letterman is still paying him back. It wasn't blackmail, it was a loan from my father, and we can prove it.'

It took Kitteridge a moment to realise what she had said. 'You mean there's proof? Real proof? Are you sure?'

'Yes. My father didn't keep watertight records, but the bank does.'

He opened the door wider, and stepped back so she was not left on the landing. Thank heaven he had left no clothes lying around. 'Come in,' he said unnecessarily.

She followed him, closing the door behind her, keeping her voice low but still without excitement. 'It's enough, because he accused Father to the authorities of blackmailing him . . . '

'Did he?' Kitteridge was struggling to make sense of it. 'I thought he just threatened Daniel . . . '

'He told Sir Thomas, and he's the head of Special Branch . . . '

'Then why me? Shouldn't you be telling him?' He thought he glimpsed the truth at last. 'If we can stop Letterman . . . '

She shook her head quickly. 'His mind is on finding Lady Pitt, and saving her life. I don't know who's really behind it, but it's not Letterman. We've got to do this, Toby. And get someone from Special Branch to arrest Letterman. He may be the man who actually has her . . . '

'With what danger to her?' He grasped it now. 'We might precipitate . . . '

'Please, Toby. Think clearly. Do you imagine they are going to let her go? Really?'

Her voice was shaking now, and he could see that she knew the nature of what she was doing, and the inevitable tragedy if she failed. 'Yes,' he said decisively, his mind made up. 'I don't have a telephone, but the chambers do. We must call someone in the police. Special Branch can't arrest anyone, and Letterman will know that.'

'We'll go direct to Special Branch, and they'll bring the police. We have to hurry. If we delay, it may be too late . . . Please . . . '

'Wait for me,' he ordered, gesturing for her to go back into the passage while he dressed. She obeyed without hesitation.

Less than five minutes later he joined her, fully dressed, but still with only vague ideas of what they were going to do.

Outside in the street, she led the way towards a small, sleek red car that was parked a few yards away, and she opened the driver's-side door and gestured for him to get into the passenger seat.

His protest died on his lips. A dim memory came to mind of Daniel telling him she was an amazing driver. It was something he did not want to think about. The early-morning air was sharp and cold. There were only delivery carts and milkmen about, and a few brewers' drays with their magnificent horses. She drove very well, but much too fast for safety, or even for comfort. He sat with his jaw clenched, but managed to keep his stomach in good order as they swept around corners and accelerated along every main road until they reached Lisson Grove and Special Branch headquarters.

There Miriam parked the car and, with Kitteridge on her heels, went inside and said she had a message for Sir Thomas Pitt, of great urgency, and needed to deliver it immediately.

'As you know,' she said. 'Lady Pitt has been kidnapped. They have searched high and low for her. I have information that cannot wait. Even an hour's delay may cost her life.' She spoke levelly, but the intensity of her fear was sharp in every word. 'I would like to speak to the man closest to him, whoever is already here . . . '

There was no prevarication to overcome; perhaps the fact that they had come to Lisson Grove at all was sufficient reason to take them seriously.

It was only fifteen minutes later that Lieutenant Livesey got into the small back seat of Miriam's car and they rode in silence to the nearest police station.

He unfolded himself and climbed out, saying he would be back immediately with the necessary policemen to make the arrest.

He returned quickly armed with Letterman's home address and accompanied by a determined young man who he introduced briefly as Sergeant Judd. There was no conversation during Miriam's nerve-wracking drive to the quiet suburb just west of Mile End, where Letterman had his home. It was now twenty minutes past six in the morning.

They pulled up outside Letterman's house. The curtains were already opened in the upstairs bedrooms, and no doubt there would be signs of life in the kitchen at the back.

'Stay here,' Kitteridge commanded Miriam. He climbed out of the car, followed by Livesey and the policeman.

Miriam climbed out immediately after them, as Kitteridge had been certain she would. He did not waste time by repeating himself.

The young policeman disappeared around the

back, to prevent any escape that way, while Livesey, Kitteridge and Miriam went to the front and knocked peremptorily.

The door was opened by a startled maid.

'Lieutenant Livesey, of Special Branch,' Livesey announced himself. 'I have a warrant to come in, and I wish to speak to Inspector Letterman immediately. Will you bring him here.' His voice fell at the end, not rising in question. It was an order.

Five minutes later, Letterman came down the stairs looking pale and grim, but in no mood to surrender. 'Who the devil are you?' He looked directly at Livesey, ignoring Kitteridge and Miriam. 'What do you mean barging in here and ordering my servants around?'

Had he looked out of a window and seen the back door? He was angry, but not yet afraid.

'Lieutenant Livesey, Special Branch,' Livesey replied.

'You have no authority here — ' Letterman began.

'No, but this police warrant and the policeman standing at your back kitchen door have.'

'On what grounds, for God's sake?' But Letterman was pale. He could control his hands, his voice, but not the blood draining from his face.

'I came here to arrest you for the attempted blackmail of Marcus fford Croft, sir. That is a serious crime, and I shall require you to come with me. It would be less distressing for your family if you come without protest . . . sir.'

'You have no proof of that idiotic charge,'

Letterman protested.

'Yes, we have, sir. The bank keeps excellent records, in detail. Jonah Drake, who was slashed to death in your jurisdiction, sir . . . ' He let the sentence fade, as if certain that Letterman got his drift.

Letterman glanced at Miriam, and his whole expression changed, as if he appreciated that this was true, and that it would be futile to deny it. A slow, ugly smile spread across his face.

'I believe you are relatively junior, Lieutenant Livesey. Have you asked permission of your superior, Sir Thomas Pitt? Don't bother to answer that, as I know you haven't. He would never have been so rash. He knows that Lady Pitt has been kidnapped.' His smile widened. 'And I am the only person who has any hope of getting her back alive . . . ' His voice was sharp with terror, but there was the knowledge of power in it also. 'How are you going to explain that to him?'

Kitteridge felt his heart lurch. He glanced at Livesey and saw him falter. Miriam looked shaken, her whole body shivering.

Kitteridge moved forward, perhaps half a step. 'At the moment, Mr Letterman, you stand to spend several years in prison, for the false accusation of blackmail. Not nice. Not at all the behaviour of an officer on the police force. But a good deal better than being tried at the Old Bailey for murder, and the swift, ugly journey to the gallows. Which, as you have just pointed out rather forcefully — and we believe you — will happen if anything more unfortunate should

369

happen to Lady Pitt than already has.'

'You're bluffing!' Letterman stumbled over the words.

'But you are not,' Kitteridge replied, as if suddenly sure of what he meant to do. 'We believe you absolutely. You have the power, and the will, to murder Lady Pitt, and if we do not stop you, that will happen. You have said so yourself. Therefore, we shall stop you, by all and every means necessary. It was foolish of you to make such a threat. Now we have heard you, and have no choice but to arrest you, and take you into custody, where we cannot have you make contact with anyone, at least not until I hear that Lady Pitt is found alive and well. You had better hope that is soon. Prison is not a nice place, especially for a man who has put so many others there . . . '

'You can't do that!' Letterman's voice was half strangled in his throat.

'I can't,' Kitteridge agreed. 'But Lieutenant Livesey can. And no doubt he will.'

'Right, Mr Kitteridge,' Livesey said. 'Get ready to meet a whole lot of old enemies, Mr Letterman, and even more new ones, I dare say.' He stepped forward and put a pair of heavy manacles on Letterman's wrists.

'You can't!' Letterman began. 'I'll have your head for this!'

Sergeant Judd appeared at the other end of the hallway. 'Everything all right, sir?' he asked Livesey.

'Ah, Sergeant, yes, thank you. I have your prisoner here for you. Have you sent for the

Black Mariah? Afraid there isn't room for you to go back in Miss fford Croft's nice sharp red car. Bit small. I'll come with you.' He looked at Letterman. 'Sorry to be so public, sir, and at this time in the morning, when everyone's still at home. Bit of a spectacle. Can't be helped.' He turned to Miriam and Kitteridge. 'Thank you for your assistance, madam, sir. We'll handle it from now on. We'll be in touch with you regarding the trial, but that won't be for a bit yet.'

Miriam gave him a slow, sweet smile.

Kitteridge was too elated, and filled with such an overwhelming relief, to speak at all.

When he arrived at chambers he was met by Hobson.

'Got it!' the young clerk declared, handing him a slip of paper. 'A receipt made out by the jeweller for the purchase of the necklace.'

Kitteridge grabbed the paper and read the name. A brief smile crossed his face. 'Good work, Hobson. Mr Drake would have been proud.' He slipped the paper into his breast pocket, the name Erasmus Faber burning hot against his chest.

★ ★ ★

The sun was well above the horizon when Daniel and Pitt reached the Faber Shipbuilding yard. It was not difficult to spot Erasmus Faber. He was standing on the edge of the scaffolding that surrounded the skeleton of a ship newly launched and waiting to be fitted. It was clearly going to be a warship for the Navy: huge, sleek and powerful enough for naval warfare in any seas on earth.

Daniel actually hesitated for a step. If there was a war, and this ship was late in being completed, what would it cost in lives? How far ahead could one look? Or what should one overlook, in the immediate moment? It was a question in the mind only.

He kept walking towards the towering edifice of the scaffolding. He did not like heights, but Faber was not moving. He had seen both Daniel and Pitt and deliberately had not climbed down.

The smell of the rising tide and the sound of gently slurping water took Daniel back to the night on the river with Evan. He did not hesitate in his pace as he climbed the ladders until he stood a yard from the edge, in front of Faber.

'Yes, Mr Pitt?' Faber spoke, eyebrows raised in question. 'I assume this must be important, for you to interrupt me here.'

Daniel looked into Faber's eyes and saw no fear at all. It awoke a very real fear in him. It also made him angry. 'I'm sure you already know that Bella Blades is dead. Probably you knew her as Belinda May, although I doubt it.'

'I don't know her at all,' Faber replied, with the shadow of a smile.

'Oh? You didn't know that she murdered Evan? You surprise me. Since I know it, I thought you would as well.'

A faint flush of anger stained Faber's cheeks, but he controlled his voice perfectly. 'I think you are closer to the case than I am, Mr Pitt. I trust the police to solve it, if it is possible. They will keep me informed.'

Daniel smiled back. 'I'm afraid they won't. No doubt Letterman would have told you, had he thought it in his own interest. Did he know she was your daughter? Did you tell him that, before sending her out to kill your son? Her brother?'

Faber's expression did not change, not even a flicker, but he could not control the ebb of colour from his skin, leaving him looking oddly pinched, somehow shrunken.

It was all Daniel needed. 'There have been quite a lot of changes,' he went on. 'My mother was kidnapped. I assume you didn't know that either?'

Faber smiled back, but it was strained, and looked false. 'How unfortunate. I'm so sorry. Can I help?'

'Not at all necessary,' Daniel replied. 'But thank you for the offer. She escaped, with the assistance of Grandma Blades. Poor old woman is devastated by your killing of her granddaughter. That was your revenge. But my mother is quite safe, and with us now. That's how we know what happened, pretty well from the beginning.' He drew a deep breath. 'Which, of course, is your murder of Marie Wesley. It must have been an unbearable blow to your vanity to know that a young woman preferred sleeping with your son, rather than with you. Especially after you gave her such an expensive necklace.'

Faber's cheeks flushed scarlet and his shoulder muscles hunched. He lunged forward and grasped Daniel by the upper arms, knocking him off balance.

For a second or two, the sky, the shipyard itself seemed to sway. Daniel knew that Faber could throw him off the edge. He could feel himself losing his balance and imagined falling through the air, and then hitting the water far below. Or worse, one of the concrete buttresses. He was certain he could not push against Faber's far greater weight, and the power of his muscles. If he tried, Faber could heave him over and then adjust his own balance and remain on the ledge.

Daniel lunged as hard as he could, catching Faber in the midsection. Faber gasped, doubling up for a moment. As his grip loosened on Daniel's arm, Daniel hit him hard, hoping to catch him on the nose. He felt bone beneath his fist, but Faber's grip did not loosen.

Daniel brought his head down and then up again sharply, catching Faber under the jaw. He staggered . . . and Daniel seized his chance. He ground the heel of his shoe into Faber's foot. Then, as the man's hands loosened for a moment, Daniel lunged at him again.

Faber lost his grip and Daniel fell forward on to the ground, expecting a crippling blow in return.

Nothing happened . . .

Except for the sound of a scream.

Daniel stood up slowly, stunned. Faber was gone. Completely. Daniel realised that he had lost his balance and, when Daniel hit him, he must have missed his footing and plunged over the edge.

Daniel was shaky, weak-legged and struggling for breath.

There were people shouting. His father was suddenly there, holding on to him. Men were gathering around them, not menacing, but cheering.

'Can you stand?' Pitt asked anxiously, not letting go of his son.

'Yes. Yes, of course I can,' Daniel replied. He looked down to see that his leg was bleeding. He could hardly feel it, but it would hurt like blazes tomorrow. He grinned. 'He was guilty,' he said, and then added, 'can we get away from the edge, please? I hate edges. And we'd better take Mother home and get her decently dressed. And feed the dog!'

Pitt did not let go of him, but eased his grip a little as he helped Daniel climb down the ladders. When they reached the ground Charlotte was there. She still looked like a tart, but to Daniel she was utterly beautiful. 'Are you all right?' she asked him anxiously.

'I'm dancing on air,' he replied, swaying a little and wincing as he put more weight on his foot, and knowing at once that it was a mistake. He turned to Pitt. 'Are you going to get into trouble for this? It was my fault, not yours. I sent him over the edge . . .'

'Probably,' Pitt answered. 'Sir James MacPherson is not a gracious loser. I don't think he can afford to fire me, although I dare say he would like to. He'll secretly be glad enough to lose Faber. He wanted a seat in the House of Lords, you know. As a beginning . . .'

'I'm sorry, I didn't mean him to go over the edge. But that's what he deserved. For Marie and Drake, and Evan, and even Bella. And Mother. We can't let that go . . . '

Daniel looked into the faces of his parents. 'Don't you agree?'

No one answered him. It was not necessary.

We do hope that you have enjoyed reading
this large print book.

Did you know that all of our titles
are available for purchase?

We publish a wide range of high quality
large print books including:
Romances, Mysteries, Classics
General Fiction
Non Fiction and Westerns

Special interest titles available in
large print are:
The Little Oxford Dictionary
Music Book
Song Book
Hymn Book
Service Book

Also available from us courtesy of
Oxford University Press:
Young Readers' Dictionary
(large print edition)
Young Readers' Thesaurus
(large print edition)

For further information or a free
brochure, please contact us at:
Ulverscroft Large Print Books Ltd.,
The Green, Bradgate Road, Anstey,
Leicester, LE7 7FU, England.
Tel: (00 44) 0116 236 4325
Fax: (00 44) 0116 234 0205

Other titles published by Ulverscroft:

ONE FATAL FLAW

Anne Perry

It is 1910 and a warehouse fire on the banks of the Thames has left one criminal dead and another charged with his murder. Convinced of his innocence, Jessie Beale begs barrister Daniel Pitt to defend the accused. It's a hopeless case — unless Daniel can find an expert witness, whose testimony on fire damage is so utterly convincing that any jury would believe him.

Daniel's friend Miriam fford Croft was taught by formidable forensic scientist Sir Barnabas Saltram, who has built his reputation on giving evidence of this kind. But when Saltram agrees to testify, thus saving an innocent man from the gallows, Daniel unwittingly starts a chain of events that has devastating consequences for all of them . . .

TRIPLE JEOPARDY

Anne Perry

Daniel Pitt is delighted that his sister is visiting London with her American husband Patrick — a policeman — and their young daughters. But Patrick's trip has another purpose, for which he enlists Daniel's help. Philip Sidney, a young British diplomat, is accused of robbery and assault in Washington, but he has taken diplomatic immunity and fled to England. The perfect opportunity to obtain justice presents itself when Sidney is charged with embezzlement at the British Embassy in America, but as Daniel digs deeper into the case, it becomes clear that vengeance is involved. When a witness is murdered in America, suspicion falls on Sidney. But is somebody trying to frame him? If so, who and why? Daniel follows a trail that uncovers another murder, and leads from Washington to a dramatic scene in court.

A CHRISTMAS RETURN

Anne Perry

As the festive season approaches, Charlotte Pitt's grandmamma, Mariah Ellison, is facing Christmas alone. When an unexpected package containing an ominous present is left on Mariah's doorstep, memories are sparked of a Christmas in Haslemere long ago, when her beloved friend Cullen Wesley died and a local vicar was brutally murdered. No killer was brought to justice. Now, the unsolved case has resurfaced and Cullen's grandson and sleuth in his own right, Peter, begs for Mariah's help to solve the crime that led to his grandfather's death. Mariah can't resist a friend in need and she returns to Haslemere to investigate the murder and heal old wounds. But evil still lurks in the picturesque village and she'll need all her wits about her to see that justice is done.